WATERI

WATERFRONT FISTS
AND OTHERS

ROBERT E. HOWARD

INTRODUCTION BY

MARK FINN

EDITED BY

PAUL HERMAN

WILDSIDE PRESS

WATERFRONT FISTS

An original publication of Wildside Press, P.O. Box 301, Holicong, PA 18928-0301. www.wildsidepress.com

"Letter to the Editor" first appeared in *The Ring*, April 1926. "Kid Lavigne is Dead" first appeared in *The Ring*, June 1928. "Dula Due to Be Champion" first appeared in *The Brownwood Bulletin*, July 18, 1928. "The Apparition in the Prize Ring" first appeared in *Ghost Stories*, April 1929. "The Pit of the Serpent" first appeared in *Fight Stories*, July 1929. "The Bull Dog Breed" first appeared in *Fight Stories*, February 1930. "Sailors' Grudge" first appeared in *Fight Stories*, March 1930. "Fist and Fang" first appeared in *Fight Stories*, May 1930. "The Iron Man" first appeared in *Fight Stories*, June 1930. "Winner Take All" first appeared in *Fight Stories*, July 1930. "Waterfront Fists" first appeared in *Fight Stories*, September 1930. "Champ of the Forecastle" first appeared in *Fight Stories*, November 1930. "Alleys of Peril" first appeared in *Fight Stories*, January 1931. "Texas Fists" first appeared in *Fight Stories*, May 1931. "Circus Fists" first appeared in *Fight Stories*, December 1931. "Vikings of the Gloves" first appeared in *Fight Stories*, February 1932. "Night of Battle" first appeared in *Fight Stories*, March 1932. "The Slugger's Game" first appeared in *Jack Dempsey's Fight Magazine*, May 1934. "General Ironfist" first appeared in *Jack Dempsey's Fight Magazine*, June 1934. "Sluggers of the Beach" first appeared in *Jack Dempsey's Fight Magazine*, August 1934. "Alleys of Darkness" first appeared in *Magic Carpet Magazine*, January 1934. Most of the boxing stories that appeared in *Fight Stories* or *Action Stories* were reprinted in *Fight Stories* between 1937 and 1942. In each case, the story was retitled, and new artwork was added. In almost every case the author's name was changed to a "house" name, either Mark Adam or John Starr.

The artwork that appears at the start of each story is the art that appeared at the start of the story in its original appearance. Artists are as follows: Allen Thomas—the stories that first appeared in *Fight Stories*. Earle K. Bergey & Allen Thomas—the stories that first appeared in *Jack Dempsey's Fight Magazine*. Unknown—"The Apparition in the Prize Ring."

FIRST EDITION

To the folks of Cross Plains, Texas, Bob's hometown,
for striving to keep the memory of REH alive,
and in appreciation of their always gracious hospitality.

CONTENTS

BARE KNUCKLES AND BULLDOGS
An Introduction to the Boxing Fiction of Robert E. Howard

As a writer working during the 1920s and 1930s, Robert E. Howard had a host of markets to choose from; indeed, there was a pulp magazine for almost every taste and sensibility. Everyone knows about the horror and "weird" pulps. They are the stuff of legends, and the market in which Howard was most successful. But Howard wrote in a variety of genres: westerns, "spicy stories," adventure, detective, and even sports.

It's no secret that Howard was a fan of boxing. He followed the prize-fighters of his day, researched and wrote about the sport, and he boxed for most of his adult life, sparring with friends and acquaintances. Howard was a regular at the local icehouse in the oil-boom town of Cross Plains, where he lived, and he spent many hours boxing with the farm hands and oil field workers. He also created a fictional boxer, Sailor Steve Costigan, about which he wrote more stories than any other character.

It's worth noting that while Howard never hacked anyone up with a sword or led an army in a charge, he did have firsthand knowledge of the sweet science. That experience had to factor into his boxing stories, more so than in any other genre in which he wrote. Many of the stories dealt with the quality of a particular fighter, or some admirable trait that separated him from the rest of his ilk. Howard's favorite boxer was Jim Jeffries, whose career had ended three decades before. Jeffries nickname, by the way, was "the Iron Man."

The boxing fiction of Robert E. Howard has been largely overlooked, due in part to the immeasurable success of his sword and sorcery fiction. However, it's in these boxing stories that we can see a very clear picture of the author's signature style, without the interference of undue editing or posthumous censoring as is the case with so much of his fantasy work.

What drives Howard's boxing fiction is first and foremost his passionate intensity that is the hallmark of his style. In Howard's work, you feel every punch, smell the sweat, and taste the blood as if you were in the ring. His flair for action can be seen in the centerpiece of the boxing stories: the fight itself. Whether it takes place in the ring, under a tent, in a cement pit, or the back alley of some Oriental port, Howard's sense of immediacy and his sparse but colorful descriptions never fail to grab the reader and pull him into the story.

These stories also give readers a more well-rounded glimpse of

REH as a writer, because the majority of them are laugh-out-loud funny. Most academics use the term "burlesque" to describe the Steve Costigan stories, and that's accurate, but Howard also uses black humor to some effect, elevating the violence of many of his stories to a cartoonish, grotesque level. The power of REH as a humorist shines in the narrative, where he employs a chatty vernacular that is an equal mix of Damon Runyan's tough-guy prattle and West Texas laconic colloquialisms. Through this style, which ventures frequently into the realm of the unreliable narrator, Howard paints a vivid, comical picture of his protagonist and his varied surroundings.

Even in the serious boxing stories, Howard doesn't shy away from his overt admiration for what he felt was the kind of fighter no longer seen in his day. Howard's boxers echo other characters in his stories in their refusal to acknowledge defeat, their stubborn determination to stay alive, stay on their feet, stay in the ring. Those stories can be held up and compared against any of Howard's other work, and the same themes, the same motivations can be seen. Regardless of how the reader may feel about the subject matter, Howard's passion for pugilism shows in every story.

Finally, it is impossible to ignore the sheer number of boxing stories that Howard wrote. Serious or funny, spooky or adventurous, these stories represent a fierce creative outburst that would pave the way later for his western hero, Breckenridge Elkins. In these stories we see Howard's craft pushed from mere construction to passionate involvement. He took all of his interests and peppered them through the various boxing stories. He wrote them faster than the magazine could print them. Clearly, he loved what he was doing. When Howard could write no more, he went on to draft Conan and the aforementioned Elkins, who owes much in style and content to the Costigan stories.

These stories are a joy to read and reread. They are funny, bawdy, picaresque, and violent. Presented here, as they were originally printed, they perfectly showcase why Robert E. Howard was one of the greatest adventure writers of the 20th century. I hope you enjoy them.

Mark Finn
Austin Texas
April 15th, 2002

EDITOR'S COMMENTS

This book contains all the works REH wrote for four different pulps and constitutes almost all of the boxing works REH sold in his day.

The Ring was apparently a magazine that REH read as a young man, as he sent them a letter in 1926, at the age of 20, and a poem a couple years later.

In 1927, REH wrote and published his first boxing story, "Cupid v. Pollux," which appeared in *The Yellow Jacket*, the school paper for Howard Payne College. This story can be found in *The Complete Yellow Jacket,* Hermanthis, 1999. "Cupid v. Pollux" already showed the typical form and formatting of most REH boxing stories. A not-too-bright boxer, usually a heavyweight, very good but not great, set in a mildly humorous story in which the boxer gets tricked by someone, sometimes even himself. It is interesting that REH's boxing characters are not the superior fighters of their universe, unlike Conan or Breckinridge Elkins. His boxers are of course the winning fighters in the stories, but the stories also regularly mention real professional boxers who REH acknowledges are superior to his character.

The next REH boxing story featured in this book is "The Apparition in the Prize Ring," and was published in *Ghost Stories* in 1929. This pulp was a little different from most. It was an oversize magazine format, 8X12, and featured stories from various people who were telling allegedly true stories. REH sold them a weird boxing story, writing as John Taverel, the mythical manager of a mythical black fighter named Ace Jessel. This is one of the few stories where the protaganist is black, as is the antagonist. For those curious about REH's views on race, this is a good story to read. This story has never been reprinted in any mainstream publication.

Also in 1929, REH began selling boxing stories to Jack Byrne at Fiction House, for their boxing pulp *Fight Stories*. As Fiction House was much more regular in their payments, and Jack Byrne enjoyed REH's work and always wanted more, REH wrote a sizable amount of material for them throughout the rest of his years.

REH's first story in *Fight Stories*, "The Pit of the Serpent," introduces us to one of REH most durable characters, Steve Costigan, A.B. (Which means "Able Bodied") seaman aboard a ship called the *Sea Girl*. REH used Costigan to tell traditional boxing stories in exotic locales, the most common being the Far East, but also including South Africa, Australia, and Texas. REH also used Costigan stories to write about Steve's dog, Mike, a pure white bulldog, a true and loyal friend, and an incredible killer when needed. REH loved his own dog, and his feelings regarding the relationship between a man and his dog shines through in several stories. REH wrote more stories featuring Steve

Costigan (or his clone, Dennis Dorgan), than any other character. REH had thirteen Costigan stories published in *Fight Stories*, the last appearing in 1932. With the creation of Breckinridge Elkins at that time, REH quit selling boxing stories to Fiction House and focused on his more genre-breaking character.

One of the last stories REH sold to *Magic Carpet Magazine* in 1933 was "Alleys of Darkness." This was a Dennis Dorgan story, a clone of the Costigan stories. Another Dorgan story had been sold to *Magic Carpet* and announced in the last issue, but the pulp folded before it could be published.

The last pulp represented here is *Jack Dempsey's Fight Magazine*. REH sold them three Costigan stories in 1934, no doubt as part of his efforts to expand the number of titles he was selling to.

As is typical of writings of this era, some word usage and attitudes are not PC, fair warning. Also, many of these stories can also be described as "brutal." The physical damage inflicted and received, and of course described, can be pretty severe.

As in previous volumes, I have tried to minimize the editing, and leave the works as much as possible as they first appeared. I have cleaned up obvious typos, of which there were few, and tried to create some consistency from inconsistent usages and words.

And as in previous volumes, I have generally left alone REH's creative variations on compound words, only changing those that are most readily apparent, or that he changed from one story to the next, to create consistency in this volume.

I hope you enjoy this book. Hopefully it will allow you to delve into one of the few true loves of REH's life. Any comments, corrections or suggestions for later printings are welcome.

Paul Herman
2002

Letter to *The Ring* Magazine

Here is my opinion on the greatest heavyweights of all time: Boxing reached its height between 1892 and 1905. That was the ring's Golden Era. The culmination of perfection, the pinnacle of achievement, the greatest heavyweight of all time was James J. Jefferies. Records prove that. During his reign there flourished the greatest collection of heavyweights ever seen, and he was the greatest of all. He defeated all manner of boxers.

In Corbett he beat the fastest heavyweight and the cleverest boxer that ever lived; in Fitzsimmons the most effective hitter of any time; in Tom Sharkey, the greatest of all near champions. While Jefferies would not rank first in skill, speed or hitting ability, for all around prowess he was invincible.

Peter Jackson never saw the day that he could have beaten Jefferies; and the idea of Johnson beating Jefferies when the white man was at his best is ridiculous. Johnson lacked both the ability and the nerve. As for Sullivan and Dempsey, they would have fought themselves out punching Jefferies, and then have been defeated. If there ever was a man who might have won from Jefferies it was Corbett, when at his prime.

This is my rating of heavyweights: James J. Jefferies; James J. Corbett; Jack Dempsey; Peter Jackson; Bob Fitzsimmons; John L. Sullivan; Tom Sharkey; Kid McCoy; Sam Langford; Jack Johnson; Louis Firpo and Jess Willard.

Robert E. Howard
Cross Plains, Texas

KID LAVIGNE IS DEAD

Hang up the battered gloves; Lavigne is dead.
Bold and erect he went into the dark.
The crown is withered and the crowds are fled,
The empty ring stands bare and lone—yet hark:
The ghostly roar of many a phantom throng
Floats down the dusty years, forgotten long.

Hot blazed the lights above the crimson ring
Where there he reigned in his full prime, a king.
The throngs' acclaim roared up beneath their sheen
And whispered down the night: "Lavigne! Lavigne!"
Red splashed the blood and fierce the crashing blows.
Men staggered to the mat and reeling rose.
Crowns glittered there in splendor, won or lost,
And bones were shattered as the sledges crossed.

Swift as a leopard, strong and fiercely lean,
Champions knew the prowess of Lavigne.
The giant dwarf Joe Walcott saw him loom
And broken, bloody, reeled before his doom.
Handler and Everhardt and rugged Burge
Saw at the last his snarling face emerge
From bloody mists that veiled their dimming sight
Ere they sank down into unlighted night.

Strong men and bold, lay vanquished at his feet.
Mighty was he in triumph and defeat.
Far fade the echoes of the ringside's cheers
And all is lost in mists of dust-dead years.
Cold breaks the dawn; the East is ghastly red.
Hand up the broken gloves; Lavigne is dead.

DULA DUE TO BE CHAMPION

From *The Brownwood Bulletin*, July 18, 1928

Arthur "Kid" Dula is due to be the middleweight champion of the world, in the opinion of Robert E. Howard of Cross Plains, who witnessed the Dula-Tramel battle in Fort Worth last week.

Howard is a close student of the boxing game, and is thoroughly posted on current boxing as well as on the history of the fight game. Writing to The Bulletin today from his home in Cross Plains, Howard says:

"Last Friday night a boy went through his baptism of blood and fire and emerged victorious. The decision went against him but the moral victory was his.

"Arthur Dula of Brownwood, in his slashing, desperate battle against Duke Tramel proved that he was of the stuff of which champions are built. I have seen challengers, champions and near champions perform but that moment in the fourth round, when Dula, his back against the ropes, pinned there by Tramel's murderous attack, and dazed from a terrific right to the temple—made a desperate rally and outslugged the most dangerous slugger the South has ever produced. Outslugged, outfought and battered him back across the ring.

"Again in the eighth, when dizzy and bloody the Kid reeled about the ring, out on his feet but with superhuman courage refusing to go down—again in the last desperate round when the Kid, weakened by cruel punishment and low blows charged recklessly across the ring, met Tramel in his own corner. And fighting like an uncaged tiger, smashed the weakening slugger from one side of the ring to the other.

Next Champion

"All this leads to the main point; that which came into my mind as I watched that bloody eighth round. Kid Dula is the next Middleweight Champion of the World.

"The Kid has much to learn of the finer points of boxing; but he is a natural hitter, a clever boxer, tough and courageous. More, he is aggressive to an extent reminiscent of Dempsey. And like all really great sluggers, like Sullivan Ketchel, Terry McGovern, Bob Fitzsimmons and Jack Dempsey, Dula never loses his punch and is most dangerous when apparently out. This quality alone is the greatest gift a fighter can have and one which has sustained Duke Tramel also, through many grim battles and made him for a time, champion of the Southwest. And Dula besides this has other qualities which Trammel lacks, mainly boxing skill and speed. His main handicap is lack of sufficient experience.

"The fight Friday night, boiled down, comes to this: a desperate battle between two iron men, the experience and sledge hammer power of one being offset by the speed and aggressiveness of the other. A draw would have been fair to both. One of the greatest fights the South has ever seen.

"And Dula is the next middleweight champion. All he needs is proper handling. He has everything else."

The APPARITION in the Prize Ring

Did a Ghost Help Win This Savage Fight? Ask Ace Jessel!

By JOHN TAVEREL
One of the Greatest Managers in the History of the Fight Game

THE APPARITION IN THE PRIZE RING

READERS OF THIS magazine will probably remember Ace Jessel, the big Negro boxer whom I managed a few years ago. He was an ebony giant, four inches over six feet tall, with a fighting weight of 230 pounds. He moved with the smooth ease of a gigantic leopard and his pliant steel muscles rippled under his shiny skin. A clever boxer for so large a man, he carried the smashing jolt of a trip-hammer in each huge fist.

It was my belief that he was the equal of any man in the ring at that time—except for one fatal defect. He lacked the killer instinct. He had courage in plenty, as he proved on more than one occasion—but he was content to box mostly, outpointing his opponents and piling up just enough lead to keep from losing.

Every so often the crowds booed him, but their taunts only broadened his good-natured grin. However, his fights continued to draw a big gate, because, on the rare occasions when he was stung out of a defensive role or when he was matched with a clever man whom he had to knock out in order to win, the fans saw a real fight that thrilled their blood. Even so, time and again he stepped away from a sagging foe, giving the beaten man time to recover and return to the attack—while the crowd raved and I tore my hair.

The one abiding loyalty in Ace's happy-go-lucky life was a fanatical worship of Tom Molyneaux, first champion of America and a sturdy fighting man of color; according to some authorities, the greatest black ringman that ever lived.

Tom Molyneaux died in Ireland a hundred years ago but the memory of his valiant deeds in American and Europe was Ace Jessel's direct incentive to action. As a boy, toiling on the wharves, he had heard an account of Tom's life and battles and the story had started him on the fistic trail.

ACE'S MOST HIGHLY prized possession was a painted portrait of the old battler. He had discovered this—a rare find indeed, since even woodcuts of Molyneaux are rare—among the collection of a London sportsman, and had prevailed on the owner to sell it. Paying for it had taken every cent that Ace made in four fights but he counted it cheap at the price. He removed the original frame and replaced it with a frame of solid silver, which, considering the portrait was full length and life size, was more than extravagant.

But no honor was too great for "Mistah Tom" and Ace merely increased the number of his bouts to meet the cost.

Finally my brains and Ace's mallet fists had cleared us a road to the top of the game. Ace loomed up as a heavyweight menace and the champion's manager was ready to sign with us—when an unexpected obstacle blocked our path.

A form hove into view on the fistic horizon that dwarfed and overshadowed all other contenders, including my man. This was "Mankiller Gomez," and he was all that his name implies. Gomez was his ring name, given him by the Spaniard who discovered him and brought him to America. He was a full-blooded Senegalese from the West Coast of Africa.

ONCE IN A century, rings fans see a man like Gomez in action—a born killer who crashes through the general ruck of fighters as a buffalo crashes through a thicket of dead wood. He was a savage, a tiger. What he lacked in actual skill, he made up by ferocity of attack, by ruggedness of body and smashing power of arm. From the time he landed in New York, with a long list of European victories behind him, it was inevitable that he should batter down all opposition—and at last the white champion looked to see the black savage looming above the broken forms of his victims. The champion saw the writing on the wall, but the public was clamoring for a match and whatever his faults, the title-holder was a fighting champion.

Ace Jessel, who alone of all the foremost challengers had not met Gomez, was shoved into discard, and as early summer dawned on New York, a title was lost and won, and Mankiller Gomez, son of the black jungle, rose up as king of all fighting men.

The sporting world and the public at large hated and feared the new champion. Boxing fans like savagery in the ring, but Gomez did not confine his ferocity to the ring. His soul was abysmal. He was apelike, primordial—the very spirit of that morass of barbarism from which mankind has so tortuously climbed, and toward which men look with so much suspicion.

There went forth a search for a White Hope, but the result was always the same. Challenger after challenger went down before the terrible onslaught of the Mankiller and at last only one man remained who had not crossed gloves with Gomez—Ace Jessel.

I hesitated to throw my man in with a battler like Gomez, for my fondness for the great good-natured negro was more than the friendship of manager for fighter. Ace was something more than a meal-ticket to me, for I knew the real nobility underlying Ace's black skin, and I hated to see him battered into a senseless ruin by a man I know in my heart to be more than Jessel's match. I wanted to wait a while, to let Gomez wear himself out with his terrific battles and the dissipations that were sure to follow the savage's success. These super-sluggers never last long, any more than a jungle native can withstand the temptations of civilization.

But the slump that follows a really great title-holder's gaining the belt was on, and matches were scarce. The public was clamoring for a title fight, sports writers were raising Cain and accusing Ace of cowardice, promoters were offering alluring purses, and at last I signed for a fifteen-round go between Mankiller Gomez and Ace Jessel.

At the training quarters I turned to Ace.

"Ace, do you think you can whip him?"

"Mistah John," Ace answered, meeting my eye with a straight gaze, "I'll do mah best, but I's mighty afeard I caint do it. Dat man ain't human."

This was bad; a man is more than half whipped when he goes into the ring in that frame of mind.

Later I went to Ace's room for something and halted in the doorway in amazement. I had heard the battler talking in a low voice as I came up, but had supposed one of the handlers or sparring partners was in the room with him. Now I saw that he was alone. He was standing before his idol—the portrait of Tom Molyneaux.

"Mistah Tom," he was saying humbly, "I ain't neveh met no man yet what could even knock me off mah feet, but I recon dat niggah can. I's gwine to need help mighty bad, Mistah Tom."

I felt almost as if I had interrupted a religious rite. It was uncanny; had it not been for Ace's evident deep sincerity, I would have felt it to be unholy. But to Ace, Tom Molyneaux was something more than a saint.

I stood in the doorway in silence, watching the strange tableaux. The unknown artist had painted the picture of Molyneaux with remarkable skill. The short black figure stood out boldly from the faded canvas. The breath of by-gone days, he seemed, clad in the long tights of that other day, the powerful legs braced far apart, the knotted arms held stiff and high—just as Molyneaux had appeared when he fought Tom Cribb of England over a hundred years ago.

Ace Jessel stood before the painted figure, his head sunk upon his mighty chest as if listening to some dim whisper inside his soul. And as I watched, a curious and fantastic idea came to me—the memory of a age-old superstition.

You know it had been said by student of the occult that statues and portraits have power to draw departed souls back from the void of eternity. I wondered if Ace had heard of this superstition and hoped to conjure his idol's spirit out of the realms of the dead, for advice and aid. I shrugged my shoulders at this ridiculous idea and turned away. As I did, I glanced again at the picture before which Ace still stood like a great image of black basalt, and was aware of a peculiar illusion; the canvas seemed to ripple slightly, like the surface of a lake across which a faint breeze is blowing. . . .

When the day of the fight arrived, I watched Ace nervously. I was more afraid than ever that I had made a mistake in permitting circumstances to force my man into the ring with Gomez. However, I was backing Ace to the limit—and I was ready to do anything under heaven to help him win that fight.

The great crowd cheered Ace to the echo as he climbed into the ring; cheered again, but not so heartily, as Gomez appeared. They afforded a strange contrast, those two negroes, alike in color but so different in all other respects!

Ace was tall, clean-limbed and rangy, long and smooth of muscle, clear of eye and broad of forehead.

Gomez seemed stocky by comparison, though he stood a good six feet two. Where Jessel's sinews were long and smooth like great cables, his were knotty and bulging. His calves, thighs, arms and shoulders stood out in great bunches of muscles. His small bullet head was set squarely between gigantic shoulders, and his forehead was so low that his kinky wool seemed to grow just above his small, bloodshot eyes. On his chest was a thick grizzle of matted black hair.

He grinned insolently, thumped his breast and flexed his mighty arms with the assurance of the savage. Ace, in his corner, grinned at the crowd, but an ashy tint was on his dusky face and his knees were trembling.

THE USUAL FORMALITIES were carried out: instructions given by the referee, weights announced—230 for Ace, 248 for Gomez. Then over the great stadium the lights went off except those over the ring where two black giants faced each other like men alone on the ridge of the world.

At the gong Gomez whirled in his corner and came out with a breath-taking roar of pure ferocity. Ace, frightened though he must have been, rushed to meet him with the courage of a cave man charging a gorilla. They met headlong in the center of the ring.

The first blow was the Mankiller's, a left swing that glanced from Ace's ribs. Ace came back with a long left to the face and a stinging right to the body. Gomez "bulled in," swinging both hands; and Ace, after one futile attempt to mix it with him, gave back. The champion drove him across the ring, sending a savage left to the body as Ace clinched. As they broke, Gomez shot a terrible right to the chin and Ace reeled into the ropes.

A great "Ahhh!" went up from the crowd as the champion plunged after him like a famished wolf, but Ace manage to get between the lashing arms and clinch, shaking his head to clear it. Gomez sent in a left, which Ace's clutching arms partly smothered, and the referee warned the Senegalese.

At the break Ace stepped back, jabbing swiftly and cleverly with his left. The round ended with the champion bellowing like a buffalo, trying to get past the rapier-like arm.

Between rounds I cautioned Ace to keep away from in-fighting as much as possible, where Gomez' superior strength would count heavily, and to use his footwork to avoid punishment.

The second round started much like the first, Gomez rushing and Ace using all his skill to stave him off and avoid those terrible smashes. It's hard to get a shifty boxer like Ace in a corner, when he is fresh and unweakened, and at long range he had the advantage over Gomez, whose one idea was to get in close and batter down his foes by sheer strength and ferocity. Still, in spite of Ace's speed and skill, just before the gong sounded Gomez got the range and sank a vicious left in Ace's midriff and the tall negro weaved slightly as he returned to his corner.

I felt that it was the beginning of the end. The vitality and power of Gomez seemed endless; there was no wearing him down and it would not take many such blows to rob Ace of his speed of foot and accuracy of eye. If forced to stand and trade punches, he was finished.

Gomez came plunging out for the third round with murder in his eye. He ducked a straight left, took a hard right uppercut square in the face and hooked both hands to Ace's body, then straightened with a terrific right to the chin, which Ace robbed of most of its force by swaying with the blow.

WHILE THE CHAMPION was still off balance, Ace measure him coolly and shot in a fierce right hook, flush on the chin. Gomez' head flew back as if hinged to his shoulders and he was stopped in his tracks! But even as the crowd rose, hands clenched, lips parted, hoping he would go down, the champion shook his bullet head and came in, roaring. The round ended with both men locked in a clinch in the center of the ring.

At the beginning of the fourth round Gomez drove Ace about the ring almost at will. Stung and desperate, Ace made a stand in a neutral corner and sent Gomez back on his heels with a left and right to the body, but he received a savage left in the face in return. Then suddenly the champion crashed through with a deadly left to the solar plexus, and as Ace staggered, shot a killing right to the chin. Ace fell back into the ropes, instinctively raising his hands. Gomez' short, fierce smashes were partly blocked by his shielding gloves—and suddenly, pinned on the ropes as he was, and still dazed from the Mankiller's attack, Ace went into terrific action and, slugging toe to toe with the champion, beat him off and drove him back across the ring!

The crowd went mad. Ace was fighting as he had never fought before, but I waited miserably for the end. I knew no man could stand the pace the champion was setting.

Battling along the ropes, Ace sent a savage left to the body and a right and left to the face, but was repaid by a right-hand smash to the ribs that made him wince in spite of himself. Just at the gong, Gomez landed another of those deadly left-handers to the body.

Ace's handlers worked over him swiftly, but I saw that the tall black was weakening.

"Ace, can't you keep away from those body smashes?" I asked.

"Mistah John, suh, I'll try," he answered.

The gong!

Ace came in with a rush, his magnificent body vibrating with dynamic energy. Gomez met him, his iron muscles bunching into a compact fighting unit. Crash—crash—and again, crash! A clinch. As they broke, Gomez drew back his great right arm and launched a terrible blow to Ace's mouth. The tall negro reeled—went down. Then without stopping for the count which I was screaming of him to take, he gathered his long, steely legs under him and was up with a bound, blood gushing down his black chest. Gomez leaped in and Ace, with the fury of desperation, met him with a terrific right, square to the jaw. And Gomez crashed to the canvas on his shoulder blades!

The crowd rose screaming! In the space of ten seconds both men had been floored for the first time in the life of each!

"One! Two! Three! Four!" The referee's arm rose and fell.

GOMEZ WAS UP, unhurt, wild with fury. Roaring like a wild beast, he plunged in, brushed aside Ace's hammering arms and crashed his right hand with the full wieght of his mighty shoulder behind it, full into Ace's midriff. Ace went an ashy color—he swayed like a tall tree, and Gomez beat him to his knees with rights and lefts which sounded like the blow of caulking mallets.

"One! Two! Three! Four—"

Ace was writhing on the canvas, trying to get up. The roar of the fans was an ocean of noise which drowned all thought.

"—Five! Six! Seven—"

Ace was up! Gomez came charging across the stained canvas, gibbering his pagan fury. His blows beat upon the staggering challenger like a hail of sledges. A left—a right—another left which Ace had not the strength to duck.

He went down again.

"One! Two! Three! Four! Five! Six! Seven! Eight—"

Again Ace was up, weaving, staring blankly, helpless. A swinging left hurled him back into the ropes and, rebounding from them, he went to his knees—then the gong sounded!

As his handlers and I sprang into the ring Ace groped blindly for his corner and dropped limply upon the stool.

"Ace, he's too much for you," I said.

A weak grin spread over Ace's face and his indomitable spirit shone in his blood-shot eyes.

"Mistah John, please, suh, don't throw in de sponge. If I mus' take it, I takes it standin'. Dat boy caint last at dis pace all night, suh."

No—but neither could Ace Jessel, in spite of his remarkable vitality and his marvelous recuperative powers, which sent him into the next round with a show of renewed strength and freshness.

The sixth and seventh were comparatively tame. Perhaps Gomez really was fatigued from the terrific pace he had been setting. At any rate, Ace managed to make it more or less of a sparring match at long range and the crowd was treated to an exhibition illustrating how long a brainy boxer can stand off and keep away from a slugger bent solely on his destruction Even I marveled at the brand of boxing which Ace was showing, though I knew that Gomez was fighting cautiously for him. The champion had sampled the power of Ace's right hand in that frenzied fifth round and perhaps he was wary of a trick. For the first time in his life he had sprawled on the canvas. He was content to rest a couple of rounds, take his time and gather his energies for a final onslaught.

This began as the gong sounded for the eighth round. Gomez launched his usual sledge-hammer attack, drove Ace about the ring and floored him in a neutral corner. His style of fighting was such that when he was determined to annihilate a foe, skill, speed and science could do no more than postpone the eventual outcome. Ace took the count of nine and rose, back-pedaling.

BUT GOMEZ WAS after him; the champion missed twice with his left and then sank a right under the heart that turned Ace ashy. A left to the jaw made his knees buckle and he clinched desperately.

On the break-away Ace sent a straight left to the face and right hook to the chin, but the blows lacked force. Gomez shook them off and sank his left wrist deep in Ace's midsection. Ace again clinched but the champion shoved him away and drove him across the right with savage hooks to the body. At the gong they were slugging along the ropes.

Ace reeled to the wrong corner, and when his handlers led him to his own, he sank down on the stool, his legs trembling and his great dusky chest heaving from his exertions. I glanced across at the champion, who was glowering at his foe. He too was showing signs of the fray, but he was much fresher than Ace. The referee walked over, looked hesitantly at Ace, and then spoke to me.

Through the mists that veiled his muddled brain, Ace realized the significance of these words and struggled to rise, a kind of fear showing in his eyes.

"Mistah John, don' let him stop it, suh! Don' let him do it; I ain't hu't nuthin' like dat would hu't me!"

The referee shrugged his shoulders and walked back to the center of the ring.

There was little use giving advice to Ace. He was too battered to understand—in his numbed brain there was room only for one thought—to fight and fight, and keep on fighting—the old primal instinct that is stronger than all things except death.

At the sound of the gong he reeled out to meet his doom with an indomitable courage that brought the crowd to its feet yelling. He struck, a wild aimless left, and the champion plunged in, hitting with both hands until Ace sent down. At "nine" he was up, back-pedaling instinctively until Gomez reached him with a long straight right and sent him down again. Again he took "nine" before he reeled up and now the crowd was silent. Not one voice was raised in an urge for the kill. This was butchery—primitive slaughter—but the courage of Ace Jessel took their breath as it gripped my heart.

Ace fell blindly into a clinch, and another and another, till the Mankiller, furious, shook him off and sank his right to the body. Ace's ribs gave way like rotten wood, with a dry crack heard distinctly all over the stadium. A strangled cry went up from the crowd and Ace gasped thickly and fell to his knees.

"—Seven! Eight—" The great black form was still writhing on the canvas.

"—Nine!" And then a miracle happened; Ace was on his feet, swaying, jaw sagging, arms hanging limply.

Gomez glared at him, as if unable to understand how his foe could have risen again, then came plunging in to finish him. Ace was in dire straits. Blood blinded him. Both eyes were nearly closed, and when he breathed through his smashed nose, a red haze surrounded him. Deep cuts gashed cheek and cheek bones and his left side was a mass of torn flesh. He was going on fighting instinct alone now, and never again would any man doubt that Ace Jessel had a fighting heart.

Yet a fighting heart alone is not enough when the body is broken and battered, and mists of unconsciousness veil the brain. Before Gomez' terrific onslaught, Ace went down—broken—and the crowd knew that this time it was final.

When a man has taken the beating that Ace had taken, something more than body and heart must come into the game to carry him through. Something to inspire and stimulate him—to fire him to heights of superhuman effort!

Before leaving the training quarters, I had, unknown to Ace, removed the picture of Tom Molyneaux from its frame, rolled it up carefully and brought it to the stadium with me. I now took this, and as Ace's dazed eyes instinctively sought his corner, I held the portrait up, just outside the flare of the ring lights, so while illumined by them it appeared illusive and dim. It may be thought that I acted wrongly and selfishly, to thus seek to bring a broken man to his feet for more punishment—but the outsider cannot fathom the souls of the children of the fight game, to whom winning is greater than life, and losing, worse than death.

All eyes were glued on the prostrate form in the center of the ring, on the exhausted champion sagging against the ropes, on the referee's arm which rose and fell with the regularity of doom. I doubt if four men in the audience saw my action—but Ace Jessel did!

I caught the gleam that came into his blood-shot eyes. I saw him shake his head violently. I saw him begin sluggishly to gather his long legs under him, while the drone of the referee rose as it neared its climax.

And as I live today, *the picture in my hands shook suddenly and violently!*

A cold wind passed like death across me and I heard the man next to me shiver involuntarily as he drew his coat close about him. But it was no cold wind that gripped my soul as I looked, wide-eyed and staring, into the ring where the greatest drama of the boxing world was being enacted.

Ace, struggling, got his elbows under him. Bloody mists masked his vision; then, far away but coming nearer, he saw a form looming through the fog. A man—a short, massive black man, barrel-chested and might-limbed, clad in the long tights of another day—stood beside him in the ring! It was Tom Molyneaux, stepping down through the dead years to aid his worshiper—Tom Molyneaux, attired and ready as when he fought Tom Cribb so long ago!

AND JESSEL WAS up! The crowd went insane and screaming. A supernatural might fired his weary limbs and lit his dazed brain. Let Gomez do his worst now—how could he beat a man for whom the ghost of the greatest of all black warriors was fighting?

For to Ace Jessel, falling on the astounded Mankiller like a blast from the Arctic, Tom Molyneaux's mighty arm was about his waist, Tom's eye guided his blows, Tom's bare fists fell with Ace's on the head and body of the champion.

The Mankiller was dazed by his opponent's sudden come-back—he was bewildered by the uncanny strength of the man who should have been fainting on the canvas. And before he could rally, he was beaten down by the long, straight smashes sent in with the speed and power of a pile-driver. The last blow, a straight right, would have felled an ox—and it felled Gomez for the long count.

As the astonished referee lifted Ace's hand, proclaiming him champion, the tall negro smiled and collapsed, mumbling the words, "Thanks, Mistah Tom."

Yes, to all concerned, Ace's come-back seemed inhuman and unnatural—though no one saw the phantom figure except Tom—and one other. I am not going to claim that I saw the ghost myself—because I didn't, though I did feel the uncanny movement of that picture. If it hadn't been for the strange thing that happened just after the fight, I would say that the whole affair might be naturally explained—that Ace's strength was miraculously renewed by a delusion resulting from his glimpse of the picture. For after all, who knows the strange depths of the human soul and to what apparently superhuman heights the body may be lifted by the mind?

BUT AFTER THE bout the referee, a steely-nerved, cold-eyed sportsman of the old school, said to me:

"Listen here! Am I crazy—or was there a fourth man in that ring when Ace Jessel dropped Gomez? For a minute I thought I saw a broad, squat, funny-looking negro standing there beside Ace! Don't grin, you bum! It wasn't that picture you were holding up—I saw that, too. It was a real man—and he looked like the one in the picture. He was standing there a moment—and then he was gone! God! That fight must have got on my nerves."

And these are the cold facts, told without any attempt to distort the truth or mislead the reader. I leave the problem up to you:

Was it Ace's numbed brain that created the hallucination of ghostly aid—or did the phantom of Tom Molyneaux actually stand beside him, as he believes to this day?

As far as I am concerned, the old superstition is justified. I believe firmly today that a portrait is a door through which astral beings may pass back and forth between this world and the next—whatever the next world may be—and that a great, unselfish love is strong enough to summon the spirits of the dead to the aid of the living.

The Pit of the Serpent

By ROBERT E. HOWARD

All rules went by the board when these two Yankee sailor-men bared their fists in the mystery pit, and battled for the favor of a dark-eyed señorita.

THE PIT OF THE SERPENT

THE MINUTE I stepped ashore from the *Sea Girl*, merchantman, I had a hunch that there would be trouble. This hunch was caused by seeing some of the crew of the *Dauntless*. The men on the *Dauntless* have disliked the *Sea Girl*'s crew ever since our skipper took their captain to a cleaning on the wharfs of Zanzibar—them being narrow-minded that way. They claimed that the old man had a knuckle-duster on his right, which is ridiculous and a dirty lie. He had it on his left.

Seeing these roughnecks in Manila, I had no illusions about them, but I was not looking for no trouble. I am heavyweight champion of the *Sea Girl*, and before you make any wisecracks about the non-importance of that title, I want you to come down to the forecastle and look over Mushy Hansen and One-Round Grannigan and Flat-Face O'Toole and Swede Hjonning and the rest of the mankillers that make up the *Sea Girl*'s crew. But for all that, no one can never accuse me of being quarrelsome, and so instead of following my natural instinct and knocking seven or eight of these bezarks for a row, just to be ornery, I avoided them and went to the nearest American bar.

After a while I found myself in a dance hall, and while it is kind of hazy just how I got there, I assure you I had not no great amount of liquor under my belt—some beer, a few whiskeys, a little brandy, and maybe a slug of wine for a chaser like. No, I was the perfect chevalier in all my actions, as was proven when I found myself dancing with the prettiest girl I have yet to see in Manila or elsewhere. She had red lips and black hair, and oh, what a face!

"Say, miss," said I, the soul of politeness, "where have you been all my life?"

"Oooh, la!" said she, with a silvery ripple of laughter. "You Americans say such theengs. Oooh, so huge and strong you are, señor!"

I let her feel of my biceps, and she give squeals of surprise and pleasure, clapping her little white hands just like a child what has found a new pretty.

"Oooh! You could just snatch little me oop and walk away weeth me, couldn't you, señor?"

"You needn't not be afraid," said I, kindly. "I am the soul of politeness around frails, and never pull no rough stuff. I have never soaked a woman in my life, not even that dame in Suez that throwed a knife at me. Baby, has anybody ever give you a hint about what knockouts your eyes is?"

"Ah, go 'long," said she, coyly—"Ouch!"

"Did somebody step on your foot?" I ask, looking about for somebody to crown.

"Yes—let's sit theese one out, señor. Where did you learn to dance?"

"It comes natural, I reckon," I admitted modestly. "I never knew I could till now. This is the first time I ever tried."

From the foregoing you will see that I am carrying on a quiet conversation, not starting nothing with nobody. It is not my fault, what happened.

Me and this girl, whose name is Raquel La Costa, her being Spanish that way, are sitting peacefully at a table and I am just beginning to get started good telling her how her eyes are like dark pools of night (pretty hot, that one; I got it offa Mushy Hansen, who is all poetical like), when I notice her looking over my shoulder at somebody. This irritates me slightly, but I ignore it, and having forgotten what I was saying, my mind being slightly hazy for some reason, I continue:

"Listen, cutey—hey, who are you winkin' at? Oh, somethin' in your eye, you say? All right, as I was sayin', we got a feller named Hansen on board the *Sea Girl* what writes po'try. Listen to this:

"Oh, the road to glory lay
Over old Manila Bay,
Where the Irish whipped the Spanish
On a sultry summer day."

At this moment some bezark came barging up to our table and, ignoring me, leaned over and leered engagingly at my girl.

"Let's shake a hoof, baby," said this skate, whom I recognized instantly as Bat Slade, champion box fighter of the *Dauntless*.

Miss La Costa said nothing, and I arose and shoved Slade back from the table.

"The lady is engaged at present, stupid," says I, poking my jaw out. "If you got any business, you better 'tend to it."

"Don't get gay with me, Costigan," says he, nastily. "Since when is dames choosin' gorillas instead of humans?"

By this time quite a crowd had formed, and I restrained my natural indignation and said, "Listen, bird, take that map outa my line uh vision before I bust it."

Bat is a handsome galoot who has a way with the dames, and I knew if he danced one dance with my girl he would figure out some way to do me dirt. I did not see any more of the *Dauntless* men; on the other hand, I was the only one of the *Sea Girl*'s crew in the joint.

"Suppose we let the lady choose between us," said Bat. Can you beat that for nerve? Him butting in that way and then giving himself equal rights with me. That was too much. With a bellow, I started my left from the hip, but somehow he wasn't there—the shifty crook! I miss by a yard, and he slams me with a left to the nose that knocks me over a chair.

My brain instantly cleared, and I realized that I had been slightly lit. I arose with an irritated roar, but before hostilities could be renewed, Miss La Costa stepped between us.

"Zut," said she, tapping us with her fan. "Zut! What is theese? Am I a common girl to be so insult' by two great tramps who make fight over me in public? Bah! Eef you wanta fight, go out in ze woods or some place where no one make scandal, and wham each other all you want. May ze best man win! I will not be fight over in public, no sir!"

AND WITH THAT she turned back and walked away. At the same time, up came an oily-looking fellow, rubbing his hands together. I mistrust a bird what goes around rubbing his hands together like he was in a state of perpetual self-satisfaction.

"Now, now, boys," said this bezark, "le's do this right! You boys wanta fight. Tut! Tut! Too bad, too bad! But if you gotta fight, le's do it right, that's what I say! Let fellers live together in peace and enmity if they can, but if they gotta fight, let it be did right!"

"Gi' me leeway—and I'll do this blankety-blank right," says I, fairly shaking with rage. It always irritates me to be hit on the nose without a return and in front of ladies.

"Oh, will you?" said Bat, putting up his mitts. "Let's see you get goin', you—"

"Now, now, boys," said the oily bird, "le's do this right! Costigan, will you and Slade fight for me in my club?"

"Anywheres!" I roar. "Bare-knuckles, gloves, or marlin-spikes!"

"Fine," says the oily bird, rubbing his hands worse than ever. "Ah, fine! Ah—um—ah, Costigan, will you fight Slade in the pit of the serpent?"

Now, I should have noticed that he didn't ask Slade if he'd fight, and I saw Slade grin quietly, but I was too crazy with rage to think straight.

"I'll fight him in the pit of Hades with the devil for a referee!" I roared. "Bring on your fight club—ring, deck, or whatever! Let's get goin'."

"That's the way to talk!" says the oily bird. "Come on."

He turned around and started for the exit, and me and Slade and a few more followed him. Had I of thought, I would have seen right off that this was all working too smooth to have happened impromptu, as it were. But I was still seething with rage and in no shape to think properly.

Howthesomever, I did give a few thoughts as to the chances I had against Slade. As for size, I had the advantage. I'm six feet, and Slade is two inches shorter; I am also a few pounds heavier but not enough to make much difference, us being heavyweights that way. But Slade,

I knew, was the shiftiest, trickiest leather-slinger in the whole merchant marine. I had never met him for the simple reason that no match-maker in any port would stage a bout between a *Sea Girl* man and a *Dauntless* tramp, since that night in Singapore when the bout between Slade and One-Round Grannigan started a free-for-all that plumb wrecked the Wharfside A. C. Slade knocked Grannigan out that night, and Grannigan was then champion slugger aboard the *Sea Girl*. Later, I beat Grannigan.

As for dope, you couldn't tell much, as usual. I'd won a decision over Boatswain Hagney, the champion of the British Asiatic naval fleet, who'd knocked Slade out in Hong Kong, but on the other hand, Slade had knocked out Mike Leary of the Blue Whale, who'd given me a terrible beating at Bombay.

These cogitations was interrupted at that minute by the oily bird. We had come out of the joint and was standing on the curb. Several autos was parked there, and the crowd piled into them. The oily bird motioned me to get in one, and I done so.

Next, we was speeding through the streets, where the lights was beginning to glow, and I asked no questions, even when we left the business section behind and then went right on through the suburbs and out on a road which didn't appear to be used very much. I said nothing, however.

AT LAST WE stopped at a large building some distance outside the city, which looked more like an ex-palace than anything else. All the crowd alighted, and I done likewise, though I was completely mystified. There was no other houses near, trees grew dense on all sides, the house itself was dark and gloomy-looking. All together I did not like the looks of things but would not let on, with Bat Slade gazing at me in his supercilious way. Anyway, I thought, they are not intending to assassinate me because Slade ain't that crooked, though he would stop at nothing else.

We went up the walk, lined on each side by tropical trees, and into the house. There the oily bird struck a light and we went down in the basement. This was a large, roomy affair, with a concrete floor, and in the center was a pit about seven feet deep, and about ten by eight in dimensions. I did not pay no great attention to it at that time, but I did later, I want to tell you.

"Say," I says, "I'm in no mood for foolishness. What you bring me away out here for? Where's your arena?"

"This here's it," said the oily bird.

"Huh! Where's the ring? Where do we fight?"

"Down in there," says the oily bird, pointing at the pit.

"What!" I yell. "What are you tryin' to hand me?"

"Aw, pipe down," interrupted Bat Slade. "Didn't you agree to fight me in the serpent pit? Stop grouchin' and get your duds off."

"All right," I says, plumb burned up by this deal. "I don't know what you're tryin' to put over, but lemme get that handsome map in front of my right and that's all I want!"

"Grahhh!" snarled Slade, and started toward the other end of the pit. He had a couple of yeggs with him as handlers. Shows his caliber, how he always knows some thug; no matter how crooked the crowd may be, he's never without acquaintances. I looked around and recognized a pickpocket I used to know in Cuba, and asked him to handle me. He said he would, though, he added, they wasn't much a handler could do under the circumstances.

"What kind of a deal have I got into?" I asked him as I stripped. "What kind of a joint is this?"

"This house used to be owned by a crazy Spaniard with more mazuma than brains," said the dip, helping me undress. "He yearned for bull fightin' and the like, and he thought up a brand new one. He rigged up this pit and had his servants go out and bring in all kinds of snakes. He'd put two snakes in the pit and let 'em fight till they killed each other."

"What! I got to fight in a snake den?"

"Aw, don't worry. They ain't been no snakes in there for years. The Spaniard got killed, and the old place went to ruin. They held cock fights here and a few years ago the fellow that's stagin' this bout got the idea of buyin' the house and stagin' grudge fights."

"How's he make any money? I didn't see nobody buyin' tickets, and they ain't more'n thirty or forty here."

"Aw, he didn't have no time to work it up. He'll make his money bettin'. He never picks a loser! And he always referees himself. He knows your ship sails tomorrow, and he didn't have no time for ballyhooin'. This fight club is just for a select few who is too sated or too vicious to enjoy a ordinary legitimate prize fight. They ain't but a few in the know—all this is illegal, of course—just a few sports which don't mind payin' for their pleasure. The night Slade fought Sailor Handler they was forty-five men here, each payin' a hundred and twenty-five dollars for admission. Figure it out for yourself."

"Has Slade fought here before?" I ask, beginning to see a light.

"Sure. He's the champion of the pit. Only last month he knocked out Sailor Handler in nine rounds."

Jerusha! And only a few months ago me and the Sailor—who stood six-four and weighed two-twenty—had done everything but knife each other in a twenty-round draw.

"Ho! So that's the way it is," said I. "Slade deliberately come and started trouble with me, knowin' I wouldn't get a square deal here, him bein' the favorite and—"

"No," said the dip, "I don't think so. He just fell for that Spanish frail. Had they been any malice aforethought, word would have circulated among the wealthy sports of the town. As it is, the fellow that owns the joint is throwin' the party free of charge. He didn't have time to work it up. Figure it out—he ain't losing nothin'. Here's two tough sailors wanting to fight a grudge fight—willin' to fight for nothin'. It costs him nothin' to stage the riot. It's a great boost for his club, and he'll win plenty on bets."

The confidence with which the dip said that last gave me cold shivers.

"And who will he bet on?" I asked.

"Slade, of course. Ain't he the pit champion?"

While I was considering this cheering piece of information, Bat Slade yelled at me from the other end of the pit:

"Hey, you blankey dash-dot-blank, ain't you ready yet?"

He was in his socks, shoes and underpants, and no gloves on his hands.

"Where's the gloves?" I asked. "Ain't we goin' to tape our hands?"

"They ain't no gloves," said Slade, with a satisfied grin. "This little riot is goin' to be a bare-knuckle affair. Don't you know the rules of the pit?"

"You see, Costigan," says the oily bird, kinda nervous, "in the fights we put on here, the fighters don't wear no gloves—regular he-man grudge stuff, see?"

"Aw, get goin'!" the crowd began to bellow, having paid nothing to get in and wanting their money's worth. "Lessee some action! What do you think this is? Start somethin'!"

"Shut up!" I ordered, cowing them with one menacing look. "What kind of a deal am I getting here, anyhow?"

"Didn't you agree to fight Slade in the serpent pit?"

"Yes but—"

"Tryin' to back out," said Slade nastily, as usual. "That's like you *Sea Girl* tramps, you—"

"Blank, exclamation point, and asterisk!" I roared, tearing off my undershirt and bounding into the pit. "Get down in here you blank-blank semicolon, and I'll make you look like the last rose of summer, you—"

Slade hopped down into the pit at the other end, and the crowd began to fight for places at the edge. It was a cinch that some of them was not going to get to see all of it. The sides of the pit were hard and rough, and the floor was the same way, like you'd expect a pit in a concrete floor to be. Of course they was no stools or anything.

"Now then," says the oily bird, "this is a finish fight between

Steve Costigan of the *Sea Girl*, weight one-eighty-eight, and Battling Slade, one-seventy-nine, of the *Dauntless*, bare-knuckle champion of the Philippine Islands, in as far as he's proved it in this here pit. They will fight three-minute rounds, one minute rest, no limit to the number of rounds. There will be no decision. They will fight till one of 'em goes out. Referee, me.

"The rules is, nothing barred except hittin' below the belt—in the way of punches, I mean. Break when I say so, and hit on the breakaway if you wanta. Seconds will kindly refrain from hittin' the other man with the water bucket. Ready?"

"A hundred I lay you like a rug," says Slade.

"I see you and raise you a hundred," I snarl.

The crowd began to yell and curse, the timekeeper hit a piece of iron with a six-shooter stock, and the riot was on.

NOW, UNDERSTAND, THIS was a very different fight from any I ever engaged in. It combined the viciousness of a rough-and-tumble with that of a legitimate ring bout. No room for any footwork, concrete to land on if you went down, the uncertain flare of the lights which was hung on the ceiling over us, and the feeling of being crowded for space, to say nothing of thinking about all the snakes which had fought there. Ugh! And me hating snakes that way.

I had figured that I'd have the advantage, being heavier and stronger. Slade couldn't use his shifty footwork to keep out of my way. I'd pin him in a corner and smash him like a cat does a rat. But the bout hadn't been on two seconds before I saw I was all wrong. Slade was just an overgrown Young Griffo. His footwork was second to his ducking and slipping. He had fought in the pit before, and had found that kind of fighting just suited to his peculiar style. He shifted on his feet just enough to keep weaving, while he let my punches go under his arms, around his neck, over his head or across his shoulder.

At the sound of the gong I'd stepped forward, crouching, with both hands going in the only way I knew.

Slade took my left on his shoulder, my right on his elbow, and, *blip-blip!* his left landed twice to my face. Now I want to tell you that a blow from a bare fist is much different than a blow from a glove, and while less stunning, is more of a punisher in its way. Still, I was used to being hit with bare knuckles, and I kept boring in. I swung a left to the ribs that made Slade grunt, and missed a right in the same direction.

This was the beginning of a cruel, bruising fight with no favor. I felt like a wild animal, when I had time to feel anything but Slade's left, battling down there in the pit, with a ring of yelling, distorted faces leering down at us. The oily bird, referee, leaned over the edge at the risk of falling on top of us, and when we clinched he would yell, "Break, you blank-blanks!" and prod us with a cane. He would dance around the edge of the pit trying to keep in prodding distance, and cussing when the crowd got in his way, which was all the time. There was no room in the pit for him; wasn't scarcely room enough for us.

Following that left I landed, Slade tied me up in a clinch, stamped on my instep, thumbed me in the eye, and swished a right to my chin on the breakaway. Slightly infuriated at this treatment, I curled my lip back and sank a left to the wrist in his midriff. He showed no signs at all of liking this, and retaliated with a left to the body and a right to the side of the head. Then he settled down to work.

He ducked a right and came in close, pounding my waist line with short jolts. When, in desperation, I clinched, he shot a right uppercut between my arms that set me back on my heels. And while I was off balance he threw all his weight against me and scraped me against the wall, which procedure removed a large area of hide from my shoulder. With a roar, I tore loose and threw him the full length of the pit, but, charging after him, he side-stepped somehow and I crashed against the pit wall, head-first. *Wham!* I was on the floor, with seventeen million stars flashing before me, and the oily bird was counting as fast as he could, "Onetwothreefourfive—"

I bounded up again, not hurt but slightly dizzy. *Wham, wham, wham!* Bat came slugging in to finish me. I swished loose a right that was labeled T.N.T., but he ducked.

"Look out, Bat! That bird's dangerous!" yelled the oily bird in fright.

"So am I!" snarled Bat, cutting my lip with a straight left and weaving away from my right counter. He whipped a right to the wind that made me grunt, flashed two lefts to my already battered face, and somehow missed with a venomous right. All the time, get me, I was swinging fast and heavy, but it was like hitting at a ghost. Bat had maneuvered me into a corner, where I couldn't get set or defend myself. When I drew back for a punch, my elbow hit the wall. Finally I wrapped both arms around my jaw and plunged forward, breaking through Slade's barrage by sheer weight. As we came together, I threw my arms about him and together we crashed to the floor.

Slade, being the quicker that way, was the first up, and hit me with a roundhouse left to the side of the head while I was still on one knee.

"Foul!" yells some of the crowd.

"Shut up!" bellowed the oily bird. "I'm refereein' this bout!"

As I found my feet, Slade was right on me and we traded rights. Just then the gong sounded. I went back to my end of the pit and sat down on the floor, leaning my back against the wall. The dip peered over the edge.

"Anything I can do?" said he.

"Yeah," said I, "knock the daylights out of the blank-blank that's pretendin' to referee this bout."

Meanwhile the aforesaid blank-blank shoved his snoot over the other end of the pit, and shouted anxiously, "Slade, you reckon you can take him in a couple more rounds?"

"Sure," said Bat. "Double your bets; triple 'em. I'll lay him in the next round."

"You'd better!" admonished this fair-minded referee.

"How can he get anybody to bet with him?" I asked.

"Oh," says the dip, handing me down a sponge to wipe off the blood, "some fellers will bet on anything. For instance, I just laid ten smackers on you, myself."

"That I'll win?"

"Naw; that you'll last five rounds."

AT THIS MOMENT the gong sounded and I rushed for the other end of the pit, with the worthy intention of effacing Slade from the face of the earth. But, as usual, I underestimated the force of my rush and the length of the pit. There didn't seem to be room enough for Slade to get out of my way, but he solved this problem by dropping on his knees, and allowing me to fall over him, which I did.

"Foul!" yelled the dip. "He went down without bein' hit!"

"Foul my eye!" squawked the oily bird. "A blind man could tell he slipped, accidental."

We arose at the same time, me none the better for my fiasco. Slade took my left over his shoulder and hooked a left to the body. He followed this with a straight right to the mouth and a left hook to the side of the head. I clinched and clubbed him with my right to the ribs until the referee prodded us apart.

Again Slade managed to get me into a corner. You see, he was used to the dimensions whereas I, accustomed to a regular ring, kept forgetting about the size of the blasted pit. It seemed like with every movement I bumped my hip or shoulder or scraped my arms against the rough cement of the walls. To date, Slade hadn't a mark to show he'd been in a fight, except for the bruise on his ribs. What with his thumbing and his straight lefts, both my eyes were in a fair way to close, my lips were cut, and I was bunged up generally, but was not otherwise badly hurt.

I fought my way out of the corner, and the gong found us slugging toe to toe in the center of the pit, where I had the pleasure of staggering Bat with a left to the temple. Not an awful lot of action in that round; mostly clinching.

The third started like a whirlwind. At the tap of the gong Slade bounded from his end and was in mine before I could get up. He slammed me with a left and right that shook me clean to my toes, and ducked my left. He also ducked a couple of rights, and then rammed a left to my wind which bent me double. No doubt—this baby could hit!

I came up with a left swing to the head, and in a wild mix-up took four right and left hooks to land my right to the ribs. Slade grunted and tried to back-heel me, failing which he lowered his head and butted me in the belly, kicked me on the shin, and would have did more, likely, only I halted the proceedings temporarily by swinging an overhand right to the back of his neck which took the steam out of him for a minute.

We clinched, and I never saw a critter short of a octopus which could appear to have so many arms when clinching. He always managed to not only tie me up and render me helpless for the time being, but to stamp on my insteps, thumb me in the eye and pound the back of my neck with the edge of his hand. Add to this the fact that he frequently shoved me against the wall, and you can get a idea what kind of a bezark I was fighting. My superior weight and bulk did not have no advantage. What was needed was skill and speed, and the fact that Bat was somewhat smaller than me was an advantage to him.

Still, I was managing to hand out some punishment. Near the end of that round Bat had a beautiful black eye and some more bruises on his ribs. Then it happened. I had plunged after him, swinging; he sidestepped out of the corner, and the next instant was left-jabbing me to death while I floundered along the wall trying to get set for a smash.

I swished a right to his body, and while I didn't think it landed solid, he staggered and dropped his hands slightly. I straightened out of my defensive crouch and cocked my right, and, simultaneous, I realized I had been took. Slade had tricked me. The minute I raised by chin in this careless manner, he beat me to the punch with a right that smashed my head back against the wall, laying open the scalp. Dazed and only partly conscious of what was going on I rebounded right into Slade, ramming my jaw flush into his left. *Zam!* At the same instant I hooked a trip-hammer right under his heart, and we hit the floor together.

Zowie! I could hear the yelling and cursing as if from a great distance, and the lights on the ceiling high above seemed dancing in a thick fog. All I knew was that I had to get back on my feet as quick as I could.

"One—two—three—four," the oily bird was counting over the both of us, "five—Bat, you blank-blank, get up!—Six—seven—Bat, blast it, get your feet under you!—eight—Juan, hit that gong! What kind of a timekeeper are you?"

"The round ain't over yet!" yelled the dip, seeing I had begun to get my legs under me.

"Who's refereein' this?" roared the oily bird, jerking out a .45. "Juan, hit that gong!—Nine!"

Juan hit the gong and Bat's seconds hopped down into the pit and dragged him to his end, where they started working over him. I crawled back to mine. Splash! The dip emptied a bucket of water over me. That freshened me up a lot.

"How you comin'?" he asked.

"Great!" said I, still dizzy. "I'll lay this bird like a rug in the next round! For honor and the love of a dame! 'Oh, the road to glory lay—'"

"I've seen 'em knocked even more cuckoo," said the dip, tearing off a cud of tobacco.

THE FOURTH! SLADE came up weakened, but with fire in his eye. I was all right, but my legs wouldn't work like they should. Slade was in far better condition. Seeing this, or probably feeling that he was weakening, he threw caution to the winds and rushed in to slug with me.

The crowd went crazy. Left-right-left-right! I was taking four to one, but mine carried the most steam. It couldn't last long at this rate.

The oily bird was yelling advice and dashing about the pit's edge like a lunatic. We went into a clinch, and he leaned over to prod us apart as usual. He leaned far over, and I don't know if he slipped or somebody shoved him. Anyway, he crashed down on top of us just as we broke and started slugging. He fell between us, stopped somebody's right with his chin, and flopped, face down—through for the night!

By mutual consent, Bat and me suspended hostilities, grabbed the fallen referee by his neck and the slack of his pants, and hove him up into the crowd. Then, without a word, we began again. The end was in sight.

Bat suddenly broke and backed away. I followed, swinging with both hands. Now I saw the wall was at his back. Ha! He couldn't duck now! I shot my right straight for his face. He dropped to his knees. *Wham!* My fist just cleared the top of his skull and crashed against the concrete wall.

I heard the bones shatter and a dark tide of agony surged up my arm, which dropped helpless at my side. Slade was up and springing for me, but the torture I was in made me forget all about him. I was nauseated, done up—out on my feet, if you get what I mean. He swung his left with everything he had—my foot slipped in some blood on the floor—his left landed high on the side of my skull instead of my jaw. I went down, but I heard him squawk and looked up to see him dancing and wringing his left hand.

The knockdown had cleared my brain somewhat. My hand was numb and not hurting so much, and I realized that Bat had broke his left hand on my skull like many a man has did. Fair enough! I came surging up, and Bat, with the light of desperation in his eyes, rushed in wide open, staking everything on one right swing.

I stepped inside it, sank my left to the wrist in his midriff, and brought the same hand up to his jaw. He staggered, his arms fell, and I swung my left flush to the button with everything I had behind it. Bat hit the floor.

About eight men shoved their snoots over the edge and started counting, the oily bird being still out. They wasn't all counting together, so somehow I managed to prop myself up against the wall, not wanting to make no mistake, until the last man had said "ten!" Then everything began to whirl, and I flopped down on top of Slade and went out like a candle.

LET'S PASS OVER the immediate events. I don't remember much about them anyhow. I slept until the middle of the next afternoon, and I know the only thing that dragged me out of the bed where the dip had dumped me was the knowledge that the *Sea Girl* sailed that night and that Raquel La Costa probably would be waiting for the victor—me.

Outside the joint where I first met her, who should I come upon but Bat Slade!

"Huh!" says I, giving him the once over. "Are you able to be out?"

"You ain't no beauty yourself," he retorted.

I admit it. My right was in a sling, both eyes was black, and I was generally cut and bruised. Still, Slade had no right to give himself airs. His left was all bandaged, he too had a black eye, and moreover his features was about as battered as mine. I hope it hurt him as much to move as it did me. But he had the edge on me in one way—he hadn't rubbed as much hide off against the walls.

"Where's that two hundred we bet?" I snarled.

"Heh, heh!" sneered he. "Try and get it! They told me I wasn't counted out officially. The referee didn't count me out. You didn't whip me."

"Let the money go, you dirty, yellow crook," I snarled, "but I whipped you, and I can prove it by thirty men. What you doin' here, anyway?"

"I come to see my girl."

"Your girl? What was we fightin' about last night?"

"Just because you had the sap's luck to knock me stiff don't mean

Raquel chooses you," he answered savagely. "This time, she names the man she likes, see? And when she does, I want you to get out!"

"All right," I snarled. "I whipped you fair and can prove it. Come in here; she'll get a chance to choose between us, and if she don't pick the best man, why, I can whip you all over again. Come on, you—"

Saying no more, we kicked the door open and went on in. We swept the interior with a eagle glance, and then sighted Raquel sitting at a table, leaning on her elbows and gazing soulfully into the eyes of a handsome bird in the uniform of a Spanish naval officer.

We barged across the room and come to a halt at her table. She glanced up in some surprise, but she could not have been blamed had she failed to recognize us.

"Raquel," said I, "we went forth and fought for your fair hand just like you said. As might be expected, I won. Still, this incomprehensible bezark thinks that you might still have some lurkin' fondness for him, and he requires to hear from your own rosy lips that you love another—meanin' me, of course. Say the word and I toss him out. My ship sails tonight, and I got a lot to say to you."

"Santa Maria!" said Raquel. "What ees theese? What kind of a bizness is theese, you two tramps coming looking like theese and talking gibberish? Am I to blame eef two great tramps go pound each other's maps, ha? What ees that to me?"

"But you said—" I began, completely at sea, "you said, go fight and the best man—"

"I say, may the best man win! Bah! Did I geeve any promise? What do I care about Yankee tramps what make the fist-fight? Bah! Go home and beefsteak the eye. You insult me, talking to me in public with the punch' nose and bung' up face."

"Then you don't love either of us?" said Bat.

"Me love two gorillas? Bah! Here is my man—Don Jose y Balsa Santa Maria Gonzales."

She then gave a screech, for at that moment Bat and me hit Don Jose y Balsa Santa Maria Gonzales simultaneous, him with the right and me with the left. And then, turning our backs on the dumfounded Raquel, we linked arms and, stepping over the fallen lover, strode haughtily to the door and vanished from her life.

"AND THAT," SAID I, as we leaned upon the bar to which we had made our mutual and unspoke agreement, "ends our romance, and the glory road leads only to disappointment and hokum."

"Women," said Bat gloomily, "are the bunk."

"Listen," said I, remembering something, "how about that two hundred you owe me?"

"What for?"

"For knockin' you cold."

"Steve," said Bat, laying his hand on my shoulder in brotherly fashion, "you know I been intendin' to pay you that all along. After all, Steve, we are seamen together, and we have just been did dirt by a woman of another race. We are both American sailors, even if you are a harp, and we got to stand by each other. Let bygones be bygones, says I. The fortunes of war, you know. We fought a fair, clean fight, and you was lucky enough to win. Let's have one more drink and then part in peace an' amity."

"You ain't holdin' no grudge account of me layin' you out?" I asked, suspiciously.

"Steve," said Bat, waxing oratorical, "all men is brothers, and the fact that you was lucky enough to crown me don't alter my admiration and affection. Tomorrow we will be sailin' the high seas, many miles apart. Let our thoughts of each other be gentle and fraternal. Let us forgit old feuds and old differences. Let this be the dawn of a new age of brotherly affection and square dealin'."

"And how about my two hundred?"

"Steve, you know I am always broke at the end of my shore leave. I give you my word I'll pay you them two hundred smackers. Ain't the word of a comrade enough? Now le's drink to our future friendship and the amicable relations of the crews of our respective ships. Steve, here's my hand! Let this here shake be a symbol of our friendship. May no women ever come between us again! Good-bye, Steve! Good luck! Good luck!"

And so saying, we shook and turned away. That is, I turned and then whirled back as quick as I could—just in time to duck the right swing he'd started the minute my back was turned, and to knock him cold with a bottle I snatched off the bar.

The Bull Dog Breed

By ROBERT E. HOWARD

Author of "The Pit of the Serpent"

Staring into the savage black eyes of Tiger Valois, Costigan thought of his abused bulldog, Mike, and then the ring of the Napoleon Club became a shambles.

THE BULL DOG BREED

"AND SO," CONCLUDED the Old Man, "this big bully ducked the seltzer bottle and the next thing I knowed I knowed nothin'. I come to with the general idee that the *Sea Girl* was sinkin' with all hands and I was drownin'—but it was only some chump pourin' water all over me to bring me to. Oh, yeah, the big French cluck I had the row with was nobody much, I learned—just only merely nobody but Tiger Valois, the heavyweight champion of the French navy—"

Me and the crew winked at each other. Until the captain decided to unburden to Penrhyn, the first mate, in our hearing, we'd wondered about the black eye he'd sported following his night ashore in Manila. He'd been in an unusual bad temper ever since, which means he'd been acting like a sore-tailed hyena. The Old Man was a Welshman, and he hated a Frenchman like he hated a snake. He now turned on me.

"If you was any part of a man, you big mick ham," he said bitterly, "you wouldn't stand around and let a blankety-blank French so-on and so-forth layout your captain. Oh, yeah, I know you wasn't there, then, but if you'll fight him—"

"Aragh!" I said with sarcasm, "leavin' out the fact that I'd stand a great chance of gettin' matched with Valois—why not pick me somethin' easy, like Dempsey? Do you realize you're askin' me, a ordinary ham-an'-egger, to climb the original and only Tiger Valois that's whipped everything in European and the Asian waters and looks like a sure bet for the world's title?"

"Gerahh!" snarled the Old Man. "Me that's boasted in every port of the Seven Seas that I shipped the toughest crew since the days of Harry Morgan—" He turned his back in disgust and immediately fell over my white bulldog, Mike, who was taking a snooze by the hatch. The Old Man give a howl as he come up and booted the innocent pup most severe. Mike instantly attached hisself to the Old Man's leg, from which I at last succeeded in prying him with a loss of some meat and the pants leg.

The captain danced hither and yon about the deck on one foot while he expressed his feelings at some length and the crew stopped work to listen and admire.

"And get me right, Steve Costigan," he wound up, "the *Sea Girl* is too small for me and that double-dash dog. He goes ashore at the next port. Do you hear me?"

"Then I go ashore with him," I answered with dignity. "It was not Mike what caused you to get a black eye, and if you had not been so taken up in abusin' me you would not have fell over him.

"Mike is a Dublin gentleman, and no Welsh water rat can boot *him* and get away with it. If you want to banish your best A.B. mariner, it's up to you. Till we make port you keep your boots off of Mike, or I will personally kick you loose from your spine. If that's mutiny, make the most of it—and, Mister First Mate, I see you easin' toward that belayin' pin on the rail, and I call to your mind what I done to the last man that hit me with a belayin' pin."

There was a coolness between me and the Old Man thereafter. The old nut was pretty rough and rugged, but good at heart, and likely he was ashamed of himself, but he was too stubborn to admit it, besides still being sore at me and Mike. Well, he paid me off without a word at Hong Kong, and I went down the gangplank with Mike at my heels, feeling kind of queer and empty, though I wouldn't show it for nothing, and acted like I was glad to get off the old tub. But since I growed up, the *Sea Girl*'s been the only home I knowed, and though I've left her from time to time to prowl around loose or to make a fight tour, I've always come back to her.

Now I knowed I couldn't come back, and it hit me hard. The *Sea Girl* is the only thing I'm champion of, and as I went ashore I heard the sound of Mushy Hansen and Bill O'Brien trying to decide which should succeed to my place of honor.

WELL, MAYBE SOME will say I should of sent Mike ashore and stayed on, but to my mind, a man that won't stand by his dog is lower down than one which won't stand by his fellow man.

Some years ago I'd picked Mike up wandering around the wharfs of Dublin and fighting everything he met on four legs and not averse to tackling two-legged critters. I named him Mike after a brother of mine, Iron Mike Costigan, rather well known in them higher fight circles where I've never gotten to.

Well, I wandered around the dives and presently fell in with Tom Roche, a lean, fighting engineer that I once knocked out in Liverpool. We meandered around, drinking here and there, though not very much, and presently found ourselves in a dump a little different from the general run. A French joint, kinda more highbrow, if you get me. A lot of swell-looking fellows was in there drinking, and the bartenders and waiters, all French, scowled at Mike, but said nothing. I was unburdening my woes to Tom, when I noticed a tall, elegant young man with a dress suit, cane and gloves stroll by our table. He seemed well known in the dump, because birds all around was jumping up from their tables and waving their glasses and yelling at him in French. He smiled back in a superior manner and flourished his cane in a way which irritated me. This galoot rubbed me the wrong way right from the start, see?

Well, Mike was snoozing close to my chair as usual, and, like any other fighter, Mike was never very particular where he chose to snooze. This big bimbo could have stepped over him or around him, but he stopped and prodded Mike with his cane. Mike opened one eye, looked up and lifted his lip in a polite manner, just like he was sayin': "We don't want no trouble; go 'long and leave me alone."

Then this French dipthong drawed back his patent leather shoe and kicked Mike hard in the ribs. I was out of my chair in a second, seeing red, but Mike was quicker. He shot up off the floor, not for the Frenchman's leg, but for his throat. But the Frenchman, quick as a flash, crashed his heavy cane down across Mike's head, and the bulldog hit the floor and laid still. The next minute the Frenchman hit the floor, and believe me he laid still! My right-hander to the jaw put him down, and the crack his head got against the corner of the bar kept him there.

I bent over Mike, but he was already coming around, in spite of the fact that a loaded cane had been broken over his head. It took a blow like that to put Mike out, even for a few seconds. The instant he got his bearings, his eyes went red and he started out to find what hit him and tear it up. I grabbed him, and for a minute it was all I could do to hold him. Then the red faded out of his eyes and he wagged his stump of a tail and licked my nose. But I knowed the first good chance he had at the Frenchman he'd rip out his throat or die trying. The only way you can lick a bulldog is to kill him.

Being taken up with Mike I hadn't had much time to notice what was going on. But a gang of French sailors had tried to rush me and had stopped at the sight of a gun in Tom Roche's hand. A real fighting man was Tom, and a bad egg to fool with.

By this time the Frenchman had woke up; he was standing with a handkerchief at his mouth, which latter was trickling blood, and honest to Jupiter I never saw such a pair of eyes on a human! His face was dead white, and those black, burning eyes blazed out at me—say, fellows!—they carried more than hate and a desire to muss me up! They was mutilation and sudden death! Once I seen a famous duelist in Heidelberg who'd killed ten men in sword fights—he had just such eyes as this fellow.

A gang of Frenchies was around him all whooping and yelling and jabbering at once, and I couldn't understand a word none of them said. Now one come prancing up to Tom Roche and shook his fist in Tom's face and pointed at me and yelled, and pretty soon Tom turned around to me and said: "Steve, this yam is challengin' you to a duel—what about?"

I thought of the German duelist and said to myself: "I bet this bird was born with a fencin' sword in one hand and a duelin' pistol in the other." I opened my mouth to say "Nothin' doin'—" when Tom pipes: "You're the challenged party—the choice of weapons is up to you."

At that I hove a sigh of relief and a broad smile flitted across my homely but honest countenance. "Tell him I'll fight him," I said, "with five-ounce boxin' gloves."

Of course I figured this bird never saw a boxing glove. Now, maybe you think I was doing him dirty, pulling a fast one like that—but what about him? All I was figuring on was mussing him up a little, counting on him not knowing a left hook from a neutral corner—takin' a mean advantage, maybe, but he was counting on killing me, and I'd never had a sword in my hand, and couldn't hit the side of a barn with a gun.

Well, Tom told them what I said and the cackling and gibbering bust out all over again, and to my astonishment I saw a cold, deadly smile waft itself across the sinister, handsome face of my tête-à-tête.

"They ask who you are," said Tom. "I told 'em Steve Costigan, of America. This bird says his name is Francois, which he opines is enough for *you.* He says that he'll fight you right away at the exclusive Napoleon Club, which it seems has a ring account of it occasionally sponsoring prize fights."

AS WE WENDED our way toward the aforesaid club, I thought deeply. It seemed very possible that this Francois, whoever he was, knew something of the manly art. Likely, I thought, a rich clubman who took up boxing for a hobby. Well, I reckoned he hadn't heard of me, because no amateur, however rich, would think he had a chance against Steve Costigan, known in all ports as the toughest sailor in the Asian waters—if I do say so myself—and champion of—what I mean—ex-champion of the *Sea Girl,* the toughest of all the trading vessels.

A kind of pang went through me just then at the thought that my days with the old tub was ended, and I wondered what sort of a dub would take my place at mess and sleep in my bunk, and how the forecastle gang would haze him, and how all the crew would miss me—I wondered if Bill O'Brien had licked Mushy Hansen or if the Dane had won, and who called hisself champion of the craft now—

Well, I felt low in spirits, and Mike knowed it, because he snuggled up closer to me in the 'rickshaw that was carrying us to the Napoleon Club, and licked my hand. I pulled his ears and felt better. Anyway, Mike wouldn't never desert me.

Pretty ritzy affair this club. Footmen or butlers or something in uniform at the doors, and they didn't want to let Mike in. But they did—oh, yeah, they did.

In the dressing room they give me, which was the swellest of its sort I ever see, and looked more like a girl's boodwar than a fighter's dressing room, I said to Tom: "This big ham must have lots of dough—notice what a hand they all give him? Reckon I'll get a square deal? Who's goin' to referee? If it's a Frenchman, how'm I gonna follow the count?"

"Well, gee whiz!" Tom said, "you ain't expectin' him to count over you, are you?"

"No," I said. "But I'd like to keep count of what he tolls off over the other fellow."

"Well," said Tom, helping me into the green trunks they'd give me, "don't worry none. I understand Francois can speak English, so I'll specify that the referee shall converse entirely in that language."

"Then why didn't this Francois ham talk English to me?" I wanted to know.

"He didn't talk to you in anything," Tom reminded me. "He's a swell and thinks you're beneath his notice—except only to knock your head off."

"H'mm," said I thoughtfully, gently touching the slight cut which Francois' cane had made on Mike's incredibly hard head. A slight red mist, I will admit, waved in front of my eyes.

When I climbed into the ring I noticed several things: mainly the room was small and elegantly furnished; second, there was only a small crowd there, mostly French, with a scattering of English and one Chink in English clothes. There was high hats, frock-tailed coats and gold-knobbed canes everywhere, and I noted with some surprise that they was also a sprinkling of French sailors.

I sat in my corner, and Mike took his stand just outside, like he always does when I fight, standing on his hind legs with his head and forepaws resting on the edge of the canvas, and looking under the ropes. On the street, if a man soaks me he's likely to have Mike at his throat, but the old dog knows how to act in the ring. He won't interfere, though sometimes when I'm on the canvas or bleeding bad his eyes get red and he rumbles away down deep in his throat.

TOM WAS MASSAGING my muscles light-like and I was scratching Mike's ears when into the ring comes Francois the Mysterious. *Oui! Oui!* I noted now how much of a man he was, and Tom whispers to me to pull in my chin a couple of feet and stop looking so goofy. When Francois threw off his silk embroidered bathrobe I saw I was in for a rough session, even if this bird was only an amateur. He was one of these fellows that *look* like a fighting man, even if they've never seen a glove before.

A good six one and a half he stood, or an inch and a half taller than me. A powerful neck sloped into broad, flexible shoulders, a limber steel body tapered to a girlishly slender waist. His legs was slim, strong and shapely, with narrow feet that looked speedy and sure; his arms was long, thick, but perfectly molded. Oh, I tell you, this Francois looked more like a champion than any man I'd seen since I saw Dempsey last.

And the face—his sleek black hair was combed straight back and lay smooth on his head, adding to his sinister good looks. From under narrow black brows them eyes burned at me, and now they wasn't a duelist's eyes—they was tiger eyes. And when he gripped the ropes and dipped a couple of times, flexing his muscles, them muscles rippled under his satiny skin most beautiful, and he looked just like a big cat sharpening his claws on a tree.

"Looks fast, Steve," Tom Roche said, looking serious. "May know somethin'; you better crowd him from the gong and keep rushin'—"

"How else did I ever fight?" I asked.

A sleek-looking Frenchman with a sheik mustache got in the ring and, waving his hands to the crowd, which was still jabbering for Francois, he bust into a gush of French.

"What's he mean?" I asked Tom, and Tom said, "Aw, he's just sayin' what everybody knows—that this ain't a regular prize fight, but an affair of honor between you and—uh—that Francois fellow there."

Tom called him and talked to him in French, and he turned around and called an Englishman out of the crowd. Tom asked me was it all right with me for the Englishman to referee, and I tells him yes, and they asked Francois and he nodded in a supercilious manner. So the referee asked me what I weighed and I told him, and he hollered: "This bout is to be at catch weights, Marquis of Queensberry rules. Three-minute rounds, one minute rest; to a finish, if it takes all night. In this corner, Monsieur Francois, weight 205 pounds; in this corner, Steve Costigan of America, weight 190 pounds. Are you ready, gentlemen?"

'Stead of standing outside the ring, English style, the referee stayed in with us, American fashion. The gong sounded and I was out of my corner. All I seen was that cold, sneering, handsome face, and all I wanted to do was to spoil it. And I very nearly done it the first charge. I came in like a house afire and I walloped Francois with an overhand right hook to the chin—more by sheer luck than anything, and it landed high. But it shook him to his toes, and the sneering smile faded.

TOO QUICK FOR the eye to follow, his straight left beat my left hook, and it packed the jarring kick that marks a puncher. The next minute, when I missed with both hands and got that left in my pan again, I knowed I was up against a master boxer, too.

I saw in a second I couldn't match him for speed and skill. He was like a cat; each move he made was a blur of speed, and when he hit he hit quick and hard. He was a brainy fighter—he thought out each move while traveling at high speed, and he was never at a loss what to do next.

Well, my only chance was to keep on top of him, and I kept crowding him, hitting fast and heavy. He wouldn't stand up to me, but backpedaled all around the ring. Still, I got the idea that he wasn't afraid of me, but was retreating with a purpose of his own. But I never stop to figure out why the other bird does something.

He kept reaching me with that straight left, until finally I dived under it and sank my right deep into his midriff. It shook him—it should of brought him down. But he clinched and tied me up so I couldn't hit or do nothing. As the referee broke us Francois scraped his glove laces across my eyes. With an appropriate remark, I threw my right at his head with everything I had, but he drifted out of the way, and I fell into the ropes from the force of my own swing. The crowd howled with laughter, and then the gong sounded.

"This baby's tough," said Tom, back in my corner, as he rubbed my belly muscles, "but keep crowdin' him, get inside that left, if you can. And watch the right."

I reached back to scratch Mike's nose and said, "You watch this round."

Well, I reckon it was worth watching. Francois changed his tactics, and as I come in he met me with a left to the nose that started the claret and filled my eyes full of water and stars. While I was thinking about that he opened a cut under my left eye with a venomous right-hander and then stuck the same hand into my midriff. I woke up and bent him double with a savage left hook to the liver, crashing him with an overhand right behind the ear before he could straighten. He shook his head, snarled a French cuss word and drifted back behind that straight left where I couldn't reach him.

I went into him like a whirlwind, lamming head on full into that left jab again and again, trying to get to him, but always my swings were short. Them jabs wasn't hurting me yet, because it takes a lot of them to weaken a man. But it was like running into a floating brick wall, if you get what I mean. Then he started crossing his right—and oh, baby, what a right he had! Blip! Blim! Blam!

His rally was so unexpected and he hit so quick that he took me clean off my guard and caught me wide open. That right was lightning! In a second I was groggy, and Francois beat me back across the ring with both hands going too fast for me to block more than about a fourth of the blows. He was wild for the kill now and hitting wide open.

Then the ropes was at my back and I caught a flashing glimpse of him, crouching like a big tiger in front of me, wide open and starting his right. In that flash of a second I shot my right from the hip, beat his punch and landed solid to the button. Francois went down like he'd been hit with a pile driver—the referee leaped forward—the gong sounded!

As I went to my corner the crowd was clean ory-eyed and not responsible; and I saw Francois stagger up, glassy-eyed, and walk to his stool with one arm thrown over the shoulder of his handler.

But he come out fresh as ever for the third round. He'd found out that I could hit as hard as he could and that I was dangerous when groggy, like most sluggers. He was wild with rage, his smile was gone, his face dead white again, his eyes was like black fires—but he was cautious. He side-stepped my rush, hooking me viciously on the ear as I shot past him, and ducking when I slewed around and hooked my right. He backed away, shooting that left to my face. It went that way the whole round; him keeping the right reserved and marking me up with left jabs while I worked for his body and usually missed or was blocked. Just before the gong he rallied, staggered me with a flashing right hook to the head and took a crushing left hook to the ribs in return.

THE FOURTH ROUND come and he was more aggressive. He began to trade punches with me again. He'd shoot a straight left to my face, then hook the same hand to my body. Or he'd feint the left for my face and drop it to my ribs. Them hooks to the body didn't hurt much, because I was hard as a rock there, but a continual rain of them wouldn't do me no good, and them jabs to the face was beginning to irritate me. I was already pretty well marked up.

He shot his blows so quick I usually couldn't block or duck, so every time he'd make a motion with the left I'd throw my right for his head haphazard. After rocking his head back several times this way he quit feinting so much and began to devote most of his time to body blows.

Now I found out this about him: he had more claws than sand, as the saying goes. I mean he had everything, including a lot of stuff I didn't, but he didn't like to take it. In a mix-up he always landed three blows to my one, and he hit about as hard as I did, but he was always the one to back away.

Well, come the seventh round. I'd taken plenty. My left eye was closing fast and I had a nasty gash over the other one. My ribs was beginning to feel the body punishment he was handing out when in close, and my right ear was rapidly assuming the shape of a cabbage. Outside of some ugly welts on his torso, my dancing partner had only one mark on him—the small cut on his chin where I'd landed with my bare fist earlier in the evening.

But I was not beginning to weaken for I'm used to punishment; in fact I eat it up, if I do say so. I crowded Francois into a corner before I let go. I wrapped my arms around my neck, worked in close and then unwound with a looping left to the head.

Francois countered with a sickening right under the heart and I was wild with another left. Francois stepped inside my right swing, dug his heel into my instep, gouged me in the eye with his thumb and, holding with his left, battered away at my ribs with his right. The referee showed no inclination to interfere with this pastime, so, with a hearty oath, I wrenched my right loose and nearly tore off Francois' head with a torrid uppercut.

His sneer changed to a snarl and he began pistoning me in the face again with his left. Maddened, I crashed into him headlong and smashed my right under his heart—I felt his ribs bend, he went white and sick and clinched before I could follow up my advantage. I felt the drag of his body as his knees buckled, but he held on while I raged and swore, the referee would not break us, and when I tore loose, my charming playmate was almost as good as ever.

He proved this by shooting a left to my sore eye, dropping the same hand to my aching ribs and bringing up a right to the jaw that stretched me flat on my back for the first time that night. Just like that! *Biff—bim—bam!* Like a cat hitting—and I was on the canvas.

Tom Roche yelled for me to take a count, but I never stay on the canvas longer than I have to. I bounced up at "Four!" my ears still ringing and a trifle dizzy, but otherwise O.K.

Francois thought otherwise, rushed rashly in and stopped a left hook which hung him gracefully over the ropes. The gong!

The beginning of the eighth I come at Francois like we'd just started, took his right between my eyes to hook my left to his body—he broke away, spearing me with his left—I followed swinging—missed a right—*crack!*

He musta let go his right with all he had for the first time that night, and he had a clear shot to my jaw. The next thing I knowed, I was writhing around on the canvas feeling like my jaw was tore clean off and the referee was saying: "—seven—"

Somehow I got to my knees. It looked like the referee was ten miles away in a mist, but in the mist I could see Francois' face, smiling again, and I reeled up at "nine" and went for that face. *Crack! Crack!* I don't know what punch put me down again but there I was. I beat the count by a hair's breadth and swayed forward, following my only instinct and that was to walk into him!

* * *

FRANCOIS MIGHT HAVE finished me there, but he wasn't taking any chances for he knowed I was dangerous to the last drop. He speared me a couple of times with the left, and when he shot his right, I ducked it and took it high on my forehead and clinched, shaking my head to clear it. The referee broke us away and Francois lashed into me, cautious but deadly, hammering me back across the ring with me crouching and covering up the best I could.

On the ropes I unwound with a venomous looping right, but he was watching for that and ducked and countered with a terrible left to my jaw, following it with a blasting right to the side of the head. Another left hook threw me back into the ropes and there I caught the top rope with both hands to keep from falling. I was swaying and ducking but his gloves were falling on my ears and temples with a steady thunder which was growing dimmer and dimmer—then the gong sounded.

I let go of the ropes to go to my corner and when I let go I pitched to my knees. Everything was a red mist and the crowd was yelling about a million miles away. I heard Francois' scornful laugh, then Tom Roche was dragging me to my corner.

"By golly," he said, working on my cut up eyes, "you're sure a glutton for punishment; Joe Grim had nothin' on you.

"But you better lemme throw in the towel, Steve. This Frenchman's goin' to kill you—"

"He'll have to, to beat me," I snarled. "I'll take it standin'."

"But, Steve," Tom protested, mopping blood and squeezing lemon juice into my mouth, "this Frenchman is—"

But I wasn't listening. Mike knowed I was getting the worst of it and he'd shoved his nose into my right glove, growling low down in his throat. And I was thinking about something.

One time I was laid up with a broken leg in a little fishing village away up on the Alaskan coast, and looking through a window, not able to help him, I saw Mike fight a big gray devil of a sled dog—more wolf than dog. A big gray killer. They looked funny together—Mike short and thick, bow-legged and squat, and the wolf dog tall and lean, rangy and cruel.

Well, while I lay there and raved and tried to get off my bunk with four men holding me down, that blasted wolf-dog cut poor old Mike to ribbons. He was like lightning—like Francois. He fought with the slash and get away—like Francois. He was all steel and whalebone—like Francois.

Poor old Mike had kept walking into him, plunging and missing as the wolf-dog leaped aside—and every time he leaped he slashed Mike with his long sharp teeth till Mike was bloody and looking terrible. How long they fought I don't know. But Mike never give up; he never whimpered; he never took a single back step; he kept walking in on the dog.

At last he landed—crashed through the wolf-dog's defense and clamped his jaws like a steel vise and tore out the wolf-dog's throat. Then Mike slumped down and they brought him into my bunk more dead than alive. But we fixed him up and finally he got well, though he'll carry the scars as long as he lives.

And I thought, as Tom Roche rubbed my belly and mopped the blood off my smashed face, and Mike rubbed his cold, wet nose in my glove, that me and Mike was both of the same breed, and the only fighting quality we had was a everlasting persistence. You got to kill a bulldog to lick him. Persistence! How'd I ever won a fight? How'd Mike ever won a fight? By walking in on our men and never giving up, no matter how bad we was hurt! Always outclassed in everything except guts and grip! Somehow the fool Irish tears burned my eyes and it wasn't the pain of the collodion Tom was rubbing into my cuts and it wasn't self-pity—it was—I don't know what it was! My grandfather used to say the Irish cried at Benburb when they were licking the socks off the English.

THEN THE GONG sounded and I was out in the ring again playing the old bulldog game with Francois—walking into him and walking into him and taking everything he handed me without flinching.

I don't remember much about that round. Francois' left was a red-hot lance in my face and his right was a hammer that battered in my ribs and crashed against my dizzy head. Toward the last my legs felt dead and my arms were like lead. I don't know how many times I went down and got up and beat the count, but I remember once in a clinch, half-sobbing through my pulped lips: "You gotta kill me to stop me, you big hash!" And I saw a strange haggard look flash into his eyes as we broke. I lashed out wild and by luck connected under his heart. Then the red fog stole back over everything and then I was back on my stool and Tom was holding me to keep me from falling off.

"What round's this comin' up?" I mumbled.

"The tenth," he said. "For th' luvva Pete, Steve, quit!"

I felt around blind for Mike and felt his cold nose on my wrist.

"Not while I can see, stand or feel," I said, deliriously. "It's bulldog and wolf—and Mike tore his throat out in the end—and I'll rip this wolf apart sooner or later."

Back in the center of the ring with my chest all crimson with my own blood, and Francois' gloves soggy and splashing blood and water at every blow, I suddenly realized that his punches were losing some of their kick. I'd been knocked down I don't know how many times, but I now knew he was hitting me his best and I still kept my feet. My legs wouldn't work right, but my shoulders were still strong. Francois played for my eyes and closed them both tight shut, but while he was doing it I landed three times under the heart, and each time he wilted a little.

"What round's comin' up?" I groped for Mike because I couldn't see.

"The eleventh—this is murder," said Tom. "I know you're one of these birds which fights twenty rounds after they've been knocked cold, but I want to tell you this Frenchman is—"

"Lance my eyelid with your pocket-knife," I broke in, for I had found Mike. "I gotta see."

Tom grumbled, but I felt a sharp pain and the pressure eased up in my right eye and I could see dim-like.

Then the gong sounded, but I couldn't get up; my legs was dead and stiff.

"Help me up, Tom Roche, you big bog-trotter," I snarled. "If you throw in that towel I'll brain you with the water bottle!"

With a shake of his head he helped me up and shoved me in the ring. I got my bearings and went forward with a funny, stiff, mechanical step, toward Francois—who got up slow, with a look on his face like he'd rather be somewhere else. Well, he'd cut me to pieces, knocked me down time and again, and here I was coming back for more. The bulldog instinct is hard to fight—it ain't just exactly courage, and it ain't exactly blood lust—it's—well, it's the bulldog breed.

NOW I WAS facing Francois and I noticed he had a black eye and a deep gash under his cheek bone, though I didn't remember putting them there. He also had welts a-plenty on his body. I'd been handing out punishment as well as taking it, I saw.

Now his eyes blazed with a desperate light and he rushed in, hitting as hard as ever for a few seconds. The blows rained so fast I couldn't think and yet I knowed I must be clean batty—punch drunk—because it seemed like I could hear familiar voices yelling my name—the voices of the crew of the *Sea Girl,* who'd never yell for me again.

I was on the canvas and this time I felt that it was to stay; dim and far away I saw Francois and somehow I could tell his legs was trembling and he shaking like he had a chill. But I couldn't reach him now. I tried to get my legs under me, but they wouldn't work. I slumped back on the canvas, crying with rage and weakness.

Then through the noise I heard one deep, mellow sound like an old Irish bell, almost. Mike's bark! He wasn't a barking dog; only on special occasions did he give tongue. This time he only barked once. I looked at him and he seemed to be swimming in a fog. If a dog ever had his soul in his eyes, he had; plain as speech them eyes said: "Steve, old kid, get up and hit one more blow for the glory of the breed!"

I tell you, the average man has got to be fighting for somebody else besides hisself. It's fighting for a flag, a nation, a woman, a kid or a dog that makes a man win. And I got up—I dunno how! But the look in Mike's eyes dragged me off the canvas just as the referee opened his mouth to say "Ten!" But before he could say it—

In the midst I saw Francois' face, white and desperate. The pace had told. Them blows I'd landed from time to time under the heart had sapped his strength—he'd punched hisself out on me—but more'n anything else, the knowledge that he was up against the old bulldog breed licked him.

I drove my right smash into his face and his head went back like it was on hinges and the blood spattered. He swung his right to my head and it was so weak I laughed, blowing out a haze of blood. I rammed my left to his ribs and as he bent forward I crashed my right to his jaw. He dropped, and crouching there on the canvas, half supporting himself on his hands, he was counted out. I reeled across the ring and collapsed with my arms around Mike, who was whining deep in his throat and trying to lick my face off.

THE FIRST THING I felt on coming to, was a cold, wet nose burrowing into my right hand, which seemed numb. Then somebody grabbed that hand and nearly shook it off and I heard a voice say: "Hey, you old shellback, you want to break a unconscious man's arm?"

I knowed I was dreaming then, because it was Bill O'Brien's voice, who was bound to be miles away at sea by this time. Then Tom Roche said: "I think he's comin' to. Hey, Steve, can you open your eyes?"

I took my fingers and pried the swollen lids apart and the first thing I saw, or wanted to see, was Mike. His stump tail was going like anything and he opened his mouth and let his tongue loll out, grinning as natural as could be. I pulled his ears and looked around and there was Tom Roche—and Bill O'Brien and Mushy Hansen, Olaf Larsen, Penrhyn, the first mate, Red O'Donnell, the second—and the Old Man!

"Steve!" yelled this last, jumping up and down and shaking my hand like he wanted to take it off, "you're a wonder! A blightin' marvel!"

"Well," said I, dazed, "why all the love fest—"

"The fact is," bust in Bill O'Brien, "just as we're about to weigh anchor, up blows a lad with the news that you're fightin' in the Napoleon Club with—"

"—and as soon as I heard who you was fightin' with I stopped everything and we all blowed down there," said the Old Man. "But the fool kid Roche had sent for us loafed on the way—"

"—and we hadda lay some Frenchies before we could get in," said Hansen.

"So we saw only the last three rounds," continued the Old Man. "But, boy, they was worth the money—he had you outclassed every way except guts—you was licked to a frazzle, but he couldn't make you realize it—and I laid a bet or two—"

And blow me, if the Old Man didn't stuff a wad of bills in my sore hand.

"Halfa what I won," he beamed. "And furthermore, the *Sea Girl* ain't sailin' till you're plumb able and fit."

"But what about Mike?" My head was swimming by this time.

"A bloomin' bow-legged angel," said the Old Man, pinching Mike's ear lovingly. "The both of you kin have my upper teeth! I owe you a lot, Steve. You've done a lot for me, but I never felt so in debt to you as I do now. When I see that big French ham, the one man in the world I would of give my right arm to see licked—"

"Hey!" I suddenly seen the light, and I went weak and limp. "You mean that was—"

"You whipped Tiger Valois, heavyweight champion of the French fleet, Steve," said Tom. "You ought to have known how he wears dude clothes and struts amongst the swells when on shore leave. He wouldn't tell you who he was for fear you wouldn't fight him; and I was afraid I'd discourage you if I told you at first and later you wouldn't give me a chance."

"I might as well tell you," I said to the Old Man, "that I didn't know this bird was the fellow that beat you up in Manila. I fought him because he kicked Mike."

"Blow the reason!" said the Old Man, raring back and beaming like a jubilant crocodile. "You licked him—that's enough. Now we'll have a bottle opened and drink to Yankee ships and Yankee sailors—especially Steve Costigan."

"Before you do," I said, "drink to the boy who stands for everything them aforesaid ships and sailors stands for—Mike of Dublin, an honest gentleman and born mascot of all fightin' men!"

SAILORS' GRUDGE

By ROBERT E. HOWARD

Author of "The Pit of the Serpent"

SAILORS' GRUDGE

I COME ASHORE AT Los Angeles for peace and quiet. Being heavyweight champion of the *Sea Girl,* whose captain boasts that he ships the toughest crews on the seven seas, ain't no joke. When we docked, I went ashore with the avowed intention of spending a couple of days in ease. I even went to the extent of leaving my white bulldog, Mike, on board. Not that I was intending to do Mike out of his shore leave, but we was to be docked a week at least, and I wanted a couple of days by myself to kinda soothe my nerves. Mike is always trying to remove somebody's leg, and then I have to either pay for the pants or lick the owner of the leg.

So I went ashore alone and drifted into the resident section along the beach. You know, where all them little summer cottages is that is occupied by nice people of modest means and habits.

I wandered up and down the beach watching the kids play in the sand and the girls sunning themselves, which many of them was knockouts, and I soon found I had got into a kind of secluded district where my kind seldom comes. I was dressed in good unassuming clothes, howthesomever, and could not understand the peculiar looks handed my way by the cottage owners.

It was with a start I heard someone say: "Oooh, sailor, yoo-hoo!"

I turned with some irritation. I am not ashamed of my profession, far from it, but I am unable to see why I am always spotted as a seaman even when I am not in my work clothes. But my irritation was removed instantly. A most beautiful little blonde flapper was coyly beckoning me and I lost no time starting in her direction. She was standing by a boat, holding a foolish little parasol over her curly head.

"Mr. Sailor, won't you row for me, please?" she cooed, letting her big baby blue eyes drift over my manly form. "I just adore sailors!"

"Miss," I said politely, rather dizzy from the look she gave me, "I will row you to Panama and back if you say the word!"

And with that I helped her in the boat and got in. That's me, always the perfect cavalier—I have lived a rough life but I always found time to notice the higher and softer things, such as courtesy and etiquette.

Well, we rowed all over the bay—leastways, I rowed, while she laid back under her little pink parasol and eyed me admiringly from under her long silky eyelashes.

We talked about such things as how hot the weather was this time of the year, and how nasty cold weather was when it was cold, and she asked me what ship I was on, and I told her and also told her my name was Steve Costigan, which was the truth; and she said her name was Marjory Harper, and she got me to tell her about my voyages and the like, like girls will. So I told her a lot of stories, most of which I got out of Mushy Hansen's dime novel library.

Being gifted with consideration, I did not tell her that I was a fighting man, well known in all ports as a tough man with the gloves, and the terror of all first mates and buckos afloat, because I could see she was a nice kid of genteel folks, and did not know nothing much about the world at large, though she was a good deal of a little flirt.

When we parted that afternoon I'll admit I had fell for her strong. She promised to meet me at the same place next day and I wended my way back to my hotel, whistling merrily.

THE NEXT MORNING found me back on the beach though I knowed I wouldn't see Marjory till afternoon. I was strolling by a shaded nook, where couples often go in to spoon, when I heard voices raised in dispute. I'm no eavesdropper, but I couldn't help but hear what was said—by the man, at least, because he had a strong voice and was using it. Some kid getting called down by her steady, I thought.

"—I told you to keep away from sailors, you little flirt!" he was saying angrily. "They're not your kind. Never mind how I know you were with some seagoing dub yesterday! That's all! Don't you talk back to me either. If I catch you with him, I'll spank you good. You're going home and stay there."

This was rather strong I ruminated, and took a dislike right away to this fellow because I despise to hear a man talking rough to a woman. But the next minute I was almost struck dead with surprise and rage. A girl and a man came out of the nook on the other side. Their backs were toward me, but I got a good look at the man's face when he turned his head for a minute, and I saw he was a big handsome young fellow, with a shock of curly golden hair—and the girl was Marjory Harper!

For an instant I stood rooted to the ground, as it were. The big ham! Forbidding a girl to go with me! Abusing sailors! Calling me a dub when he didn't even know me! I was also amazed and enraged at Marjory's actions; she comes along with him as meek as a child and didn't even talk back. Before I could get my scattered wits together, they got into a car and drove off.

Talk about seeing red! And I knowed from this young upstart's build and walk that he was a sailor, too. The hypocrite!

Well, promptly at the appointed time, I was at the place I'd met Marjory the day before, and I didn't much expect her to show up. But she did, looking rather downcast. Even her little parasol drooped.

"I just came to tell you," she said rather nervously, "that I couldn't go rowing today. I must go back home at once."

"I thought you told me you wasn't married," I said bitterly.

She looked rather startled. "I'm not!" she exclaims.

"Well," I said, "I might's well tell you: I heard you get bawled out this mornin' for bein' with me. And I don't understand how come you took it."

"You don't know Bert," she sighed. "He's a perfect tyrant and treats me like a child." She clenched her little fists angrily and tears come into her eyes. "He's a big bully! If I was a man, I'd knock his block off!"

"Where is this Bert now?" I asked with the old sinister calm.

"Over in Hollywood, somewhere," she answered. "I think he's got a small part in a movie. But I can't stay. I musn't let Bert know I've been out to see you."

"Well, ain't I ever goin' to see you again?" I asked plaintively.

"Oh, goodness, no!" she shivered, dabbing her eyes. "I wouldn't dare! It makes Bert furious for me to even look at a sailor."

I ground my teeth gently. "Ain't this boob a sailor hisself?" I asked mildly.

"Who? Bert? Yes, but he says as a rule they're no good for a nice girl to go with."

I restrained an impulse to howl and bite holes in the beach, and said with an effort at calmness: "Well, I'm goin' now. But remember, I'm comin' back to you."

"Oh, please don't!" she begged. "I'm terribly sorry, but if Bert catches us together, we'll both suffer."

Being unable to stand any more, I bowed politely and left for Hollywood at full speed. For a girl who seemed to have so much spunk, Bert sure had Marjory buffaloed. What kinda hold did he have over her, so he could talk to her like that? Why didn't she give him the gate? She couldn't love a ham like that, not with men like me around, and, anyway, if she'd loved him so much, she wouldn't have flirted with me.

I decided it must be something like I seen once in a movie called "The Curse of Rum," where the villain had so much on the heroine's old man that the heroine had to put up with his orneryness till the hero comes along and bumped him. I decided that Bert must have something on Marjory's old man, and was on the point of going back to ask her what it was, when I decided I'd make Bert tell me hisself.

WELL, I ARROVE in Hollywood and like a chump, started wandering around vaguely in the bare hopes I would run onto this Bert fellow. All to once I thought luck was with me. In a cafe three or four men was sitting talking earnestly and there was Bert! He was slicked up considerably, better dressed and even more handsome than ever. But

I recognized that curly gold hair of his.

The next minute I was at the table and had hauled him out of the seat.

"Order my girl around, will ya?" I bellowed, aiming a terrible right at his jaw. He ducked and avoided complete annihilation by a inch, then to my utmost amazement he dived under the table, yelling for help. The next minute all the waiters in the world was on top of me but I flung 'em aside like chaff and yelled: "Come out from under that table, Bert, you big yellow-headed stiff! I'll show you—!"

"Bert—nothin'," howled a little short fat fellow hanging onto my right, "that's Reginald Van Veer, the famous movie star!"

At this startling bit of information I halted in amazement, and the aforesaid star sticking his frightened face out from under the table, I seen I had made a mistake. The resemblance between him and Bert was remarkable, but they wasn't the same man.

"My mistake," I growled. "Sorry to intrude on yuh." And so saying, I throwed one waiter under the table and another into the corner and stalked out in silent majesty. Outside I ducked into a alley and beat it down a side street because I didn't know but what they'd have the cops on my neck.

Well, the street lights was burning when I decided to give it up. About this time who should I bump into but Tommy Marks, a kid I used to know in 'Frisco, and we had a reunion over a plate of corned beef and a stein of near beer. Tommy was sporting a small mustache and puttees and he told me that he was a assistant director, yes man, or something in the Tremendous Arts Movie Corporation, Inc.

"And boy," he splurged, "we are filming a peach, a pip and a wow! Is it a knockout? Oh, baby! A prize-fight picture entitled "The Honor of the Champion," starring Reginald Van Veer, with Honey Precious for the herowine. Boy, will it pack the theayters!"

"Baloney!" I sniffed. "You mean to tell me that wax-haired Van Veer will stand up and be pasted for art's sake?"

"Well, to tell you the truth." admitted Tommy, "he wouldn't; anyway, the company couldn't take a chance on a right hook ruinin' his profile. By sheer luck and wonderful chance, we found a fellow which looks enough like Reggie to be his twin brother. He's a tough sailor and a real fightin' man and we use him in the fights. For close-ups we use Reggie, made up to look sweaty and bloody, in a clinch with the other dub, y'see. We'll work the close-ups in between the long shots and nobody'll be able to tell the difference."

"Who's this double?" I asked, smit by a sudden thought.

"I dunno. I picked him up over in Los Angeles. His first name is—"

"Bert!" I yelped.

Tommy looked kinda surprised. "Yeah, it is, come to think of it."

"Ayargh!" I gnashed my teeth. "I'll be around on the lot tomorrer. I got a few words to say to this here Bert."

"Hey!" hollered Tommy, knowing something of my disposition. "You lay off him till this picture is finished! For cat's sake! Tomorrow we shoot the big fight scene. The climax of the picture, see? We got a real fighter for Reggie's opponent—Terry O'Rourke from Seattle and we're payin' him plenty. If you spoil Reggie's double, we'll be out of luck!"

"Well," I snarled, "I'll be on the lot the first thing in the mornin', see? I don't reckon they'll let me in, but I'll be waitin' for Bert when he comes out."

THE NEXT MORNING found me at the Tremendous Arts studio before it was open. Yet, early as it was, I found a group of tough looking gents collected outside the casting office. They was four of them and one I recognized as Spike Monahan, A.B. mariner on the *Hornswoggle,* merchant ship, and as tough a nut as ever walked a deck.

"How come the thug convention, Spike?" I asked.

"Ain'tcha heard?" he responded. "Last night Terry O'Rourke broke his wrist swingin' at a bouncer in a night club and we're here to cop his job. Not that I care for the money so much," he ruminated, "but I want the job uh mussin' up Reggie Van Veer's beautiful countenance."

"Well, you're outa luck," I said, "because they're usin' a double."

"No matter," said all the tough birds, "we craves to bust into the movies."

"Boys," said I, taking off my coat, "consider the matter as closed. I've decided to take the job."

"Steve," said Spike, spitting in his hands, "I have nothin' agin' you. But it is my duty to the nation to put my map on the silver screen and rest the eyes of them fans which is tired of lookin' at varnished mugs like Reggie Van Veer's, and craves to gaze upon real he-men. Don't take this personal-like, Steve."

So saying, he shot over a right hook at my chin. I ducked and dropped him with an uppercut, blocked a swing from another thug and dropped him across Spike with a left hook to the stummick.

I then turned on the other two who was making war-like gestures, stopped a fist with my eye and crashed the owner of the fist with a left hook to the button.

The fourth man now raised a large lump on my head with a glancing blow of a blackjack, and slightly irritated, I flattened his nose with a straight left, jarred loose a couple of ribs with a right, and bringing the same hand up to his jaw, laid him stiff as a wedge.

Spike was now arising and noting the annoyance in his eye and the brass knuckles on his left hand, I did not wait for him to regain his feet but dropped my right behind his ear while he was still in a stooping position. Spike curled up with a cherubic smile on his frightful countenance.

I then threw my coat over my arm and went up to the door of the casting office and about this time it was opened by a small man in spectacles.

"Who are you?" he asked with some surprise, his gaze fixed on my fast blackening eye.

"I'm your new boxer," I answered gently, "takin' the place of Terry O'Rourke."

He looked puzzled.

"I know we sent the word out rather late last night," said he, "but I rather expected several men to be here, from which we could choose."

"They was four other fellers," I answered, "but they decided they wouldn't wait."

He looked past me to where the four galoots was weaving uncertainly off the lot, and he looked back at me and shuddered slightly.

"Come around next month," said he. "We're shooting a jungle picture then."

I didn't get him, but I said: "Well, you ain't tryin' to tell me I don't get this job, are you?"

"Oh, no," he said hastily. "Oh heavens, no! Come right in!"

I FOLLOWED HIM and after winding in and out among a lot of rooms and things I didn't know the use or meaning of, we come into a place which was fixed up like a big stadium, seats, ring and everything. It was still very early, but already swarms of extras was coming in and being arranged in the seats.

The head director come bustling up and looked me over. He acted like he was about half cuckoo and I don't wonder, what with all the noise and the confusion and fellows running up every second to ask him about lights, or sets or costumes or something.

"What's your name?" he snapped. "You look like a fighter. Where're you from?"

"Steve Costi—" I began.

"All right—listen to me. You're Battling O'Hanlon, champion of the British Isles, see? Reggie Van Veer is the champion of America and you're fighting for the title of the world, see? Of course we have a double for Reggie. After we shoot the fight, we'll take some close-ups of you and Reggie in the clinches and run them in at the proper places. Tommy, take this man to the dressing room and fix him up."

Tommy Marks come up on the run and when he seen me, he stopped short and turned pale. He motioned me to follow him, but when I started to speak to him he hissed: "Shut up! I don't know you! I can see where you crumb the deal some way and if it looks like we're friends, I'll lose my job! They'll think I put you up to it!"

Seeing his point, I said nothing and he led me into a dressing room, where I allowed him to smear some kind of goo on my face and touch up my eye brows. I couldn't see that it improved my looks any, but Tommy said it didn't do them any damage because nothing could. I put on the swellest pair of trunks I ever wore and Tommy knotted a British flag about my waist which struck me funny because while I'd often fought men wearing that flag, naturally I'd never thought I'd ever wear it myself. I tried to make him put the flag of the Irish Free State on me instead, but he said they didn't have one. He then give me a fine silk bath robe to put on and so accoutered I sallied forth.

I heard a wild roar as I opened the dressing room door and peeking carefully forth, I saw Reggie Van Veer striding majestically down the aisle, dressed even sweller than I was. Two cameras was grinding away and the director was howling his lungs out, and the crowd of extras in the seats was jumping and whooping just like a fight crowd does when the favorite comes down the aisle.

He clumb into the ring with a swarm of seconds and handlers, and then Tommy told me to go into the ring. I come swaggering down the other aisle with a bigger gang than his behind me, carrying enough towels and buckets to fit out a army. I was astonished at the pains the movie people had took to make things realistic. I don't know how many extras was being used, but I saw right off that I'd never fought before a bigger crowd even in the real game itself.

I climbed through the ropes, following the instructions which the director yelled at me. I was kind of surprised. I'd always thought they was a lot of rehearsing to do. The referee called us to the center of the ring and they took a close-up of Reggie shaking hands with me, then the cameras quit grinding and Reggie skipped out of the ring, and in come—Bert! He was dressed just like Reggie had been and I was again struck by their strange resemblance.

"Now, then," bellowed the director, "this is going to be one picture that's going to look real! That's why I haven't rehearsed you boys. Go in and fight like you want to, so long as it's a fight! We got the ring well covered and can take you at any angle, so don't worry about getting out of range. This is going to be something new in pictures!

"Now, forget you're actors for the time being. Get into your solid skulls that you're fighters, like you've always been! Make this real! Put everything you got into it for four rounds. Then, Bert, when I yell at you in the fifth round, you step back and shoot your left to the body.

Steve, you drop your guard and then Bert, you crash the right to the jaw! And don't you pull the punch! I want this to be real. Steve, you drop when the right lands—"

I was thinking I'd be very likely to, anyway!

"I ain't going to have no knockout blows landing on the shoulder. The fight fans that see the shows have got so they spot 'em. This is going to appeal to those fans! If you boys get any teeth knocked out or noses broken, you get extra money. All right, get to your corners, and when the gong sounds, come out like they was a grudge between you!"

I COULD ASSURE him of that. I'd been watching Bert from under my lids while the director was talking. He stripped well and from his manner I knowed he was at home in a ring. He was broad-shouldered and lean-hipped and his muscles rolled beautifully. He was about six feet, one inch, and would weigh, I guess, a hundred and ninety-eight pounds, which was a inch taller and eight pounds heavier than me. Altogether he looked a lot like these Greek gods people rave about, but his firm square jaw and steely gray eyes told me I had my work cut out for me.

Well, the gong sounded and we went for each other. I wanted to give him fair warning, so I ducked his left and clinched.

"Never mind what that director cluck said," I snarled in his ear. "One of us is goin' out of here on a stretcher! I got your number, you big ham!"

"I don't even know you," he growled, jerking loose.

"You will!" I grinned savagely, throwing my right at his head with everything I had. He come back with a slashing left hook to the body and then we didn't have no more time for polite conversation.

This boy was fast, and cleverer than me, but he liked to mix it, too. He followed that left hook with a crashing right. I blocked it and landed hard under the eye, then went into a clinch and clubbed him with my right until the referee broke us.

We traded rights to the head and lefts to the body and he brought up a sizzling uppercut which might of tore my head off, hadst it landed. I buckled his knees with a right hook under the heart and he opened a cut under my left eye with a venomous straight right.

He then backed away, sparring and working for my wounded eye with a sharp-shooting left. Much annoyed, I followed him about the ring and suddenly dropped him to his knees with a smashing right cross to the side of the head. He bounced up without a count and flashed a straight left to my sore eye, following it instantly with a right uppercut to the body. I missed a looping right, landed with my left, took two straight rights in the face to sink my left hook into his belly, and he went into a clinch. We worked out of it and was fighting along the ropes at the gong.

By this time the extras was whooping in earnest and the director was dancing with joy and yelling for us to keep it up. I growled and flashed a meaningful look across at my dancing partner and from the way he bared his strong white teeth at me, I knowed that the director was going to have his wish.

He come out at the gong like a wildcat and had rammed a straight left to my wind and two straight rights to my face before I could get collected. I came back with a wicked right hook under the heart, and missed with the same hand for the jaw. He had evidently decided his straight right was his best ace, for he kept shooting it over my guard and inside my looping left hook. Enraged, I suddenly slipped it, let it go over my left shoulder, and crossed my left hard to his jaw.

He grunted, and I sank my right deep into his ribs before he could recover his balance. He fell into a desperate clinch and hung on, shaking his head to clear it. The referee broke us, and Bert, evidently infuriated, crashed a haymaking right swing to the side of my head which knocked me into the ropes on the opposite side of the ring. As I come out of them, still dizzy, he was on me like a enraged wildcat and lifted me clear off the floor with a slung-shot right uppercut. Now it was me that clinched and it took all the referee's strength to tear us apart.

Bert feinted a straight right again, then shot his left to my heart. I missed a right, got in a good left and then the gong sounded.

AS I SET on my stool and my handlers and seconds went through a lot of motions which wasn't needed, I glanced out over the crowd. My heart give a leap right up into my mouth! On the first row, ringside, sat Marjory!

She was staring at the ring, rather pale. I give her a grin to show she needn't worry about me, but she just looked back kind of frightened. Poor kid, I reckoned she wasn't used to such tough work and was afraid Bert would hurt me. I chuckled gayly at the thought and felt a deep feeling of satisfaction, that she should see me give the big ham the lamming he deserved.

The gong!

Bert come out kind of cautious. He feinted a left, swung his right at my head, missed and backed away. I followed him rather carelessly, ducking another right swing. I thought, the next time he does that I will block it with my left and step in with a right to the jaw. Well, he swung his left, then his right and mechanically I threw up my left to block it. Too late I noticed that he had changed his position in a curious manner and was a lot closer to me than he ought to be. *Bam!* I was on the canvas feeling like my midriff was caved in.

As I got my legs under me, I realized he'd played the old Fitzsimmons shift on me. As he swung his right for a feint, he'd stepped forward with the right leg which brought him inside my guard and in position to drive in a terrific left-hander to the solar plexus. Well, he done so, and it's a good thing for me he didn't land just where he wanted to, and that he didn't have old Fitz's trick of shooting in bone-crushers from a few inches. If he had, I'd still been out.

Well, I got up at nine, Bert rushing in eager-like to finish me. I snapped my right to his jaw and stopped him in his tracks, and followed with a left hook to the body which he partially blocked. Any man which had ever fought me could of told him that I, like most sluggers, was most dangerous when groggy. He seemed rather discouraged and played safe for the rest of the round, which was rather slow, as I wasn't in no mood to push things, myself.

On my stool I cast a jovial grin at Marjory but she didn't seem to be enjoying the game much. Poor kid, I thought, the sight of me on the canvas was too much for her tender little heart. I bet, thought I, that girl is as good as mine, right now.

So it was with visions of wedding rings and vine covered cottages dancing in my head that I went out for the fourth round. Almost instantly these beautiful visions was shook out of my head by a severe right hook and I settled down to the business at hand. Bert was inclined to end matters quick and we traded wallops toe to toe till the ring was swimming before my eyes and I could see from the glazed look in Bert's eyes that he wasn't in no better shape. We then went into a clinch and leaned on each other, shaking our heads till they was partly clear again.

Then Bert started working his old reliable straight right until I give a roar of rage, dived under it and sank my left hook into his midriff, bringing up a right from my knees that would of ended the fight had it landed. In a wild mix-up we both slipped to the canvas, but was up in a second, Bert closing my eye tight as a drum while I battered him with terrific body blows.

Baring his teeth at me, he shot a right to my bobbing head and suddenly bounded back from my return. We had got close to the ropes and he bounded right against them. The next thing he bounced off of them right into me. I'd never seen a heavyweight try that trick before and he caught me off my guard. His right crashed against my chest and I hit the canvas so hard my feet flew straight up and I thought I'd go on through the boards.

But it was the force and weight of the blow that knocked me down; I didn't fall because I was stunned or badly hurt. I was up at the count of nine and opened a cut over Bert's eye with a wild right. I didn't think he'd try that bouncing trick so quick again and he nearly fooled me there. This time he drew my left, jumped back, hit the ropes and came for me so quick I didn't have time to think. By instinct I side-stepped and met him in mid-air with a right hook to the jaw. *Crash!* He hit the canvas and rolled over and over. I ran back to the fartherest corner, but it didn't look like anybody could get up after a wallop like that. But this Bert was a tough baby. The crowd wasn't yelling now.

At seven he had his legs under him and at nine he come up, wobbly, rubber-legged and glass-eyed, still full of fight. I hesitated; I hated to hit him again, but then the thought come of what he'd said about me, and how he'd bullied poor little Marjory and the way he'd abused sailors. I heard the director yell as I shot across the ring, but I paid no heed.

Bert tried to clinch as I came in, but I dropped him face down with a right hook to the jaw. The crowd began to howl and bellow as I went back to the corner, and through the noise I heard the director, who was jumping up and down and tearing his hair. He was yelling: "Bert, get up! Hey, hey! Get up, for cat's sake! If you get knocked out, you'll rooin the picture."

Bert give no sign of obeying and the director howled: "Sound the gong and drag him to his corner! The round's half a minute to go, but the movie fans won't know the difference!"

This was done, much to my disgust and the director began to yell caustic remarks at me.

"Aw, shut up!" I growled. "You said make it real, didn't you?" So he shut up. Well, I was kind of bothered about hitting Bert and him so near helpless, but it's all in the game; he'd of done the same thing to me, and I remembered that he was blackmailing old man Harper and holding Marjory in the grip of his hand—or why else did she take so much off him? So I decided that I ought not to worry over a black hearted villain like Bert, but go out and knock his head off.

THEY GIVE AN extra long time between rounds, to give Bert time to recover and his handlers was working like mad over him. At last I saw him shake his head, then raise it and glare across the ring at me like a hungry tiger. The director was yelling instructions.

"All right now, remember! When I yell: 'Now!' Bert, you shoot the left to the body and you, Steve, drop your guard."

The gong! We rushed together and Bert clinched and gripped me like a gorilla.

"I want to know if you're going to flop this round according to schedule?" he hissed in my ear.

"Be yourself!" I snarled. "Forget that director cluck! This here's between me and you! I'm goin' to lay you like a rug!"

"But what you got it in for me for!" he snarled bewilderedly. "I never saw you before?"

"Aragh!" I roared, jerking loose and whizzing a terrible right past his jaw. He came back with a hard left to the body and another to the jaw while I planted a wicked right under the heart. He threw a right which went over my shoulder, and falling into me, clinched and tied me up.

"You see that little blonde in the first row?" I hissed. "I heard you abusin' and bullyin' her, and if you want to know, that's why I'm goin' to knock you into her lap!"

He shot a quick glance in the direction I jerked my head, and a bewildered look came over his face.

"Why, that girl—" he began, but just then the referee pulled us apart.

"Now, Bert!" howled the director, "shoot the left! Steve, be ready to flop!"

"Baloney!" I snarled over my shoulder, and stuck my own left into Bert's eye. He retaliated with a terrific right to the ribs and the director, sensing that something was going on which wasn't according to schedule, began to leap up and down and tear his hair and doin' other foolish things like cussing and weeping and screaming. But the cameras kept on grinding and we kept on slugging.

Following the right to the body, Bert swished a left which glanced from my head and I crashed a right under his heart. My continual body punching had begun to take the steam out of him, but he made one more rally, landing two blows to my one, but mine had much more kick behind them. Suddenly I threw everything I had into one ferocious burst of slugging. I snapped Bert's head back with a left uppercut I brought from my knees, and crashed my right under his heart. He staggered and I shot my right twice to his head—hooked a left under his heart and crashed another right flush to the jaw. They'd been coming so fast and hard that Bert, in his weakened condition, couldn't stop them. The last right lifted him off his feet and dropped him under the ropes, right in front of Marjory, who had leaped to her feet, with both her little hands pressed to her cheeks, and her pretty mouth wide open.

The referee mechanically started counting, but it was unnecessary. I strode over to my corner, took my bathrobe from the limp hands of a dumfounded handler and was about to climb out of the ring, when the director, who had thrown hisself on the ground and was biting the grass, come to life.

"Grab that idiot!" he howled. "Tie him up! Soak him! Get a cop! He's crazy! The picture's rooint! We're out heavy money! Grab him! If I got a friend in court, I'll send him up for life!"

"Aw, stand away!" I growled at the menials who approached me uncertainly, "this was a private matter between me and Bert."

"But it's going to cost us more than we can afford to pay!" wailed the director, plucking forth strands of his scanty locks and tossing them recklessly on the breeze. "Oh, why didn't you perform according to instructions? The first four rounds were pippins! But that finish—oh, that I should live to see this day!"

WELL, I FELT sorry for him and kind of wished that I'd waited and licked Bert outside, but I didn't see what I could do. Then up rushed Tommy Marks. He began yanking at the director's sleeve.

"Say, boss," he yelped, "I got a great idea! We'll cut that last round at the place where Bert got knocked down the last time! Then we'll start a scene with Reggie Van Veer, see? Splice the shots together—they can fix it in the cutting room, easy!"

"Yeah?" sniffed the director, wiping his eyes. "I should throw Reggie in with that man-eater. He's crazy; I think he's the maniac that tried to kill Reggie down-town yesterday."

"I thought he was Bert," I said.

"And listen," cried Tommy, "the shot will show Reggie getting up off the canvas slowly, with Steve waiting in his corner. Then Steve rushes out, Reggie meets him with a right to the jaw and Steve flops! A sensational k.o. at the end of the greatest fight ever filmed! See? Reggie won't even get hit at all. And nobody can tell the difference."

"Well, how'll I know this cave man won't take a notion to flatten Reggie when he gets him in the ring?"

"Aw, he's got nothin' against Reggie, have you, Steve? That was a private feud between him and Bert, wasn't it, Steve? You'll do it, won't you, Steve?"

"All right," muttered the director. "We'll try it, but don't rush at Reggie too ferociously or he'll jump clean out of the ring."

I had listened to this talk with much impatience. I wanted to square myself with the movie people and was willing to do what I could, but just now I had other business. I signified my willingness to do what they wanted me to do, then I hurried over to the seat where Marjory sat. She was not in it, and I seen her following close behind the handlers which was taking the still groggy blonde battler to his dressing room.

I hastened to her and laid a gentle hand on her little shoulder.

"Marjory," I said, "fear that big fellow no more! I have avenged us both! He will not be apt to bother you again! Tell your old man not to be afraid, no matter what this big flop has on him! Bert will not come between true lovers again, I bet you!"

To my utter amazement and horror, she turned on me with flashing eyes.

"What kind of gibberish are you talking?" she cried furiously. "You big brute! If you ever speak to me again, I'll call a policeman! How dare you speak to me after what you've done to poor Bert? You beast! You villain!"

And with that she swung her little hand and slapped me smack in the face, then with a stamp of her little foot and a burst of tears, she run forward and gently slipped one of Bert's arms about her slim shoulders, cooing to him gently.

I stood gaping after them like a fool, when Tommy pulled my sleeve.

"Hey, let's get on that shot, Steve."

"Say, Tommy," I said, a bit dazed as I followed him, "you see that little dame that belted me in the map just now? Well, what's that bozo, to her?"

"Him?" said Tommy, biting off a chew of tobacco. "Oh, nobody much—just only merely nobody but her big brother!"

At that I let out a howl that could of been heard in Labrador, and right after that I have to act as nurse to Tommy, he havin' swallowed his tobacco when he hears me yap.

Anyhow, I learned you never can tell when women is holdin' something out on you.

FIST AND FANG

By ROBERT E. HOWARD

Stark, savage rage pitted against white man's courage! Strange ways and dark in an island empire! But what was danger to a fighting sea-rover like Steve Costigan?

FIST AND FANG

I'VE FOUGHT ALL my life; sometimes for money, sometimes for fun—once in a while for my life. But the deadliest, most vicious fight I ever fought wasn't for none of them things; no, sir, I was fighting wild and desperate *for the privilege of getting a bullet through my brain!*

Stand by and I'll tell you why I was fighting so me and my best friend would get shot.

I'm the heavyweight champion of the *Sea Girl,* merchant ship, my name being Steve Costigan. The Old Man is partial to warm waters and island trade, see? Well, we was cruising through the Solomons on our way to Brisbane, taking our time because the Old Man practically growed up in the South Sea trade and knows all the old traders and native chiefs and the like, and is always on the lookout for bargains in pearls and such like.

Well, we hove to at a small island by the name of Roa-Toa which had a small trading post on it. This post was run by the only white man on the islands, a fellow named MacGregor, and him being an old friend of the captain's, we run in for a visit.

The minute the Old Man had stepped onto the ramshackle wharf, Bill O'Brien, my side kick, said to me, he said: "Steve, see that motor launch down there by the wharf? Let's grab it and chase over to Tamaru and see old Togo."

Tamaru was another little island so close to Roa-Toa you could see the top of the old dead volcano. Togo was the chief; that wasn't his name, but it was as near as we could come to pronouncing it. He was a wrinkled old scoundrel and was a terrible sot, but very friendly to the white men.

"The Old Man will likely stop at Tamaru," I said.

"He won't, either," said Bill. "Him and MacGregor will drink up all the whiskey we got on board before he ever weighs anchor from Roa-Toa. He won't stop by Tamaru because he won't have no liquor to give to or trade with old Togo. Come on," said Bill. "We can easy make it in that launch. If we hang around the mate will find somethin' for us to do. Let's get to that launch and scoot before the Old Man or MacGregor sees us. Mac wouldn't let us have it, like as not, if we asked him."

So in a very short time we was heading out to sea, me and Bill, and my white bulldog, Mike. I heard a kind of whooping above the sputter of the motor, and looked back to see the Old Man and MacGregor run out of the trading stores and they jumped up and down and shook their fists and hollered, but we waggled our fingers at them and kept on our course, full speed, dead ahead.

* * *

WELL, IN DUE time Tamaru grew up out of the ocean in front of us, all still and dark green, with its dead volcano, and the trees growing up the sides of the mountains.

Togo's village was right on the beach when we was there the year before, but now much to our surprise we found nothing but a heap of ruins. The huts was leveled, trees cut short close to the water's edge, and not a sign of human life.

While we was talking, four or five natives come slithering out of the jungle and approached us very friendly, with broad smiles. Mike bristled and growled, but I put it down to the fact that no white dog likes colored people. According to that, no black dog ought to like white people, but it don't work.

Anyway, these kanakas made us understand in their pidgin English that the village had been moved back in the jungle a way, and they signified for us to come with them.

"Ask 'em how come they moved the village," I told Bill, who could speak their language pretty well, and he said: "Aw, they say the salt water made the babies sick. Don't worry about that; they likely don't know theirselves why they moved. They don't often have no reason for what they do. Let's go see Togo."

"Ask 'em how Togo is," I said, and Bill did, and said: "They says he's as free from pain and sickness as a man can be."

The kanakas grinned and nodded. Well, we plodded after them, and Mike he come along and growled deep down in his throat till I asked him very irritably to please shut up. But he paid no attention.

After awhile we come on to a large open space and there was the village. Just now they wasn't a sign of life, except a few native dogs sleeping in the sun. A chill wiggled up and down my spine.

"Say," I said to Bill, "this is kind of queer; ask 'em where Togo is."

"Where at is Togo?" said Bill, and one of the natives grinned and pointed to a pole set in front of the biggest hut. At first I couldn't make out what he meant. Then I did, and I suddenly got sick at my stomach—and cold at the heart with fear. *On top of that pole was a human head!* It was all that was left of poor old Togo.

The next second two big kanakas had grabbed each of us from behind, and a couple hundred more came swarming out of the huts.

Bill, he give a yell and ducked, throwing one of his natives clean over his head, and he twisted half way round and knocked the other cold with a terrible biff on the jaw. Then the one on the ground grabbed Bill by the legs, and another hit him over the head with a club, laying his scalp open and knocking him to his knees.

MEANWHILE I WAS having my troubles. The minute them two grabbed me, Mike went for them, jerked one of them off me, got him down and nearly tore him apart. At the same instant I jammed my elbow backward, and by sheer luck connected with the other one's solar plexus. He grunted and loosened his hold, and I wheeled round to smash him, but as I did, I felt a sharp prick between my shoulders and knowed one of them was holding a spear at my back. I stopped short and stood still. The next minute me and Bill was tied hand and foot. I looked at Bill; he was bleeding plenty from the cut in his head, but he grinned.

Well, all that took something less than a minute. Three or four natives had went for Mike and pulled him off of his victim, which was howling and bleeding like a stuck hog. The said victim staggered away to the nearest hut, looking like a wreck on a lee shore, and the others danced and jumped around Mike trying to stab him with spears and hit him with clubs, without losing a leg at the same time; while Mike tried to eat his way through them to me.

Then while I watched with my heart in my mouth, *crack!* went a pistol and Mike went down, rolling over and over till he lay still with the blood oozing from his head. I give a terrible cry and began to rave and tear at my ropes; I struggled so wild and desperate that I jerked loose from the kanakas which was holding me, and fell on the ground, being tied up like I was.

Then they pulled me and Bill roughly around to face a big dark fellow who came swaggering up, a smoking pistol in his hand. At first glance it struck me I'd seen him before, but all I wanted to do now was get loose and tear his throat out with my bare hands for killing Mike.

This bezark stopped in front of us, twirling his gun on his forefinger and I looked close at him. If looks and wishes would kill, he would of dropped dead three times in succession. A big, tall, beautifully built native he was, but he didn't look like the rest. He had a kind of yellow tint to his skin, whereas they was golden brown. And his face wasn't open and good natured like theirs was in repose; it was cruel and slant-eyed and thin-lipped. Malay blood there, I quickly seen. A half breed, with the worst blood of both races. He was dressed in just a loin cloth, like the rest, but somewhere, I knowed, I'd seen him in different clothes and different surroundings. Well, if I hadn't been so grieved and mad on account of Mike, I guess I'd have knowed him right off.

"Well, Meestah Costigan," said the big ham, in a kind of throaty voice, "you visit my island, eh? You like my welcome, maybeso? Maybeso you stay a long time, eh? Glad you come, me; I rather see you than any other man in the world!"

He was still grinning, but when he said the last his heavy jaws come together like the snap of a alligator. And then Bill, who was glaring at him like he couldn't believe his eyes, yelled: "Santos!"

* * *

IT ALL COME back to me in a flash! And I would of fell over from sheer surprise, hadst I not been tied and held up. Sure, I remembered! And you ought to, too, if you keep up with even part of the fighters that comes and goes.

A couple of years ago I'd met Santos in a Frisco ring. Yeah! Battling Santos, the Borneo Tiger, that Abie Hussenstein had discovered slaughtering second-raters in Asiatic ports. Abie brought him to America after Santos had cleaned up everything in sight over there.

They is no doubt that the big boy was good. In America he went through his first rank of set-ups like a sickle through wheat. He was fast, fairly clever for a big man, and strong as a bull.

Well, his first first-rater was Tom York, you remember, and Tom outboxed him easy in the first round, but in the second Santos landed a crusher that broke Tom's nose and knocked out four teeth. From then on it was a butchery, and the referee stopped it in the fifth to keep York from being killed. After that the scribes raved over Santos more than ever, called him a second Firpo and said he couldn't miss being champion.

Abie was sparring for matches in the Garden and he sent Santos back to Frisco to pad his k.o. record and keep in trim by toppling some ham-and-eggers. Then, enter a dark man, the villain of the play—otherwise Steve Costigan.

Santos was matched to meet Joe Handler ten rounds in San Francisco. The very day of the fight, Handler sprained his ankle, and they substituted me the last minute. I needn't tell you I went into the ring on the short end of about a hundred to one, with no takers—except the *Sea Girl*'s crew, who seem to think I can lick anybody, simply because I've licked all of them.

Well, I reckon the praise and hurrah and all had went to Santos' head. He come out clowning and playing up to the crowd. He feinted at me with his big long brown arms and made faces and wise-cracks, as I come out of my corner. He dropped his gloves, stuck out his jaw and motioned me to hit him. This got a big laugh out of the crowd, and while he was doing that, with his mouth wide open, laughing, I hit him!

I reckon I was closer to him than he thought, for it was a wide open shot. I crashed my right from my knee, and I plunged in behind it with everything I had. I smashed solid on his sagging jaw so hard it numbed my whole arm. I don't see how I come not to tear his jaw clean off. Anyway, he hit the canvas like he figured on staying there indefinite, and they had to carry him to his dressing room to bring him to.

When everybody got their breath back, they yelled "fluke! fluke!" And it was, because Santos would of licked me, if he'd watched hisself. But it finished him; he'd lost his heart, or something.

His next start he dropped a decision to Kid Allison, and he lost two more fights in a row that way. Hussenstein give him the bounce and he dropped out of view. Santos had gone back to stoking, people supposed; the public had forgot all about him, and I had too, nearly. But here he was!

ALL THIS FLASHED through my brain as I stood and gawped at the big cheese. Say, if Santos had looked tigerish in the ring, in civilized settings, he looked deadly now.

He stuck the pistol back into his girdle and said, easy and lazy: "Well, Meestah Costigan, you remember me, eh?"

"Yeah, I do, you dirty half-breed!" I roared. "What you mean shootin' my dog? Lem'me loose, and I'll rip your heart out!"

He bared his white teeth in a kind of venomous smile and gestured lazily toward the pole where old Togo's head was.

"You come to see your old friend, eh? Well, there he is! What left of him. Now Santos is chief! The old man was fool; the young men, they follow Santos. Now we make palaver; you my guests!"

And with that he laughed in a cold deadly way and said something to the kanakas which was holding us. He turned his back and walked toward his hut, them dragging us along anyway. I looked back, though, and my heart give a jump. Old Mike got to his feet kind of groggy and glassy-eyed, and shook his head and looked around for me. He seen me and started toward me; then he seen Santos, and sneaked away among the trees. I give a sigh of relief. Must be the bullet just grazed him enough to knock him out; nobody had seen him get up and hide but me, and he was safe for the time being, at least—which was something me and Bill O'Brien wasn't—and I guess Bill felt the same way for he looked kind of white.

Santos sat down in a chair, which was one the Old Man had give poor old Togo, and we was propped up in front of him.

"Once we meet before, Costigan," he said, "in your country. Now we meet in mine. This my country. I born here. Big fool, me. I leave with white men on ship when very young. I scrub decks; then shovel coal. I fight with other stokers. I meet Hus'stein and fight for him. He take me to Australia—America; I lick everybody. Everybody yell when I come in ring."

The grin had faded off his map and a wild light was growing in his eyes; they was getting red.

"Then I meet you!" his voice had dropped to a kind of hiss. "They tell me you one big ham. Nothing in the head! I think make people laugh! I hold out my face, say: 'Hit me!' Then I think maybeso the roof fall on me."

He was snarling like a wild beast now; his chest was heaving with rage and his big hands was working like my throat was between them.

"After that, I not so good. People say dirty things now at me. They say: 'Yellow! Glass chin! Throw him out!' Hus'stein say: 'Get out! You no drawing card now!' I go to stoking again. I work my way back to my people; my island."

He give a short grim laugh. He hit his breast with his fist.

"Me king, now! Togo old fool; friend to white man! Bah! I say to young men: make me king! We kill white men, and take rum and cloth and guns like our people did long ago. So I kill Togo, and old men that follow him! And you—" His eyes burned into me.

"You make fool of me," he said slowly. "Aaahhh! I pay you back!" He looked like a madman, gnashing his teeth and rolling his eyes as he roared at us.

I LOOKED AT Bill, uncertain like, and Bill says, nervy enough, but in a kind of unsteady voice: "You don't dast harm a white man. You may be king of this one-horse hunk of mud, but you know blame well if you knock us off, you'll have a British gunboat on your neck."

Santos grinned like a ogre and sank back in his chair. If he'd ever been half way civilized, which I doubt, he had sure reverted back to type again.

"The British have come," said he. "They knocked our village to pieces and killed a few pigs. But we ran away into the jungle and they could no find us. They shoot some shells around and then steam away, the white swine! That was because we fire on a trading boat and kill a sailor."

"Well," said Bill, "the *Sea Girl*'s anchored off Roa-Toa and if you harm us, the crew won't leave nobody alive on this island. They won't shoot at you from long range. They'll land and mop up."

"Soon I go to Roa-Toa," said Santos, very placid. "I think I like to be king of Roa-Toa too; I kill MacGregor, and take his guns and all. If your ship come here, I take her, too. You think I no dare kill white man? Eh? Big fool, you."

"Well," I roared, the suspense being too much for me, "what you goin' to do with us, you yellow-bellied half-breed!"

"I kill you both!" he hissed, smiling and playing with his gun.

"Then do it, and get it over with," I snarled, being afraid I'd blow up if he dragged it out too long. "But, lem'me tell you somethin'—"

"Oh, no," he smiled, "not with the pistol. That is too easy, eh? I want you to suffer like I suffered."

"I don't get yuh," I growled. "It's all in the game. I don't see why you got it in for me. If you'd a-licked me, I wouldn't of kicked. Anyway, you got no cause to bump off Bill, too."

"I kill you all!" he shouted, leaping up again. "And you two—you will howl for death before I get through. *Arrgh!* You will scream to die—but you will no die till I am ready."

He came close to me and his wild beast eyes burned into mine.

"Slow you will die," he whispered. "Slow—slow! For that blow you strike me, you suffer—and for all I suffer at the hands of your people, you shall suffer ten times ten!"

He stopped and glared at me.

"The Death of a Thousand Cuts shall be yours," he purred. "You know that, eh? Ah, you been to China! I know you know it, because your face go white now!" I reckon mine did, all right. I knew what he meant, and so did Bill. "Me, I show them where to cut," went on Santos, "for I have seen the Chinese torture like those."

I felt froze solid and my clothes were damp with sweat; also I was mad, like a caged rat.

"All right, you black swine!" I yelled at him, kind of off my bat, I reckon. "Go ahead—do your worst! But remember one thing—remember that I licked you! I knocked you cold! Killin' me won't alter the fact that I'm the best man!"

He screamed like a maddened jungle cat and I thought he'd go clean nuts. I'd sure touched him to the quick there!

"You did no beat me!" he howled. "I was big fool! I let you hit me! White pig, I break you with my hands! I tear your heart out and give it to the dogs!"

"Well, why didn't you?" I asked bitterly. "You had your chance, and you sure muffed it! I licked you then, and I can lick you now. You wouldn't dare look at me crost-wise if my hands wasn't tied. I'll die knowin' that I licked you."

His eyes was red as a blood-mad tiger's now, and they glittered at me from under his thick black brows. He grinned, but they was no mirth in it.

"I fight you again," he whispered. "We fight before I kill you. I give you something to fight for, too: if I whip you, and no kill you—you die under the knives; and your friend, too. If I whip you, and kill you with my hands—your friend die under the cuts. But if you whip me, then I no torture you, but kill you both quick." He tapped his pistol.

Anything sounded better than the thousand cuts business, and, anyway, I'd have a chance to go out fighting.

"And suppose I kill you?" I asked.

He laughed contemptuously. "No chance. But if you do, my people shoot you quick."

"Take him up, Steve," said Bill. "It's the best of a bad bargain, any way you look at it."

"I'll fight you on your own terms," I said to Santos.

He grunted, yelled some orders in his own tongue, and the stage was set for the strangest battle I ever had.

In the open space between the huts, the natives made a big ring, standing shoulder to shoulder, about three deep, the men behind looking over the shoulders of those in front. The kids and women come out of the huts and tried to watch the fight between the men's legs.

A sort of oval-shaped space was left clear. At each end of this space stood a thick post, set deep in the ground. They tied Bill to one of these posts.

"I can't be in your corner this fight, old sea horse," said Bill, kind of drawn-faced, but still grinning.

"Well, in a way you are," I said. "You can't sponge my cuts and wave a towel, but you can yell advice when the goin's rough. Anyway," I said, "you got a good view of the fight."

"Sure," he grinned, "I got a ringside seat."

About that time the kanakas unfastened my ropes, and I worked my hands and fingers to get the circulation started again. Bill's hands was tied, so we couldn't shake hands, but I clapped him on the shoulder, and we looked at each other a second. Seafaring men ain't much on showing their emotions, and they ain't very demonstrative, but each of us knew how the other felt. We'd kicked around a good many years together—

Well, I turned around and walked to the middle of the oval, and waited. I didn't have to wait long. Santos came from the other end, his head lowered, his red eyes blazing, a terrible smile on his lips. All he wore was a loin cloth; all I had on was an old pair of pants. We was both bare-footed; and, of course, bare-handed.

I'D NEVER SEEN anything like this in my life before. They was no bright lights except the merciless tropic sun; they was no cheering crowds—nothing but a band of savages that wanted our blood; they was no seconds, no referee—only a hard-faced kanaka with gaudy feathers in his hair, holding Santos' pistol. They was no purse but death. A quick death if I won; a long, slow, terrible death if I lost.

Santos was rangy, big, tapering from wide shoulders to lean legs. Speed and power there was in them smooth, heavy muscles. He was six feet one and a half inch tall; heavier than when I first fought him, but the extra weight was hard muscle. I don't believe he had a ounce of fat on him. He must have weighed two hundred, which gave him about ten pounds on me.

For a second we moved in a half circle, wary and deadly, and then he roared and come lashing in like a tidal wave. He shot left and right to my head so fast that for a second I was too busy ducking and blocking to think. He was crazy to knock my head off; he was shipping everything he had in that direction. Well, it's hard to knock a tough man cold with bare-knuckled head punches. The raw 'uns cut and bruise, but they ain't got the numbing shock the padded glove has. You'll notice most of the knock-outs in the old bare-knuckle days was from blows to the body and throat.

The moment I had a breathing space, I hooked a wicked left to the belly. His ridged muscles felt like flexible steel bands under my knuckles, and he merely snarled and lashed back with a right-hander which bruised my forearm when I blocked it. He was fast and his left was chain lightning—he shot it straight, he uppercut, and he hooked, just like that—*zip! blip! blam!*

The hook flattened my right ear, and almost simultaneously he threw his right with everything he had. I ducked and he missed by a hair's lash. Jerusha! I heard that right sing past my head like a slung shot, and Santos spun off balance and went to his knees from the force of it. He was up like a cat, spitting and snarling, and I heard Bill yell: "For the love of Mike, Steve, watch that right, or he'll knock your head clean off!"

Well, I guess in a ring with ordinary stakes, Santos would have finished me; but this was different. I'm tough any time; now I was fighting for the privilege of me and my pard going out clean. The thought of them sharp little knives put steel in me.

Santos grinned like a devil as he came in again. This time he didn't rush, he edged craftily, left hand out, watching for a chance to shoot his deadly right over. That's once I wished I was clever! But I ain't, and I knew if I tried to box him, I wouldn't have a chance. So I come in sudden and wide open; his right swished through the air and looped around my neck as I ducked and I braced my feet and ripped both hands to his midriff—*bam—bam!* The next second his left chopped down on the back of my head. I went into a clinch, and his teeth snapped like a wolf's at my throat as I tied him up. He was snarling at me in his language as we worked out of the clinch, and he nailed me on the breakaway with a straight left to the mouth, which instantly began to bleed.

The sight of the blood maddened the kanakas, and they began to yell like jungle beasts. Santos laughed wild and fierce, and began swinging at my head again with both hands. To date he hadn't tried a single body blow. Three times he landed to the side of my head with a swinging left, and I dug my right into his midriff. His right came over, and I blocked it with my elbow, then shot my own right to his belly again. He'd give a kind of sway with his whole body as he let go the right to give it extra force, and his arm would snap through the air like a big steel spring released.

Crash! His left landed on the side of my head, and I seen ten thousand stars. *Bam!* His right followed, and I blocked it. But this time it landed flush on the upper arm instead of the elbow, and for a second I thought the bone was broke. The whole arm was numb, and, desperate, I crashed into close quarters and ripped short-arm rights to his belly, while he slashed at my head with short hooks. He wasn't so good in close; he didn't like it, and he broke away and backed off, spearing me with his long left as I followed.

BUT MY BLOOD was up now and I kept right on top of him. I slashed a left hook to his face, sank a straight right under his heart—*wham!* He brought up a left uppercut that nearly ripped my head off. He flailed in with a torrid right, and I hunched my left shoulder just in time to save my jaw. At the same time I shot my right for his jaw and landed solid, but a little high. He swayed like a tall tree, his eyes rolled, but he come back with a screech like a tree cat and flashed a vicious left to my already bleeding mouth. The right came in behind it like a thunderbolt and I done the only thing I could—ducked, and took it high on the front part of my head. Jerusha! It felt like my skull was unjointed! I heard Bill scream as I hit the ground so hard it nearly knocked the breath clean outa me.

It was just like being hit with a hammer. A stream of blood trickled down into my eyes from where the scalp had been laid open.

I dunno why Santos stepped back and let me get up. Force of habit, I guess. Anyway, as I scrambled up, shaking the blood outa my eyes, he give me a ferocious grin and said: "Now I kill you, white man!" And come slithering in to do it. He feinted his left, drew it back, and as he feinted again, I threw my right, wild and overhand, desperate like, and caught him under the cheek bone. Blood spurted and he went back on his heels. I ripped a left to his belly and he grabbed me and held on like a big python, clubbing me with his left till I tore loose.

He nailed me with the right as I went away from him, but it lacked the old jar. I got a hard skull. No man could of landed like he did without hurting his hand some, anyway. But his left was so fast it looked and felt like twins. He shot it at one of my eyes in straight jabs till I felt that eye closing, and then, as I stepped in with a slashing right to the ribs, he came back with a terrible left hook that split my other eyebrow wide open and the lid sagged down like a curtain halfway over the eye.

"Work in close, Steve!" I heard Bill yell, above the howling of the kanakas. "If he keeps you at long range, he'll kill you!"

I'd already decided that! I wrapped both arms around my head and plunged in till my forehead bumped his chin, and then I started ripping both hands to the belly and heart. His left was beating my right cauliflower to a pulp, but I kept blasting away with both hands till the whole world was blind and red; but he was softening. My fists were sinking deeper into his belly at every blow, and I heard him gasp. Then he wrapped his long, snaky arms around me and pinned me tight. As we tussled back and forth, with his breath hot in my ear, he sunk his teeth into my shoulder and worried it like a dog shaking a rat, growling deep in his throat till I tore away by main strength, and brought a stream of blood from his lips with a smashing right hook.

Then Santos went clean crazy. He howled like a wolf and began throwing punches wild and terrible, without aim or timing. He wasn't thinking about that sore right no more. It was like the air was full of flying sledge-hammers. Some he missed from sheer wildness; I blocked till my arms and shoulders ached. Plenty landed. I slashed a left to his face—and *crack!*—his right bashed into mine, smashing my nose flat. I heard the bones crackle and snap and a red mist waved in front of my eyes so I couldn't see. I felt faintly the impact of another blow, and then I felt the ground under my shoulders.

I lay there, counting to myself; my head was clearing fast. Nobody ever accused me of not being tough! Having my nose broke was a old story. I said to myself: "Nine!" and got to my feet, wrapping both arms around my head and crouching. Santos yelled and battered at my arms while I glared at him over them, and suddenly I unwound and sank my right to the wrist in his belly. Yes, he was getting soft from my continued batterings! His body muscles was getting too sore to contract hard and my fists sank in deep. Santos bent double, but came up with a punishing left uppercut to the jaw that dazed me and before I could recover, he ripped over that sledge-hammer right. It tore my left ear loose from my head and I felt it flap against my cheek.

I was out on my feet; just fighting from the old battle instinct, now. Some kind of a smash sent me back on my heels, and I felt myself falling backward and couldn't stop. Then I fell against something and heard a fierce voice in my ear: "Steve! He's weakening! Just one more smash, old sea horse, and he's yours!"

We had fought back to the end of the oval space and I was leaning against the post where Bill was tied. I made a desperate effort to right myself. Santos was watching me with his hands down and a nasty sneer on his face. He put his hands out and gripped my shoulders. He was marked pretty well hisself.

"You licked now," he said. "The little knives, now they feast! The Death of a Thousand Cuts, it is yours!"

AT THAT I went kind of crazy, too. I lunged away from the post, and missed with a wild right, and the slaughter recommenced. Santos was mad and bewildered. Well, he wasn't the first fighter who couldn't understand why I kept getting up. My eyes was full of blood and sweat; one was nearly closed, and the sagging lid nearly hid the other. My nose was busted flat, one ear was hanging loose and the other swole out of all proportions. My left shoulder and arm was so numbed from blocking Santos' terrible right, I couldn't lift it but a few inches above my waist line. My wind was giving out; I didn't know how long the fight had been going on; it seemed to me like we'd been fighting for centuries. I dunno what kept me on my feet; I dunno what kept me going. I'd almost got to where I didn't know nor care what they did to me. Sometimes I'd forget what we was fighting for. Sometimes I'd think it was because Santos had killed Mike, then again it would be Bill I'd think he'd killed. Once I thought we was back in the ring in Frisco.

Then I was down on my back, and Santos was kneeling on my chest, strangling me. I tore his hold loose and threw him off, and then we was standing toe to toe, trading slow, hard smashes. Then suddenly Santos shifted his attack for the first time and catapulted a blasting right to my body. Something snapped like a dead stick and I went to my knees with a red-hot knife cutting into my left side.

Santos standing over me, kicked at me with his big bare feet till I caught his legs, and as I clung on and he rained blows down at my head, I heard Bill's voice above the uproar: *"You got his goat, Steve! Get up! Get up once and he's licked!"*

I got up. I climbed that Malay devil's legs, paying no attention to the punches he showered on me, and as I leaned on his chest and our eyes glared into each other's, I saw a wild, terrible light had come into his—the light that's in a trapped tiger's—scared and bewildered, and dangerous as death. I'd fought him to a standstill—I had his number! And at them thoughts, strength flowed back into my arms. He flailed at me, but the kick was going from his blows; he was nearly punched out.

I stepped back and then drove in again. He was snarling between his teeth, and then he took a deep breath. The instant I saw his midriff go in, I sank my left in to the wrist, and as he bent forward I slugged him behind the ear, and he dropped to his knees. But he come up, gasping and wild. He'd forgot all the boxing he ever knowed, now. I stepped inside his wild swings and crashed my right under his heart, and though it was the most fearful agony to do it, brought up my left to his jaw. He went down on his haunches and I heard, in the deathly silence which had fell, Bill yelling for me to give him the boots. But I don't fight that way—even if I'd of had any boots on.

But Santos wasn't through. He was all savage now, and too primitive to be stopped by ordinary means. I'd fought him to a standstill; he was licked at this game. And he went clean back to the Stone Age. He leaped off the ground, howling and slavering at the mouth, and sprang at me with his fingers spread like talons; not to hit, but to strangle, tear, claw and gnash. And as he came in wide open, I met him with the same kind of punch I'd flattened him with once; a blasting right I brought up from my knee. *Crack!* I felt his jaw-bone and my hand give way as I landed, and he turned a complete somersault, heels over head, and crashed down on his back a dozen feet away. You'd think that would hold a man, wouldn't you? Well, it would—a man.

It's possible to break a man's jaw with your bare fist, and still not knock him unconscious. Any ordinary man wouldn't be able to do nothing more after that. But Santos wasn't a man, no more; he was a jungle varmint, and he'd gone mad.

BEFORE I COULD tell what he was going to do, he whirled and tore a long-handled battle-axe from the hand of a warrior in the front rank. He must have been on the point of collapse; he'd taken fearful punishment. Where he found strength for his last effort, I dunno. But it all happened in a flash. He had the axe and was looming over me like a black cloud of death before I could move. As he bounded in and swung up the thing above his head, I threw up my right arm. That saved my life; and the axe head missed the arm, but the heavy handle broke my forearm like a match, and knocked me flat on my shoulders.

Santos howled, swung up the axe and leaped again—and a white thunderbolt shot across me and met him in mid-air! Square on the Malay's chest Mike landed, and the impact knocked Santos flat on his back. One terrible scream he gave, and then Mike's iron jaws closed on his throat.

In a second it was the craziest confusion you ever seen. Kanakas whooping and yelling and running and falling over each other doing nothing, and Bill swearing something terrible and tearing at his bonds—and Mike making a bloody mess out of Santos in the middle of all of it. I tried to get up, but I was done. I got to my knees and slumped over again.

THE REST IS all like a dream. I saw the kanaka with the pistol shoot at Mike, and miss—and then, like an echo, come another shot—and the kanaka whooped, clapped his hand to the seat of his loin cloth, and scooted. I heard yelling in white men's voices, shots and a hurrah generally and then into my line of vision—considerably blurred—hove the Old Man, MacGregor, and Penrhyn, the mate, all cursing and whooping, with the whole crew behind them.

"Great Jupiter!" squawked the Old Man, red faced and puffing, as he leaned over me.

"They've kilt Steve! They've beat him to death with axes!"

"He ain't dead!" snarled Bill, twisting at his ropes. "He has just fit the toughest fight I ever seen—will some of you salt pork and biscuit eaters untie me from this post?"

"Rig a stretcher," said the Old Man. "If Steve ain't dead, he's the next thing to it. Hey, what the—!"

At this moment Mike came sauntering over and sat down beside me, licking my hand.

"Wh-who—who is—*was*—that?" asked the Old Man, kind of white-faced, pointing to what Mike had left.

"That there is what's left of Battlin' Santos, the Borneo Tiger," said Bill, stretching his arms with relish. "History repeats itself, and Steve has just handed him a most artistic trimmin'—are you goopin' swabs goin' to let Steve die here? Get him on board ship, will you?"

"Look about Mike first," I mumbled. "Santos shot him with a pistol."

"Just a graze," pronounced MacGregor, examining Mike's unusually hard head. "Shot him with a pistol, eh? Guess if he'd used a rifle the dawg would of slaughtered the whole tribe. Wait, don't put Costigan on the stretcher till I mop off some of his blood."

I felt his hands feeling around over me, and I cussed when he'd gouge me.

"He'll be all right," he pronounced, "soon's we've set his arm and this rib here, and stitched his ear back on, and took up a few more gashes. And that nose'll need some attention, though I ain't set many noses."

I kind of dimly remember being carried back to the ship, with Mike trotting alongside, and I heard Bill and the Old Man yappin' at each other back and forth.

"—and no sooner had Mac here got through tellin' me that Santos had killed old Togo and set hisself up as king, than we heard the motor launch sputter, and see you two prize jackasses scootin' away into the jaws uh death. We yelled and whooped but you was too smart to listen—"

"How in the name of seven dizzy mermaids did you expect us to hear you with the motor goin'?"

"—and I says, 'Mac,' I says, 'it ain't worth it to save their useless hides, but we got to do it.' And it bein' a well-known fact that a fast motor launch can make more speed than a sailin' vessel, includin' even the *Sea Girl,* which is all we had to rescue you in, we have just now arrove at the village. Hadst it not been for me—"

"Hadst it not been for Steve, you would of found only a few hunks of raw beef. Santos was goin' to carve us, and believe you me when I tell yuh Steve fought him to a standstill! Steve was licked to a frazzle, and didn't know it! Santos had everything, and he made Steve into the hash which now lies on that stretcher, but the old sea horse just naturally outgamed him. Accordin' to rights, Steve shoulda been knocked cold five times."

"Arrumph, arrumph!" growled the Old Man, but I could tell he was that proud he couldn't hardly keep his feet on the ground. "I'd of give the price of a cargo to see that fight. Well, we didn't do like the British gunboat did—anchor off-shore and shell a few huts. We went through that jungle like Neptune goes through the water, and all of the bucks was too interested to know we was comin' till we swarmed out on 'em.

"I'm tellin' you, we'd of scuppered a flock of them, if my crew wasn't the worst aggregation of poor shots on the Seven Seas—"

"Well, hey," said the crew, "we didn't notice you bringin' down nobody on the fly."

"Shut up!" roared the Old Man. "I'm boss here and I'll be respected."

"For cats' sake," I snarled through my pulped lips, "will you cockeyed sea horses dry up and let a sufferin' man suffer in his own way?"

"Don't think you rate so high, just because you're a little bunged up," growled Bill; but they was a catch in his voice. From the way he gripped my hand, I knowed exactly how he felt.

THE IRON MAN

By ROBERT E. HOWARD

Mike Brennon's defense was a granite jaw and iron ribs. He took 'em all on, wearing 'em down. Fierce incentives stung him to action—the greatest of which he did not understand, until—

Complete Fight Novel

THE IRON MAN

A CANNON-BALL for a left and a thunderbolt for a right! A granite jaw, and chilled steel body! The ferocity of a tiger, and the greatest fighting heart that ever beat in an iron-ribbed breast! That was Mike Brennon, heavyweight contender.

Long before the sports writers ever heard the name of Brennon, I sat in the "athletic tent" of a carnival performing in a small Nevada town, grinning at the antics of the barker, who was volubly offering fifty dollars to anyone who could stay four rounds with "Young Firpo, the California Assassin, champeen of Los Angeles and the East Indies!" Young Firpo, a huge hairy fellow, with the bulging muscles of a weight-lifter and whose real name was doubtless Leary, stood by with a bored and contemptuous expression on his heavy features. This was an old game to him.

"Now, friends," shouted the spieler, "is they any young man here what wants to risk his life in this here ring? Remember, the management ain't responsible for life or limb! But if anybody'll git in here at his own risk—"

I saw a rough-looking fellow start up—one of the usual "plants" secretly connected with the show, of course—but at that moment the crowd set up a yell, "Brennon! Brennon! Go on, Mike!"

At last a young fellow rose from his seat, and with an embarrassed grin, vaulted over the ropes. The "plant" hesitated—Young Firpo evinced some interest, and from the hawk-like manner in which the barker eyed the newcomer, and from the roar of the crowd, I knew that he was on the "up-and-up"—a local boy, in other words.

"You a professional boxer?" asked the barker.

"I've fought some here, and in other places," answered Brennon. "But you said you barred no one."

"We don't," grunted the showman, noting the difference in the sizes of the fighters.

While the usual rigmarole of argument was gone through, I wondered how the carnival men intended saving their money if the boy happened to be too good for their man. The ring was set in the middle of the tent; the dressing-rooms were in another part. There was no curtain across the back of the ring where the local fighter could be pressed to receive a blackjack blow from the confederate behind the curtain.

Brennon, after a short trip to the dressing-room, climbed into the ring and was given a wild ovation. He was a finely built lad, six feet one in height, slim-waisted and tapering of limb, with remarkably broad shoulders and heavy arms. Dark, with narrow gray eyes, and a shock of black hair falling over a low, broad forehead, his was the true fighting face—broad across the cheekbones—with thin lips and a firm jaw. His long, smooth muscles rippled as he moved with the ease of a huge tiger. Opposed to him Young Firpo looked sluggish and ape-like.

Their weights were announced, Brennon 189, Young Firpo 191. The crowd hissed; anyone could see that the carnival boxed weighed at least 210.

THE BATTLE WAS short, fierce and sensational, and with a bedlam-like ending. At the gong Brennon sprang from his corner, coming in wide open, like a bar-room brawler. Young Firpo met him with a hard left hook to the chin, stopping him in his tracks. Brennon staggered, and the carnival boxer swung his right flush to the jaw—a terrific blow which, strangely enough, did not seem to worry Brennon as had the other. He shook his head and plunged in again, but as he did so, his foe drew back the deadly left and crashed it once more to his jaw. Brennon dropped like a log, face first. The crowd was frenzied. The barker, who was also referee, began counting swiftly, Young Firpo standing directly over the fallen warrior.

At "five!" Brennon had not twitched. At "seven!" he stirred and began making aimless motions. At "eight!" he reeled to his knees, and his reddened, dazed eyes fixed themselves on his conqueror. Instantly they blazed with the fury of the killer. As the spieler opened his mouth to say "ten!" Brennon reeled up in a blast of breath-taking ferocity that stunned the crowd.

Young Firpo, too, seemed stunned. Face whitening, he began a hurried retreat. But Brennon was after him like a blood-crazed tiger, and before the carnival fighter could lift his hands, Brennon's wide-looping left smashed under his heart and a sweeping right found his chin, crashing him face down on the canvas with a force that shook the ring.

The astounded barker mechanically began counting, but Brennon, moving like a man in a trance, pushed him away and stooping, tore the glove from Young Firpo's limp left hand. Removing something therefrom, held it up to the crowd. It was a heavy iron affair, resembling brass knuckles, and known in the parlance of the ring as a knuckle-duster. I gasped. No wonder Young Firpo had been unnerved when his victim rose! That iron-laden glove crashing twice against Brennon's jaw should have shattered the bone, yet he had been able to rise within ten seconds and finish his man with two blows!

Now all was bedlam. The barker tried to snatch the knuckle-duster from Brennon, and one of Young Firpo's seconds rushed across the ring and struck at the winner. The crowd, sensing injustice to their favorite, surged into the ring with the avowed intention of wrecking the show! As I made my way to the nearest exit I saw an infuriated townsman swing up a chair to strike the still prostrate Young Firpo. Brennon sprang forward and caught the blow on his own shoulder, going to his knees under it; then I was outside and as I walked away, laughing, I still heard the turmoil and the shouts of the policemen.

Some time later I saw Brennon fight again, in a small club on the West Coast. His opponent was a second-rater named Mulcahy. During the fight my old interest in Brennon was renewed. With incredible stamina, with as terrific a punch as I ever saw, it was evident his one failing was an absolute lack of science. Mulcahy, though strong and tough, was a mere dub, yet he clearly outboxed Brennon for nearly two rounds, and hit him with everything he had, though his best blows did not even make the dark-browed lad wince. With the second round a half minute to go, one of Brennon's sweeping swings landed and the fight was over.

I thought to myself: that lad looks like a champion, but he fights like a longshoreman, but I won't attach too much importance to that. Many a fighter stumbles through life and never learns anything, simply because of an ignorant or negligent manager.

I went to Brennon's dressing-room and spoke to him.

"My name is Steve Amber. I've seen you fight a couple of times."

"I've heard of you," he answered. "What do you want?"

Overlooking his abrupt manner, I asked: "Who's your manager?"

"I haven't any."

"How would you like me to manage you?"

"I'd as soon have you as anybody," he answered shortly. "But this was my last fight. I'm through. I'm sick of flattening dubs in fourth-rate joints."

"Tie up with me. Maybe I'll get you better matches."

"No use. I had my chance twice. Once against Sailor Slade; once against Johnny Varella. I flopped. No, don't start to argue. I don't want to talk to you—or to anybody. I'm through, and I want to go to bed."

"Suit yourself," I answered. "I never coax—but here's my card. If you change your mind, look me up."

CHAPTER II

Scenting the Kill

Weeks stretched into months. But Mike Brennon was not a man one could forget easily. When I dreamed, as all fight fans and fighters' managers dream, of a super-fighter, the form of Mike Brennon rose unbidden—a dark, brooding figure, charged with the abysmal fighting fury of the primitive.

Then one day Brennon came to me—not in a day-dream, but in the flesh. He stood in the office of my training camp, his crumpled hat in his hand, an eager grin on his dark face—a very different man from the morose and moody youth to whom I had talked before.

"Mr. Amber," he said directly, "if you still want me, I'd like to have you manage me."

"That's fine," I answered.

Brennon appeared nervous.

"Can you get me a fight right away?" he asked. "I need money."

"Not so fast," I said. "I can advance you some money if you're in debt—"

He made an impatient gesture. "It's not that—can you get me a fight this week?"

"Are you in trim? How long since you've been in the ring?"

"Not since you saw me last; but I always stay in shape."

I took Brennon to my open-air ring where Spike Ganlon, a clever middleweight, was working out, and instructed them to step for a few fast rounds. Brennon was eager enough, and I was astonished to see him put up a very fair sort of boxing against the shifty Ganlon. True, he was far out-stepped and out-classed, but that was to be expected, as Ganlon was a rather prominent figure in the fistic world. But I did not like the way Mike sent in his punches. They lacked the old trip-hammer force, and he was slower than I had remembered him to be. However, when I had him slug the heavy bag he flashed his old form, nearly tearing the bag loose from its moorings, and I decided that he had been pulling his punches against Ganlon.

The days that followed were full of hard work and careful coaching. Brennon listened carefully to what Ganlon and I told him, but the result was far from satisfying. He was intelligent, but he could not seem to apply practically the things he learned easily in theory.

Still, I did not expect too much of him at first. I worked with him patiently for several weeks, importing a fairly clever heavyweight for his sparring partner. The first time they really let go, I was amazed and disappointed. Mike shuffled and floundered awkwardly with futile, flabby blows. When a sharp jab on the nose stung him, he quit trying to box and went back to his old style of wild and aimless swinging. However, these swings were the old sledge-hammer type, and his erratic speed had returned to him. I quickly called a halt.

"I'm wrong," I said. "I've been trying to make a boxing wizard out of you. But you're a natural slugger, though you seem to have little of the natural slugger's aptitude. Looks like you'd have learned something from your actual experience in the ring.

"Well, anyway, I'm going to make a real slugger like Dempsey,

Sullivan and McGovern out of you. I know how you are; you've got the slugger's instinct. You can box fairly well with a friend when you're just doing it for fun, but when you're in the ring, or somebody stings you, you forget everything but your natural style. It's no discredit to a man's mentality. Dempsey was a clever boxer when he was sparring, but he never boxed in the ring. And he swung like you do, till DeForest taught him to hit straight.

"Still, Mike, I'll tell you frankly that at his crudest, Dempsey showed more aptitude for the game than you do. Now, this is for your own good. Dempsey, Ketchell and McGovern, even when they were just starting, used instinctive footwork and kept stepping around their men. They ducked and weaved and hit accurately. You go in straight up and wide open, and a blind man could duck your swings. You've unusual speed, but you don't know how to use it. But now that I know where I've been making my mistake, I'll change my tactics."

FOR A TIME it seemed as though my dreams were coming true—that Mike was a second Dempsey. In spite of his urging that I get him a fight, I kept him idle for three months—that is, he was not fighting. For hours each day I had him practice hooking the heavy bag with short smashes to straighten his punches and eliminate so much aimless swinging. He would never learn to put force behind a straight punch, but I intended making him a vicious hooker like Dempsey. And I tried to teach him the weave of that old master and the trick of boring in, protected by a barricade of gloves and elbows until in close; and the fundamentals of footwork and feinting. It was not easy.

"Mike," said Ganlon to me, "is a queer nut. He's got a fighter's heart and body, but he ain't got a fighter's brain. He understands, but he can't do what you teach him. He has to work for hours on the simplest trick—and then he's liable to forget it. If he was a bonehead, I'd understand it. But he's brainy in other ways."

"Maybe he fought so long in second-rate clubs he formed habits he can't break."

"Partly. But it goes deeper. They's a kink in his brain."

"What do you mean, a kink?" I asked uneasily.

"I dunno. But it's somethin' that breaks down his coordination and keeps his mind from workin' with his muscles. When he tries to box he has to stop and think, and in the ring you ain't got time. You see a punch comin' and in that split-second you got to know what you can't do and what you can do to get outa the way and counter. 'Course, you don't exactly study it all out, but you *know,* see? That is, if you're a fast boxer. If you're a wide-open slugger like Mike, you don't think nothin'. You just take the punch as a matter of course, spit out your teeth and keep borin' in."

"But any slugger is that way," I objected. "And we're not trying to teach Mike to be clever, in the technical sense of the word."

Ganlon shook his head. "I know. But Mike's different. He ain't cut out for this game. Even these simple tricks are too complicated for him. Well, he's got to learn some defense, or he'll be punched cuckoo in a few years. All the great sluggers had some. Some weaved and crouched, like Dempsey; some wrapped their arms around their skull and barged in, like Nelson and Paolino. Them that fought wide open didn't last no time, 'specially among the heavies. The padded cell and paper-doll cut-outs for most of 'em. It don't stand to reason a human skull can stand up under the beatin's it gets like that."

"You're a born croaker. Mike's rugged but intelligent. He'll learn."

"At anything else, yes—at this game—maybe."

NOT LONG AFTER my talk with Spike, Brennon came to me.

"Steve," he said, "I've got to have a fight. I need money—bad."

"Mike," said I, "it's none of my business, but I don't see why you should be so desperately insistent. You've been at no expense at all, here in the camp. You said you weren't in debt, and you've refused my offer to loan you—"

"What business is it of yours?" he broke in, white at the lips.

"None at all," I hastened to assure him. "Only as your manager, I've got your financial interests at heart, naturally. I apologize."

"I apologize, too, Steve," he answered abruptly, his manner changing. "I should have known you weren't trying to pry into my private affairs. But I've got to have at least—" And he named a sum of money which rather surprised me.

"There's only one way to get that much," I answered. "Understand, I don't believe you're ready to go in with a first-string man. But since money is the object—Monk Barota is on the coast now, padding his kayo record. He'll be looking for set-ups. The promoter at the Hopi A.C. is a friend of mine. I can get you a match with him at close to the figure you named. You understand that a bad defeat now might ruin you. Don't say I didn't warn you. But you're in fine shape, and if you fight as we've taught you, I believe you can whip him."

"I'll whip him," Mike nodded grimly.

I hoped he was more sincere in his belief than I was. I really felt in my heart that he was not ready for a first-rater and I had intended building him up more gradually. But there was fierce, driving intensity about him when he spoke of the money he needed that broke down my resolution. Brennon was, in many ways, a character of terrific magnetic force. Like Sullivan, he dominated all about him, trainers, handlers and matchmakers. But only in the matter of money was he unreasonable, and this quirk in his nature amounted to an obsession.

Mainly through my influence, Brennon, an entirely unknown quantity, was matched with Barota for a ten-rounder; at ringside the odds were three to one on the Italian, with no takers. My last instructions to Mike were: "Remember! Use the crouch and guard Ganlon taught you. If you don't have some defense, he'll ruin you!"

The lights went out except those over the ring. The gong sounded. The crowd fell silent—that breathless, momentary silence that marks the beginning of the fight. The men slid out of their corners and—

"Oh, my gosh!" wailed Ganlon at my side. "He's doin' everything backward!"

Mike wore his old uncertain manner. Under the lights, with his foe before him and the roar of the crowd deafening him, he was like a trapped jungle beast, bewildered and confused. Barota led—Mike ducked clumsily the wrong way, and took the punch in the eye. That flicking left was hard for any man to avoid, but Mike incessantly ducked into it.

Ganlon was raving at my side. "After all these months of work, he forgets! You better throw in the sponge now. Look there!" as Mike tried a left of his own. "He can't even hook right. The whole house knows what's comin'. Same as writin' a letter about it."

BAROTA WAS TAKING his time. In spite of the fact that his foe seemed to have nothing but a scowl, no man could look into Mike Brennon's face and take him lightly. But a round of clumsy floundering and ineffectual pawing lulled his suspicions. Meanwhile, he flitted around the bewildered slugger, showering him with stinging left jabs. Ganlon was nearly weeping with rage as if his pupil's inaptness somehow reflected on him.

"All I know, I taught him, and there's that wop makin' a monkey outa him!"

With the round thirty seconds to go, Barota suddenly tore in with one of his famous attacks. Mike abandoned all attempts at science and began swinging wildly and futilely. Barota worked untouched between his flailing arms, beating a rattling barrage against Brennon's head and body. The gong stopped the punishment.

Mike's face was somewhat cut, but he was as fresh as if he had not just gone through a severe beating. He broke in on Ganlon's impassioned soliloquy to remark: "This fellow can't hit."

"Can't hit!" Ganlon nearly dropped the sponge. "Why, he's got a kayo record as long as a subway! Ain't he just pounded you all over the ring?"

"I didn't feel his punches, anyway," answered Mike, and then the gong sounded.

Barota came out fast, in a mood to bring this fight to a sudden close. He launched a swift attack, cut Mike's lips with a right; then began hammering at his body with the left-handed assault which had softened so many of his opponents for the kayo. The crowd went wild as he battered Mike around the ring, but suddenly I felt Ganlon's fingers sink into my arm.

"Bat Nelson true to life!" he whispered, his voice vibrating with excitement. "The crowd thinks, and Barota thinks, them left hooks is hurtin' Mike—but he ain't even feelin' 'em. He's got one chance—when Barota shoots the right—"

At this moment Barota stepped back, feinted swiftly and shot the right. He was proud of the bone-crushing quality of that right hand. He had a clear opening and every ounce of his weight went behind it. The leather-guarded knuckles backed by spar-like arm and heavy shoulder, crashed flush against Mike's jaw. The impact was plainly heard in every part of the house. A gasp went up, nails sank deep into clenching palms. Mike swayed drunkenly, but he did not fall.

Barota stopped short for a flashing instant—frozen by the realization that he had failed to even floor his man. And in that second Mike swung a wild left and landed for the first time—high on the cheek bone, but Barota went down. The crowd rose screaming. Dazed, the Italian rose without a count and Mike tore into him with the ferocity of a tiger that scents the kill. Barota, blinded and dizzy, was in no condition to defend himself, yet Mike missed with both hands until a mine-sweeping right-hander caught his man flush on the temple, and he dropped—not merely out, but senseless.

The crowd was in a frenzy, but Ganlon said to me: "He's an iron man, don't you see? A natural-born freak like Grim and Goddard. He'll never learn anything, not if he trains a hundred years."

CHAPTER III

White Hot Fighting Fury

THE DAY AFTER Mike Brennon had shocked the sporting world by his victory, he, Ganlon and I sat at breakfast, and we were a far from merry gang. Ganlon read the morning papers and growled.

"The whole country's on fire," he muttered. "Sports writers goin' cuckoo over the new find. Tellin' Barota cried and took on in his dressin'-room when he come to; and talkin' about how Mike 'fooled' his man in the first round by lookin' like a dub—callin' him a second Fitzsimmons! Applesauce. But here's a old-timer that knows his stuff.

"'If I am not much mistaken,'" he read, "'this Brennon is the same who looked like a deckhand against Sailor Slade in Los Angeles last year. His kayo of Barota had all the ear-marks of a fluke. He is, however, incredibly tough.'

"Uhmhuh," said Ganlon, laying down the paper. "Quite true. Mike, I hate to say it, but as a fighter you're a false alarm. It ain't your fault. You got the heart and the body, but you got no more natural talent than a ribbon clerk, and you can't learn. You got the fightin' instinct, but not the fighter's instinct—and they's a flock of difference.

"You're just a heavyweight Joe Grim. A iron man; never was one but Jeffries who could learn anything. I'm advisin' you to quit the ring—now. Your kind don't come to no good end. Too many punches on the head. They get permanently punch drunk. You don't have to go around countin' your fingers; you got brains enough to succeed somewhere else.

"You got three courses to follow: first, you can go around fightin' set-ups at the small clubs. You can make a livin' that way, and last a long time. Second, you can sign up with some of the offers you're bound to get now. Fightin' clever first-raters you won't win much, if any, but you'll be an attraction like Grim was. But you won't last. You'll crack under the incessant fire of smashes, and wind up in the booby hatch. Third and best, you can take what money you got and step out. Me and Steve will gladly lend you enough to start in business in a modest way."

I nodded. Mike shook his head and spread his iron fingers on the table in front of him. As usual he dominated the scene—a great somber figure of unknown potentialities.

"You're right, Spike, in everything you've said. I've always known there was a deficiency somewhere. No man could be as impervious to punishment as I am and have a perfectly normal brain. Not alone at boxing; I've failed at everything else I've tried. As for boxing, the crowd dazes me, for one thing. But that isn't all. I just can't remember what to do next, and have to struggle through the best way I can.

"But—I *can take it!* That's my one hope. That's why I'm not quitting the game. At the cost of my reflexes, maybe, Nature gave me an unusual constitution. You admit I'd be a drawing card. Well, I'm like Battling Nelson—not human when it comes to taking punishment. The only man that ever hurt me was Sailor Slade, and he couldn't stop me. Nobody can now. Eventually, after years of battering, someone will knock me out. But before that time, I'm going to cash in on my ruggedness. Capitalize on the fact that no man can keep me down for the count. I'll accumulate a fortune if I'm handled right."

"Great heavens, man!" I exclaimed. "Do you realize what that means—the frightful punishment, the mutilations? You'll be fighting first-raters now—men with skill and terrific punches. You have no defense. You sap, they'd hammer you to a red pulp."

"My defense is a granite jaw and iron ribs," he answered. "I'll take them all on and wear them down."

"Maybe," I answered. "A man can wear himself down punching a granite boulder, as I've seen men do with Tom Sharkey and Joe Goddard, but what about the boulder! You were lucky with Barota. The next man will watch his step."

"They can't hurt me. And I can beat any man I can hit. Win or lose, I'll be a drawing card, and that means big purses. That's what I'm after. Do you think I'd go through this purgatory if the need wasn't great?"

"If it's poverty—" I began.

"What do you know about poverty?" he cried in a strange passion. "Were you left in a basket on the steps of an orphanage almost as soon as you were born? Did you spend your childhood mixed in with five hundred others, where the needs of all were so great that no one of you got more than the barest necessities? Did you pass your boyhood as a tramp and hobo worker, riding the rods and starving? I did!

"But that's neither here nor there; nor it isn't my own personal poverty so much that drove me back in the ring—but let it pass. As my manager, I want you to get busy. If I can win another fight it will increase my prestige. I don't expect to win many. Later on, they'll come packing in to see me, for the same reason they went to see Joe Grim—to see if I can be knocked out. Until the fans find out I'm a freak, I'll have to go on my merits. Barota wants a return match. I don't want him now, or any other clever man who'll outpoint me and make me look even worse than I am. I want the fans to see me bloody and staggering—and still carrying on! That's what draws the crowd. Get me a mankiller—a puncher who'll come in and try to murder me. Get me Jack Maloney!"

"It's suicide!" I cried. "Maloney'll kill you! I won't have anything to do with it!"

"Then, by heaven," Brennon roared, heaving erect and crashing his fist on the table, "our ways part here! You could help me better than anyone else—you know the ballyhoo. But if you fail me—"

"If you're determined," I said huskily, my mind almost numbed by the driving force of his will-power, "I'll do all I can. But I warn you, you'll leave this game with a clouded brain."

His nervous grip nearly crushed my fingers as he said shortly: "I knew you'd stand by me. Never mind my brain; it's cased in solid iron."

As he strode out Ganlon, slightly pale, said to me in a low voice: "A twist in his head sure. Money—all the time—money. I'm no dude, but he dresses like a wharfhand. What's he do with his money? He ain't supportin' no aged mother, it's a cinch. You heard him say he was left on a doorstep."

I shook my head. Brennon was an enigma beyond my comprehension.

THE RISE OF Iron Mike Brennon is now ring history, and of all the vivid pages in the annals of this heart-stirring game, I hold that the story of this greatest of all iron men makes the most lurid, fantastic and pulse-quickening chapter.

Iron Mike Brennon! Look at him as he was when his exploits swept the country. Six feet one from his narrow feet to the black tousled shock of his hair; one hundred and ninety pounds of steel springs and whalebone. With his terrible eyes glaring from under heavy black brows, thin, blood-smeared lips writhed in snarl of battle fury—still when I dream of the super-fighter there rises the picture of Mike Brennon—a dream charged with bitterness. Take a man with incredible stamina and hitting power; take from him the ability to remember one iota of science in actual combat and leave out of his make-up the instinct of the natural fighter, and you have Iron Mike Brennon. A man who would have been the greatest champion of all time, but for that flaw in his make-up.

His first fight, after that memorable breakfast table conversation, was with Jack Maloney—one hundred and ninety-five pounds of white-hot fighting fury, with a right hand like a caulking mallet. They met at San Francisco.

With the aid of Ganlon and friendly scribes, I set the old ballyhoo working. The papers were full of Mike Brennon. They pointed out that he had over twenty knockouts to his credit, ignoring the fact that all of these victims, except one, were unknown dubs. They glossed over the fact that he had been out-pointed by second-raters and beaten to a pulp by Sailor Slade. They angrily refuted charges that his kayo of Barota was a fluke.

The stadium was packed that night. The crowd paid their money, and they got its worth. Before the bell I was whispering a few instructions which I knew would be useless, when Mike cut in with fierce eagerness: "What a sell-out! Look at that crowd! If I win it'll mean more sell-outs and bigger purses! I've *got* to win!" His eyes gleamed with ferocious avidity.

Two giants crashed from their corners as the gong sounded. Maloney came in like the great slugger he was, body crouched, chin tucked behind his shoulder, hands high. Brennon, forgetting everything before the blast of the crowd and his own fighting fury, rushed like a longshoreman, head lifted, hands clenched at his hips, wide open—as iron men have fought since time immemorial—with but one thought—to get to his foe and crush him.

Maloney landed first, a terrific left hook which spattered Brennon with blood and brought the crowd to its feet, roaring. I heard a note of relief in the shouts of Maloney's manager. This bird was going to be easy, after all! Like most sluggers, when they find a man they can hit easily, Maloney had gone fighting crazy. He lashed Brennon about the ring, hitting so hard and fast that Mike had no time to get set. The few swings he did try swished harmlessly over Maloney's bobbing head.

"He's slowin' down," muttered Ganlon as the first round drew to a close. "The old iron man game! Maloney's punchin' hisself out."

True, Jack's blows were coming not weaker, but slower. No man could keep up the pace he was setting. Brennon was as strong as ever, and just before the gong he staggered Maloney with a sweeping left to the body—his first blow.

Back in his corner Ganlon wiped the blood from Mike's battered face and grinned savagely: "Joe Goddard had nothin' on you. I'm beginnin' to believe you'll beat him. You've took plenty and you'll take more; he'll come out strong but each round he'll get weaker; he'll be fought out."

THE FANS THUNDERED acclaim as Maloney rushed out for the second. But he had sensed something they had not. He had hit this man with everything he possessed and had failed to even floor him. So he tore in like a wild man, and again drove Brennon about the ring before a torrent of left and right hooks that sounded like the kicks of a mule. Brennon, eyes nearly closed, lips pulped, nose broken, showed no sign of distress until the latter part of the round, when Maloney landed repeatedly to the jaw with his maul-like right. Then Mike's knees trembled momentarily, but he straightened and cut his foe's cheek with a glancing right.

At the gong the crowd began to realize what was going on. The timbre of their yells changed. They began to inquire at the top of their voices if Maloney was losing his famed punch, or if Brennon was made of solid iron.

Ganlon, wiping Brennon's gory features and offering the smelling salts, which he pushed away, said swiftly: "Maloney's legs trembled as he went back to his corner; he looked back over his shoulder like he couldn't believe it when he saw you walk to your corner without a quiver. He knows he ain't lost his punch! He knows you're the first man ever stood up to him wide open; he knows you been through a tough grind and ain't even saggin'. You got his goat. Now go get *him!*"

The gong sounded. Maloney came in, the light of desperation in his eyes, to redeem his slipping fame as a knocker-out. His blows were like a rain of sledge-hammers and before that rain Mike Brennon went down. The referee began counting. Maloney reeled back against the ropes, breath coming in great gasps—completely fought out.

"He'll get up," said Ganlon calmly.

Brennon was half crouching on his knees, dazed, not hurt. I saw his lips move and I read their motion: "More fights—more money—"

He bounded erect. Maloney's whole body sagged. Brennon's rising took more morale out of Jack than any sort of a blow would have done. Mike, sensing the mental condition and physical weariness of Maloney, tore in like a tiger. Left, right, he missed, shaking off Maloney's weakening blows as if they had been slaps from a girl. At last he landed—a wide left hook to the head. Maloney tottered, and a wild over-hand right crashed under his cheek bone, dashing him to his knees. At "nine!" he staggered up, but another right that a blind man in good condition could have ducked, dropped him again. The referee hesitated, then raised Mike's hand, beckoning to Maloney's seconds.

As Maloney, aided by his handlers, reeled to his corner on buckling legs, I noted the ironical fact: the winner was a gory, battered wreck, while the loser had only a single cut on his cheek. I thought of the old fights in which iron men of another day had figured: of Joe Goddard, the old Barrier Champion, outlasting the great Choynski, finishing each of their terrible battles a bloody travesty of a man, but winner. I thought of Sharkey dropping Kid McCoy; of Nelson outlasting Gans; Young Corbett—Herrerra. And I sighed. Of all the men who relied on their ruggedness to carry them through, Brennon was the most wide open, the most erratic.

As I sponged his cuts in the dressing-room, I could not help saying: "You see what fighting a first-string hitter means; you won't be able to answer the gong for months."

"Months!" he mumbled through smashed lips. "You'll sign me up with Johnny Varella for a bout next week!"

CHAPTER IV

Iron Mike's Dread

AFTER THE MALONEY fight, fans and scribes realized what he was—an iron man—and as such his fame grew. He became a drawing card just as he had predicted—one of the greatest of his day. And his inordinate lust for money grew with his power as an attraction. He haggled over prices, held out for every cent he could get, and rather than pass up a fight, would always lower his price. For the first and only time in my life, I was merely a figure-head. Brennon was the real power behind the curtain. And he insisted on fighting at least once a month.

"You'll crack three times as quickly fighting so often," I protested. "Otherwise you might last for years."

"But why stretch it out if I can make the same amount of money in a few months that I could make in that many years?"

"But consider the strain on you!" I cried.

"I'm not considering anything about myself," he answered roughly. "Get me a match."

The matches came readily. He had caught the crowd's fancy and no matter whom he fought, the fans flocked to see him. He met them all—ferocious sluggers, clever dancers, and dangerous fighters who combined the qualities of slugger and boxer. When first-rate opponents were not forthcoming quickly enough, he went into the sticks and pushed over second-raters. As long as he was making money, no matter how much or how little, he was satisfied. What he did with that money, I did not know. He was honest, always shot square with his obligations; but beyond that he was a miser. He lived at the training camps or at the cheapest hotels, in spite of my protests; he bought cheap clothes and allowed himself no luxuries whatever.

At first he won consistently. He was dangerous to any man. Coupled with his abnormal endurance was a mental state—a driving, savage determination—which dragged him off the canvas time and again. This was above and beyond his natural fighting fury, and he had acquired it between the time he had first retired and the next time I saw him.

At the time he was in his prime, there was a wealth of material in the heavyweight ranks, and Brennon loomed among them as the one man none of them could stop. That fact alone put him on equal footing with men in every other way his superiors.

Following the Maloney fight, the public clamored for a match between my iron man and Yon Van Heeren, the Durable Dutchman, who was considered, up to that time, the toughest man in the world, one who had never been knocked out, and whose only claim to fame, like Brennon's, was his ruggedness. A certain famous scribe, referring to this fight as "a brawl between two bar-room thugs," said: "This unfortunate affair has set the game back twenty years. No sensitive person seeing this slaughter for his or her first fight, could ever be tempted to see another. People who do not know the game are likely to judge it by the two gorillas, who, utterly devoid of science, turned the ring into a shambles."

Before the men went into the ring they made the referee promise not to stop the fight under any circumstances—an unusual proceeding, but easily understood in their case.

*　*　*

THE FIGHT WAS a strange experience to Mike; most of the punishment was on the other side. Van Heeren, six feet two and weighing 210 pounds, was a terrific hitter, but lacked Mike's dynamic speed and fury. Those sweeping haymakers which had missed so many others, crashed blindingly against the Dutchman's head or sank agonizingly into his body. At the end of the first round his face was a gory wreck. At the end of the fourth his features had lost all human semblance; his body was a mass of reddened flesh.

Toe to toe they stood, round after round, neither taking a back step. The fifth, sixth and seventh rounds were nightmares, in which Mike was dropped three times, and Van Heeren went down twice that many times. All over the stadium women were fainting or being helped out; fans were shrieking for the fight to be stopped.

In the ninth, Van Heeren, a hideous and inhuman sight, dropped for the last time. Four ribs broken, features permanently ruined, he lay writhing, still trying to rise as the referee tolled off the "Ten!" that marked his finish as a fighting man.

Mike Brennon, clinging to the ropes, dizzy and nearly punched out for the only time in his life, stood above his victim, acknowledged king of all iron men. This fight finished Van Heeren, and nearly finished boxing in the state, but it added to Brennon's fame, and his real pity for the broken Dutchman was mingled with a fierce exultation of realized power. More money—more packed houses! The world's greatest iron man! In the three years he fought under my management he met them all, except the champion of his division. He lost about as many as he won, but the only thing that could impair his drawing power was a knockout—and this seemed postponed indefinitely. He won more of his fights against the hard punchers than against the light tappers, as the latter took no chances. Many a slugger, after battering him to a red ruin, blew up and fell before his aimless but merciless attack. He broke the hands and he broke the hearts of the men who tried to stop him.

The light hitters outboxed him, but did not hurt him, and his wild swings were dangerous even to them. Barota outpointed him, and Jackie Finnegan, Frankie Grogan and Flash Sullivan, the lightheavy champion.

The hard hitters made the mistake of trading punches with him. Soldier Handler dropped him five times in four rounds, and then stopped a right-hander that knocked him clear out of the ring and into fistic oblivion. Jose Gonzales, the great South American, punched himself out on the iron tiger and went down to defeat. Gunboat Sloan battered out a red decision over him, but still believing he could achieve the impossible, went in to trade punches in a return bout, and lasted less than a round. Brennon finished Ricardo Diaz, the Spanish Giant, and beat down Snake Calberson after his toughness had broken the Brown Phantom's heart. Johnny Varella and several lesser lights broke their hands on him and quit. He met Whitey Broad and Kid Allison in no decision bouts; knocked out Young Hansen, and fought a fierce fifteen-round draw with Sailor Steve Costigan, who never rated better than a second-class man, but who gave some first-raters terrific battles.

To those who doubt that flesh and blood can endure the punishment which Brennon endured, I beg you to look at the records of the ring's iron men. I point to your attention, Tom Sharkey plunging headlong into the terrible blows of Jeffries; that same Sharkey shooting headlong over the ropes onto the concrete floor from the blows of Choynski, yet finishing the fight a winner.

I call to your attention Mike Boden, who had no more defense than had Brennon, staying the limit with Choynski; and Joe Grim taking all Fitzsimmons could hand him—was it fifteen or sixteen times he was floored? Yet he finished that fight standing. No man can understand the iron men of the ring. Theirs is a long, hard, bloody trail, with oftentimes only poverty and a clouded mind at the end, but the red chapter their clan has written across the chronicles of the game will never be effaced.

And so Brennon fought on, taking all his cruel punishment, hoarding his money, saying little—as much a mystery to me as ever. Sports writers discovered his passion for money, and raked him. They accused him of being miserly and refusing aid to his less fortunate fellows—the battered tramps who will occasionally touch a successful fighter for a hand-out. This was only partly true. He did sometimes give money to men who needed it desperately, but the occasions were infrequent.

Then he began to crack. Ganlon, his continual champion, first sensed it. Crouching beside me the night Mike fought Kid Allison, Spike whispered to me out of the corner of his mouth: "He's slowin' down. It's the beginnin' of the end."

THAT NIGHT SPIKE spoke plainly to his friend.

"Mike, you're about through. You're slippin'. Punches jar you worse than they used to. You've lasted three years of terrible hard goin'. You got to quit."

"When I'm knocked out," said Mike stubbornly. "I haven't taken the count yet."

"When a bird like you takes the count, it means he's a punch-drunk wreck," said Ganlon. "When the blows begin to hurt you, it means the shock of them is reachin' the brain and hurtin' it. Remember Van Heeren, that you finished? He's wanderin' around, sayin' he's trainin' to fight Fitzsimmons, that's been dead for years."

A shadow crossed Mike's dark face at the mention of the Dutchman's name. The beatings he had taken had disfigured him and given him a peculiarly sinister look, which however, did not rob his face of its strange dominating quality.

"I'm good for a few more fights," he answered. "I need money—"

"Always money!" I exclaimed. "You must have half a million dollars at least. I'm beginning to believe you *are* a miser—"

"Steve," said Ganlon suddenly, "Van Heeren was around here yesterday."

"What of it?"

Ganlon continued almost accusingly, "Mike gave him a thousand dollars."

"What if I did?" cried Brennon in one of his rare inexplicable passions. "The fellow was broke—in no condition to earn any money—I finished him—why shouldn't I help him a little? Whose business is it?"

"Nobody's," I answered. "But it shows you're not a miser. And it deepens the mystery about you. Won't you tell me why you need more money?"

He made a quick impatient gesture. "There's no need. You get the matches—I do the fighting. We split the money, and that's all there is to it."

"But, Mike," I said as kindly as I could, "there is more to it. You've made me more money than either of the champions I've managed, and if I didn't sincerely wish for your own good, I'd say for you to stay in the ring.

"But you *ought* to quit. You can even get your features fixed up—plastic face building is a wonderful art. Fight even one more time, and you may spend your days in a padded cell."

"I'm tougher than you think," he answered. "I'm as good as I ever was and I'll prove it. Get me Sailor Slade."

"He beat you once before, when you were better than you are now. How do you expect—"

"I didn't have the incentive to win then, that I have now."

I nodded. What this incentive was I did not know, but I had seen him rise again and again from what looked like certain defeat—had seen him, writhing on the canvas, turn white, his eyes blue with sudden terror as he dragged himself upright. Terror? Of losing! A terror that kept him going when even his iron body was tottering on the verge of collapse and when the old fighting frenzy had ceased to function in the numbed brain. What prompted this dread? It was a mystery I could not fathom, but that in some way it was connected with his strange money-lust, I knew.

"You'll sign me for four fights," Brennon was saying. "With Sailor Slade, Young Hansen, Jack Slattery and Mike Costigan."

"You're out of your head!" I exclaimed sharply. "You've picked the four most dangerous battlers in the world!"

"Hansen, it'll be easy. I beat him once, and I can do it again. I don't know about Slattery. I want to take him on last. First, I've got to hurdle Slade. After him, I'll fight Costigan. He's the least scientific of the four, but the hardest hitter. If I'm slipping I want to get him before I've gone too far."

"It's suicide!" I cried. "If you've got to fight, pass up these mankillers and take on some set-ups. If Slade don't knock you out, he'll soften you up so Costigan will punch you right into the bughouse. He's a murderer. They call him Iron Mike, too."

"I'll pack them in," he answered heedlessly. "Slade's nearly the drawing card I am, and as for Costigan, the fans always turn out to see two iron men meet."

As usual, there was no answer to be made.

CHAPTER V

The Roll of the Iron Men

IT WAS A few nights before the Brennon-Slade fight. I had wandered into Mike's room and my eye fell on a partially completed letter on his writing table. Without any intention of spying, I idly noted that it was addressed to a girl named Marjory Walshire, at a very fashionable girls' school in New York state.

I saw that a letter from this girl lay beside the other one, and though it was an atrocious breach of manners, in my curiosity to know why a girl in a society school like that would be writing a prize-fighter, I picked up the partially completed letter and glanced idly over it. The next moment I was reading it with fierce intensity, all scruples, forgotten. Having finished it, I snatched up the other and ruthlessly tore it open.

I had scarcely finished reading this when Mike entered with Ganlon. His eyes blazed with sudden fury, but before he could say a word I launched an offensive of my own—for one of the few times in my life, wild with rage.

"You born fool!" I snarled. "So this is why you've been crucifying yourself!"

"What do you mean by getting into my private correspondence?" his voice was husky with fury.

I sneered. "I'm not going to enter into a discussion of etiquette.

You can beat me up afterward, but just now I'm going to have my say.

"You've been keeping some girl in a ritzy finishing school back East. Finishing school! It's nearly finished you! What kind of a girl is she, to let you go through this mill for her? I'd like for her to see your battered map now! While she's been lolling at ease in the most expensive school she could find, you've been flattening out the resin with your shoulders and soaking it down with your blood—"

"Shut up!" roared Brennon, white and shaking.

He leaned back against the table, gripping the edge so hard his knuckles whitened as he fought for control. At last he spoke more calmly.

"Yes, that's the incentive that's kept me going. That girl is the only girl I ever loved—the only thing I ever had to love.

"Listen, do you know how lonely a kid is when he has absolutely nobody in the world to love? The folks in the home were kind, but there were so many children—I got the beginnings of a good education. That's all.

"Out in the world it was worse. I worked, tramped, starved. I fought for everything I ever got. I have a better education than most, you say. I worked my way through high school, and read all the books in my spare time that I could beg, steal or borrow. Many a time I went hungry to buy a book.

"I drifted into the ring from fighting in carnivals and the like. I never got anywhere. After I whipped Mulcahy the night you talked to me, I quit. Drifted. Then in a little town on the Arizona desert I met Marjory Walshire.

"Poverty? She knew poverty! Working her fingers to the bone in a cafe. Good blood in her too, just as there is in me, somewhere. She should have been born to the satins and velvets—instead she was born to the greasy dishes and dirty tables of a second-class cafe. I loved her, and she loved me. She told me her dreams that she never believed would come true—of education—nice clothes—refined companions—every thing that any girl wants.

"Where was I to turn? I could take her out of the cafe—only to introduce her to the drudgery of a laboring man's wife. So I went back into the ring. As soon as I could, I sent her to school. I've been sending her money enough to live as well as any girl there, and I've saved too, so when she gets out of school and I have to quit the ring, we can be married and start in business that won't mean drudgery and poverty.

"Poverty is the cause of more crimes, cruelty and suffering than anything else. Poverty kept me from having a home and people like other kids. You know how it is in the slums—parents toiling for a living and too many children. They can't support them all. Mine left me on the door-step of the orphanage with a note: 'He's honest born. We love him, but we can't keep him. Call him Michael Brennon.'

"Poverty can be as cruel in a small town as in a city—Marjory, who'd never been out of the town where she was born—with her soul starved and her little white hands reddened and callused—

"It's the thought of her that's kept me on my feet when the whole world was blind and red and the fists of my opponent were like hammers on my shattering brain—that's the thought that dragged me off the canvas when my body was without feeling and my arms hung like lead, to strike down the man I could no longer see. And as long as she's waiting for me at the end of the long trail, there's no man on earth can make me take the count!"

His voice crashed through the room like a clarion call of victory, but my old doubts returned.

"But how can she love you so much," I exclaimed, "when she's willing for you to go through all this for her?"

"What does she know of fighting? I made her believe boxing was more or less of a dancing and tapping affair. She'd heard of Corbett and Tunney, clever fellows who could step twenty rounds without a mark, and she supposed I was like them. She hasn't seen me in nearly four years—not since I left the town where she worked. I've put her off when she's wanted to come and see me, or for me to come to her. When she does see my battered face it'll be a terrible shock to her, but I was never very handsome anyway—"

"Do you mean to tell me," I broke in, "that she never tunes in on one of your fights, never reads an account of them, when the papers are full of your doings?"

"She don't know my real name. After I quit the game the first time, I went under the name of Mike Flynn to duck the two-by-four promoters I'd fought for, and who were always pestering me to fight for them again. The first time I saw Marjory I began to think of fighting again, and I never told her differently. The money I've sent has been in cashier's checks. To her, I'm simply Mike Flynn, a fighter she never hears of. She wouldn't recognize my picture in the papers."

"But her letters are addressed to Mike Brennon."

"You didn't look closely. They're addressed to Michael Flynn, care of Mike Brennon, this camp. She thinks Brennon is merely a friend of her Mike. Well, now you know why I've fought on and stinted myself. With Van Heeren, it was different. I'm responsible for his condition. I had to help him.

"These four fights now; one of them may be my last. I've got money, but I want more. I intend that Marjory shall never want again for anything. I'm to get a hundred grand for this fight. My third purse of that size. With good management, thanks to you, I've made more money than many champions. If I whip these four men, I'll fight on. If I'm knocked out, I'll have to quit. Let's drop the matter."

I HAVEN'T THE heart to tell of the Brennon-Slade fight in detail. Even today the thought of the punishment Mike took that night takes the stiffening out of my knees. He had slipped even more than we had thought. The steel-spring legs, which had carried him through so many whirlwind battles, had slowed down. His sweeping haymakers crashed over with their old power, but they did not continually wing through the air as of old. Blows that should not have jarred him, staggered him. The squat sailor, wild with the thought of a knockout, threw caution to the winds. How many times he floored Mike I never dared try to remember, but Brennon was still Iron Mike. Again and again the gong saved him; in the fourteenth round Slade went to pieces, and the iron tiger he had punched into a red smear, found him in the crimson mist and blindly blasted him into unconsciousness.

Brennon collapsed in his corner after Slade was counted out, and both men were carried senseless from the ring. I sat by Mike's side that night while he lay in a semi-conscious state, occasionally muttering brokenly as his bruised brain conjured up red visions. He lay, both eyes closed, his oft-broken nose a crushed ruin, cut and gashed all about the head and face, now and then stirring uneasily as the pain of three broken ribs stabbed him.

For the first time he spoke the name of the girl he loved, groping out his hands like a lost child. Again he fought over his fearful battles and his mighty fists clenched until the knuckles showed white and low bestial snarls tore through his battered lips.

In his delirium he raised himself painfully on one elbow, his burning, unseeing eyes gleaming like slits of flame between the battered lids; he spoke in a low voice as if answering and listening to the murmur of ghosts: "Joe Grim! Battling Nelson! Mike Boden! Joe Goddard! Iron Mike Brennon!"

My flesh crawled. I cannot impart to you the uncanniness of hearing the roll call of those iron men of days gone by, muttered in the stillness of night through the pulped and delirious lips of the grimmest of them all.

At last he fell silent, and went into a natural slumber. As I went softly into the other room, Ganlon entered, his savage eyes blazing with fierce triumph. With him was a girl—a darling of high society she seemed, with her costly garments and air of culture, but she exhibited an elemental anxiety such as no pampered and sophisticated debutante would, or could have done.

"Where is he?" she cried desperately. "Where is Mike? I must see him!"

"He's asleep now," I said shortly, and added in my cruel bitterness: "You've done enough to him already. He wouldn't want you to see him like he is now."

She cringed as from a blow. "Oh, let me just look in from the door," she begged, twining her white hands together—and I thought of how often Mike's hands had been bathed in blood for her—"I won't wake him."

I hesitated and her eyes flamed; now she was the primal woman.

"Try to stop me and I'll kill you!" she cried, and rushed past me into the room.

CHAPTER VI

A Cinch to Win!

THE GIRL STOPPED short on the threshold. Mike muttered restlessly in his sleep and turned his blind eyes toward the door, but did not waken. As the girl's eyes fell on that frightfully disfigured face, she swayed drunkenly; her hands went to her temples and a low whimper like an animal in pain escaped her. Then, her face corpse-white and her eyes set in a deathly stare, she stole to the bedside and with a heart-rending sob, sank to her knees, cradling that battered head in her arms.

Mike muttered, but still he did not waken. At last I drew her gently away and led her into the next room, closing the door behind us. There she burst into a torrent of weeping. "I didn't know!" she kept sobbing over and over. "I didn't know fighting was like that! He told me never to go to a fight, or listen to one over the radio, and I obeyed him. Why, how could I know—here's one of the few letters in which he even mentioned his fights. I've kept them all."

The date was over three years old. I read: "Last night I stopped Jack Maloney, a foremost contender. He scarcely laid a glove on me. Don't worry about me, darling, this game is a cinch."

I laughed bitterly, remembering the gory wreck Maloney had made of Mike before he went out.

"I've been doing you an injustice," I said. "I didn't think a man could keep a girl in such ignorance as to the real state of things, but it's true. You're O.K. Maybe you can persuade Mike to give up the game—we can't."

"Surely he can't be thinking of fighting again if he lives?" she cried.

I laughed. "He won't die. He'll be laid up a while, that's all. Now I'll take you to a hotel—"

"I'm going to stay here close to Mike," she answered passionately.

"I could kill myself when I think how he's suffered for me. Tomorrow I'm going to marry him and take him away."

After she was settled in a spare room, I turned to Spike: "I guess you're responsible for this. You might have waited till Mike was out of bed. That was a terrible shock for her."

"I intended it should be," he snarled. "I wrote and told her did she know her boy Mike Flynn was really Mike Brennon which was swiftly bein' punched into the booby-hatch? And I gave her some graphic accounts of his battles. I wrote her in time for her to get here to see the fight, but she says she missed a train."

"Let him fight," Spike spat. "Costigan will kill him, if they fight. I've seen these iron men crack before. I was in Tom Berg's corner the night Jose Gonzales knocked him out, and he died while the referee was countin' over him. Some men you got to kill to stop. Mike Brennon's one of 'em. If the girl's got a spark of real womanhood in her, she'll persuade him to quit."

Morning found the battered iron man clear of mind, his superhuman recuperative powers already asserting themselves. I brought Marjory to his bedside and before he could say anything, I left them alone. Later she came to me, her eyes red with weeping.

"I've argued and begged," she cried desperately, "but he won't give in!"

All of us surrounded Mike's bedside. "Mike," I said, "you're a fool. The punches have gone to your head. You can't mean you'll fight again!"

"I'm good for some more big purses," he replied with a grin.

Marjory cried out as if he had stabbed her. "Mike—oh, Mike! We have more money now than we'll ever use. You haven't been fair to me. I'd have rather gone in rags, and worked my fingers to the bone in the lowest kind of drudgery than to have you suffer!"

His face lighted with a rare smile. He reached out a hand, amazingly gentle, and took one of the girl's soft hands in his own.

"White little hands," he murmured. "Soft, as they were meant to be, now. Why, just looking at you repays me a thousand times for all I've gone through. And what have I gone through? A few beatings. The old-timers took worse, and got little or nothing."

"But there's no reason for your crucifying yourself—and me—any longer."

He shook his head with that strange abnormal stubbornness which was the worst defect in his character.

"As long as I can draw down a hundred thousand dollars a fight, I'd be a fool to quit. I'm tougher than any of you think. A hundred thousand dollars!" His eyes gleamed with the old light. "The crowd roaring! And Iron Mike Brennon taking everything that's handed out, and finishing on his feet! No! No! I'll quit when I'm counted out—not before!"

"Mike!" the girl cried piercingly. "If you fight again, I'll swear I'll go away and never see you again!"

His gaze beat her eyes down, and her head sank on her breast. I never saw the human being—except one—who could stand the stare of Mike Brennon's magnetic eyes.

"Marjory," his deep voice vibrated with confidence, "you're just trying to bluff me into doing what you want me to do. But you're mine, and you always will be. You won't leave me, now. You can't!"

She hid her tear-blinded face in her hands and sobbed weakly. He stroked her bowed head tenderly. A failure in the ring perhaps, but outside of it Brennon had a power over those with whom he came in contact that none could overcome. The way he had beaten down the girl's weak pretense was almost brutal.

"Mike!" snarled Ganlon, speaking harshly and bitterly to hide his emotions; for a moment the hard-faced middleweight with his two hundred savage ring battles behind him, dominated the scene: "Mike, you're crazy! You got everything a man could want—things that most men work their lives out for and never get. You're on the borderline. You couldn't whip a second-rater.

"Costigan's as tough as you ever were. If I thought he'd flatten you with a punch or two, I'd say, go to it. But he won't. He'll knock you out, but it'll be after a smashin' that'll ruin you for life. You'll die, or you'll go to the bughouse. What good will your money, or Marjory's love do you then?"

Mike took his time about replying, and again his strange influence was felt like a cloud over the group.

"Costigan's over-rated. I'll show him up. He never saw the day he could take as much as I can, or hit as hard."

Spike made a despairing gesture, and turned away. Later he said to the girl and me: "No use arguin'. He thinks it's the money, but it ain't. The game's in his blood. And he's jealous of Mike Costigan. These iron men is terrible proud of their toughness. Remember how Van Heeren fought?"

"Win or lose, ten rounds with Costigan means Mike's finish. Each is too tough to be knocked out quick. It'll be a long, bloody grind, and it *may* finish Costigan, but it'll *sure* finish Mike. He'll end that fight dead, or punched nutty. At his best, Brennon would likely have wore Costigan down like he did Van Heeren. But Mike's gone away back, and Costigan is young—in his prime—which in a iron man is the same as sayin' you couldn't hurt him with a pile-driver."

MIKE BRENNON TRAINED conscientiously, as always. I discharged his sparring partners and had him punch the light bag for speed, and do a great deal of road work in a vain effort to recover some of the former steel spring quality of his weakening legs. But I knew it was useless. It was not a matter of conditioning—his trouble lay behind him in the thousands of cruel blows he had absorbed. A clever boxer may get out of condition, lose fights and come back; but when an iron man slips there is no comeback.

In the four months which preceded the Costigan fight, an air of gloom surrounded the camp which affected all but Mike himself. Marjory, after days of passionate pleading, sank into a sort of apathy. That he was being bitterly cruel to the girl never occurred to Mike, and we could not make him see it. He laughed at our fears as foolish, and insisted that he was practically in his prime. He swore that his fight with Slade, far from showing that he had slipped, proved that he was better than ever! For had he not beaten Slade, the most dangerous man in the ring? As for Costigan—a few rounds of savage slugging would send him down and out.

Mike was aware of his fistic faults; he frankly admitted that any second-rater who could avoid his swings could outpoint him; but he sincerely believed that he was still superior in ruggedness to any man that ever lived. And deep in his heart, I doubt if Mike really believed he would ever be knocked out.

One thing he insisted on; that Marjory should not see the fight. And she made one last plea for him to give it up.

"No use to start all that," he answered calmly. "Think, Marjory! My fourth hundred-thousand-dollar purse! That's a record few champions have set! One hundred thousand with Flash Sullivan—Gonzales—Slade—and now Costigan! Thousands of tickets sold in advance! I've got to go on now, anyhow. And I'm a cinch to win!"

CHAPTER VII

Framed

AS IF IT were yesterday I visualize the scene; the ring bathed in the white glow above it; while the great crowd that filled the huge outside bowl swept away into the darkness of each side. A circle of white faces looked up from the ringside seats. Farther out only a twinkling army of glowing cigarettes evidenced the multitude, and a vast rippling undertone came from the soft darkness.

"Iron Mike Brennon, 190 pounds; in this corner, Iron Mike Costigan, 195!"

Brennon sat in his corner, head bowed, a contrast to the nervous, feline-like picture he had offered when he had paced the floor in his dressing-room. I wondered if he was still seeing the tear-stained face of Marjory as she kissed him in his dressing-room before he came into the ring.

When the men were called to the center of the ring for instructions, Mike, to my surprise, seemed apathetic. He walked with dragging feet. However, in front of his foe he came awake with fierce energy. Iron Mike Costigan was dark, with tousled black hair. Five feet eleven, and heavier than Brennon, what he lacked in lithe ranginess he made up in oak and iron massiveness.

The eyes of the two men burned into each other with savage intensity. Volcanic blue for Costigan; cold steel gray for Brennon. Their sun-browned faces were set in unconscious snarls. But as they stood facing each other, Brennon's stare of concentrated cold ferocity wavered and fell momentarily before Costigan's savage blue eyes. I realized that this was the first man who had ever looked Mike down, and I thought of Corbett staring down Sullivan—of McGovern's eyes falling before Young Corbett's.

Then the men were back in their corners, and the seconds and handlers were climbing through the ropes. I hissed to Mike that I was going to throw in the sponge if the going got too rough, but he made no reply. He seemed to have sunk into that strange apathy again.

The gong!

Costigan hurtled from his corner, a compact bulk of fighting fury. Brennon came out more slowly. At my side Ganlon hissed: "What's the matter with Mike? He acts like he was drunk!"

The two Iron Mikes had met in the center of the ring. Costigan might have been slightly awed by the fame of the man he faced. At any rate he hesitated. Brennon walked toward his foe, but his feet dragged.

Then Costigan suddenly launched an attack, and shot a straight left to Brennon's face. As if the blow had roused him to his full tigerish fury, Mike went into action. The old sweeping haymakers began to thunder with all their ancient power. Costigan had, of course, no defense. A sweeping left-hander crashed under his heart with a sound like a caulking mallet striking a ship's side; a blasting right that whistled through the air, cannon-balled against his jaw. Costigan went down as though struck by a thunderbolt.

Then even as the crowd rose, he reeled up again. But I was watching Brennon. As though that sudden burst of action had taken all the strength out of him, he sagged against the ropes, limp, cloudy-eyed. Now sensing that his foe was up, he dragged himself forward with halting and uncertain motions.

Costigan, still dizzy from that terrific knockdown, was conscious of only one urge—the old instinct of the iron man—bore in and hit until somebody falls! Now he crashed through Brennon's groping arms and shot a right hook to the chin. Brennon swayed and fell, just as a drunken man falls when a prop against which he has been leaning is removed.

Over his motionless form the referee was counting: "Eight! Nine! Ten!"And the ring career of Iron Mike Brennon was at an end. A stunned silence reigned, and Iron Mike Costigan, new king of all iron men, leaned against the ropes, unable to believe his senses. *Mike Brennon had been knocked out!*

AROUND THE RING the typewriters of the reporters were ticking out the fall of a king: "Evidently Mike Brennon's famous iron jaw has at last turned to crockery after years of incredible bombardings. . . ."

We carried Mike, still senseless, to his dressing-room. Ganlon was muttering under his breath, and as soon as we had Mike safe on a cot with a physician looking to him, the middleweight vanished. Marjory had been waiting for us and now she stood, white-faced and silent, by the cot where her lover lay.

At last he opened his eyes, and instantly he leaped erect, hands up. Then he halted, swayed and rubbed his eyes. Marjory was at his side in an instant and gently forced him back on the cot.

"What happened? Did I win?" he asked dazedly.

"You were knocked out in the first round, Mike." I felt it better to answer him directly. His eyes widened with amazement.

"I? Knocked out? Impossible!"

"Yes, Mike, you were," I assured him, expecting him to do any of the things I have seen fighters do on learning of their first knock-out—weep terribly, faint, rave and curse, or rush out looking for the conqueror. But being Mike Brennon and a never-to-be-solved enigma, he did none of these things. He merely rubbed his chin and laughed cynically.

"Guess I'd gone farther back than I thought. I don't remember the punch that put me out; funny thing—I've come through my last fight without a mark."

"And now you'll quit!" cried Marjory. "This is the best thing that could have happened to you. You promised you'd quit if you were knocked out, Mike." Her voice was painful in its intensity.

"Why, I wouldn't draw half a house now," Mike was beginning ruefully, when Ganlon burst in, eyes blazing.

"Mike!" he snarled. "Steve! Don't you two boneheads see there's somethin' wrong here? Mike, when did you begin feelin' drowsy?"

Brennon started. "That's right. I'd forgotten. I began feeling queer when I climbed in the ring. I sort of woke up when the referee was talking to us, and I remember how Costigan's eyes blazed. Then when I went back to my corner I got dizzy and drunken. Then I knew I was moving out in the ring and I saw Costigan through a fog. He hit me a hummer and I woke up and started swinging and saw him go down. That's the last I remember until I came to here."

Ganlon laughed bitterly. "Sure. You was out on your feet before Costigan hit you. A girl coulda pushed you over, and that's all Costigan done!"

"Doped!" I cried. "Costigan's crowd—or the gambling ring—"

"Naw—Mike's been crossed by the last person you'd think of. I been doin' some detective work. Mike, just before you left your dressin'-room, you drunk a small cup of tea, didn't you? Kinda unusual preparation for a hard fight, eh? But you drunk it to please somebody—"

Marjory was cowering in the corner. Mike was troubled and puzzled.

"But Spike, Marjory made that tea herself—"

"Yeah, and she doped it herself! She framed you to lose!"

OUR EYES TURNED on the shrinking girl—amazement in mine, anger in Ganlon's, and a deep hurt in Mike's.

"Marjory, why did you do that?" asked Mike, bewildered. "I might have won—"

"Yes, you might have won!" she cried in a sudden gust of desperate and despairing defiance. "After Costigan had battered you to a red ruin! Yes, I drugged the tea. It's my fault you were knocked out. You can't go back now, for you've lost your only attraction. You can't draw the crowds. I've gone through tortures since I first saw you lying on that cot after your fight with Slade—but you've only laughed at me. Now you'll have to quit. You're out of the game with a sound mind—that's all I care. I've saved you from your mad avarice and cruel pride in spite of yourself! And you can beat me now, or kill me—I don't care!"

For a moment she stood panting before us, her small fists clenched, then as no one spoke, all the fire went out of her. She wilted visibly and moved droopingly and forlornly toward the door. The wrap which enveloped her slender form, slid to the floor as she fumbled at the door-knob, revealing her in a cheap gingham dress. Mike, like a man awakening from a trance, started forward:

"Marjory! Where are you going? What are you doing in that rig?"

"It's the dress I was wearing when you first met me," she answered listlessly, "I wrote and got back my old job at the cafe."

He crossed the room with one stride, caught her slim shoulders and spun her around to face him, with unconsciously brutal force. "What do you mean?" he said.

She collapsed suddenly in a storm of weeping. "Don't you hate me for drugging you?" she sobbed. "I didn't think you'd ever want to see me again."

He crushed her to him hungrily. "Girl, I swear I didn't realize how it was hurting you. I thought you were foolish—willful. I couldn't see how you were suffering. But you've opened my eyes. I must have been insane! You're right—it was pride—senseless vanity—I couldn't see it then, but I do now. I didn't understand that I was ruining your happiness. And that's all that matters now, dear. We've got our life and love before us, and if it rests with me, you're going to be happy all the rest of your life."

Ganlon beckoned me and I followed him out. For the only time since I had known him, Mike's hard face had softened. The sentiment that lies at the base of the Irish nature, however deeply hidden sometimes, made his steely eyes almost tender.

"I had her down all wrong," Ganlon said softly. "I take back everything I might have said about her. She's a regular—and Mike—well, he's the only iron man I ever knew that got the right breaks at last."

WINNER TAKE ALL

By

ROBERT E. HOWARD

Wow! What a night for Costigan! Singapore—dark alleys—Chinese tongs—the Arena, and the smashing fists of Panther Cortez. . . .

WINNER TAKE ALL

ME AND BILL O'Brien was flat broke when we come out of Jerry Rourke's American Bar. Yes, sir—half a hour ashore, and cleaned along by of a land shark with a pair of educated dice. Not having the coin to pay his fine in case my white bulldog Mike followed his usual custom of tearing off some cop's pants leg, I left him with Jerry till I could raise some dough.

Well, me and Bill sallied forth into the night looking for anything that might mean money, experience having told us that you can find mighty near anything in the wharf-side streets of Singapore. Well, what we did find was the last thing we'd of expected.

We was passing a dark alley in the native quarters when we heard a woman screaming: "Help! Help! Help!"

We dashed into the alley immediately, and in the faint light we seen a girl struggling with a big Chinee. I seen the flash of a knife and I yelled and dived for him, but he dropped the frail and scooted down the alley like a scared rabbit, ducking the cobble-stone Bill heaved after him.

"Are you hurt, Miss?" I asked with my usual courtesy, lifting her to her feet.

"No, but I'm scared stiff," she answered. "That was a close call—let's get out of here before the big Chinee comes back with a mob."

So we legged it out into the street. Under the light of the street lamps we saw she was a white girl—American by her accent, and not hard to look at either, with her big grey eyes and wavy black hair.

"Where at shall we take you to, Miss?" asked Bill.

"I dance at the Bristol Cabaret," said she. "But let's go into the saloon—the bar-keep's a friend of mine and I want to buy you men a drink. It's the least I can do, for saving my life."

"Don't mention it, Miss," said I with a courtly bow. "We was glad to be of service. Howthesomever, if it will give you any pleasure to buy us a drink, we would not think of refusin'."

"More especially as we have just lost all our jack in a crap game, and are slowly but surely perishin' of thirst," said Bill, who ain't got my natural tact.

So we went in and got a back room to ourselves, and while we was downing our liquor—me and Bill, that is, because the girl said she never even tasted the stuff—she cupped her chin in her hands and rested her elbows on the table and gazing deep in my eyes, she sighed deeply.

"If I had a big strong man like you to protect me," she said in open admiration, "I wouldn't have to work in joints like the Bristol, and be abused by such swipes as tried to slit my gullet tonight."

I involuntarily expanded my enormous chest and said: "Well, lady, as long as Steve Costigan, A.B. mariner, can stand on his feet and hit with either maulie, you got no call to be afraid of anybody. The best thing, next to fightin', that me and Bill O'Brien here do is aid ladies in distress."

She shook her head wistfully. "You've been very kind to me, but you sailors are all alike—a girl in every port. But—I haven't even introduced myself—my name is Joan Wells, and I'm from Philadelphia."

"We're mighty glad to meet somebody from the States," said Bill. "But why was that slant-eye tryin' to knife you?"

"I—I really shouldn't tell," said she, looking kind of frightened.

"We ain't tryin' to intrude in your private affairs none," I hastened to add.

"I couldn't keep a secret from a man like you," said she with a languishing glance that made my heart skip a beat, "so I'll tell you. Take a look out the door to see that nobody's listening at the key-hole."

Nobody wasn't, so she went on.

"Did you ever hear of the No Sen Tong?" We shook our heads. We knowed in a general way about the big tongs, or merchant houses, which just about controls the Orient, but we hadn't had no experience with them.

"Well," said she, "it's the richest, most secret tong in the world. When I first came here I worked as private secretary for old To Ying, who's one of its highest secret officials. He fired me because I wouldn't let him get fresh with me—the old slant-eyed snake—and I went to work at the Bristol. But once you've been on the inside of an organization like that, you have ways of knowing things that other people don't."

Her eyes sparkled and her fists clenched as she got all excited. "I'm in on the biggest coup of the century!" she exclaimed. "If I live, I'll be a rich woman! Did you ever hear of the Korean Copper Company? No? Well, it's about to go bankrupt. They've never paid a single dividend. Stock's selling at a dollar a share, with no buyers. But, listen! They've hit the biggest copper mine that the world has ever seen! The No Sens are quietly buying up all the stock they can get—at a dollar a share! As soon as I found this out I ran down to the broker's and bought a hundred shares. It took every cent I had. But one of the No Sen spies saw me, and that's why old To Ying tried to have me bumped off. He's afraid I'll squeal.

"Think what a riot there'll be on the stock market tomorrow when the word gets in! Tonight Korean Copper's selling for a dollar! Tomorrow it'll be worth a thousand dollars a share!"

"Hold everything!" I said, kind of dizzy. "You mean you shoot a buck and get a thousand on the spin of the wheel?"

"I sure do—say, why don't you men buy some stock? It's the chance of a lifetime! Most of it has been bought up by the No Sens, but I know where I can get you a few hundred shares."

Bill laughed bitterly. "Sister, it might as well be sellin' for a thousand per right now as far as we're concerned. We ain't got a dime! And my watch is in a pawn-shop in Hong Kong."

"I'd gladly lend you some money," said she, "but I spent all mine on stock—"

"Wait a minute," said I, getting on my feet, "I got a idee. Miss Wells—Joan, is it safe for you to be left alone for a few hours?"

"Sure; the bar-keep goes off duty in a few minutes, and he can see me home."

"All right. I think we can raise some dough. Where can we see you, in say about three hours?"

"Come to the Alley of the Seven Mandarins," said she, "and knock on the door with the green dragon carved on it. I'm going to hide there till the No Sens quit looking for me. I'll be waiting for you," said she, giving my rugged hand a timid, shy little squeeze that made my big, honest heart flutter like a boy's.

THEN ME AND Bill was out in the foggy dim lighted streets and making tracks. I led the way through narrow streets and garbage-strewn back alleys till we was in the toughest section of Singapore's waterfront. It's dangerous in the daytime; it's pure Hades at night.

Right on the wharfs we come to a big ramshackle building, which a struggling sign announced as Heinie Steinman's Grand International Fight Arena. This dump was all lighted up, and was shaking with the ferocious roars which went up inside.

"Hello, Steve; hello, Bill," said the fellow at the door, a dip who knowed us well. "How 'bout a couple good ringside seats?"

"Gangway," said I. "We ain't got no money—but I'm fightin' here tonight."

"G'wan," said he, "you ain't even matched with nobody—"

"One side!" I roared, drawing back my famous right. "I'm fightin' *somebody* here tonight, get me?"

"Well, go in and fight somebody that's paid to git mutilated!" he squawked, turning slightly pale and climbing up on the ticket counter, so me and Bill stalked haughtily within.

If you want to study humanity in its crudest and most uncivilized form, take in one of Heinie Steinman's fight shows. The usual crowd was there—sailors, longshoremen, beach-combers, thugs and crooks; men of every breed and color and description, from the toughest ships and the worst ports in the world. Undoubtedly, the men which fights at the International performs to the toughest crowds in the world. The fighters is mostly sailors trying to pick up a few dollars by massacring each other.

Well, as me and Bill entered, the fans was voicing their disapproval in a tone that would of curled the hair of a head-hunter. The main event had just driven the patrons into a frenzy by going to the limit, and they was howling like a pack of wolves because they'd been no knockout. The crowd that comes to Heinie's Arena don't make no talk about being wishful to see a exhibition of boxing. What they want is gore and busted noses, and if somebody don't get just about killed they think they have been gypped, and wreck the joint.

Just as me and Bill come in, the principals scurried out of the ring followed by a offering of chair bottoms, bricks and dead cats, and Heinie, who'd been acting as referee, tried to calm the mob—which only irritated them more and somebody hit Heinie square between the eyes with a rotten tomato. The maddened crowd was fast reaching a point where they was liable to do anything, when me and Bill climbed into the ring. They knowed us, and they kind of quieted down a minute and then started yelling fiercer than ever.

"For my sake, Steve," said Heinie, kind of pale, wiping the vegetable out of his eyes, "say somethin' to 'em before they start a riot. Them two hams that just faded away only cake-walked through the bout and these wolves is ready to lynch everybody concerned, particularly includin' me."

"Have you got somebody I can fight?" I asked.

"No, I ain't," he said, "But I'll announce—"

"I don't see no announcer," I growled, and turning to the crowd I silenced them by the simple process of roaring: "*Shut up!*" in a voice which drowned them all out.

"Listen here, you tin-horn sports!" I bellered. "You've already paid your dough, but do you think you've got your money's worth?"

"*No!*" they thundered in a voice that started Heinie's knees to knocking. "We been robbed! We been rooked! We been gypped! Give us our money back! Wreck the dump! Hang that Dutchman!"

"Shut up, you Port Mahon baboons!" I roared. "If you're sports enough to jar loose and make up a purse of twenty-five dollars, I'll fight any man in the house to a finish, winner take all!"

At that they lifted the roof. "'At's the stuff!" they whooped. "Shower down gents. We know Steve! He always gives us a run for our money!"

Coins and a few bills began to shower on the canvas, and two men jumped up from among the crowd and started for the ring. One was a red-headed Englishman and the other was a lithe black-haired fellow. They met just outside the ropes.

"One side, bloke," growled the red-head. "H'I'm fightin' this bloody Yank!"

Black-head's right shot out like a battering ram and red-head kissed the floor, and laid still. The mob went into hysterics of joy and the winner hopped over the ropes, followed by three or four of the most villainous looking mugs I ever hope to see.

"I weel fight Costigan!" said he, and Heinie give a deep sigh of relief. But Bill swore under his breath.

"That's Panther Cortez," said he. "And you know you ain't been trainin' close lately."

"Never mind," I growled. "Count the money. Heinie, you keep your hands off that dough till Bill counts it."

"Thirty-six dollars and fifty cents," announced Bill, and I turned to the slit-eyed devil which called hisself Panther Cortez, and growled: "You willin' to fight for that much—winner take all, loser gets nothin' but a headache?"

He grinned with a flash of white fangs. "Sure!—I fight you just for the fun of knocking you cold!"

I turned my back on him with a snarl and, giving Heinie the money to hold, though it was a terrible risk to take, I strode to one of the make-shift dressing rooms, where I was given a pair of dingy trunks, which Heinie pulled off a preliminary boy which had gone on earlier in the evening and was still out.

I gave little thought to my opponent, though Bill kept grouching about the fact that I was going to get so little for knocking out such a man as Cortez.

"You oughta be gettin' at least a hundred and fifty," Bill grumbled. "This Cortez is a mean puncher, and shifty and dirty. He ain't never been knocked out."

"Well," said I, "it ain't never too late to begin. All I want you to do is watch and see that none of his handlers don't sneak around and hit me with a water bottle. Thirty-six shares means thirty-six thousand dollars for us. Tomorrer we'll kick the Old Man in the slats for a token of farewell, and start livin'! No more standin' watch and gettin' sunburnt and froze for somebody else—"

"Hey!" yelled Heinie, looking in at the door, "hurry up, will ya? This crowd's goin' clean nuts waitin'. The Panther's already in the ring."

AS I CLIMBED through the ropes I was greeted by a roar such as must of resembled them given by the Roman mobs when a favorite gladiator was throwed to the lions. Cortez was seated in his corner, smiling like a big lazy jungle cat, the lids drooping down over his glittering eyes in a way that always irritated me.

He was a mixed breed—Spanish, French, Malay and heck knows what else, but all devil. He was the choice fighting man aboard the *Water Snake,* a British vessel with a shady reputation, and though I'd never fought him, I knowed he was a dangerous man. But, gosh, all he represented to me just then was thirty-six dollars and fifty cents, which in turn represented thirty-six thousand dollars.

Heinie waved his arms and said: "Gents, you all know these boys! Both of them has fought here plenty of times before, and—"

The crowd rose up and drowned him out: "Yeah, we know 'em. Cut the introductions and le's see gore spilt!"

"Weights," yelled Heinie to make hisself heard. "Sailor Costigan of the *Sea Girl,* one hundred ninety pounds! Panther Cortez of the *Water Snake,* one hundred eighty-five pounds!"

"That's a lie!" roared Bill. "He weighs one-ninety if he weighs a ounce!"

"Aw, stow yer gab, ye bleedin' mick!" snarled one of the Panther seconds, shoving out his lantern jaw. Bill bent his right on that jaw and the limey went over the ropes on his head. The mob applauded madly; things was going just to their taste! All they needed to make it a perfect evening was for me or Cortez to get our neck broke—preferably both of us.

Well, Heinie chased Cortez' handlers out of the ring, and Bill climbed out, and the slaughter was on. Heinie was referee, but he didn't give us no instructions. We'd fought enough there to know what we was supposed to do, and that was to sock and keep on socking till somebody kissed the canvas and stayed there. The gloves we wore was at least a ounce and a half lighter than the regular style, and nothing was a foul at the International as long as both fellows could stand on their feet.

The Panther was lithe, rangy, quick; taller than me, but not so heavy. We come together in the middle of the ring, and he hit with catlike speed. Left to the face, right to the body and left to the jaw. Simultaneous I shot my right to his chin, and he hit the canvas on the seat of his trunks. The crowd howled, but he wasn't hurt much, mainly surprised and mad. His eyes blazed. He took the count of nine, though he could of got up sooner, and bounced up, stopping me in my tracks with a hard left to the mouth. I missed with a looping left, took a right to the ribs and landed hard under the heart. He spat in my face and began working his arms like pistons—left, right, left, right, to the face and body while the crowd went nuts. But that was my game; I grinned savagely and braced my feet, boring in and slugging hard with both hands.

A minute of this, and he backed away in a hurry, blood trickling from a cut on his cheek. I was after him and sank a left deep in his midriff that made him clinch and hold on. On the break he nailed me with a straight right to the head, and followed it up with a hard left to the eye, but failed to land his right, and got a wicked right hook to the ribs. I battered away at his body, but he was all elbows, and, irritated, I switched to his head and nearly tore it off with a blazing right hook just at the gong.

"That round was yours by a mile," said Bill, between exchanging insults with Cortez' handlers. "But watch out; he's dangerous and dirty—"

"I'm goin' to ask Joan to marry me," I said. "I can tell she's fell for me, right off. I dunno why it is, but it seems like they's a fatal fascination about me for women. They can't keep from floppin' for me at first sight—"

The gong sounded and I dashed out to collect that $36.50.

Well, the Panther had found out that he couldn't trade wallops with me, so he come out boxing. I don't mean he tin-canned and rode his bicycle, like some prominent fighters I could mention. He was one baby that could fight and box at the same time, if you get me. When I say he boxed, I mean he feinted me out of position, kept me off balance, speared me with cutting left jabs, ducked my ferocious returns, tied me up in the clinches, nearly ripped my head off with right uppercuts in close, stayed inside my wings, and generally made a sap outa me.

Inside of a minute he had me bleeding at the mouth and nose, and I hadn't landed solid once. The crowd was howling like wolves and Bill was cussing something terrible, but I wasn't worried. I had all night to lick him in, and I knowed I'd connect sooner or later, and I did quicker than I'd thought. It was a smashing right hook under the heart, and it bent Señor Cortez double. While in this position I clouted him heartily behind the ear and drove him to his knees. He was up without a count, slipped the terrible swing I threw at him, and having clinched and tied me up, scraped his glove laces across my eyes and ground his heel into my instep. He hung on like a regular octopus regardless of my cruel and unusual oaths. Heinie wouldn't pull him loose, and finally we both went to the canvas still clinched in a vise-like embrace.

This mishap threw the crowd into a perfect delirium of delight, which was increased by Cortez earnestly chewing my ear while we writhed on the mat. Driven to frenzy I tore loose, arose and closed the Panther's left eye with a terrible right swing the minute he was on his feet. He came back with a slashing left hook to the body, ripped the same hand to my already battered face, and stopped a straight left with his own map. At that moment the gong rang.

* * *

"I'M GOIN' TO kick Heinie Steinman loose from his britches after the fight!" snarled Bill, shaking with rage as he mopped the blood off my mangled ear. "If that wasn't the dirtiest foul I ever seen—"

"I wonder if we couldn't buy a half share with that fifty cents," I meditated. "That'd be five hundred dollars—"

I rushed out for the third frame inclined to settle matters quick, but Cortez had other plans. He opened a cut over my eye with a left hook, ripped a right hook to my sore ear and went under my return. He come up with a venomous right under the heart, ducked my left swing and jabbed me three times on the nose without a return. Maddened, I hurtled into him headlong, grabbed him with my left and clubbed him with my right till he tied me up.

At close quarters we traded short arm rights and lefts to the body and he was the first to back away, not forgetting to flick me in the eye with his long left as he did so. I was right on top of him and suddenly he lowered his head and butted me square in the mouth, bringing a flow of claret that dyed my chin. He instantly ripped in a right uppercut that loosened a bunch of my teeth and backed me into the ropes with a perfect whirlwind of left and right hooks to the head.

With the ropes cutting into my back I rallied, steadied myself and smashed a right under his heart that stopped him in his tracks. A left to the jaw set him back on his heels and rattled his teeth like a castinet, and before I could hit again the gong sounded.

"This is lastin' considerably longer than I thought," I said to Bill, who was mopping blood and talking to Heinie with some heat.

"My gosh, Bill," said Heinie. "Be reasonable! If I stopped this fight and awarded it to Steve or anybody else on a foul, these thugs wouldst tear this buildin' down and hang me to the rafters. They craves a knockout—"

"They're goin' to get one!" I snarled. "Never mind the fouls. Say, Bill, did you ever see such clear, honest eyes as Joan's got? I know women, I wanta tell you, and I never seen a straighter, squarer jane in my life—"

At the gong we went into a clinch and pounded each other's midsections till Heinie broke us. Cortez wasn't taking much chances, fighting wary and cautious. He slashed away with his left, but he kept his right high and never let it go unless he was sure of landing. He was using his elbows plenty in the clinches, and butting every chance he got, but Heinie pretended not to see. The crowd didn't care; as long as a man fought, they didn't care *how* he fought. Bill was making remarks that would of curled the toes of a Hottentot, but nobody seemed to mind.

About the middle of the lap, Cortez began making remarks about my ancestors that made me good and mad. My Irish got up, and I went for him like a wild bull, head down and arms hammering. He shot his left and side-stepped, but the left ain't made that can stop me when my temper's up, and I was right on top of him too fast for him to get away. I battered him across the ring, but just as I thought I had him pinned on the ropes he side-stepped and I fell into them myself.

This highly amused the crowd, and Cortez hooked three lefts to my head while I was untangling myself, and when I slewed around and swung, he ducked and crashed my jaw with a right hook he brought up from the floor and which had me groggy for the first time that night. Sensing victory, he shot the same hand three times to my head, knocking me back into the ropes where he sank his left to the wrist in my midriff.

I was dizzy and slightly sick, but I saw Cortez' snarling face in a sort of red haze and I smashed my right square into the middle of that face. He was off his guard—not expecting a return like that and his head went back like it was hinged. The blood splattered, and the crowd howled with relish. I plunged after him, but he crouched and as I came in he went under my swing and hooked his right hard to my groin. Oh Jerusha! I dropped like my legs had been cut from under me, and writhed and twisted on the canvas like a snake with a broken back.

I had to clench my teeth to keep from vomiting and I was sick—nauseated if you get what I mean. I looked up and Heinie, with his face white, was fixing to count over me.

"One!" he said. "Two! Three!"

"You hog-fat nit-wit!" screamed Bill. "If you count him out I'll blow your brains through the back of your skull!"

Heinie shivered like he had a chill; he took a quick look at Bill, then he shot a scared glance at the ravening crowd, and he ducked his head like a tortoise, shut his eyes and kept on counting.

"Four! Five! Six!"

"Thirty-six thousand dollars!" I groaned, reaching for the ropes. The cold sweat was standing out on my brow as I pulled myself up.

"Seven! Eight! Nine!"

I was up, feet braced wide, holding the top rope to keep from falling. Cortez came lunging in to finish me, and I knowed if I let go I'd fall again. I hunched my shoulder and blocked his right, but he ripped his left to my chin and crashed his right high on my temple—and then the gong sounded. He socked me again after the gong, before he went to his corner—but a little thing like that don't cause no comment in the International Fight Arena.

BILL HELPED ME to my corner, cursing between clenched teeth, but, with my usual recuperative powers, I was already recovering from the effects of that foul blow. Bill emptied a bucket-full of cold water over me, and much to Cortez' disgust I come out for the fifth frame as good as new. He didn't think so at first, but a wicked right-hander under the heart shook him to the toes and made him back pedal in a hurry.

I went for him like a whirlwind and, seeming somewhat discouraged, he began his old tactics of hit and run. A sudden thought hit me that maybe all the shares was bought up. This fight looked like it was going on forever; here I was chasing Panther Cortez around the ring and doing no damage, while the No Sens was buying up all the Korean Copper in sight. Every minute a fortune was slipping that much farther away from me, and this rat refused to stand up and be knocked out like a man. I nearly went crazy with fury.

"Come on and fight, you yellow skunk!" I raged, while the crowd yelled blood-thirstily, beginning to be irritated at Cortez' tactics, which was beginning to be more run than hit. "Stand up to it, you white-livered, yellow-bellied, Porchugeeze half-caste!"

They's always something that'll get under a fellow's hide. This got under Cortez'. Maybe he did have some breed blood in him. Anyway, he went clean crazy. He give a howl like a blood-mad jungle-cat, and in spite of the wild yells from his corner, he tore in with his eyes glaring and froth on his lips. *Biff! Bim! Bam!* I was caught in a perfect whirlwind of punches; it was like being clawed by a real panther. But, with a savage grin, I slugged it out with him. That's my game! He hit three blows to my one, but mine were the ones that counted.

There was the salty tang of blood in my mouth, and blood in my eyes; it reddened Heinie's shirt, and stained the canvas under our feet. It spattered in the faces of the yelling ring-siders at every blow. But my gloves were sinking deep at every sock, and I was satisfied. Toe to toe we slashed and smashed, till the ring swum red and the thunder of our blows could be heard all over the house. But it couldn't last; flesh and blood couldn't stand it. Somebody had to go—and it was Cortez.

Flat on his back he hit, and bounced back up without a count. But I was on him like a blood-mad tiger. I took his left and right in the face without hardly feeling them, and smashed my right under his heart and my left to his jaw. He staggered, glassy eyed; a crashing right to the jaw dropped him under the ropes on his face. Maybe he's there yet. Anyhow, up to the count of ten he didn't bat an eyelash.

"Gimme that dough!" I snarled, jerking it out of Heinie's reluctant hand.

"Hey!" he protested. "What about my cut? Didn't I promote this show? Didn't I stand all the expense? You think you can fight in my ring for nothin'—"

"If I had your nerve I'd be King of Siam," I growled, shaking the blood outa my eyes, and at that moment Bill's right met Heinie's jaw like a caulking mallet meeting a ship's hull, and Heinie went to sleep. The crowd filed out, gabbling incoherently. That last touch was all that was needed to make the night a perfect success for them.

"Here, give this to Cortez when he wakes up!" I snarled, shoving a five-dollar bill—American money—into the hand of one of the Panther's seconds. "He's dirty, but he's game. And he don't know it, but it's the same as me givin' him five thousand dollars. Come on, Bill."

I CHANGED MY clothes in the dressing-room, noting in a cracked mirror that my face looked like I'd fallen afoul a wildcat, and likewise that I had a beautiful black eye or two. We skinned out a side door, but I reckon some thugs in the crowd had seen us get the money—and they's plenty of men in the Singapore waterfront who'd cut your throat for a dime. The second I stepped out into the dark alley-way something crashed against my head, and I went to my knees seeing about a million stars. I come up again and felt a knife-edge lick along my arm. I hit out blind and landed by sheer luck. My right lifted my unseen attacker clean off his feet and dropped him like a sack on the ground. Meanwhile Bill had grappled with two more and I heard the crack as he knocked their heads together.

"You hurt, Steve?" he asked, feeling for me, because it was that dark you couldn't see your hand before you.

"Scratched a little," I said, my head still ringing from the blackjack sock. "Let's get outa here. Looks like we got to lick everybody in Singapore before we get that stock."

We got out of the alley and beat it down the street, people looking kind of funny at us. Well, I guess I was a sight, what with my black eye and cut and battered face, the bump on my head, and my arm bleeding from the knife wound. But nobody said nothing. People in places like that have got a way of minding their own business that politer folks could well copy.

"We better stop by the Waterfront Mission before we go for that stock, Steve," said Bill. "The gospel-shark will bandage your arm and not charge a cent—and keep his mouth shut afterward."

"No, no, no!" said I, becoming irascible because of my hurts and the delay. "We're goin' to get that stock before we do anything else."

We was passing a gambling hall and Bill's eyes lighted as he heard the click and whir of the roulette wheel.

"I feel lucky tonight," he muttered. "I betcha I could run that thirty bucks up to a hundred in no time."

"And I'd give my arm for a shot of licker," I snapped. "But I tell you, we ain't takin' no chances. We can guzzle and play fan-tan and roulette all we want to after we get rich."

After what seemed a century we arrived at the dismal, dark and vile smelling alley that the Chinese call the Alley of the Seven Mandarins—why, I never could figure. We found the door with the green dragon and knocked, and my heart stood still for fear Joan wouldn't be there. But she was. The door opened and she give a gasp as she saw me.

"Quick, don't keep us in suspense," Bill gasped. "Is the stock all took up?"

"Why, no," she said. "I can get you—"

"Then do it, quick," I said, pressing the money into her hand. "There's thirty-one dollars and fifty-cents—"

"Is that all?" she said, like she was considerably disappointed.

"If you'd a seen how I won it, you'd think it was a lot," I said.

"Well," she said. "Wait a minute. The man who owns that stock lives down the alley."

She vanished down the dark alley-way, and we waited with our hearts knocking holes in our ribs for what seemed like hours. Then she came out of the darkness, looking kind of white and ghostly in the shadows, and slipped a long envelope into my hot and sweaty hand. I hove a vast sigh of relief and started to say something, but she put her finger to her lips.

"Shhh! I musn't be seen with you. I must go, now." And before I could say a word, she'd vanished in the dark.

"Open the envelope, Steve," urged Bill. "Let's see what a fortune looks like!"

I opened it and pulled out a slip of paper. I moved over to the lamp-light in the street to read what was wrote on it. Then I give a roar that brought faces to every window on the street. Bill jerked the paper from me and glared at it and then he give a maddened howl and joined me in a frenzied burst of horrible talk that brought a dozen cops on the run. We wasn't in no condition to make any coherent reply, and the ensuing riot didn't end till the reserves was called out.

On the paper which was in the envelope Joan Wells gave me in return for my hard-earned money was wrote:

This is to certify that you are entitled to thirty-one and a half shares of stock in the Korean Copper Company which was dissolved in the year 1875. Don't worry about the No Sen Tong; it was extinct before the Boxer Rebellion. Of all the suckers that have fallen for this graft, you saps were the easiest. But cheer up; you're out only $31.50, and I took one bonehead for $300. A girl has got to live.

WATERFRONT FISTS

By ROBERT E. HOWARD

Author of "The Iron Man"

Trouble never troubled Steve Costigan, for trouble meant action with a capital A—and action was what Steve craved. This time it was Honolulu, waterfront cabarets, and—guess what—a beautiful girl!

WATERFRONT FISTS

THE *SEA GIRL* hadn't been docked in Honolulu more'n three hours before Bill O'Brien come legging it down to the pool hall where I was showing Mushy Hansen the fine points of the game, to tell me that he'd got me matched to fight some has-been at the American Arena that night.

"The *Ruffian* is in," said Bill, "and they got a fellow which they swear can take any man aboard the *Sea Girl* to a royal cleanin'. I ain't seen him, but they say he growed up in the back country of Australia and run wild with the kangaroos till he was shanghaied aboard a ship at an early age. They say he's licked everybody aboard the *Ruffian* from the cap'n down to the mess boy—"

"Stow the gab and lead me to some *Ruffian* idjits which is cravin' to risk their jack on this tramp," I interrupted. "I got a hundred and fifty bucks that's burnin' my pockets up."

Well, it was easy to find some lunatics from the *Ruffian,* and after putting up our money at even odds, with a bartender for stakeholder, and knowing I had a tough battle ahead of me and needed some training, I got me a haircut and then went down to the Hibernian Bar for a few shots of hard licker. While me and Bill and Mushy was lapping up our drinks, in come Sven Larsen. This huge and useless Swede has long been laboring under the hallucination that *he* oughta be champion of the *Sea Girl,* and no amount of battering has been able to quite wipe the idee outa what he supposes to be his brain.

Well, this big mistake come up to me, and scowling down at me, he said: "You Irisher, put oop your hands!"

I set my licker down with a short sigh of annoyance. "With a thousand sailors in port itchin' for a scrap," I said, "you got to pick on me. G'wan—I don't want to fight no shipmate now. Anyway, I got to fight the *Ruffian*'s man in a few hours."

"Aye shood be fightin' him," persisted the deluded maniac. "Aye ought to be champ of dey *Sea Girl.* Come on, you big stiffer!" And so saying he squared off in what he fondly believed was a fighting pose. At this moment my white bulldog, Mike, sensing trouble, bristled and looked up from the bowl of beer he was lapping up on the floor, but seeing it was nobody but Sven, he curled up and went to sleep.

"Don't risk your hands on the big chump, Steve," said Bill disgustedly. "I'll fix him—"

"You stay oot of dis, Bill O'Brien," said the Swede waving his huge fists around menacingly. "Aye will see to you after Aye lick Steve."

"Aw, you're drunk," I said. "A fine shipmate you are."

"Aye am not droonk!" he roared. "My girl told me—"

"I didn't know you had a girl here," said Bill.

"Well, Aye have. And she said a big man like me shood be champion of his ship and she wouldn't have nothings to do with me till Aye was. So put oop your hands—"

"Aw, you're crazy," I snapped, turning back to the bar, but watching him close from the corner of my eye. Which was a good thing because he started a wild right swing that had destruction wrote all over it. I side-stepped and he crashed into the bar. Rebounding with a bloodthirsty beller he lunged at me, and seeing they was no arguing with the misguided heathen, I stepped inside his swing and brought up a right uppercut to the jaw that lifted his whole two hundred and forty-five pounds clean off the floor and stood him on the back of his neck, out cold. Mike, awakened by the crash, opened one eye, raised one ear, and then went back to sleep with a sort of gentle canine smile.

"Y'oughta be careful," growled Bill, while Mushy sloshed a pitcher of dirty water over the Swede. "You mighta busted yore hand. Whyn't you hit him in the stummick?"

"I didn't wanta upset his stummick," I said. "I've skinned my knuckles a little, but they ain't even bruised much. I've had 'em in too many buckets uh brine."

AT LAST SVEN was able to sit up and cuss me, and he mumbled something I didn't catch.

"He says he's got a date with his girl tonight," Mushy said, "but he's ashamed to go back to her with that welt on his jaw and tell her he got licked."

"Ya," said Sven, rubbing his jaw, "you got to go tell her I can't come, Steve."

"Aw, well," I said, "all right. I'll tell her you fell off the docks and sprained your ankle. Where's she live?"

"She dances at the Striped Cat Cabaret," said Sven.

After downing a finger of Old Jersey Cream, I tightened my belt and me and Mike sauntered forth.

Bill followed me out into the street and said: "Dawg-gone it, Steve, you ought not to go cruisin' off this way, with the fight just a few hours in the offin'. That *Ruffian* crew is crooked as a buncha snakes—and you know what a soft head you are where women is concerned."

"Your remarks is highly insultin', Bill," I returned with my well-known quiet dignity. "I don't reckon no woman ever made a fool outa me. I know 'em like a book. Anyhow, you don't think I'd fall for a dame as encouraged a sap like Sven, do you? Heck, she's probably some big fat wench with a face like a bull terrier. What'd he say her name was—oh, yes, Gloria Flynn. Don't you worry about me. I'll be at the American in plenty uh time."

It was after dark when me and Mike got to the Striped Cat Cabaret which is located in a tough waterfront section of the city. I asked the manager for Gloria Flynn, and he said she'd just finished a dance and was in her dressing room, changing to street clothes. He told me to wait for her at the back exit, which I done. I was standing there when the door opened and some girls come out. I said, taking off my cap, politely, "Which one of you frails is Gloria Flynn, if any?"

You could of knocked me over with a pile-driver when the snappiest, prettiest one of the bunch up and said, "I'm her—and what of it?"

"Well," I said, eyeing her with great admiration, "all I can say is, what does a girl like you want to waste her time with such tripe as Sven Larsen when they is men like me in port?"

"Don't get fresh!" she snapped.

"Oh, I ain't fresh," I assured her. "I just come to tell you that Sven fell off a dock and broke his neck—I mean sprained his ankle, and he can't make the date tonight."

"Oh," she murmured. Then looking close at me, she said, "Who are you?"

"I'm Steve Costigan, the fellow that licked him," I replied thoughtlessly.

"Oh!" she said, kind of breathlessly. "So you're Steve Costigan!"

"Yeah, I am," I said, having spilled the beans anyway. "Steve Costigan, A. B. mariner, and heavyweight champion aboard the trader *Sea Girl*. I knowed you didn't know me, or you wouldn't of persuaded your boy friend to risk his life by takin' a swing at me."

She looked kind of bewildered. "I don't know what you're talking about."

"Oh, it's all right," I hastened to assure her. "Sven told me about you urgin' him to climb me, but it's natural for a frail to want her fellow to be a champ of somethin'. What I can't understand is, what you see in a galoot like Sven."

She gave a kind of hysterical laugh. "Oh, I see. Why, Mr. Costigan—"

"Call me Steve," I beamed.

"Well—Steve," she said with a little embarrassed laugh, "I didn't urge him anything of the sort. I just said he was such a big fellow I bet he could whip anybody aboard his ship—and he said one of the other sailors, Steve Costigan, was champion, and I said I was surprised that anybody could lick him—Sven, I mean. Why, I had no idea he'd get it into his head I wanted him to fight anybody. I do hope you didn't hurt the poor boy."

"Oh, not much," I said, unconsciously swelling out my huge chest,

"I always handle my shipmates easy as possible. Though uh course, I'm so powerful some times I hit harder'n I intend to. But say, sister, I know a swell little girl like you wasn't takin' that big squarehead serious. You was just sorry for him because he's so kind of big and awkward and dumb, wasn't you?"

"Well," she admitted, "that was the way of it; he looked lonesome—"

"Well, that's mighty fine of you," I said. "But forget about him now; after the beltin' I give him, he won't want to come back to you, and anyway, he'll find a native girl or a Chinese or somethin'. He ain't like me; a woman's a woman to him and he'll fall for anything in skirts that comes along. Me, I'm a one-woman man. Anyway, kid, it ain't right for you to trail around with a galoot like him. You owe it to yourself to keep company with only the best—me, for instance."

"Maybe you're right," she said, with downcast eyes.

"Sure, I'm always right," I answered modestly. "Now what say we go in and lap up something. All this talkin' I been doin's got my throat dry."

"Oh, I never drink intoxicants," she said with a bright smile. "If you don't mind let's go over here to this ice-cream parlor."

"O.K. with me," I said, "but first lemme introduce you to Mike who can lick his weight both in wildcats and dog biscuits."

Well, Mike, he shook hands with her but he wasn't particular enthusiastic. He ain't no ladies' dog; he treats 'em politely but coldly. Then we went over to the joint where they sold ice cream, and while we was dawdling over the stuff, I let my eyes wander over my charming companion. She was a beauty, no doubt about it; curly yellow hair and big trusting violet eyes.

"WHAT'S A NICE girl like you doin' workin' in a dump like the Striped Cat?" I asked her, and she kind of sighed and hung her head.

"A girl has to do lots of things she don't like to," she said. "I was in a high class stock company which went broke here on account of the manager getting delirium tremens and having to be sent back to his home in England. I had to eat, and this was the only job open for me. Some day I'm going home; my folks live on a dairy farm in New Jersey, and I was a fool ever to leave there. Right now I can see the old white farm house, and the green meadows with the babbling brooks running through them, and the cows grazing."

I thought she was going to cry for a minute, then she kind of sighed and smiled: "It's all in a lifetime, isn't it?"

"You're a brave kid," I said, touched to my shoe soles, "and I wanta see more of you. I'm fightin' some guy at the American Arena in a little while. How about holdin' down a nice ringside seat there, and then havin' supper and a little dancin' afterwards? I can't dance much, but I'm a bear at the supper table."

"Oh," said she, "you're the man that's going to fight Red Roach?"

"Is that his name?" I asked. "Yeah, if he's the man from the *Ruffian*."

"I'd like to go," she said, "but I have to go on in another dance number in half an hour."

"Well," I said, "the fight can't last more'n three or four rounds, not with me in there. How 'bout me droppin' around the Striped Cat afterwards? If you ain't through then, I'll wait for you."

"That's fine," she said, and noting my slightly unsatisfied expression, she said: "If I'd known you were going to fight so soon, I wouldn't have let you eat that ice cream."

"Oh, that won't interfere with my punchin' ability any," I said. "But I would like a shot of hard licker to kind of settle it on my stummick."

That's the truth; sailors is supposed to be hawgs about ice cream and I have seen navy boys eat it in digusting quantities, but it's poor stuff for my belly. Mike had ate the bowl full I give him, but he'd a sight rather had a pan of slush.

"Let's don't go in any of these saloons," said Gloria. "These waterfront bars sell you the same stuff rattlesnakes have in their teeth. I tell you, I've got a bottle of rare old wine not very far from here. I never touch it myself, but I keep it for my special friends and they say it's great. You've time for a nip, haven't you?"

"Lead on, sister," I said, "I've always got time to take a drink, or oblige a beautiful girl!"

"Ah, you flatterer," she said, giving me a little push. "I bet you tell that to every girl you meet."

WELL, TO MY surprise we halted before a kind of ramshackle gymnasium, and Gloria took out a key and unlocked the door.

"I didn't tell you I had a kid brother with me," she said in answer to my surprised glance. "He's a weakly sort of kid, and I have to support him as well as myself. Poor kid, he would come with me when I left home. Well, Mr. Salana, who owns the gym, lets him use the equipment to build himself up; it's healthy for him. This is the boy's key. I keep the wine hidden in one of the lockers."

"Ain't this where Tony Andrada trains?" I asked suspiciously. "'Cause if it is, it ain't no place for a nice girl. They is fighters and fighters, my child, and Tony is no credit to no business."

"He's always been a perfect gentleman towards me," she answered. "Of course I come here only occasionally when my brother is working out—" She opened the door and we went in and then she shut it. To my slight surprise I heard the click as she locked it. She switched on a light and I seen her bending over something. Then she swung around and—wow!—I got the most unexpected, dumfounding surprise of my life to date! When she turned she had a heavy Indian club in both hands, and she heaved it up and crashed it down on my head with everything she had behind it!

Well, I was so utterly dumfounded I just stood and gaped at her, and Mike, he nearly had a fit. I'd always taught him never to bite a woman, and he just didn't know what to do. Gloria was staring at me with eyes that looked like they was going to jump right out of her head. She glanced down at the broken fragments of the Indian club in a kind of stunned way, and then the color all ebbed out of her face, leaving her white as a ghost.

"That's a nice way to do a friend!" I said reproachfully. "I don't mind a joke, but you've made me bite my tongue."

She cringed back against the wall and held out both hands pitifully: "Don't hit me!" she cried, "please don't hit me! I had to do it!"

Well, if I ever seen a scared girl, it was then. She was shaking in every limb.

"You don't need to insult me on top of busting a club on my skull," I said with my quiet dignity. "I never hit no woman in my life and I ain't figurin' on it."

All to once she began to cry. "Oh," said she, "I'm ashamed of myself. But please listen—I've lied to you. My brother is a fighter too, and he just about had this fight with Red Roach, when the promoter at the American changed his mind and signed you up instead. This fight would have given us enough to get back to New Jersey where those cows are grazing by the babbling meadows. I—I—thought, when you told me you were the one that's going to fight Roach, I'd fix it so you wouldn't show up, and they'd have to use Billy—that's my brother—after all. I was going to knock you unconscious and tie you up till after the fight. Oh, I know you'll hate me, but I'm desperate. I'll die if I have to live this life much longer," she said passionately. And then she starts to bawl.

Well, I can't see as it was my fault, but I felt like a horse thief anyhow.

"Don't cry," I said. "I'd help you all I can, but I got all my jack sunk on the imbroblio to win by a k.o."

She lifted her tear stained face. "Oh, Steve, you can help me! Just stay here with me! Don't show up at the Arena! Then Billy will get the fight and we can go home! Please, Steve, please, please, *please!"*

She had her arms around my neck and was fairly shaking me in her eagerness. Well, I admit I got a soft spot in my heart for the weaker sex, but gee whiz!

"Great cats, Gloria," I said, "I'd dive off the Statue uh Liberty for you, but I can't do this. My shipmates has got every cent they got bet on me. I can't throw 'em down that way."

"You don't love me!" she mourned.

"Aw, I do too," I protested. "But dawg-gone it, Gloria, I just can't do it, and please don't coax me, 'cause it's like jerkin' a heart-string loose to say 'No' to you. Wait a minute! I got a idee! You and your brother got some money saved up, ain't cha?"

"Yes, some," she sniffed, dabbing at her eyes with a foolish little lace handkerchief.

"Well, listen," I said, "you can double it—sink every cent you got on me to win by a kayo! It'll be a cinch placin' the dough. Everybody on the waterfront's bettin' one way or the other."

"But what if you lose?" said she.

"Me lose?" I snorted. "Don't make me laugh! You do that—and I can't stay another minute, kid—I'm due at the Arena right now. And say, I'll have some dough myself after the battle, and I'm goin' to help you and your brother get back to them green cows and babblin' farm houses. Now I got to go!"

And before she had time to say another word, I kicked the lock off the door, being in too big a hurry to have her unlock it, and the next second me and Mike was sprinting for the Arena.

I FOUND BILL tearing his hair and walking the dressing room floor.

"Here you are at last, are you, you blankety-blank mick dipthong!" he yelled blood-thirstily. "Where you been? You want to make a nervous wreck outa me? You realize you been committin' the one unpardonable sin, by keepin' the crowd waitin' for fifteen minutes? They're yellin' bloody murder and the crew which is all out front in ringside seats, has been throwin' chairs at the *Ruffian*'s men which has been howlin' you'd run out on us. The promoter says if you ain't in that ring in five minutes, he'll run in a substitute."

"And I'll run him into the bay," said I, sitting down and shucking my shoes. "I gotta get my wind back a little. Boy, we had Sven's girl down all wrong! She's a peach, as well as bein' a square-shootin'—"

"Shut up, and get into them trunks!" howled Bill, doing a war-dance on the cap I'd just took off. "You'll never learn nothin'. Listen to that crowd! We'll be lucky if they don't lynch all of us!"

Well, the maddened fans was making a noise like a flock of hungry lions, but that didn't worry me none. I'd just got into my fighting togs when the door opened and the manager of the Arena stuck a pale face in.

"I got a man in place of Costigan—" he began, when he saw me and stopped.

"Gangway!" I snarled, and as I pushed by him, I saw a fellow in trunks coming out of another dressing room. To my amazement it was Tony Andrada, which even had his hands taped. His jaw fell when he seen me, and his manager, Abe Gold, give a howl. They was two other thugs with them—Salana and Joe Cromwell—I'd been in Honolulu enough to know them yeggs.

"What do you think you're doin' here?" I snarled, facing Tony.

"They want me to fight Roach, when you run out—" he begun.

Bill grabbed my arm as I was making ready to slug him. "For cats' sake!" he snarled, "you can lick him after you flatten Roach if you want to! *Come on!*"

"It's mighty funny he should turn up, right at this time," I growled. "I thought Billy Flynn was to fight Roach if I didn't show up."

"Who's Billy Flynn?" asked Bill as he rushed me up the aisle between howling rows of infuriated fans.

"My new girl's kid brother," I answered as I clumb through the ropes. "If they've did anything to him, I'll—"

My meditations was drowned by the thunders of the mob, who give me cheers because I'd got there, and razzes because I hadn't got there sooner.

On one side of the ring the *Sea Girl*'s crew lifted the roof with their wild whoops and on the other side the *Ruffian*'s roughnecks greeted me with coarse, rude squawks and impolite remarks.

Well, I glanced over to the opposite corner and saw Red Roach for the first, and I hope the last, time. He was tall and raw-boned, and the ugliest human I ever seen. He had freckles as big as mess pans all over him; his nose was flat, and his low slanting forehead was topped by a shock of the most scandalously red hair I ever looked at. When he rose from his stool I seen he was knock-kneed and when we came to the center of the ring to pretend to listen to instructions, I was disgusted to note that he was also cross-eyed. At first I thought he was counting the crowd, and it was slightly disconcerting to finally decide he was glaring at me!

WE WENT BACK to our corners, the gong sounded, the scrap started and I got another jolt.

Roach come out, right foot and right hand forward. He was left-handed! I was so disgusted I come near lighting in and giving him a good cussing. Red-headed, cross-eyed—and left-handed! And he was the first good port-sider I'd ever met in a ring.

I forgot to say our weights was 190 for me, and 193 for him. In addition, he was six feet three, or just three inches taller'n me, and he musta had a reach of anyways fifteen fathoms. We was still so far apart I didn't think he could reach me with a pole when—*bam!* his right licked out to my chin. I give a roar and plunged in, meaning to make it a quick fight. I wanted to crush this inhuman freak before the sight of him got on my nerves and rattled me.

But I was all at sea. A left-hander does everything backwards. He leads with his right and crosses his left. He side-steps to the left instead of the right ordinarily. This guy done everything a port-sider's supposed to do, and a lot more stuff he thought up for hisself. He had a fast hard straight right and a wicked left swing—oh boy, how he could hit with that left! Seemed like every time I did anything, I got that right in the eye or the mouth or on the nose, and whilst I was thinking about that, *bam!* come the left and nearly ripped my head clean off.

The long, lanky mutt—it looked like if I ever landed solid I'd bust him in two. But I couldn't get past that long straight right. My swings were all short and his straight right beat my left hook every time. When I tried trading jabs with him, his extra reach ruint that—anyway, I'm a natural hooker. My straight left is got force, but it ain't as accurate as it should be.

At the end of the first round my right ear was nearly mangled. In the second frame he half closed my eye with a sizzling right hook, and opened a deep gash on my forehead. At the beginning of the third he dropped me for no-count with a left hook to the body that nearly caved me in. The *Ruffian*'s crew was getting crazier every second and the *Sea Girl*'s gang was yelling bloody murder. But I wasn't worried. I'm used to more punishment than I was getting and I wasn't weakening any.

But dawg-gone it, it did make me mad not to be able to hit Roach. To date I hadn't landed a single solid punch. He was a clever boxer in his way, and his style woulda made Dempsey look like a one-armed paperhanger carryin' a bucket.

He managed to keep me at long range, and he belted me plenty, but it wasn't his speed nor his punch that kept me all at sea; it was his cruel and unusual appearance! Dawg-gone—them eyes of his nearly had me batty. I couldn't keep from looking at 'em. I tried to watch his waist-line or his feet, but every time my gaze wouldst wander back to his distorted optics. They had a kinda fatal attraction for me. Whilst I wouldst be trying to figure out where they was looking—*wham!* would come that left winging in from a entirely unexpected direction—and this continued.

WELL, AFTER ARISING from that knock-down in the third frame, I was infuriated. And after chasing him all around the ring, and getting only another black eye for my pains, I got desperate. With the round half a minute to go, I wowed the audience by closing both my eyes and tearing in, swinging wild and regardless.

He was pelting me plenty, but I didn't care; that visage of his wasn't upsetting all my calculations as long as I couldn't see it, and in a second I felt my left crash against what I knew to be a human jaw. Instantly the crowd went into hystericals and I opened my eyes and looked for the corpse.

My eyes rested on a recumbent figure, but it was not Red Roach. To my annoyance I realized that one of my blind swings had connected with the referee. At the same instant Roach's swinging left crashed against my jaw and I hit the canvas. But even as I went down I swung a wild dying effort right which sunk in just above Red's waistline. The round ended with all three of us on the canvas.

Our respective handlers dragged us to our corners, and somebody throwed a bucket of water on the referee, who was able to answer the gong with us battlers by holding on to the ropes.

Well, as I sat in my corner sniffing the smelling salts and watching Red's handlers massaging his suffering belly, I thought deeply, a very rare habit of mine while fighting. I do not believe in too much thinking; it gives a fighter the headache. Still and all, with my jaw aching from Red's left and my eyes getting strained from watching his unholy face, I rubbed the nose Mike stuck into my glove, and meditated. A left-hander is a right-hander backwards. Nine times out of ten his straight right will beat your left jab. If you lead your right to a right-hander, he'll beat you to the punch with his left; but you can lead your right to a left-hander, because his left has as far to travel as your right.

So when we come out for the fourth round, instead of tearing in, I went in cautious-like for me, ignoring the yells of the *Ruffian*'s crew that I was getting scared of their man. Red feinted with his right so clumsy even I knowed it was a feint and instantly shot my right with everything I had behind it. It beat his left swing and landed solid, but high. He staggered and I dropped him to his all fours with a whistling left hook under the heart. He was up at "Nine" and caught me with a wild left swing as I rushed in. It dizzied me but I kept coming, and every time he made a motion with his left I shot my right. Sometimes I landed first and sometimes he did, and sometimes we landed simultaneous, but my smashes had the most kick behind them. Like most port-siders when they're groggy, he'd clean forgot he had a right hand and was staking everything on his left swing.

I battered him back across the ring, and he rallied and smashed over a sledge-hammer left hook that rocked me to my heels and made the blood spatter, but I bored right in with a sizzling left hook under the heart. He gasped, his knees buckled, then he steadied hisself and shot over his left just as I crashed in with a right. *Bam!* Something exploded in my head, and then I heard the referee counting. To my chagrin I found I was on the canvas, but Roach was there too.

The still weaving and glassy-eyed referee was holding onto the ropes with one hand and counting over us both, but I managed to reel up at "Six!" Me and Red had landed square to the button at just the same second, but my jaw was just naturally tougher than his. He hadn't twitched at "Ten" and they had to carry him to his dressing room to bring him to.

Well, a few minutes' work on me with smelling salts, ammonia, sponges and the like made me as good as new. I couldn't hardly wait for Bill to dress my cuts with collodion, but the minute I got my clothes on and collected my winnings and bets from the bartender, who'd come to the ring under escort from both ships, I ducked out the back way. I even left Mike with Bill because he's always scrapping with some other dog on the streets and I was in a big hurry.

I was on my way to see if Gloria had followed my advice, also something else. One hundred and fifty bucks I won; with what I had that made three hundred. I got a hundred and fifty for the fracas. Altogether I had four hundred and fifty dollars all in greenbacks of large denomination in my jacket pocket. And I was going to give Gloria every cent of it, if she'd take it, so she could go back to New Jersey and the cows. This sure wasn't no place for a nice girl to be in, and I'll admit I indulged in some dreams as I hurried along—about the time I'd retire from the sea and maybe go into the dairy farming business in New Jersey.

I WAS HEADED for the Striped Cat, but on my way I passed Salana's gym, and I noticed that they was a light in one of the small rooms which served as a kind of office. As I passed the door I distinctly heard a voice I knowed was Gloria's. I stopped short and started to knock on the door, then something made me steal up close and listen—though I ain't a eavesdropper by nature. From the voices five people was in the room—Gloria, Salana, Abe Gold, Joe Cromwell, and Tony.

"Don't hand us no line, sister," Gold was saying in his nasty rasping voice. "You said leave it to you. Yeah, we did! And look what it got us! You was goin' to keep Costigan outa the way, so's we could run Tony in at the last minute. You know the promoter at the American was all set to match Tony with Roach when Costigan's ship docked and the big cheese changed his mind and matched the Mick instead, because the fool sailors wanted the scrap.

"Roach woulda been a spread for Tony, because the wop eats these port-siders up. The town sports know that, and they woulda sunk heavy on Tony. We was goin' to bet our shirts on Roach, and Tony would flop along about the third. Then we coulda all left this dump and gone to Australia.

"Well, we left it up to you to get rid of Costigan. And what does he do, I ask you? He walks in as big as you please, just when Tony was fixing to go in for him. I ask you!"

"Well, don't rag me," said Gloria in a voice which startled me, it was that hard, "I did my best. I got hold of a Swede aboard the *Sea Girl* and primed the big stiff proper. I stirred him up and sent him down to climb Costigan, thinking he'd bung the mick up so he couldn't come on tonight, or that Costigan would at least break his hands on him.

"But the harp flattened him without even spraining a thumb, and the first thing I knew, he was waiting for me outside the cabaret. I thought he'd come to smack me down for sicking the Swede on him, but the big slob had just come to tell me the square-head couldn't keep his date. Can you feature that? Well, he fell for me right off, naturally, and I got him into the gym here, intending to lay him cold and lock him up till after the fight. But say! That big mick must have a skull made of reinforced battleship steel! I shattered a five-pound Indian club over his dome without even making him bat his eyes!

"Well, I hope I never have a half-minute like that again! When I failed to even stagger him with that clout, I thought I was a gone goose! I had visions of him twisting my head off and feeding it to that ugly cannibal he calls his bulldog.

"But you can't tell about those tough looking sluggers like him. He didn't even offer to lay a hand on me, and when I got my second wind, I spun him a yarn about having a kid brother that needed this fight to get back home. He fell for it so easy that I thought I could coax him to run out on his own accord, but he balked there. All he'd do was to advise me to bet on him, and then all at once he said it was time for him to be at the stadium, and he busted right out through the door and took it on the lam, making some crack about coming back after the fight."

"A fine mess you've made!" sneered Salana. "You've gummed things up proper! We had everything set for a killing—"

"A high class brand of sports you are!" she snapped. "I'm ashamed to be seen with you, you cheap grafters! A big killing! You don't know what one is. Anyway, what do you want me to do, cry?"

"We want you to give back that hundred we paid you in advance," snarled Salana, "and if you don't, you'll cry plenty."

"And I guess you think I risk my life for such cheap welchers as you for nothing?" she sneered. "Not one cent—"

There was the sound of a blow and Gloria give a short, sharp cry which was cut short in a sort of gasp.

"Give her the works, Joe," Salana snarled. "You can't cross me, you little—!"

* * *

NEVER MIND WHAT he called her. I'd have half killed him for that alone. I tore the door clean off the hinges as I went through it, and I seen a sight that made a red mist wave in front of me so everything in that room looked bloody and grim.

Salana had Gloria down on a chair and was twisting both her arms up behind her back till it looked like they'd break. Joe Cromwell had the fingers of his left hand sunk deep in her white throat and his right drawed back to smash in her face. Tony and Abe Gold was looking on with callous, contemptuous sneers.

They all turned to look as the door crashed in, and I saw Salana go white as I give one roar and went into action. He turned loose of the girl, but before he could get his hands up, I crashed him with a left-hander that crushed his nose and knocked out four teeth, and my next smash tore Joe Cromwell's ear loose and left it hanging by a shred. Another of the same sort stood him on his head in a corner with a cracked jaw-bone, and almost simultaneous Abe Gold barely missed me with a pair of brass knuckles, and Tony landed hard on my ear. But I straightened with a right-hander that dropped Gold across Salana with three broken ribs, and missed a left swing that wouldst of decapitated Tony hadst it landed.

I ain't one of these fellows which has to be crazy mad to put up a good fight, but when I *am* crazy mad, they's no limit to the destruction I can hand out. Maybe in the ring, under ordinary circumstances, Tony could of cut me to ribbons, but here he never had a chance. I didn't even feel the punches he was raining on me, and after missing a flock of swings in a row, I landed under his jaw with a hay-making right-hander that I brought up from the floor. Tony turned a complete somersault in the air, and when he come down his head hit the wall with a force that laid his scalp open and wouldst of knocked him cold, if he hadn't already been unconscious before he landed.

Maybe a minute and a half after I busted through the door, I stood alone in the middle of the carnage, panting and glaring down at the four silent figures which littered the room. All I craved was for all the other yeggs in Honolulu to come busting in. Pretty soon I looked around for Gloria and saw her cringing in a corner like she was trying to flatten herself out against the wall. She was white-faced and her eyes was blazing with terror.

She give a kind of hunted cry when I looked at her. "Don't! Please, don't!"

"Please don't what?" I snapped in some irritation. "Ain't you learned by this time that I don't clout frails? I come in here to rescue you from these gypes, and you insult me!"

"Forgive me," she begged. "I can't help but be a little afraid of you—you look so much like a gorilla—"

"What!"

"I mean you're such a terrible fighter," she hastily amended. "Come on—let's get out of here before these welchers come to."

"Would that they wouldst," I brooded. "What I done to 'em was just a sample of what I'm goin' to do to 'em. Dawg-gone it, some of these days somebody's goin' to upset my temper, then I'll lose control of myself and hurt somebody."

Well, we went out on the street, which was mostly deserted and rather dimly lighted, and Gloria said pretty soon: "Thank you for rescuing me. If my brother had been there—"

"Gloria," I said wearily, "ain't you ever goin' to stop lyin'? I was outside the door and heard it all."

"Oh," said she.

"Well," I said, "I reckon I'm a fool when it comes to women. I thought I was stuck on you, and didn't have sense enough to know you was stringin' me. Why, I even brung the four hundred and fifty bucks I won, intendin' to give it to you."

And so saying I threw out the wad of bills, waved it reproachfully in front of her eyes and replaced it in my jacket pocket. All at once she started crying.

"Oh, Steve, you make me ashamed of myself! You're so fine and noble—"

"Well," I said with my quiet dignity, "I know it, but I can't help it. It's just my nature."

"I'm so ashamed," she sobbed. "There's no use lying; Salana paid me a hundred dollars to get you out of the way. But, Steve, I'm changing my ways right here! I'm not asking you to forgive me, because I guess it's too much to ask, and you've done enough for me. But I'm going home tomorrow. That stuff I told you about the dairy farm in New Jersey was the only thing I told you that wasn't a lie. I'm going home and live straight, and I want to kiss you, just once, because you've showed me the error of my ways."

And so saying, she threw her arms around me and kissed me vigorously—and me not objectin' in no manner.

"I'm going back to the old, pure simple life," she said. "Back to the green meadows and babbling cows!"

And she made off down the street at a surprising rate of speed. I watched her go and a warm glow spread over me. After all, I thought, I do know women, and the hardest of them is softened by the influence of a strong, honest, manly heart like mine.

She vanished around a corner and I turned back toward the Hibernian Bar, at the same time reaching for my bank roll. Then I give a yell that woke up everybody in that section of Honolulu with cold sweat standing out on them. Now I knowed why she wanted to put her arms around me. My money was gone! She loved me—she loved me *not!*

Champ of the Forecastle

By ROBERT E. HOWARD

Author of "Sailor's Grudge"

Along the docks they used to say: "That's Steve Costigan, champ of the Sea Girl, the toughest ship afloat." It was a title to cherish, won and held by dint of raw courage and ready fists. And now Steve, groggy and battered but still on his feet, saw it slipping . . . slipping . . .

CHAMP OF THE FORECASTLE

I DON'T HAVE to have a man tell me he craves war. I can tell it by the set of his jaw, the glare in his eyes. So, when Sven Larson raised his huge frame on his bunk and accused me of swiping his tobaccer, I knowed very well what his idee was. But I didn't want to fight Sven. Havin' licked the big cheese three or four times already, I seen no need in mauling him any more. So somewhat to the surprise of the rest of the crew, I said:

"Sven, that's purty crude. You didn't need to think up no lie to pick a fight with me. I know you crave to be champion of the *Sea Girl*, but they ain't a chance, and I don't want to hurt you—"

I got no further, because with a bull's beller he heaved hisself offa his bunk and come for me like a wild man. Gosh, what a familiar scene that was—the fierce, hard faces ringing us, the rough bunks along the wall, the dim light of the lantern swinging overhead, and me standing in the middle, barefooted and stripped to the waist, holding my only title against all comers! They ain't a inch of that forecastle floor that I ain't reddened with my blood. They ain't a edge of a upper bunk that I ain't had my head smashed against. And since I been a man grown they ain't a sailor on the Seven Seas that can say he stood up to me in that forecastle and beat me down.

The lurching of the ship and the unsteady footing don't bother me none, nor the close space and foul, smoke-laden air. That's my element, and if I couldst fight in the ring like I can in the forecastle, with nothing barred, I'd be champion of something besides a tramp windjammer.

Well, Sven come at me with his old style—straight up, wide open, with a wild swinging right. I ducked inside it and smashed my left under his heart, following instantly with a blasting right hook to the jaw as he sagged. He started falling and a lurch of the ship throwed him half under a opposite bunk. They's no mercy ast, give or expected in a forecastle fight; it's always to the finish. I was right after him, and no sooner hadst he got to his feet than I smashed him down again before he could get his hands up.

"Let's call it a day, Sven," I growled. "I don't want to punch you no more."

But he come weaving up, spitting blood and roaring in his own tongue. He tried to clinch and gouge, but another right hook to the jaw sent him down and out. I shook the sweat outa my eyes and glared down at him in some irritation, which was mixed with the satisfaction of knowing that again I hadst proved my right to the title of champion of the toughest ship afloat. Maybe you think that's a mighty small thing, but it's the only title I got and I'm proud of it.

But I couldn't get onto Sven. Me and him was good friends ordinarily, but ever so often he'd get the idee he couldst lick me. So the next day I looked him up between watches and found him sulking and brooding. I looked over his enormous frame and shook my head in wonder to think that I hadst gotten no further in the legitimate ring than I have, when I can lay out such incredible monsters as Sven so easy.

Six feet four he was in his socks, and his two hundred and forty-five pounds was all muscle. I can bend coins between my fingers, tear up decks of cards and twist horseshoes in two, but Sven's so much stronger'n me they's no comparison. But size and strength ain't everything.

"Sven," said I, "how come you forever got to be fightin' me?"

Well, at first he wouldn't say, but at last it come out.

"AYE BANE GOT girl at Stockholm. She bane like me purty good, but they bane another faller. His name bane Olaf Ericson and he own fishing smack. Always when Aye go out with my girl, he bane yump on me and he always lick me. Aye tank if Aye ever lick you, Aye can lick Olaf."

"So you practice on me, hey?" I said. "Well, Sven, you never will lick me nor Olaf nor any man which can use his hands unless you change your style. Oh, uh course, you're a bear-cat when it comes to fightin' ignorant dock-wallopers and deck-hands which never seen a glove and can't do nothin' but bite and gouge. But you see what happens when you get up against a real fightin' man. Sven," said I on a sudden impulse, like I usually do, "far be it from me to see a deep water seaman get beat up regular by a Baltic fish-grabber. It's a reflection on the profession and on the ship. Sven," said I, "I'm goin' to train you to lick this big cheese."

Well, I hadn't never give much thought to Sven before, only in a general way—you can't pay close attention to every square-head which comes and goes aboard a trading ship—but in the weeks which followed I done my best to make a fighting man of him. I rigged up a punching bag for him and sparred with him between watches. When him or me wasn't doing our trick at the wheel or holystoning the deck, or scraping the cable or hauling on a rope, or trimming sail or exchanging insults with the mates, I tried to teach him all I knowed.

Understand, I didn't try to make no boxing wizard outa him. The big slob couldn't of learned even if I could of taught him. And I didn't know how myself. I ain't a clever boxer. I'm a rough and willing mixer in the ring, but compared to such rough-house scrappers as Sven, I'm a wonder. The simple ducking, slipping and blocking, which even the crudest slugger does in the ring, is beyond the ken of the average untrained man, and as for scientific hitting, they never heard of it. They just draw back the right and let it go without any aim, timing nor nothing. Well, I just taught Sven the fundamentals—to stand with his left foot forward and not get his legs crossed, to lead with his left and to time and aim a little. I got him outa the habit of swinging wild and wide open with his right all the time, and by constant drilling I taught him the knack of hooking and hitting straight. I also give him a lot of training to harden his body muscles, which was his weak spot.

Well, the big Swede took to it like a duck takes to water, and after I'd explained each simple move upwards of a thousand times, he'd understand it and apply it and he wouldn't forget. Like lots of squareheads, he was slow to learn, but once he had learned, he remembered what he'd learned. And his great size and strength was a big asset.

Bill O'Brien says, "Steve, you're trainin' the big sap to take your title away from you." But I merely laughed with great merriment at the idee.

Sven had a wallop like a mule's kick in either hand, and when he learned to use it, he was dangerous to any man. He was pretty tough, too, or got so before I got through with him. He wasn't very fast, and I taught him a kind of deep defensive crouch like Jeffries used. He took to it natural and developed a surprising left for the body.

After six months of hard work on him, I felt sure that he could lick the average alley-fighter easy. And about this time we was cruising Baltic waters and headed for Stockholm.

As we approached his native heath, Sven grew impatient and restless. He had a lot more self-confidence now and he craved another chance at Olaf, the demon rival. Sven wasn't just a big unwieldy slob no more. Constant sparring with me and Bill O'Brien had taught him how to handle hisself and how to use his bulk and strength. A few days outa Stockholm he had a row with Mushy Hansen, which was two hundred pounds of fighting man, and he knocked the Dane so cold it took us a hour and a half to bring him to.

Well, that cheered Sven up considerable and when we docked, he said to me: "Aye go see Segrida, my girl, and find out if Olaf bane in port. He bane hang out at dey Fisherman's Tavern. Aye go past with Segrida and he come out and yump on me, like usual. Only diss time Aye bane lick him."

Well, at the appointed time me and Bill and Mushy was loafing around the Fisherman's Tavern, a kind of bar where a lot of tough Swedish fishermen hung out, and pretty soon, along come Sven.

He had his girl with him, all right, a fine, big blonde girl—one of these tall, slender yet well-built girls which is overflowing with health and vitality. She was so pretty I was plumb astounded as to what she seen in a big boob like Sven. But women is that way. They fall for the dubs and pass up the real prizes—like me, for instance.

Segrida looked kind of worried just now and as they neared the Tavern, she cast a apprehensive eye that way. Well, they was abreast of the door when a kind of irritated roar sounded from within and out bulged what could of been nobody but Olaf the Menace, hisself, in person.

THERE WAS A man for you! He was fully as tall as Sven, though not as heavy. Tall, lithe and powerful he was, like a big, blond tiger. He was so handsome I couldst easily see why Segrida hesitated between him and Sven—or rather I couldn't see why she hesitated at all! Olaf looked like one of these here Vikings you read about which rampaged around in old times, licking everybody. But he had a hard, cruel eye, which I reckon goes with that kind of nature.

He had some fellers with him, but they stayed back in the doorway while he swaggered out and stopped square in front of Sven. He had a most contemptuous sneer and he said something which of course I couldn't understand, but as Mushy later translated the conversation to me, I'll give it like Mushy told to me and Bill.

"Well, well," said Olaf, "looking for another licking, eh? Your deep sea boy friend is back in port looking for his usual trouncing, eh, Segrida?"

"Olaf, please," said Segrida, frightened. "Don't fight, please!"

"I warned you what would happen to him," said Olaf, "if you went out with him—"

At this moment Sven, who had said nothing, shocked his bold rival by growling: "Too much talk; put up your hands!"

Olaf, though surprised, immediately done so, and cut Sven's lip with a flashing straight left before the big boy couldst get in position. Segrida screamed but no cops was in sight and the battle was on.

Olaf had learned boxing some place, and was one of the fastest men for his size I ever seen. For the first few seconds he plastered Sven plenty, but from the way the big fellow hunched his shoulders and surged in, I hadst no doubt about the outcome.

Sven dropped into the deep, defensive crouch I'd taught him, and I seen Olaf was puzzled. He hisself fought in the straight-up English sparring position and this was the first time he'd ever met a man who fought American style, I could see. With Sven's crouch protecting his body and his big right arm curved around his jaw, all Olaf couldst see to hit was his eyes glaring over the arm.

He battered away futilely at Sven's hard head, doing no damage whatever, and then Sven waded in and drove his ponderous left to the wrist in Olaf's midriff. Olaf gasped, went white, swayed and shook like a leaf. He sure couldn't take it there and I yelled for Sven to hit him again in the same place, but the big dumb-bell tried a heavy swing for the jaw, half straightening out of his crouch as he swung and Olaf ducked and staggered him with a sizzling right to the ear. Sven immediately went back into his shell and planted another battering-ram left under Olaf's heart.

Olaf broke ground gasping and his knees trembling, but Sven kept right on top of him in his plodding sort of way. Olaf jarred him with a dying-effort swing to the jaw, but them months of punching hadst toughened Sven and the big fellow shook his head and leaned on a right to the ribs.

That finished Olaf; his knees give way and he started falling, grabbing feebly at Sven as he done so. But Sven, with one of the few laughs I ever heard him give, pushed him away and crashed a tremendous right-hander to his jaw. Olaf straightened out on the board-walk and he didn't even quiver.

A LOW RUMBLE of fury warned us and we turned to see Olaf's amazed but wrathful cronies surging towards the victor. But me and Bill and Mushy and Mike kind of drifted in between and at the sight of three hard-eyed American seamen and a harder-eyed Irish bulldog, they stopped short and signified their intention of merely taking Olaf into the Tavern and bringing him to.

At this Sven, grinning placidly and turning to Segrida with open arms, got the shock of his life. Instead of falling on to his manly bosom, Segrida, who hadst stood there like she was froze, woke up all at once and bust into a perfect torrent of speech. I would of give a lot to understand it. Sven stood gaping with his mouth wide open and even the rescue party which had picked up Olaf, stood listening. Then with one grand burst of oratory, she handed Sven a full-armed, open-handed slap that cracked like a bull-whip, and busting into tears, she run forward to help with Olaf. They vanished inside the Tavern.

"What'd she say? What's the idee?" I asked, burnt up with curiosity.

"She say she bane through with me," Sven answered dazedly. "She say Aye bane a brute. She say she ain't bane want to see me no more."

"Well, keel-haul me," said I profanely. "Can ya beat that? First she wouldn't choose Sven because he got licked by Olaf all the time; now she won't have him because he licked Olaf. Women are all crazy."

"Never mind, old timer," said Bill, slapping the dejected Sven on the back. "Anyway, you licked Olaf to a fare-you-well. Come along, and we'll buy you a drink."

But Sven just shook his head sullen-like and moped off by hisself; so after arguing with him unsuccessfully, me and Bill and Mushy betook ourselves to a place where we couldst get some real whiskey and not the stuff they make in them Scandinavian countries. The barkeep kicked at first because I give my white bulldog, Mike, a pan-full of beer on the floor, but we overcome that objection and fell to talking about Sven.

"I don't savvy dames," I said. "If she gives Sven the bounce for beatin' up Olaf, whyn't she give Olaf the bounce long ago for beatin' up Sven so much?"

"It's Olaf she really loves," said Mushy.

"Maybe," said Bill. "And maybe he's just persistent. But women is kind-hearted. They pities a poor boob which has just got punched in the nose, and as long as Sven was gettin' licked all the time, he got all her pity. But now her pity and affections is transferred to Olaf, naturally."

Well, we didn't see no more of Sven till kind of late that night, when in come one of our square-head ship-mates named Fritz to the bar where me and Bill and Mushy was, and said he: "Steve, Sven he say maybeso you bane come down to a place on Hjolmer Street; he bane got something to show you."

"Now what could that Swede want now?" said Bill testily, but I said, "Oh well, we got nothin' else to do." So we went to Hjolmer Street, a kind of narrow street just out of the waterfront section. It wasn't no particularly genteel place—kind of dirty and dingy for a Swedish street, with little crumby shops along the way, all closed up and deserted that time of night. The square-head, Fritz, led us to a place which was lighted up, though the shutters was closed. He knocked on the door and a short fat Swede opened it and closed it behind us.

To my surprise I seen the place was a kind of third-rate gymnasium. They was a decrepit punching bag, a horizontal bar and a lot of bar-bells, dumb-bells, kettle bells—in fact, all the lifting weights you couldst imagine. They was also a rastling mat and, in the middle of the floor, a canvas covered space about the size of a small ring. And in the middle of this stood Sven, in fighting togs and with his hands taped.

"Who you goin' to fight, Sven?" I asked curiously.

He scowled slightly, flexed his mighty arms kind of embarrassed-like, swelled out his barrel chest and said: "You!"

You could of bowled me over with a jib boom.

"Me?" I said in amazement. "What kind of joke is this?"

"It bane no yoke," he answered stolidly. "Mine friend Knut bane own diss gym and teach rastlin' and weight liftin'. He bane let us fight here."

Knut, a stocky Swede with the massive arms and pot belly of a retired weight lifter, give me a kind of apologetic look, but I glared at him.

"But what you want to fight me for?" I snarled in perplexity. "Ain't I taught you all you know? Didn't I teach you to lick Olaf? You ungrateful—"

"Aye ain't got no grudge for you, Steve," the big cheese answered placidly. "But Aye tank Aye like be champion of dass *Sea Girl.* Aye got to lick you to be it, ain't it? Sure!"

Bill and Mushy was looking at me expectantly, but I was all at sea. After you've worked six months teaching a man your trade and built him up and made something outa him, you don't want to undo it all by rocking him to sleep.

"Why're you so set on bein' champ of the *Sea Girl?*" I asked irritably.

"Well," said the overgrown heathen, "Aye tank Aye lick you and then Aye can lick Olaf, and Segrida she like me. But Aye lick Olaf, and Segrida she give me dass gate. Dass bane your fault, for teach me to lick Olaf. But Aye ain't blame you. Aye like you fine, Steve, but now Aye tank Aye be champ of dass *Sea Girl.* Aye ain't got no girl no more, so Aye got to be something. Aye lick Olaf so Aye can lick you. Aye lick you and be champ and we be good friends, ya?"

"But I don't want to fight you, you big mutton-head!" I snarled in wrathful perplexity.

"Then Aye fight you on the street or the fo'c's'le or wherever Aye meet you," he said cheerfully.

At that my small stock of temper was plumb exhausted. With a blood thirsty howl I ripped off my shirt. "Bring on the gloves, you square-headed ape!" I roared. "If I got to batter some sense into your solid ivory skull I might as well start now!"

A FEW MINUTES later I was clad in a dingy pair of trunks which Knut dragged out of somewhere for me, and we was donning the gloves a set lighter than the standard weight, which Knut hadst probably got as a present from John L. Sullivan or somebody.

We agreed on Bill as referee, but Sven being afraid of Mike, made me agree to have Mushy hold him, though I assured him Mike wouldn't interfere in a glove fight. They was no ropes around the canvas space, no stools nor gong. However, as it happened, they wasn't needed.

As we advanced toward each other I realized more'n ever how much of a man Sven was. Six feet four—245 pounds—all bone and muscle. He towered over me like a giant, and I musta looked kinda small beside him, though I'm six feet tall and weigh 190 pounds. Under his white skin the great muscles rolled and billowed like flexible iron, and his chest looked more like a gorilla's than a human's.

But size ain't everything. Old Fitz used to flatten men which outweighed him over a hundred pounds, and lookit what Dempsey and

Sharkey used to do to such like giants—and I'm as tough as Sharkey and can hit as hard as either of them other palookas, even if I ain't quite as accurate or scientific.

No, I hadst no worries about Sven, but I'd got over being mad at him and I seen his point of view. Sven wasn't sore at me, nor nothing. He just wanted to be champ of his ship, which was a natural wish. Since his girl give him the air, he wanted to more'n ever to kind of soothe his wounded vanity, as they say.

No, I cooled down and kind of sympathized with Sven's point of view which is a bad state of mind to enter into any kind of a scrap. They ain't nothing more helpful than a good righteous anger and a feeling like the other bird is a complete rascal and absolutely in the wrong.

As we come together, Sven said: "No rounds, Steve; we fight to dass finish, yes?"

"All right," I said with very little enthusiasm. "But, Sven, for the last time—have you just got to fight me?"

His reply was a left which he shot for my jaw so sudden like I just barely managed to slip it. I come back with a slashing right which he blocked, clumsy but effective. He then dropped into the deep crouch I'd taught him and rammed his left for my wind. But I knowed the counter to that, having seen pictures of the second Fitzsimmons-Jeffries riot. I stepped around and inside his ramming left, slapping a left uppercut inside the crook of his right arm, to his jaw, cracking his teeth together and rocking his head up and back for a right hook which I opened a gash on his temple with.

He give a deafening roar and immediately abandoned his defensive posture and come for me like a mad bull. I figured, here's where I end this scrap quick, like always. But in half a second I seen my error.

Sven didn't rush wide open, flailing wild, like he used to. He come plunging in, bunched in a compact bulk of iron muscles and fighting fury; he hooked and hit straight, and he kept his chin clamped down on his hairy chest and his shoulders hunched to guard it, half crouching to protect his body. Even the rudiments of boxing science he'd learned, coupled with his enormous size and strength made him plenty formidable to any man.

I don't know how to tin-can and back pedal. If Jeffries hisself was to rush me, all I'd know to do wouldst be to stand up to him and trade punches until I went out cold. I met Sven with a right smash that was high, but stopped him in his tracks. Blood spattered and he swayed like a big tree about to crash, but before I could follow up, he plunged in again, hitting with both hands. He hit and he hit—and—he—hit!

He throwed both hands as fast as he could drive one after the other and every blow had all his weight behind it. Outa the depths of his fighting fit he'd conjured up amazing speed. It happens some time.

I never seen a man his size hit that fast before or since. It was just like being in a rain of sledge-hammers that never quit coming. All I couldst see was his glaring eyes, his big shoulders hunched and rocking as he hit—and a perfect whirlwind of big glove-covered clubs.

He wasn't timing or aiming much—hitting too fast for that. But even when he landed glancing-like, he shook me, with that advantage of fifty-five pounds. And he landed solid too often to suit me.

Try as I would, I couldn't get in a solid smash under the heart, or on the jaw. He kept his head down, and my vicious uppercuts merely glanced off his face, too high to do much good. Black and blue bruises showed on his ribs and shoulders, but his awkward half crouch kept his vitals protected.

It's mighty hard to hammer a giant like him out of position—especially when you're trying to keep him from tearing off your head at the same time. I bored in close, letting Sven's blows go around my neck while I blasted away with both hands. No—they was little science used on either side. It was mostly a wild exchange of sledge-hammer wallops.

In one of our rare clinches, Sven lifted me off my feet and throwed me the full width of the room where I hit the wall—*wham!*—like I was going on through. This made Bill, as referee, very mad at Sven and he cussed him and kicked him heartily in the pants, but the big cheese never paid no attention.

I WAS LANDING the most blows and they rocked Sven from stem to stern, but they wasn't vital ones. Already his face was beef. One eye was closed, his lips were pulped and his nose was bleeding; his left side was raw, but, if anything, he seemed to be getting stronger. My training hadst toughened him a lot more than I'd realized!

Blim! A glancing slam on my jaw made me see plenty of stars. *Wham!* His right met the side of my head and I shot back half-way across the room to crash into the wall. Long ago we'd got off the canvas; we was fighting all over the joint.

Sven was after me like a mad bull, and I braced myself and stopped him in his tracks with a left hook that ripped his ear loose and made his knees sag for a second. But the Swede had worked hisself into one of them berserk rages where you got to mighty near kill a man to stop him. His right, curving up from his hip, banged solid on my temple and I thought for a second my skull was caved in like an egg-shell.

Blood gushed down my neck when he drawed his glove back, and, desperate, I hooked my right to his body with everything I had behind it. I reckon that was when I cracked his rib, because I heard something snap and he kind of grunted.

Both of us was terrible looking by this time and kind of in a dream like, I saw Knut wringing his hands and begging Bill and Mushy and Fritz to stop it—I reckon he'd never saw a real glove battle before and it was so different from lifting weights! Naturally, they, who was clean goggle-eyed and yelling theirselves deaf and dumb, paid no attention to him at all, and so in a second Knut turned and run out into the street like he was going for the cops.

But I paid no heed. For the first time in many a day I was fighting with my back to the wall against one of my own crew. Sven was inhuman—it was like fighting a bull or an elephant. He was landing solid now, and even if them blows was clumsy, with 245 pounds of crazy Swede behind them, they was like the blows of a pile-driver.

He knowed only one kind of footwork—going forward. And he kept plunging and hitting, plunging and hitting till the world was blind and red. I shook my head and the blood flew like spray. The sheer weight of his plunges hurtled me back in spite of myself.

Once more I tried to rock his head up for a solid shot to the jaw. My left uppercut split his lips and rattled his teeth, but his bowed neck was like iron. In desperation I banged him square on the side of the head where his skull was hardest.

Blood spurted like I'd hit him with a hand spike, and he swayed drunkenly—then he dropped into a deep crouch and shot his left to my midriff with all his weight behind it. Judas! It was so unexpected I couldn't get away from it. I was standing nearly upright and that huge fist sank into my solar-plexus till I felt it banged against my spine. I dropped like a sack and writhed on the floor like a snake with a busted back, fighting for air. Bill said later I was purple in the face.

Like I was looking through a thick fog, I seen Bill, dazed and white-faced, counting over me. I dunno how I got up again. I was sick—I thought I was dying. But Sven was standing right over me, and looking up at him, a lot of thoughts surged through my numbed and battered brain in a kind of flash.

The new champion of the *Sea Girl*, I thought, after all these years I've held my title against all comers. After all the men I've fought and licked to hold the only title I got. All the cruel punishment I've took, all the blood I've spilt, now I lose my only title to this square-head that I've licked half a dozen times. Like a dream it all come back—the dim-lighted, smelly, dingy forecastle, the yelling, cursing seamen—and me in the middle of it all—the bully of the forecastle. And now—never no more to defend my title—never to hear folks along the docks say: "That's Steve Costigan, champ of the toughest ship afloat!"

WITH A KIND of gasping sob, I grabbed Sven's legs and climbed up, up, till I was on my feet, leaning against him chest to chest, till he shook me off and smashed me down like he was driving a nail into the floor. I reeled up just as Bill began to count, and this time I ducked Sven's swing and clinched him with a grip even he couldn't break.

And as I held on and drew in air in great racking gasps, I looked over his straining shoulder and seen Knut come rushing in through the door with a white-faced girl behind him—Segrida. But I was too near out to even realize that Sven's ex-girl was there.

Sven pushed me away finally and dropped me once more with a punch that was more a push than anything else. This time I took the count of nine, resting, as my incredible vitality, the wonder of manys the sporting scribe, began to assert itself.

I rose suddenly and beat Sven to the punch with a wild right that smashed his nose. Like most sluggers, I never lose my punch, no matter how badly beaten I am. I'm dangerous right to the last second, as better men than Sven Larson has found out.

Sven wasn't going so strong hisself as he had been. He moved stiff and mechanical and swung his arms awkwardly, like they was dead. He walked in stolidly and smashed a club-like right to my face. Blood spattered and I went back on my heels, but surged in and ripped my right under the heart, landing square there for the first time.

Another right smashed full on Sven's already battered mouth, and, spitting out the fragments of a tooth, he crashed a flailing left to my body, which I distinctly felt bend my ribs to the breaking point.

I ripped a left to his temple, and he flattened my ear with a swinging right, rocking drunkenly like a tall ship in the Trades with all sails set. Another right glanced offa the top of my head as I ducked and for the first time I seen his unguarded jaw as he loomed above me where I crouched.

I straightened, crashing my right from the hip, with every ounce of my weight behind it, and all the drive they was in leg, waist, shoulder and arm. I landed solid on the button with a jolt that burst my glove and numbed my whole arm—I heard a scream—I seen Sven's eyes go blank—I seen him sway like a falling mast— I seen him pitching forward—*bang!* The lights went out.

I WAS PROPPED up in a chair and Bill was sloshing me with water. I looked around at the dingy gym; then I remember. A queer, sad, cold feeling come over me. I felt old and worn out. After all, I wasn't a boy no more. All the hard, bitter years of fighting the sea and fighting men come over me and settled like a cold cloud on my shoulders. All the life kind of went out of me.

"Believe me, Steve," said Bill, slapping at me with his towel, "that fight sure set Sven solid with Segrida. Right now she's weepin' over his busted nose and black eye and the like, and huggin' him and kissin' him and vowin' everlastin' love. I knowed I was right all the time. Knut run after her to get her to stop the bout. Gosh, the Marines couldn't a stopped it! Mushy clean chawed Mike's collar in two, he was that excited! Say, would you uh thought a slob like Sven coulda made the fightin' man he has in six months?"

"Yeah," I said listlessly, scratching Mike's ear as he licked my hand. "Well, he had it comin'. He worked hard enough. And he was lucky havin' somebody to teach him. All I know, I learned for myself in cruel hard battles. But, Bill, I can't stay on the *Sea Girl* now; I just can't get used to bein' just a contender on a ship where I was champion."

Bill dropped his towel and glared at me: "What you talkin' about?"

"Why, Sven's the new champ of the *Sea Girl*, lickin' me this way. Strange, what a come-back he made just as I thought he was goin' down."

"You're clean crazy!" snorted Bill. "By golly, a rap on the dome has a funny effect on some skates. Sven's just now comin' to. Mushy and Fritz and Knut has been sloshin' him with water for ten minutes. You knocked him stiff as a wedge with that last right hook."

I come erect with a bound! "What? Then I licked Sven? I'm still champion? But if he didn't knock me out, who did?"

Bill grinned. "Don't you know no man can hit you hard enough with his fist to knock you out? Swedish girls is impulsive. Segrida done that—with a iron dumb-bell!"

ALLEYS OF PERIL

A scrap was a scrap to Steve Costigan. Yellow men or white, it was all one, for Steve feared no living soul the whole length of the China coast. And that went for the White Tigress, too!

By ROBERT E. HOWARD

Author of "Waterfront Fists"

ALLEYS OF PERIL

THE MINUTE I seen the man they'd picked to referee the fight between me and Red McCoy, I didn't like his looks. His name was Jack Ridley and he was first mate aboard the *Castleton,* one of them lines which acts very high tone, making their officers wear uniforms. Bah! The first cap'n I ever sailed with never wore nothing at sea but a pair of old breeches, a ragged undershirt and a month's growth of whiskers. He used to say uniforms was all right for navy admirals and bellhops but they was a superflooity anywheres else.

Well, this Ridley was a young fellow, slim and straight as a spar, with cold eyes and a abrupt manner. I seen right off that he was a bucko which wouldn't even let his crew shoot craps on deck if he could help it. But I decided not to let his appearance get on my nerves, but to ignore him and knock McCoy stiff as quick as possible so I couldst have the rest of the night to myself.

They is a old feud between the *Sea Girl* and McCoy's ship, the *Whale.* The minute the promoter of the Waterfront Fight Arena heard both our ships had docked, he rushed down and signed us up for a fifteen-round go—billed it as a grudge fight, which it wasn't nothing but, and packed the house.

The crews of both ships was holding down ringside seats and the special police was having a merry time keeping 'em from wrecking the place. The Old Man was rared back on the front row and ever few seconds he'd take a long swig out of a bottle, and yell: "Knock the flat-footed ape's lousy head off, Steve!" And then he'd shake his fist across at Cap'n Branner of the *Whale,* and the compliments them two old sea horses wouldst exchange wouldst have curled a Hottentot's hair.

You can judge by this that the Waterfront Fight Arena is kinda free and easy in its management. It is. It caters to a rough and ready class, which yearns for fast action, in the ring or out. Its performers is mostly fighting sailors and longshoremen, but, if you can stand the crowd that fills the place, you'll see more real mayhem committed there in one evening than you'll see in a year in the politer clubs of the world.

Well, it looked like every sailor in Hong Kong was there that night. Finally the announcer managed to make hisself heard above the howls of the mob, and he bellered: "The main attrackshun of the evenin'! Sailor Costigan, one hunnerd an' ninety pounds, of the *Sea Girl*—"

"The trimmest craft afloat!" roared the Old Man, heaving his empty bottle at Cap'n Branner.

"And Red McCoy, one hunnerd an' eighty-five pounds, of the *Whale,*" went on the announcer, being used to such interruption. "Referee, First Mate Ridley of the steamship *Castleton,* the management havin' requested him to officiate this evenin'. Now, gents, this is a grudge fight, as you all know. You has seen both these boys perform, an'—"

"And if you don't shut up and give us some action we'll wreck the dump and toss your mangled carcass amongst the ruins!" screamed the maddened fans. "Start somethin' before we do!"

The announcer smiled gently, the gong sounded, and me and Red went together like a couple of wildcats. He was a tough baby, one of them squat, wide-built fellows. I'm six feet; he was four inches shorter, but they wasn't much difference in our weight. He was tough and fast, with one of these here bulldog faces, and how that sawed-off brick-top could hit!

Well, nothing much of interest happened in the first three rounds. Of course, we was fighting hard, neither of us being clever, but both strong on mixing it. But we was both too tough to show much damage that early in the fight. He'd cut my lip and skinned my ear and loosened some teeth, and I'd dropped him for no-count a couple of times, but outside of that nothing much had happened.

We'd stood toe-to-toe for three rounds, flailing away right and left and neither giving back a step, but, just before the end of the third, my incessant body punching began to show even on that chunk of granite they called Red McCoy. For the first time he backed out of a mix-up, and just before the gong I caught him with a swinging right to the belly that made him grunt and bat his eyes.

SO I COME out for the fourth round full of snap and ginger and promptly run into a right hook that knocked me flat on my back. The crowd went crazy, and the *Whale's* men begun to kiss each other in their ecstasy, but I arose without a count and, ducking the cruel and unusual right swing McCoy tossed at me, I sunk my left to the wrist in his belly and crashed my right under his heart.

This shook Red from stem to stern and, realizing that my body blows was going to beat him if he didn't do something radical, he heaved over a hay-making right with everything he had behind it. It had murder writ all over it, and when it banged solid on my ear so you could hear it all over the house, the crowd jumped up and yelled: "There he goes!" But I'm a glutton for punishment if I do say so, and I merely tittered amusedly, shook my head to clear it, and caressed Red with a left hook that broke his nose.

The baffled look on his face caused me to bust into hearty laughter, in the midst of which Red closed my left eye with a right-hander he started in Mesopotamia. Enraged for the first time that night, I rammed a blasting left hook to his midriff, snapped his head back between his shoulders with another left, and sank my terrible right mauler to the wrist in his belly just above the waist-line.

He immediately went to the canvas like he figured on staying there indefinitely, and his gang jumped up and yelled "Foul!" till I bet they was plainly heard in Bombay. They knowed it wasn't no foul, but when Red heard 'em, he immediately put both hands over his groin and writhed around like a snake with a busted back.

The referee came over, and as I stood smiling amusedly to hear them howl about fouls, I suddenly noticed he wasn't counting.

"Say, you, ain't you goin' to count this ham out?" I asked.

"Shut up, you cad!" he snapped to my utter amazement. "Get out of this ring. You're disqualified!"

And while I gaped at him, he helped Red to his feet and raised his hand.

"McCoy wins on a foul!" he shouted. The crowd sat speechless for a second and then went into hysterics. The Old Man went for the *Whale's* skipper, the two crews pitched in free and hearty, the rest of the crowd took sides and began to bash noses, and Red's handlers started working over him. The smug look he give me and the wink he wunk, drove me clean cuckoo. I grabbed Ridley's shoulder as he started through the ropes.

"You double-crossin' louse," I ground. "You can't get away with that! You know that wasn't no foul!"

"Take your hands off me," he snapped. "You deliberately hit low, Costigan."

"You're a liar!" I roared, maddened, and *crack* come his fist in my mouth quick as lightning, and I hit the canvas on the seat of my trunks. Before I could hop up, a bunch of men pounced on me and held me whilst I writhed and yelled and cussed till the air was blue.

"I'll get you for this!" I bellered. "I'll take you apart and scatter the pieces to the sharks, you gyppin', lyin', thievin' son of a skunk!"

He looked down at me very scornful. "A fine specimen of sportsmanship you are," he sneered, and his tongue cut me like a keen knife. "Keep out of my way, or I'll give you a belly-full of what you want. Let him loose—I'll handle him!"

"Handle him my eye!" said one of the fellows holding me. "Get outa here while gettin's good. They ain't but ten of us settin' on him and we're givin' out. Either beat it or get seven or eight other birds to help hold him!"

He laughed kind of short, and, climbing from the ring, strode out of the building between rassling, slugging and cursing groups of bellering fans, many of which was yellin' for his blood. Funny how some men can get by with anything. Here was hundreds of tough birds which was raving mad at Ridley, yet he just looked 'em in the eye and they give back and let him past. Good thing for him, though, that my white bulldog Mike was too busy licking Cap'n Branner's police dog to go for him.

WELL, EVENTUALLY THE cops had things quieted, separated the dogs and even pried the Old Man and Cap'n Branner apart, with their hands full of whiskers they had tore off each other.

I didn't take no part in the rough-house. As quick as I could get dressed and put some collodion on my cuts, I slipped out the back way by myself. I even left Mike with Bill O'Brien because I didn't want him interfering and chewing up my man; I wanted nobody but me to get hold of Mister Jack Ridley and beat him into a red hash. He wasn't going to cow me with the cold stare of his eyes, because I was going to close both of 'em.

Honest to cats, I dunno when I ever been so mad in my life. I was sure he'd deliberately jobbed me and throwed the fight to McCoy, and what was worse, he'd slugged me in the face and got away with it. A red haze swum in front of me and I growled deep black curses which made people stop and stare at me as I swaggered along the waterfront streets.

After a while I seen a barkeep I knowed and I asked him if he'd seen Ridley.

"No," said he, "but if you're after him, I'll give you a tip. Lay off him. He's a hard man to fool with."

That only made me madder. "I'll lay off him," I snarled, "after I've made hash for the fishes outa him, the dirty, double-crossin', thievin' rat! I'll—"

At this minute the barkeep commenced to shine glasses like he was trying for a record, and I turned around to see a girl standing just behind me. She was a white girl and she was a beauty. Her face very white, all except her red lips and her hair was blacker than mine. Her eyes was deep and a light gray, shaded by heavy lashes. And them eyes was the tip-off. At first glance she mighta been a ordinary American flapper, but no flapper ever had eyes like them. They was deep but they was hard. They was yellow sparks of light dancing in them, and I had a funny feeling that they'd shine in the dark like a cat's.

"You were speaking of Mr. Jack Ridley, of the *Castleton*?" she asked.

"Yeah, I was, Miss," I said, dragging off my ragged old cap.

"Who are you?"

"Steve Costigan, A. B. mariner aboard the trader *Sea Girl,* outa San Francisco."

"You hate Ridley?"

"Well, to be frank, I ain't got no love for him," I said. "He just robbed me of a fight I won fair and square."

She eyed me for a minute. I ain't no beauty. In fact, I been told by my closest enemies that I look more like a gorilla than a human being. But she seemed plenty satisfied.

"Come into the back room," she said, and, to the bartender: "Send us a couple of whisky-and-sodas."

In the back room, as we sipped our drinks, she said, "You hate Ridley, eh? What would you do to him if you could?"

"Anything," I said bitterly. "Hangin's too good for a rat like him."

She rested her elbows on the table and her chin in her hands, and, looking into my eyes, she said, "Do you know who I am?"

"Yeah," I answered. "I ain't never seen you before, but you couldn't be nobody else but the girl the Chinese call the 'White Tigress.'"

Her narrow eyes glittered a little and she nodded.

"Yes. And would you like to know what drove a decent white girl into the shadows of the Orient—made an innocent, trusting child into one of a band of international criminals, and the leader of desperate tongmen? Well, I'll tell you in a few words. It was the heartlessness of a man—the man who took me from my home in England, lied to me, deceived me, and finally left me to the tender mercies of a yellow mandarin in interior China."

I shuffled my feet kind of restless; I felt sorry for her and didn't know what to say. She leaned toward me, her voice dropped almost to whisper, while her eyes burned into mine: "The man who betrayed and deserted me was the man who robbed you tonight—Jack Ridley!"

"Why, the low-down swine!" I ejaculated.

"I, too, want revenge," she breathed. "We can be useful to each other. I will send a note to Ridley asking him to come to a certain place in the Alley of Rats. He will come. There you will meet him. There will be no one to hold you this time."

I grinned—kinda wolfishly, I reckon. "Leave the rest to me."

"No one will ever know," she murmured, which kind of puzzled me. "Hong Kong's waterfront has many secrets and many mysteries. I will send a man with you to guide you to the place. Then, come to me here tomorrow night; I can use you. A man like you need not work away his life on a trading schooner."

She clapped her hands. A Chinaboy come in. She spoke to him in the language for a minute, and he bowed and beat it. She arose: "I am going now. In a few minutes your guide will come. Do as he says. Good luck to you; may you avenge us both."

SHE GLIDED OUT and left me sitting there sipping my licker and wondering what it was all about. I'd heard of the White Tigress; who in China ain't? A white girl who had more power amongst the yellow boys than the Chinese government did. Who was she? How come her to get so much pull? Them as knowed didn't say. That she was a international crook she'd just admitted. Some said she was a pirate on the sly; some said she was the secret wife of a big mandarin; some said she was a spy for a big European power. Anyway, nobody knowed for sure, but everybody agreed that anybody which crossed her was outa luck.

Well, I set there and guzzled my licker, and pretty soon in come the meanest, scrawniest looking piece uh humanity I ever seen. A ragged, dirty shrimp he was, with a evil, furtive face.

"Bli'me, mate," said he, "le's be up and doin'. It's a nice night's work we got ahead of us."

"Suits me," said I, and I follered him out of the saloon by a side door into the nasty, dimly lighted streets, and through twisty alleys which wasn't lighted at all. They stunk like sin and I couldst hear the stealthy rustling noises which always goes on in such places. Rats, maybe, but if a yellow-faced ghost hadda jumped around my neck, I wouldn'ta been surprised a bit.

Well, the cockney seemed to know his way, though my sense of direction got clean bumfuzzled. At last he opened a door and I follered him into a squalid, ramshackle room which was as dark as the alleys. He struck a light and lit a candle on a rough table. They was chairs there, and he brought out a bottle. A door opened out of the room into some other part of the place, I guess; the windows was heavily barred and I saw a trap door in the middle of the floor. I could hear the slow, slimy waves sucking and lapping under us, and I knowed the house was built out over the water.

"Mate," said the Cockney, after we'd finished about half the bottle, "it comes to me that we're a couple o' blightin' idjits to be workin' for a skirt."

"What d'ya mean?" I asked, taking a pull at the bottle.

"Well, 'ere's us, two red-blooded 'e-men, takin' orders from a lousy little frail, 'andin' the swag h'over to 'er, and takin' wot she warnts to 'and us, w'en we could 'ave the 'ole lot. Take this job 'ere now—"

I stared at him. "I don't get you."

He glanced around furtive-like, and lowered his voice: "Mate, let's cop the sparkler for ourselves and shove out! We can get back to Hengland or the States and live like blurry lords for a while. Hi'm sick o' this bloody dump."

"Say, you," I snarled, "what'r you drivin' at? What sparkler?"

"W'y, lorlumme," said he, "the sparkler we takes off Mate Ridley afore we dumps his carcass through that trapdoor."

"Hold everything!" I was up on my feet, all in a muddle. "I didn't contract to do no murder."

"Wot!" said the Cockney. "Bli'me! The Tigress says as you was yearnin' for Ridley's gore!"

'Well, I am," I growled, "but she didn't get my meanin'. I didn't mean I wanted to kill him, though, come to think about it, it mighta sounded like it. But I ain't no murderer, though killin' is what he needs after the way he treated that poor kid. When he comes through that door, I'm goin' to hammer him within a inch of his life, understand, but they ain't goin' to be no murder done—not tonight. You can bump him later, if you want to. But you got to let me pound him first, and I ain't goin' to be in on no assassination."

"But we got to finish him," argued the Cockney, "or him and To Yan will have all the bobbies in the world after us."

"Say," I said, "the Tigress didn't say nothin' about no jewel nor no To Yan. What's they got to do with it? She said Ridley brung her into China and left her flat—"

"Banan orl!" sneered the Cockney. "She was spoofin' you proper, mate. Ridley never even seen 'er. Hi dunno 'ow she got into so much power in China myself, but she's got somethin' on a mandarin and a clique o' government officials. She's been a crook ever since she was big enough to steal the blinkin' paint orf 'er bloomin' cradle.

"Listen to me, mate, and we 'ands 'er the double-cross proper. I wasn't to spill this to you, y'understand. I was to cop the sparkler after you'd bumped Ridley, and say nuthin' to you about it, see? But Hi'm sick o' takin' orders orf the 'ussy.

"Old To Yan, the chief of the Yan Tong, 'as a great fancy to Ridley. Fact is, Ridley's old man and the old Chinee 'as been close friends for years. Right now, To Yan's oldest darter is in Hengland gettin' a Western eddication. Old To Yan's that progressive and hup to the times. Well, it's the yellow girl's birthday soon, and To Yan's sendin' 'er a birthday present as would make your heyes bug out. Bli'me! It's the famous Ting ruby, worth ten thousand pounds—maybe more. Old To Yan give it to Jack Ridley to take to the girl, bein' as Ridley's ship weighs anchor for Hengland tomorrer. I dunno 'ow the Tigress found hout habout it, but that's wot she's hafter."

"I see," said I, grinding my teeth. "I was the catspaw, hey? She handed me a line to rub me up to do her dirty work. She thought I wanted to bump Ridley, anyway. Why'n't she have some of her own thugs do it?"

"That's the blightin' smoothness o' 'er," said the Cockney. "Why risk one o' her own men on a job like that, w'en 'ere was a tough sailor sizzlin' for the blinkin' hopportunity? She really thought you was wantin' to bump Ridley; she didn't know you just warnted to beat 'im hup. If you'd bumped 'im and got caught, she wouldn't a been connected with it, so's it could be proved, because you ain't one o' 'er regular men. She thought you was the right man for the job, anyway, because, mate, if Hi may say so, you looks like a natural-born murderer. But look 'ere—let's cross 'er, and do the trick hon our hown."

"Not a chance," I snapped. "Unlock that door and let me out!"

"Let you hout to squeal hon me," he whined, a red light beginning to gleam in his little rat eyes. "Not me, says you! Watch hout, you Yankee swine—!"

I saw the flash of his knife as he came at me, and I kicked a chair into his legs; and while he was spitting curses like a cat and trying to untangle hisself, I bent my right on his jaw and he took the count.

WITH SCARCELY A glance at his recumbent form, I twisted the lock off the door and stalked forth into the darkness. I groped around in a lot of twisty back alleys for a while, expecting any minute to get a knife in my back or fall into the bay, but finally I blundered into a narrow street which was dimly lit and soon found myself back in a more civilized portion of the waterfront. And a few minutes later who do I see emerging from a saloon but a man I recognized as a stoker aboard the *Castleton.*

"Hey, you," I accosted him politely, "where is that lousy first mate of yours?"

"Try and find out, you boneheaded mick," he answered rudely. "What d'ya think uh that?"

"Chew on this awhile," I growled, clouting him heartily in the mush, and for a few seconds a merry time was had by all. But pretty quick I smashed a right hook under his heart that took all the fight out of him, along with his wind.

Having brung him to by a liberal deluge of water from a nearby horse trough, I said: "All right, if you got to be so stubborn you won't answer a civil question, I won't insist. But lemme tell you somethin', and you can pass it on to that four-flushin' mate—when I get my hands on him, I'm goin' make him eat that foul decision. And say, you better find him and tell him that if he keeps packin' around what To Yan give him, he's goin' to lose it, along with his life. He'll understand what I mean. And tell him to stay away from the Alley of Rats, if he ain't already gone there."

Well, it was mighty late by this time. The streets was nearly deserted, even them which usually has a crowd of revelers on 'em all night. I was sleepy, but knowing that the *Castleton* was sailing the next morning, I took one more stroll around, hoping to run onto the mate. I was sure he hadn't gone aboard yet, because he always spent his nights ashore when he could.

After hunting for maybe an hour or more, I was about to give it up. I was passing a dark alleyway when something come slipping out, looking like a slim white ghost. It was the White Tigress.

"Wait a minute, Costigan," she said, as friendly as you please. "May I speak to you just a moment?"

"You got a nerve, Miss," I said reproachfully, "after the bunk you handed me—"

"Ah, don't be angry at me," she cooed, patting my arm. "Forget it. I'll make it up to you, if you'll just come with me. You're the kind of a man I admire."

I'm the prize boob of the Asiatics. I follered her along the little, dark, smelly alley, through an arched doorway and into a kind of small court, lighted by smoky lamps. Then she turned on me and I got a chill.

Boy, all the cat-spirit in her eyes was up and blazing. Her face was whiter than ever, her red lips writhed into a snarl, and of all the concentrated venom I ever seen flaming out of a woman's eyes, it was there! Murder, destruction, torture, sudden death and damnation she looked at me.

"I reckon maybe I better be going Miss," I said, kind of nervous. "It's gettin' late and the Old Man'll be expectin' me back—"

"Stand where you are!" she said in a voice so low it was almost a whisper.

"But the cook may be drunk and I'll have to make breakfast for the crew!" I said wildly, beginning to get desperate.

"Shut up, you fool!" she exclaimed in a voice which plumb shook with passion. "I'll fix you, you dumb, imbecilic, boneheaded, double-crossing beast! It was you who warned Ridley, wasn't it? And he ditched the ruby and never showed up at the Alley of Rats. It was just by pure luck that we got him at all. But he'll tell what he did with the gem before we get through with him. And as for you—"

She stopped a minute and her eyes ran up and down my huge frame gloatingly; she actually licked her lips like a cat over a mouse.

"When I finish with you, you'll have learned not to interfere with my affairs," she added, taking a long, thin raw-hide whip from somewhere and flicking it through the air. "I'm going to lash you within an inch of your life," she announced. "You won't be the first, either. I'm going to flay you and cut you to pieces. I'm going to whip you until you're a blind, whimpering, writhing mass of raw flesh."

"Now listen, Miss," I said, with quiet dignity, "I like to oblige a lady but they is such a thing as carryin' curtesy too far. I ain't goin' to let you even touch me with that cat."

"I didn't suppose you would," she sneered, "so I provided for that." She clapped her hands and into the courtyard from nowhere come five big Chinese. They was big, too; the smallest was larger than me and the biggest looked more like a elephant than a man. They come for me from all sides like shadows.

"Grab him, boys," she snapped in English, and I give a wolfish grin. I was plumb at ease now I had men to deal with. They was reaching for me when I went into action. A trained fighter can clean up a roomful of white civilians—and a Chinee can't take a punch. Quick as a flash I threw my whole shoulder-weight behind the left I smashed into the yellow map of the one in front of me; blood spattered and he sagged down, out cold. The next instant the rest was on me like a pack of wolves, but I whirled, ducking under a pair of arms and dropping the owner with a right hook to the heart. For the next few seconds it was a kind of whirlwind of flailing arms and legs, with me as the center.

At first they tried to capture me alive, but, being convinced of the futility of this endeavor, they tried to kill me. A knife licked along my arm, and the sting of the wound maddened me. With a roar, I crashed my right down on the neck of the Chinee which had me around the legs, driving him against the ground so hard his face splattered like a tomato. Then, reaching back and getting a good hold on the yellow boy which was both strangling me from behind and trying to knife me, I tossed him over my head. He hit on his neck and didn't get up. I then ducked a hatchet swiped at me by the biggest of the gang, and, rising on my toes, I reached his jaw and crashed him with a torrid left hook. I didn't need to hit him again.

THE FIGHT HAD took maybe a minute and a half. I glanced scornfully at the prostrate figures of my victims, and then looked around for the Tigress. She was crouched back in a angle of the wall, with a kind of stunned look in her eyes, the whip dangling from her limp fingers. She give me one horrified look and shuddered and murmured something about a gorilla.

"Well," I said, kind of sarcastic, "it don't look like they is goin' to be no whippin' tonight—or have you got some more hatchet-men hid away somewheres? If you have, trot 'em out. Action is what I crave."

"Great heavens," she murmured, "are you human? Do you realize that you've just laid out five professional murderers? And—and—*what are you going to do with me*?"

Seeing that she was scared gave me a idea. Maybe I could make her tell something about Ridley.

"You come with me," I growled, and taking her arm, I marched her out of the courtyard by another way, until we come to another courtyard similar to the one we'd left, but open enough so I couldst see if anybody tried to slip up on me. Spite of what she'd did, I felt kind of ashamed of myself, because if I ever seen a scared girl, it was the White Tigress. Her knees knocked together and she looked like she thought I'd eat her. When she thought I wasn't looking, she dropped the whip like it was hot, giving me a most guilty glance. I reckon she thought maybe I'd use it on her, and I felt clean insulted.

"Where's Jack Ridley?" I asked her, and she named a place I'd never heard of.

"Don't hit me," she begged, though I never hit a woman and hadst made not the slightest threatening motion at her. "I'll tell you about it. I sent the note to Ridley and waited for the Cockney to come and report to me. He had orders to hide you in a safe place after you'd turned the trick, and then come back and tell me about it. But after a while the Cockney turned up with a welt on his jaw, and said you'd balked on the job. He said you knew about the ruby somehow and that you proposed that you and he kill Ridley, take the stone and skip—"

"Aha," thought I to myself, "I bet he lied hisself into a jamb!"

"—but I realized that you couldn't have known about it unless he told you, so I laid into him with the raw-hide and pretty soon he admitted that he let it slip about the ruby. But he said you wanted him to double-cross me, and he wouldn't do it, and you knocked him out and left. He said that after he came to he waited a while, intending to kill Ridley himself, but the mate never showed up. I knew the Cockney was lying about part of it, at least, but I believed him when he said that likely you had killed Ridley yourself and skipped. I started my gang out looking for you, but they caught Ridley instead. It was just by chance.

"They brought him to the hang-out and we searched him, but he didn't have the ruby on him and he wouldn't tell what he'd done with it. We did worm it out of him that he was on his way to the Alley of Rats in answer to the note he got, when a stoker on his ship met him and warned him to keep away. While we were getting ready to *make* him talk, one of my boys brought me word that he'd just seen you on the streets, and I thought I'd settle the score between us. I'm sorry; I'll never try it again. What are you going to do with me?"

"How do I know you're tellin' the truth?" I asked.

She shuddered. "I'd be afraid to lie to you. You're the only man I ever saw that I was afraid of. Don't be angry—but I saw a gorilla kill six or seven niggers on the West African Coast once, and, when you were fighting those China-boys, you looked just like him."

I was too offended to say anything for a second, and she kind of whimpered: "Please, what *are* you going to do with me? Please let me go!"

"I'm goin' to let you take me to where you got Jack Ridley," I growled, mopping the blood off my cut arm, and working it so it wouldn't get stiff. "I got a account to settle with the big cheese—and you ain't goin' to torture no Americans while I can stand on my two feet. Lead the way!"

* * *

WELL, I'D OF been in a jamb if she'd refused, because I don't know what I coulda done to make her—it just ain't in me to be rough with no women—but my bluff worked. She didn't argue at all. She led me out of the courtyard, down three or four narrow, deserted streets, across a bunch of back alleys, and finally through a narrow doorway.

Here she stopped. The room was very dimly lighted by a street lamp that burned just outside and through the cracks in the wall I could see they was a light in the room beyond.

I had my hand on her arm, just so she wouldn't try to give me the slip, but I guess she thought I'd wring her neck if she crossed me, because she whispered: "Ridley's in there, but there's a gang of men with him."

"How many and who all are they?" I whispered.

"Smoky and Squint-Eye and Snake and the Dutchman; and then there's Wladek and—"

Just then I heard a nasty voice rise that I recognized as belonging to the said Smoky—a shady character but one which I hadn't known was mixed up in the Tigress game: "Orl right, you bloody Yank, we'll see wot you says after we've touched yer up a bit wiv a 'ot h'iron, eh, mates?"

I let go the girl's arm and slid to the door, soft and easy. And then I found out the Tigress wasn't near as scared as she'd pretended, because she jumped back and yelled: "Look out, boys!"

Secrecy being now out of the question, the best thing was to get in the first punch. I hit that door like a typhoon and crashed right through it. I had a fleeting glimpse of a smoky lamp in a bracket on the wall, of a rope-wrapped figure on a bunk and a ring of startled, evil faces.

"Ow, murder!" howled somebody I seen was the Cockney. "It's that bloody sailor again!" And he dived through the nearest window.

In that room they was a Chinee, a Malay, a big Russian and six thugs which was a mixed mess of English, Dutch and American. As I come through the door, I slugged the big Russian on the jaw and finished him for the evening, and grabbing the Chinee and the Malay by their necks, I disposed of them by slammin' their heads together. Then the rest of the merry men rose up and come down on me like a wolf on the fold, and the real hilarity commenced.

It was just a whirlwind. Fists, boots, bottles and chairs! And a few knives and brass knuckles throwed in for good measure. We romped all over the room and busted the chairs and shattered the table, and it was while I was on the floor, on top of three of them while the other three was dancing a horn-pipe on me, that I got hold of a heavy chair-leg. Shaking off my assailants for a instant, I arose and smote Dutchy over the head with a joyous abandon that instantly reduced the number of my foes to five. Another swat broke Snake's arm, and at that moment a squint-eyed yegg ran in and knifed me in the ribs. I give a roar of irritation and handed him one that finished him and the chair-leg simultaneous.

At this moment a red-headed thug laid my scalp open with a pair of brass knuckles, and Smoky planted his hob-nailed boots in my ribs so hard it put me on my back again, where the survivors leaped on me with howls of delirious joy. But I was far from through, though rather breathless.

Biting a large hunk out of the thumb a scar-faced beachcomber tried to shove in my eyes, I staggered up again. Doing this meant lifting Smoky too, as he was on my back, industriously gnawing my ear. With a murmur of resentment, I shook him off and flattened him with a right-handed smash that broke three ribs; and, ducking the chair Scar-Face swung at me, I crashed him with a left that smashed his nose and knocked out all his front teeth.

Red-Head was still swinging at me with the brass knuckles, and he contrived to gash my jaw pretty deep before I broke *his* jaw with a hay-making right swing. As the poem says, the tumult and the clouting died, and, standing panting in the body-littered room, I shook the blood and sweat outa my eyes and glared around for more thugs to conquer.

But I was the only man on his feet. I musta been a sight. All my clothes was tore off except my pants, and they wasn't enough of them left to amount to anything. I was bleeding from a dozen cuts. I was bruised all over and I had another black eye to go with the one McCoy had give me earlier in the evening. I looked around for Ridley and seen him lying on the bunk where he was tied up, staring at me like he'd never seen a critter like me before. I looked for the Tigress but she was gone.

SO I WENT over and untied Ridley, and he never said a word; acted like he was kinda stunned. He worked his fingers and glanced at the victims on the floor, some of which was groaning and cussing, and some of which was slumbering peaceful.

"Gettin' the circulation back in your hands?" I asked, and he nodded.

"All right," said I, "Put up your mitts; I'm goin' to knock you into the middle of Kingdom Come."

"Good Lord, man," he cried, "you've saved my life—and you mean you want to fight me?"

"What the hell did you think?" I roared. "Think I come around to thank you for jobbin' me out of a rightful decision? I never fouled nobody in my life!"

"But you're in no shape to fight now!" he exclaimed. "You've just whipped a roomful of men and taken more punishment than I thought any human being could take, and live! You're bleeding like a stuck hog. Both your eyes are half-closed, your lips are pulped, your scalp's laid open, one of your ears is mangled, and you've got half a dozen knife cuts on you. I saw one of those fellows stab you in the ribs—"

"Aw, it just slid along 'em," I said. "If you think I'm marked up, you oughta seen me after I went fifteen rounds to a draw with Iron Mike Brennon. But listen, that ain't neither here nor there. You ain't as big as I am, but you got the reputation of a fighter. Now you put up your mitts like a man."

Instead, he dropped his hands to his sides. "I won't fight you. Not after what you've just done for me. Do you realize that you've burst into the secret den of the most dangerous crook in China—and cleaned up nine of her most desperate gangmen, practically bare-handed?"

"But what about that foul?" I asked petulantly.

"I was wrong," he said. "I was standing behind McCoy and didn't really get a good look at the blow you dropped him with. Honestly, it looked low to me, and when McCoy began to writhe around on the canvas, I thought you had fouled him. But if you did, it wasn't intentional. A man like you wouldn't deliberately hit another fighter low. You didn't even hit these thugs below the belt, though God knows you had every right. Now then, I apologize for that foul decision, and for hitting you, and for what I said to you. If you want to take a swing at me anyway, I won't blame you, but I'm not going to fight you."

He looked at me with steady eyes and I seen he wasn't afraid of me, or handing me no bluff. And, somehow, I was satisfied.

"Well," I said, mopping the blood off my scalp, "that's all right. I just wanted you to know I don't fight foul. Now let's get outa here. Say—the White Tigress was here with me—where'd she go, do you reckon?"

"I don't know. And I don't want to know. If I don't see her again, it will be soon enough. It must have been she who sent me that note earlier in the night."

"It was. And I don't understand, if you was goin' to do what it said, why it took you so long. You shoulda been at the Alley of Rats before the stoker had time to find you and give you my warnin'."

"Well," he said, "I hesitated for nearly an hour after getting the note, as to whether I'd go or not, but finally decided I would. But I left the To Yan ruby with the captain. On the way, the stoker met me and gave me your tip, which he didn't understand but thought I ought to know nevertheless. So I didn't go to the Alley of Rats, but later on a gang jumped me, tied me up and brought me here. And say, how is it that you're mixed up in all this?"

"It's a long story," I said, as we come out into one of the politer streets, "and—"

"And just now you need those cuts and bruises dressed. Come with me and I'll attend to that. You can tell me all about it while I bandage you."

"All right," I said, "but let's make it snappy 'cause I got business."

"Got a girl in this port, have you?"

"Naw," I said. "I think I can find the promoter of the Waterfront Fight Arena at his saloon about now, and I want to ask him to get Red McCoy to fight me at the Arena again tomorrow night."

TEXAS FISTS

By ROBERT E. HOWARD

Author of "The Pit of the Serpent"

Seaman versus miner! The best two-fisted he-man who ever stalked a forecastle versus the fightin'est buckaroo in the great Southwest! What a match! What a match! But Steve Costigan, in port after a hard voyage, said no. And then other fists began to fly.

TEXAS FISTS

THE *SEA GIRL* hadn't been docked in Tampico more'n a few hours when I got into a argument with a big squarehead off a tramp steamer. I forget what the row was about—sailing vessels versus steam, I think. Anyway, the discussion got so heated he took a swing at me. He musta weighed nearly three hundred pounds, but he was meat for me. I socked him just once and he went to sleep under the ruins of a table.

As I turned back to my beer mug in high disgust, I noticed that a gang of fellers which had just come in was gawping at me in wonder. They was cow-punchers, in from the ranges, all white men, tall, hard and rangy, with broad-brimmed hats, leather chaps, big Mexican spurs, guns an' everything; about ten of them, altogether.

"By the gizzard uh Sam Bass," said the tallest one, "I plumb believe we've found our man, hombres. Hey, pardner, have a drink! Come on—set down at this here table. I wanta talk to you."

So we all set down and, while we was drinking some beer, the tall cow-puncher glanced admiringly at the squarehead which was just coming to from the bar-keep pouring water on him, and the cow-puncher said:

"Lemme introduce us: we're the hands of the Diamond J—old Bill Dornley's ranch, way back up in the hills. I'm Slim, and these is Red, Tex, Joe, Yuma, Buck, Jim, Shorty, Pete and the Kid. We're in town for a purpose, pardner, which is soon stated.

"Back up in the hills, not far from the Diamond J, is a minin' company, and them miners has got the fightin'est buckaroo in these parts. They're backin' him agin all comers, and I hates to say what he's did to such Diamond J boys as has locked horns with him. Them miners has got a ring rigged up in the hills where this gent takes on such as is wishful to mingle with him, but he ain't particular. He knocked out Joe, here, in that ring, but he plumb mopped up a mesquite flat with Red, which challenged him to a rough-and-tumble brawl with bare fists. He's a bear-cat, and the way them miners is puttin' on airs around us boys is somethin' fierce.

"We've found we ain't got no man on the ranch which can stand up to that grizzly, and so we come into town to find some feller which could use his fists. Us boys is more used to slingin' guns than knuckles. Well, the minute I seen you layin' down that big Swede, I says to myself, I says, 'Slim, there's your man!'

"How about it, amigo? Will you mosey back up in the hills with us and flatten this big false alarm? We aim to bet heavy, and we'll make it worth yore while."

"And how far is this here ranch?" I asked.

"'Bout a day's ride, hossback—maybe a little better'n that."

"That's out," I decided. "I can't navigate them four-legged craft. I ain't never been on a horse more'n three or four times, and I ain't figgerin' on repeatin' the experiment."

"Well," said Slim, "we'll get hold of a auteymobeel and take you out in style."

"No," I said, "I don't believe I'll take you up; I wanta rest whilst I'm in port. I've had a hard voyage; we run into nasty weather and had one squall after another. Then the Old Man picked up a substitute second mate in place of our regular mate which is in jail in Melbourne, and this new mate and me has fought clean across the Pacific, from Melbourne to Panama, where he give it up and quit the ship."

The cow-punchers all started arguing at the same time, but Slim said:

"Aw, that's all right boys; I reckon the gent knows what he wants to do. We can find somebody else, I reckon. No hard feelin's. Have another drink."

I kinda imagined he had a mysterious gleam in his eye, and it looked like to me that when he motioned to the bartender, he made some sort of a signal; but I didn't think nothing about it. The bar-keep brought a bottle of hard licker, and Slim poured it, saying: "What did you say yore name was, amigo?"

"Steve Costigan, A. B. on the sailing vessel *Sea Girl,"* I answered. "I want you fellers to hang around and meet Bill O'Brien and Mushy Hanson, my shipmates, they'll be around purty soon with my bulldog Mike. I'm waitin' for 'em. Say, this stuff tastes funny."

"That's just high-grade tequila," said Slim. "Costigan, I shore wish you'd change yore mind about goin' out to the ranch and fightin' for us."

"No chance," said I. "I crave peace and quiet . . . Say, what the heck . . . ?"

I hadn't took but one nip of that funny-tasting stuff, but the barroom had begun to shimmy and dance. I shook my head to clear it and saw the cowboys, kinda misty and dim, they had their heads together, whispering, and one of 'em said, kinda low-like: "He's fixin' to pass out. Grab him!"

At that, I give a roar of rage and heaved up, upsetting the table and a couple of cow-hands.

"You low-down land-sharks," I roared. "You doped my grog!"

"Grab him, boys!" yelled Slim, and three or four nabbed me. But I throwed 'em off like chaff and caught Slim on the chin with a clout that sprawled him on the back of his neck. I socked Red on the nose and it spattered like a busted tomater, and at this instant Pete belted me over the head with a gun-barrel.

With a maddened howl, I turned on him, and he gasped, turned pale and dropped the gun for some reason or other. I sunk my left mauler to the wrist in his midriff, and about that time six or seven of them cow-punchers jumped on my neck and throwed me by sheer weight of man-power.

I got Yuma's thumb in my mouth and nearly chawed it off, but they managed to sling some ropes around me, and the drug, from which I was already weak and groggy, took full effect about this time and I passed clean out.

I musta been out a long time. I kinda dimly remember a sensation of bumping and jouncing along, like I was in a car going over a rough road, and I remember being laid on a bunk and the ropes took off, but that's all.

I WAS WOKE up by voices. I set up and cussed. I had a headache and a nasty taste in my mouth, and, feeling the back of my head, I found a bandage, which I tore off with irritation. Keel haul me! As if a scalp cut like that gun-barrel had give me needed dressing!

I was sitting on a rough bunk in a kinda small shack which was built of heavy planks. Outside I heered Slim talking:

"No, Miss Joan, I don't dast let you in to look at him. He ain't come to, I don't reckon 'cause they ain't no walls kicked outa the shack, yet; but he might come to hisself whilst you was in there, and they's no tellin' what he might do, even to you. The critter ain't human, I'm tellin' you, Miss Joan."

"Well," said a feminine voice, "I think it was just horrid of you boys to kidnap a poor ignorant sailor and bring him away off up here just to whip that miner."

"Golly, Miss Joan," said Slim, kinda like he was hurt, "if you got any sympathy to spend, don't go wastin' it on that gorilla. Us boys needs yore sympathy. I winked at the bar-keep for the dope when I ordered the drinks, and, when I poured the sailor's, I put enough of it in his licker to knock out three or four men. It hit him quick, but he was wise to it and started sluggin'. With all them knockout drops in him, he near wrecked the joint! Lookit this welt on my chin—when he socked me I looked right down my own spine for a second. He busted Red's nose flat, and you oughta see it this mornin'. Pete lammed him over the bean so hard he bent the barrel of his forty-five, but all it done was make Costigan mad. Pete's still sick at his stummick from the sock the sailor give him. I tell you, Miss Joan, us boys oughta have medals pinned on us; we took our lives in our hands, though we didn't know it at the start, and, if it hadn't been for the dope, Costigan would have destroyed us all. If yore dad ever fires me, I'm goin' to git a job with a circus, capturin' tigers and things. After that ruckus, it oughta be a cinch."

At this point, I decided to let folks know I was awake and fighting mad about the way I'd been treated, so I give a roar, tore the bunk loose from the wall and throwed it through the door. I heard the girl give a kind of scream, and then Slim pulled open what was left of the door and come through. Over his shoulder I seen a slim nice-looking girl legging it for the ranch-house.

"What you mean scarin' Miss Joan?" snarled Slim, tenderly fingering a big blue welt on his jaw.

"I didn't go to scare no lady," I growled. "But in about a minute I'm goin' to scatter your remnants all over the landscape. You think you can shanghai me and get away with it? I want a big breakfast and a way back to port."

"You'll git all the grub you want if you'll agree to do like we says," said Slim; "but you ain't goin' to git a bite till you does."

"You'd keep a man from mess, as well as shanghai him, hey?" I roared. "Well, lemme tell you, you long-sparred, leather-rigged son of a sea-cock, I'm goin' to—"

"You ain't goin' to do nothin'," snarled Slim, whipping out a long-barreled gun and poking it in my face.

"You're goin' to do just what I says or get the daylight let through you—"

Having a gun shoved in my face always did enrage me. I knocked it out of his hand with one mitt, and him flat on his back with the other, and, jumping on his prostrate frame with a blood-thirsty yell of joy, I hammered him into a pulp.

His wild yells for help brought the rest of the crew on the jump, and they all piled on me for to haul me off. Well, I was the center of a whirlwind of fists, boots, and blood-curdling howls of pain and rage for some minutes, but they was just too many of them and they was too handy with them lassoes. When they finally had me hawg-tied again, the side wall was knocked clean out of the shack, the roof was sagging down and Joe, Shorty, Jim and Buck was out cold.

SLIM, LOOKING A lee-sore wreck, limped over and glared down at me with his one good eye whilst the other boys felt theirselves for broken bones and throwed water over the fallen gladiators.

"You snortin' buffalo," Slim snarled. "How I hones to kick yore ribs in! What do you say? Do you fight or stay tied up?"

The cook-shack was near and I could smell the bacon and eggs sizzling. I hadn't eat nothing since dinner the day before and I was hungry enough to eat a raw sea lion.

"Lemme loose," I growled. "I gotta have food. I'll lick this miner for you, and when I've did that, I'm going to kick down your bunkhouse and knock the block offa every man, cook and steer on this fool ranch."

"Boy," said Slim with a grin, spitting out a loose tooth, "does you lick that miner, us boys will each give you a free swing at us. Come on—you're loose now—let's go get it."

"Let's send somebody over to the Bueno Oro Mine and tell them mavericks 'bout us gittin' a slugger," suggested Pete, trying to work back a thumb he'd knocked outa place on my jaw.

"Good idee," said Slim. "Hey, Kid, ride over and tell 'em we got a man as can make hash outa their longhorn. Guess we can stage the scrap in about five days, hey, Sailor?"

"Five days my eye," I grunted. "The *Sea Girl* sails day after tomorrow and I gotta be on her. Tell 'em to get set for the go this evenin'."

"But, gee whiz!" expostulated Slim. "Don't you want a few days to train?"

"If I was outa trainin', five days wouldn't help me none," I said. "But I'm allus in shape. Lead on the mess table. I crave nutriment."

Well, them boys didn't hold no grudge at all account of me knocking 'em around. The Kid got on a broom-tailed bronc and cruised off across the hills, and the rest of us went for the cook-shack. Joe yelled after the Kid: "Look out for Lopez the Terrible!" And they all laughed.

Well, we set down at the table and the cook brung aigs and bacon and fried steak and sour-dough bread and coffee and canned corn and milk till you never seen such a spread. I lay to and ate till they looked at me kinda bewildered.

"Hey!" said Slim, "ain't you eatin' too much for a tough scrap this evenin'?"

"What you cow-pilots know about trainin'?" I said. "I gotta keep up my strength. Gimme some more of them beans, and tell the cook to scramble me five or six more aigs and bring me in another stack of buckwheats. And say," I added as another thought struck me, "who's this here Lopez you-all was jokin' about?"

"By golly," said Tex, "I thought you cussed a lot like a Texan. 'You-all,' huh? Where was you born?"

"Galveston," I said.

"Zowie!" yelled Tex. "Put 'er there, pard; I aims for to triple my bets on you! Lopez? Oh, he's just a Mex bandit—handsome cuss, I'll admit, and purty mean. He ranges around in them hills up there and he's stole some of our stock and made a raid or so on the Bueno Oro. He's allus braggin' 'bout how he aims for to raid the Diamond J some day and ride off with Joan—that's old Bill Dornley's gal. But heck, he ain't got the guts for that."

"Not much he ain't," said Jim. "Say, I wish old Bill was at the ranch now, 'steada him and Miz Dornley visitin' their son at Zacatlan. They'd shore enjoy the scrap this evenin'. But Miss Joan'll be there, you bet."

"Is she the dame I scared when I called you?" I asked Slim.

"Called me? Was you callin' me?" said he. "Golly, I'd of thought a bull was in the old shack, only a bull couldn't beller like that. Yeah, that was her."

"Well," said I, "tell her I didn't go for to scare her. I just naturally got a deep voice from makin' myself heard in gales at sea."

Well, we finished breakfast and Slim says: "Now what you goin' to do, Costigan? Us boys wants to help you train all we can."

"Good," I said. "Fix me up a bunk; nothing like a good long nap when trainin' for a tough scrap."

"All right," said they. "We reckons you knows what you wants; while you git yore rest, we'll ride over and lay some bets with the Bueno Oro mavericks."

SO THEY SHOWED me where I couldst take a nap in their bunkhouse and I was soon snoozing. Maybe I should of kinda described the ranch. They was a nice big house, Spanish style, but made of stone, not 'dobe, and down to one side was the corrals, the cook-shack, the long bunkhouse where the cowboys stayed, and a few Mexican huts. But they wasn't many Mexes working on the Diamond J. They's quite a few ranches in Old Mexico owned and run altogether by white men. All around was big rolling country, rough ranges of sagebrush, mesquite, cactus and chaparral, sloping in the west to hills which further on became right good-sized mountains.

Well, I was woke up by the scent of victuals; the cook was fixing dinner. I sat up on the bunk and—lo, and behold—there was the frail they called Miss Joan in the door of the bunkhouse, staring at me wide-eyed like I was a sea horse or something.

I started to tell her I was sorry I scared her that morning, but when she seen I was awake she give a gasp and steered for the ranch-house under full sail.

I was bewildered and slightly irritated. I could see that she got a erroneous idee about me from listening to Slim's hokum, and, having probably never seen a sailor at close range before, she thought I was some kind of a varmint.

Well, I realized I was purty hungry, having ate nothing since breakfast, so I started for the cook-shack and about that time the cow-punchers rode up, plumb happy and hilarious.

"Hot dawg!" yelled Slim. "Oh, baby, did them miners bite! They grabbed everything in sight and we has done sunk every cent we had, as well bettin' our hosses, saddles, bridles and shirts."

"And believe me," snarled Red, tenderly fingering what I'd made outa his nose, and kinda hitching his gun prominently, *"you better win!"*

"Don't go makin' no grandstand plays at me," I snorted. "If I can't lick a man on my own inisheyative, no gun-business can make me do it. But don't worry; I can flatten anything in these hills, includin' you and all your relatives. Let's get into that mess gallery before I clean starve."

While we ate, Slim said all was arranged; the miners had knocked off work to get ready and the scrap would take place about the middle of the evening. Then the punchers started talking and telling me things they hadst did and seen, and of all the triple-decked, full-rigged liars I ever listened to, them was the beatenest. The Kid said onst he come onto a mountain lion and didn't have no rope nor gun, so he caught rattlesnakes with his bare hands and tied 'em together and made a lariat and roped the lion and branded it, and he said how they was a whole breed of mountain lions in the hills with the Diamond J brand on 'em and the next time I seen one, if I would catch it and look on its flank, I would see it was so.

So I told them that once when I was cruising in the Persian Gulf, the wind blowed so hard it picked the ship right outa the water and carried it clean across Arabia and dropped it in the Mediterranean Sea; all the riggings was blown off, I said, and the masts outa her, so we caught sharks and hitched them to the bows and made 'em tow us into port.

Well, they looked kinda weak and dizzy then, and Slim said: "Don't you want to work out a little to kinda loosen up your muscles?"

Well, I was still sore at them cow-wranglers for shanghaing me the way they done, so I grinned wickedly and said: "Yeah, I reckon I better; my muscles is purty stiff, so you boys will just naturally have to spar some with me."

Well they looked kinda sick, but they was game. They brung out a battered old pair of gloves and first Joe sparred with me. Whilst they was pouring water on Joe they argued some about who was to spar with me next and they drawed straws and Slim was it.

"By golly," said Slim looking at his watch, "I'd shore admire to box with you, Costigan, but it's gettin' about time for us to start dustin' the trail for the Bueno Oro."

"Heck, we got plenty uh time," said Buck.

Slim glowered at him. "I reckon the foreman—which is me—knows what time uh day it is," said Slim. "I says we starts for the mine. Miss Joan has done said she'd drive Costigan over in her car, and me and Shorty will ride with 'em. I kinda like to be close around Miss Joan when she's out in the hills. You can't tell; Lopez might git it into his haid to make a bad play. You boys will foller on your broncs."

* * *

WELL, THAT'S THE way it was. Joan was a mighty nice looking girl and she was very nice to me when Slim interjuced me to her, but I couldst see she was nervous being that close to me, and it offended me very much, though I didn't show it none.

Slim set on the front seat with her, and me and Shorty on the back seat, and we drove over the roughest country I ever seen. Mostly they wasn't no road at all, but Joan knowed the channel and didn't need no chart to navigate it, and eventually we come to the mine.

The mine and some houses was up in the hills, and about half a mile from it, on a kind of a broad flat, the ring was pitched. Right near where the ring stood, was a narrow canyon, leading up through the hills. We had to leave the car close to the mine and walk the rest of the way, the edge of the flat being too rough to drive on.

They was quite a crowd at the ring, which was set up in the open. I notice that the Bueno Oro was run by white men same as the ranch. The miners was all big, tough-looking men in heavy boots, bearded and wearing guns, and they was a considerable crew of 'em. They was still more cow-punchers from all the ranches in the vicinity, a lean, hard-bit gang, with even more guns on them than the miners had. By golly, I never seen so many guns in one place in my life!

They was quite a few Mexicans watching, men and women, but Joan was the only white woman I seen. All the men took their hats off to her, and I seen she was quite a favorite among them rough fellers, some of which looked more like pirates than miners or cowboys.

Well the crowd set up a wild roar when they seen me, and Slim yelled: "Well, you mine-rasslin' mavericks, here he is! I shudders to think what he's goin' to do to yore man."

All the cow-punchers yipped jubilantly and all the miners yelled mockingly, and up come the skipper of the mine—the guy that done the managing of it—a fellow named Menly.

"Our man is in his tent getting on his togs, Slim," said he. "Get your fighter ready—and we'd best be on the lookout. I've had a tip that Lopez is in the hills close by. The mine's unguarded. Everybody's here. And while there's no ore or money for him to swipe—we sent out the ore yesterday and the payroll hasn't arrived yet—he could do a good deal of damage to the buildings and machinery if he wanted to."

"We'll watch out, you bet," assured Slim, and steered me for what was to serve as my dressing room. They was two tents pitched one on each side of the ring, and they was our dressing rooms. Slim had bought a pair of trunks and ring shoes in Tampico, he said, and so I was rigged out shipshape.

As it happened, I was the first man in the ring. A most thunderous yell went up, mainly from the cow-punchers, and, at the sight of my manly physique, many began to pullout their watches and guns and bet them. The way them miners snapped up the wagers showed they had perfect faith in their man. And when he clumb in the ring a minute later they just about shook the hills with their bellerings. I glared and gasped.

"Snoots Leary or I'm a Dutchman!" I exclaimed.

"Biff Leary they call him," said Slim which, with Tex and Shorty and the Kid, was my handler. "Does you know him?"

"Know him?" said I. "Say, for the first fourteen years of my life I spent most of my time tradin' punches with him. They ain't a back-alley in Galveston that we ain't bloodied each other's noses in. I ain't seen him since we was just kids—I went to sea, and he went the other way. I heard he was mixin' minin' with fightin'. By golly, hadst I knowed this you wouldn't of had to shanghai me."

Well, Menly called us to the center of the ring for instructions and Leary gawped at me: "Steve Costigan, or I'm a liar! What you doin' fightin' for cow-wranglers? I thought you was a sailor."

"I am, Snoots," I said, "and I'm mighty glad for to see you here. You know, we ain't never settled the question as to which of us is the best man. You'll recollect in all the fights we had, neither of us ever really won; we'd generally fight till we was so give out we couldn't lift our mitts, or else till somebody fetched a cop. Now we'll have it out, once and for all!"

"Good!" said he, grinning like a ogre. "You're purty much of a man, Steve, but I figger I'm more. I ain't been swingin' a sledge all this time for nothin'. And I reckon the nickname of 'Biff' is plenty descriptive."

"You always was conceited, Biff," I scowled. "Different from me. Do I go around tellin' people how good I am? Not me; I don't have to. They can tell by lookin' at me that I'm about the best two-fisted man that ever walked a forecastle. Shake now and let's come out fightin'."

Well, the referee had been trying to give us instructions, but we hadn't paid no attention to him, so now he muttered a few mutters under his breath and told us to get ready for the gong. Meanwhile the crowd was developing hydrophobia wanting us to get going. They'd got a camp chair for Miss Joan, but the men all stood up, banked solid around the ring so close their noses was nearly through the ropes, and all yelling like wolves.

"For cat's sake, Steve," said Slim as he crawled out of the ring, "don't fail us. Leary looks even meaner than he done when he licked Red and Joe."

I'll admit Biff was a hard looking mug. He was five feet ten to my six feet, and he weighed 195 to my 190. He had shoulders as wide as a door, a deep barrel chest, huge fists and arms like a gorilla's. He was hairy and his muscles swelled like iron all over him, miner's style, and his naturally hard face hadst not been beautified by a broken nose and a cauliflower ear. Altogether, Biff looked like what he was—a rough and ready fighting man.

AT THE TAP of the gong he come out of his corner like a typhoon, and I met him in the center of the ring. By sheer luck he got in the first punch—a smashing left hook to the head that nearly snapped my neck. The crowd went howling crazy, but I come back with a sledge-hammer right hook that banged on his cauliflower ear like a gunshot. Then we went at it hammer and tongs, neither willing to take a back step, just like we fought when we was kids.

He had a trick of snapping a left uppercut inside the crook of my arm and beating my right hook. He'd had that trick when we fought in the Galveston alleys, and he hadn't forgot it. I never couldst get away from that peculiar smack. Again and again he snapped my head back with it—and I got a neck like iron, too; ain't everybody can rock my head back on it.

He wasn't neglecting his right either. In fact he was mighty fond of banging me on the ear with that hand. Meanwhile, I was ripping both hands to his liver, belly and heart, every now and then bringing up a left or right to his head. We slugged that round out without much advantage on either side, but just before the gong, one of them left up-percuts caught me square in the mouth and the claret started in streams.

"First blood, Steve," grinned Biff as he turned to his corner.

Slim wiped off the red stuff and looked kinda worried.

"He's hit you some mighty hard smacks, Steve," said he.

I snorted. "Think I been pattin' him? He'll begin to feel them body smashes in a round or so. Don't worry; I been waitin' for this chance for years."

At the tap of the gong for the second round we started right in where we left off. Biff come in like he aimed for to take me apart, but I caught him coming in with a blazing left hook to the chin. His eyes rolled, but he gritted his teeth and come driving in so hard he battered me back in spite of all I couldst do. His head was down, both arms fly-ing, legs driving like a charging bull. He caught me in the belly with a right hook that shook me some, but I braced myself and stopped him in his tracks with a right uppercut to the head.

He grunted and heaved over a right swing that started at his knees, and I didn't duck quick enough. It caught me solid but high, knocking me back into the ropes.

The miners roared with joy and the cow-punchers screamed in dismay, but I wasn't hurt. With a supercilious sneer, I met Leary's rush with a straight left which snapped his head right back between his shoulders and somehow missed a slungshot right uppercut which had all my beef behind it.

Biff hooked both hands hard to my head and shot his right under my heart, and I paid him back with a left to the midriff which brung a grunt outa him. I crashed an overhand right for his jaw but he blocked it and was short with a hard right swing. I went inside his left to blast away at his body with both hands in close, and he throwed both arms around me and smothered my punches.

We broke of ourselves before Menly couldst separate us, and I hooked both hands to Leary's head, taking a hard drive between the eyes which made me see stars. We then stood head to head in the center of the ring and traded smashes till we was both dizzy. We didn't hear the gong and Menly had to jump in and haul us apart and shove us toward our corners.

The crowd was plumb cuckoo by this time; the cowboys was all yelling that I won that round and the miners was swearing that it was Biff's by a mile. I snickered at this argument, and I noticed Biff snort in disgust. I never go into no scrap figgering to win it on points. If I can't knock the other sap stiff, he's welcome to the decision. And I knowed Biff felt the same way.

Leary was in my corner for the next round before I was offa my stool, and he missed me with a most murderous right. I was likewise wild with a right, and Biff recovered his balance and tagged me on the chin with a left uppercut. Feeling kinda hemmed in, I went for him with a roar and drove him out into the center of the ring with a series of short, vicious rushes he couldn't altogether stop.

I shook him to his heels with a left hook to the body and started a right hook for his head. Up flashed his left for that trick uppercut, and I checked my punch and dropped my right elbow to block. He checked his punch too and crashed a most tremendous right to my unguarded chin. Blood splattered and I went back on my heels, floundering and groggy, and Biff, wild for the kill and flustered by the yells, lost his head and plunged in wide open, flailing with both arms.

I caught him with a smashing left hook to the jaw and he rolled like a clipper in rough weather. I ripped a right under his heart and cracked a hard left to his ear, and he grabbed me like a grizzly and hung on, shaking his head to get rid of the dizziness. He was tough—plenty tough. By the time the referee had broke us, his head had plumb cleared and he proved it by giving a roar of rage and smacking me square on the nose with a punch that made the blood fly.

Again the gong found us slugging head-to-head. Slim and the boys was so weak and wilted from excitement they couldn't hardly see straight enough to mop off the blood and give me a piece of lemon to suck.

Well, this scrap was to be to a finish and it looked like to me it wouldst probably last fifteen or twenty more rounds. I wasn't tired or weakened any, and I knowed Biff was like a granite boulder—nearly as tough as me. I figgered on wearing him down with body punishment, but even I couldn't wear down Biff Leary in a few shakes. Just like me, he won most of his fights by simply outlasting the other fellow.

Still, with a punch like both of us carried in each hand, anything might happen—and did, as it come about.

WE OPENED THE fourth like we had the others, and slugged our way through it, on even terms. Same way with the fifth, only in this I opened a gash on Biff's temple and he split my ear. As we come up for the sixth, we both showed some wear and tear. One of my eyes was partly closed, I was bleeding at the mouth and nose, and from my cut ear; Biff had lost a tooth, had a deep cut on his temple, and his ribs on the left side was raw from my body punches.

But neither of us was weakening. We come together fast and Biff ripped my lip open with a savage left hook. His right glanced offa my head and again he tagged me with his left uppercut. I sunk my right deep in his ribs and we both shot our lefts. His started a fraction of a second before mine, and he beat me to the punch; his mitt biffed square in my already closing eye, and for a second the punch blinded me.

His right was coming behind his left, swinging from the floor with every ounce of his beef behind it. *Wham!* Square on the chin that swinging mauler tagged me, and it was like the slam of a sledge-hammer. I felt my feet fly out from under me, and the back of my head hit the canvas with a jolt that kinda knocked the cobwebs outa my brain.

I shook my head and looked around to locate Biff. He hadn't gone to no corner but was standing grinning down at me, just back of the referee a ways. The referee was counting, the crowd was clean crazy, and Biff was grinning and waving his gloves at 'em, as much as to say what had he told 'em.

The miners was dancing and capering and mighty near kissing each other in their joy, and the cowboys was white-faced, screaming at me to get up, and reaching for their guns. I believe if I hadn't of got up, they'd of started slaughtering the miners. But I got up. For the first time I was good and mad at Biff, not because he knocked me down, but because he had such a smug look on his ugly map. I knowed I was the best man, and I was seeing red.

I come up with a roar, and Biff wiped the smirk offa his map quick and met me with a straight left. But I wasn't to be stopped. I bored into close quarters where I had the advantage, and started ripping away with both hands.

Quickly seeing he couldn't match me at infighting, Biff grabbed my shoulders and shoved me away by main strength, instantly swinging hard for my head. I ducked and slashed a left hook to his head. He ripped a left to my body and smashed a right to my ear. I staggered him with a left hook to the temple, took a left on the head, and beat him to the punch with a mallet-like right hander to the jaw. I caught him wide open and landed a fraction of a second before he did. That smash had all my beef behind it and Biff dropped like a log.

But he was a glutton for punishment. Snorting and grunting, he got to his all-fours, glassy-eyed but shaking his head, and, as Menly said "nine," Leary was up. But he was groggy; such a punch as I dropped him with is one you don't often land. He rushed at me and connected with a swinging left to the ribs that shook me some, but I dropped him again with a blasting left hook to the chin.

This time I seen he'd never beat the count, so I retired to the furtherest corner and grinned at Slim and the other cowboys, who was doing a Indian scalp-dance while the miners was shrieking for Biff to get up.

Menly was counting over him, and, just as he said "seven," a sudden rattle of shots sounded. Menly stopped short and glared at the mine, half a mile away. All of us looked. A gang of men was riding around the buildings and shooting in them. Menly give a yell and hopped out of the ring.

"Gang up!" he yelled. "It's Lopez and his men! They've come to do all the damage they can while the mine's unguarded! They'll burn the office and ruin the machinery if we don't stop 'em! Come a-runnin'!"

He grabbed a horse and started smoking across the flat, and the crowd followed him, the cowboys on horses, the rest on foot, all with their guns in their hands. Slim jumped down and said to Miss Joan: "You stay here, Miss Joan. You'll be safe here and we'll be back and finish this prize fight soon's we chase them Greasers over the hill."

WELL, I WAS plumb disgusted to see them mutts all streak off across the flat, leaving me and Biff in the ring, and me with the fight practically won. Biff shook hisself and snorted and come up slugging, but I stepped back and irritably told him to can the comedy.

"What's up?" said he, glaring around. "Why, where's Menly? Where's the crowd? What's them shots?"

"The crowd's gone to chase Lopez and his merry men," I snapped. "Just as I had you out, the fool referee quits countin'."

"Well, I'd of got up anyhow," said Biff. "I see now. It is Lopez's gang, sure enough—"

The cow-punchers and miners had nearly reached the mine by this time, and guns was cracking plenty on both sides. The Mexicans was drawing off, slowly, shooting as they went, but it looked like they was about ready to break and run for it. It seemed like a fool play to me, all the way around.

"Hey, Steve," said Biff, "whatsa use waitin' till them mutts gits back? Let's me and you get our scrap over."

"Please don't start fighting till the boys come back," said Joan, nervously. "There's something funny about this. I don't feel just right. Oh—"

She give a kind of scream and turned pale. Outa the ravine behind the ring rode a Mexican. He was young and good-looking but he had a cruel, mocking face; he rode a fine horse and his clothes musta cost six months' wages. He had on tight pants which the legs flared at the bottoms and was ornamented with silver dollars, fine boots which he wore inside his pants legs, gold-chased spurs, a silk shirt and a jacket with gold lace all over it, and the costliest sombrero I ever seen. Moreover, they was a carbine in a saddle sheath, and he wore a Luger pistol at his hip.

"Murder!" said Biff. "It's Lopez the Terrible!"

"Greetings, senorita!" said he, with a flash of white teeth under his black mustache, swinging off his sombrero and making a low bow in his saddle. "Lopez keeps his word—have I not said I would come for you? Oho, I am clever. I sent my men to make a disturbance and draw the Americanos away. Now you will come with me to my lair in the hills where no gringo will ever find you!"

Joan was trembling and white-faced, but she was game. "You don't dare touch an American woman, you murderer!" she said. "My cowboys would hang you on a cactus."

"I will take the risk," he purred. "Now, senorita, come—"

"Get up here in the ring, Miss Joan," I said, leaning down to give her a hand. "That's it—right up with me and Biff. We won't let no harm come to you. Now, Mr. Lopez, if that's your name, I'm givin' you your sailin' orders—weigh anchor and steer for some other port before I bend one on your jaw."

"I echoes them sentiments," said Biff, spitting on his gloves and hitching at his trunks.

Lopez's white teeth flashed in a snarl like a wolf's. His Luger snaked into his hand.

"So," he purred, "these men of beef, these bruisers dare defy Lopez!" He reined up alongside the ring and, placing one hand on a post, vaulted over the ropes, his pistol still menacing me and Biff. Joan, at my motion, hadst retreated back to the other side of the ring. Lopez began to walk towards us, like a cat stalking a mouse.

"The girl I take," he said, soft and deadly. "Let neither of you move if you wish to live."

"Well, Biff," I said, tensing myself, "we'll rush him from both sides. He'll get one of us but the other'n'll git him."

"Oh, don't!" cried Joan. "He'll kill you. I'd rather—"

"Let's go!" roared Biff, and we plunged at Lopez simultaneous.

But that Mex was quicker than a cat; he whipped from one to the other of us and his gun cracked twice. I heard Biff swear and saw him stumble, and something that burned hit me in the left shoulder.

Before Lopez couldst fire again, I was on him, and I ripped the gun outa his hand and belted him over the head with it just as Biff smashed him on the jaw. Lopez the Terrible stretched out limp as a sail-rope, and he didn't even twitch.

"OH, YOU'RE SHOT, both of you!" wailed Joan, running across the ring toward us. "Oh, I feel like a murderer! I shouldn't have let you do it. Let me see your wounds."

Biff's left arm was hanging limp and blood was oozing from a neat round hole above the elbow. My own left was getting so stiff I couldn't lift it, and blood was trickling down my chest.

"Heck, Miss Joan," I said, "don't worry 'bout us. Lucky for us Lopez was usin' them steel-jacket bullets that make a clean wound and don't tear. But I hate about me and Biff not gettin' to finish our scrap—"

"Hey, Steve," said Biff hurriedly, "the boys has chased off the bandits and heered the shots, and here they come across the flat on the run! Let's us finish our go before they git here. They won't let us go on if we don't do it now. And we may never git another chance. You'll go off to your ship tomorrer and we may never see each other again. Come on. I'm shot through the left arm and you got a bullet through your left shoulder, but our rights is okay. Let's toss this mutt outa the ring and give each other one more good slam!"

"Fair enough, Biff," said I. "Come on, before we gets weak from losin' blood."

Joan started crying and wringing her hands.

"Oh, please, please, boys, don't fight each other any more! You'll bleed to death. Let me bandage your wounds—"

"Shucks, Miss Joan," said I, patting her slim shoulder soothingly, "me and Biff ain't hurt, but we gotta settle our argument. Don't you fret your purty head none."

We unceremoniously tossed the limp and senseless bandit outa the ring and we squared off, with our rights cocked and our lefts hanging at our sides, just as the foremost of the cow-punchers came riding up.

We heard the astounded yells of Menly, Slim and the rest, and Miss Joan begging 'em to stop us, and then we braced our legs, took a deep breath and let go.

We both crashed our rights at exactly the same instant, and we both landed—square on the button. And we both went down. I was up almost in a instant, groggy and dizzy and only partly aware of what was going on, but Biff didn't twitch.

The next minute Menly and Steve and Tex and all the rest was swarming over the ropes, yelling and hollering and demanding to know what it was all about, and Miss Joan was crying and trying to tell 'em and tend to Biff's wound.

"Hey!" yelled Yuma, outside the ring. "That *was* Lopez I seen ride up to the ring a while ago—here he is with a three-inch gash in his scalp and a fractured jawbone!"

"Ain't that what Miss Joan's been tellin' you?" I snapped. "Help her with Biff before he bleeds to death—naw, tend to him first—I'm all right."

Biff come to about that time and nearly knocked Menly's head off before he knowed where he was, and later, while they was bandaging us, Biff said: "I wanta tell you, Steve, I still don't consider you has licked me, and I'm figgerin' on lookin' you up soon's as my arm's healed up."

"Okay with me, Snoots," I grinned. "I gets more enjoyment outa fightin' you than anybody. Reckon there's fightin' Texas feud betwixt me and you."

"Well, Steve," said Slim, "we said we'd make it worth your while—what'll it be?"

"I wouldn't accept no pay for fightin' a old friend like Biff," said I. "All I wantcha to do is get me back in port in time to sail with the *Sea Girl.* And, Miss Joan, I hope you don't feel scared of me no more."

Her answer made both me and Biff blush like school-kids. She kissed us.

CIRCUS FISTS

By ROBERT E. HOWARD

Author of "Alleys of Peril"

Flattening jobbies in a circus side-show! Boy, that wasn't work for Steve Costigan; that was recreation . . . until a black-browed giant breathing fire and swift destruction heaved his hairy chest through the ropes to make a Roman holiday for Ironville fans.

CIRCUS FISTS

ME AND THE Old Man had a most violent row whilst the *Sea Girl* was tied up at the docks of a small seaport on the West Coast. Somebody put a pole-cat in the Old Man's bunk, and he accused me of doing it. I denied it indignantly, and asked him where he reckoned I would get a pole-cat, and he said well, it was a cinch *somebody* had got a pole-cat, because there it was, and it was his opinion that I was the only man of the crew which was low-down enough to do a trick like that.

This irritated me, and I told him he oughta know it wasn't me, because I had the reputation of being kind to animals, and I wouldn't put a decent skunk where it would have to associate with a critter like the Old Man.

This made him so mad that he busted a bottle of good rye whiskey over my head. Annoyed at such wanton waste of good licker, I grabbed the old walrus and soused him in a horse-trough—us being on the docks at the time.

The Old Man ariz like Neptune from the deep, and, with whiskers dripping, he shook his fists at me and yelled, "Don't never darken my decks again, Steve Costigan. If you ever try to come aboard the *Sea Girl,* I'll fill you fulla buckshot, you mutineerin' pirate!"

"Go set on a marlin-spike," I sneered. "I wouldn't sail with you again for ten bucks a watch and plum duff every mess. I'm through with the sea, anyhow. You gimme a bad taste for the whole business. A landman's life is the life for me, by golly. Me and Mike is goin' to fare forth and win fame and fortune ashore."

And so saying, I swaggered away with my white bulldog, follered clean outa sight by the Old Man's sincere maledictions.

Casting about for amusement, I soon come onto a circus which was going full blast at the edge of town. I seen a side-show poster which said, *Battling Bingo, Champion of the West Coast.* So I went in and they was considerable of a crowd there and a big dumb-looking mutt in tights standing up in a ring, flexing his arms and showing off his muscles.

"Gents," yelled the barker, a flashy-dressed young feller with a diamond horse-shoe stick-pin, "the management offers fifty dollars to any man which can stay four rounds with this tiger of the ring! Five minutes ago I made the same offer on the platform outside, and some gent took me up. But now he seems to have got cold feet, and is nowhere to be found. So here and now I again make the original proposition—fifty round, bright iron men to any guy which can stay four rounds with this man-killin' terror, this fire-breathin' murderer, this iron-fisted man-mountain, Battling Bingo, the Terror of the Rockies!"

The crowd whooped, and three or four fellers made a move like they was going to take up the challenge, but I brushed 'em scornfully aside and bellered, "I'll take that dough, mate!"

I bounced into the ring, and the barker said, "You realize that the management ain't responsible for life or limb?"

"Aw, stow that guff and gimme them gloves," I roared, ripping off my shirt. "Get ready, champeen. I'm goin' to knock your crown off!"

The gong sounded, and we went for each other. They wasn't no canvas stretched across the back of the ring where Bingo couldst shove me up against to be blackjacked by somebody behind it, so I knowed very well he had a iron knuckle-duster on one of his hands, and, from the way he dangled his right, I knowed that was the hand. So I watched his right, and, when he throwed it, I stepped inside of his swing and banged him on the whiskers with a left and a right hook which tucked him away for the evening.

The crowd roared in huge approval, and I jerked the wad of greenbacks outa the barker's hand and started away when he stopped me.

"Say," he said, "I reckernize you now. You're Sailor Costigan. How'd you like to take this tramp's place? We'll pay you good wages."

"All I got to do is flatten jobbies?" I said, and he said it was. So that's how I come to start working in Flash Larney's Gigantic Circus and Animal Show.

Each night I'd appear in fighting tights before the multitude, and the barker, Joe Beemer, wouldst go through the usual ballyhoo, and then all I had to do was to knock the blocks offa the saps which tried to collect the fifty. I wouldn't use the knuckle-duster. I wouldn't of used it even if I'd of needed it, which I didn't. If I can't sock a palooka to sleep, fair and above-board, with my own personal knuckles, then they ain't no use in trying to dint him with a load of iron.

WE WORKED UP and down the West Coast and inland, and it was mostly easy. The men which tried to lick me was practically all alley-fighters—big strong fellers, but they didn't know nothing. Mostly farmers, blacksmiths, sailors, longshoremen, miners, cowpunchers, bar-room bouncers. All I had to do was to hit 'em. More'n once I knocked out three or four men in one night.

I always got action because the crowd was always against me, just like they was against Battling Bingo when I flattened him. A crowd is always against the carnival fighter, whether they know his opponent or not. And when the opponent is some well-known local boy, they nearly have hydrophobia in their excitement.

You oughta heered the cheers they'd give their home-town pride, and the dirty remarks they'd yell at me. No matter how hard I was fighting, I generally found time to reply to their jeers with choice insults I had picked up all over the seven seas, with the result that the maddened mob wouldst spew forth more raging sluggers to be slaughtered. Some men can't fight their best when the crowd's against 'em, but I always do better, if anything. It makes me mad, and I take it out on my opponent.

When I wasn't performing in the ring, I was driving stakes, setting up or taking down tents, and fighting with my circus-mates. Larney's outfit had the name of being the toughest on the Coast, and it was. The fights I had in the ring wasn't generally a stitch to them I had on the lot.

Well, I always makes it a point to be the champeen of whatever outfit I'm with, and I done so in this case. The first day I was with the show I licked three razor-backs, the lion-tamer and a side-show barker, and from then on it was a battle practically every day till them mutts realized I was the best man on the lot.

Fighting all the time like I was, I got so hard and mean I surprised myself. They wasn't a ounce of flesh on me that wasn't like iron, and I believe I could of run ten miles at top speed without giving out. The Dutch weight-lifter figgered to give me a close scrimmage, but he was way too slow. The toughest scrap I had was with a big Japanese acrobat. We fought all over the lot one morning, and everybody postponed the parade for a hour to watch. I was about all in when I finally put the heathen away, but, with my usual recuperative powers, I was able to go on that night as usual, and flatten a farm-hand, a piano-mover and a professional football player.

Some trouble was had with Mike, which always set in my corner and bit anybody which tried to hit me through the ropes, as often happened when the local boy started reeling. Larney wanted to shave him and tattoo him and put him in a sideshow.

"The tattooed dog!" said Larney. "That would draw 'em! A novelty! Can't you see the crowds flockin' through the gates for a look at him?"

"I can see me bustin' you in the snoot," I growled. "You let Mike alone."

"Well," said Larney, "we got to make him more presentable. He looks kinda crude and uncultured alongside our trained poodles."

So the lion-trainer bathed Mike and combed him and perfumed him, and put on a little fool dog-blanket with straps and gilt buckles, and tied a big bow ribbon on his stump tail. But Mike seen himself in a mirror and tore off all that rigging and bit the lion-tamer.

Well, they had a old decrepit lion by the name of Oswald which didn't have no teeth, and Mike got to sleeping in his cage. So they fixed a place where Mike couldst get in and out without Oswald getting out, and made a kind of act out of it.

Larney advertised Mike as the dog which laid down with the lion, and wouldst have Mike and Oswald in the cage together, and spiel about how ferocious Oswald was, and how unusual it was for a friendship to spring up between such natural enemies. But the reason Mike slept in the cage was that they put more straw in it than they did in the other cages on account of Oswald being old and thin-blooded, and Mike liked a soft bed.

Larney was afraid Mike would hurt Oswald, but the only critters Mike couldn't get along with was Amir, a big African leopard which had already kilt three men, and Sultan, the man-eating tiger. They was the meanest critters in the show, and was always trying to get out and claw Mike up. But he wasn't afeard of 'em.

WELL, I WAS having a lot of fun. I thrives in a rough environment like that, though I'll admit I sometimes got kinda homesick for the *Sea Girl* and the sea, and wondered what Bill O'Brien and Mushy Hanson and Red O'Donnell was doing. But I got my pride, and I wouldn't go back after the Old Man had pratically kicked me out to shift for myself.

Anyway, it was a lot of fun. I'd stand out on the platform in front of the tent with my massive arms folded and a scowl on my battered face, whilst Joe Beemer wouldst cock his derby back on his head and start the ballyhoo.

He'd whoop and yell and interjuice me to the crowd as "Sailor Costigan, the Massive Man-mauler of the Seven Seas!" And I'd do strong-man stunts—twisting horse-shoes in two and bending coins between my fingers and etc. Then he'd rare back and holler, "Is they any man in this fair city courageous enough to try and stay four rounds with this slashin' slugger? Take a chance, boys—he's been drivin' stakes all day and maybe he's tired and feeble—heh! heh! heh!"

Then generally some big ham wouldst jump outa the crowd and roar, "I'll fight the so-and-so." And Joe wouldst rub his hands together and say under his breath, "Money, roll in! I need groceries!" And he'd holler, "Right this way, gents! Right through the door to the left. Ten cents admission—one dime! See the battle of the century! Don't crowd, folks. Don't crowd."

The tent was nearly always packed with raging fans which honed at the top of their voices for their local hope to knock my iron skull off. However small a tank-town might be, it generally had at least one huge roughneck with a reputation of some kind.

One time we hit a town in the throes of a rassling carnival. Nobody couldst be found to box with me, but a big Polack came forward claiming to be the rassling champeen of the West—I ain't never seen a rassler which wasn't champeen of something—and wanted me to rassle him. Beemer refused, and the crowd hissed, and the rassler said I was yeller.

I seen red and told him I wasn't no rassler but I'd give him more'n he could tote home. He figgered I was easy, but he got fooled. I don't know a lot about scientific rassling, but I know plenty rough-and-tumble, and I was so incredibly hard and tough, and played so rough that I broke his arm and dislocated his shoulder. And after that nobody ast me to rassle.

IT WASN'T LONG after that when we blowed into a mining town by the name of Ironville, up in the Nevada hills, and from the looks of the populace I figgered I'd have plenty of competition that night. I wasn't fooled none, neither, believe me.

Long before we was ready to start the show, a huge crowd of tough-looking mugs in boots and whiskers was congregated around the athaletic tent, which wasn't showing no interest whatever in the main-top nor the freaks nor the animals.

Joe hadn't hardly got started on his ballyhoo when through the crowd come a critter which looked more like a grizzly than a man—a big black-headed feller with shoulders as broad as a door, and arms like a bear's paw. From the way the crowd all swarmed around him, I figgered he was a man of some importance in Ironville.

I was right.

"You don't need to say no more, pard," he rumbled in a voice like a bull. "I'll take a whirl at yore tramp!"

Joe looked at the black-browed giant, and he kinda got cold feet for the first time in his career.

"Who are you?" he demanded, uneasily.

The big feller grinned wolfishly and said, "Who, me? Oh, I'm just a blacksmith around here." And the crowd all whooped and yelled and laughed like he'd said something very funny.

"Somethin's fishy about this, Steve," whispered Joe to me. "I don't like the looks of it."

About that time the crowd begun to hiss and boo, and the big feller said nastily, "Well, what's the matter—you hombres gettin' yeller?"

I seen red. "Get into this tent, you black-muzzled palooka!" I roared. "I'll show you who's yeller! Shut up, Joe. Ain't I always said I barred nobody? What's the matter with you, anyhow?"

"I tell you, Steve," he said, wiping his forehead with his bandanner, "I seen this big punk somewheres, and if he's a simple blacksmith I'm a Bohemian!"

"Gahhh!" I snorted disgustfully. "When I get through with him, he'll look like a carpet. Have I lost you a penny since I joined the show?

Naw! Come on!"

And so saying, I swaggered into the tent and bounded into the ring while the crowd gathered around, packing the place solid, applauding their man and howling insults at me, which I returned with interest, that being a game at which I ain't no amateur myself.

JOE STARTED TO lead the big feller to the dressing-room which was partitioned off with a curtain in one corner of the tent, but he snorted and began ripping off his clothes then and there, revealing ring togs under 'em. Ah, thought I, he come here with the intention of going on with me. Some local battler, no doubtless.

When he clumb into the ring, they was several men with him—one a tall cold-faced man which looked like a high-class gambler, and who they called Brelen, and three or four tough mugs which was to act as seconds. They had the game writ all over their flat noses and tin ears. In fact, it looked to me like the big feller had a right elaborate follering, even if he was a local white hope.

"Who referee's?" asked Brelen, the poker-faced gent.

"Oh, I referee," said Joe.

"Not this time you don't," said Brelen. "The crowd chooses a referee who'll give my boy a square deal, see?"

"It's against the rules of the management—" began Joe, and the crowd rumbled and begun to surge forward. "All right, all right," said Joe, hurriedly. "It's okay with me."

Brelen grinned kinda thin-like, and turned to the crowd and said, "Well, boys, who do you want to referee?"

"Honest Jim Donovan!" they roared, and pushed forward a baldheaded old sea-lion which had the crookedest face I ever seen on a human. Joe give him a look and clasped his head and groaned. The crowd was nasty—itching for trouble. Joe was kinda white around the gills, and my handlers was uneasy. I was glad I'd locked Mike up in Oswald's cage before the show started, being suspicious of the customers. Mike ain't got much discretion; when the crowd starts throwing things at me, he's likely to go for 'em.

"Gents," yelled Joe, who, being a natural-born barker, couldn't keep his mouth shut if he swung for it, "you are now about to witness the battle of the centu-ree, wherein the Fighting Blacksmith of your fair city endeavors to stay four actual rounds with Sailor Costigan, the Terror of the Seven Seas—"

"Aw, shut up and get out of this ring," snarled Brelen. "Let the massacre commence!"

THE GONG SOUNDED and the Blacksmith come swinging outa his corner. Jerusha, he was a man! He stood six feet one and a quarter and weighed not less than two hundred and ten pounds to my six feet and one ninety. With a broad chest matted with black hair, arms knotted with muscles like full-sized cables, legs like trees, a heavy jutting jaw, a broad fighting face with wicked gray eyes glittering from under thick black brows, and a shock of coarse black hair piled up on top of his low, broad forehead—I wanta tell you I ain't never seen a more formidable-looking fighter in my life!

We rushed together like a pair of mad bulls. *Bang!* In a shower of stars I felt myself flying through the air, and I landed on my shoulders with a jolt that shook the ring. Zowie! I sprawled about, almost petrified with dumfoundment. The crowd was whooping and cheering and laughing like all get-out.

I glared in wild amazement at the black-headed giant which was standing almost over me, with a nasty grin on his lips. A light dawned.

"Blacksmith my eye!" I roared, leaping up at him. "They ain't but one man in the world can hit a lick like that—*Bill Cairn!*"

I heard Joe's despairing howl as I slashed into my foe. *Wham! Wham!* I was on the resin again before I even got a chance to connect. The yells sounded kinda jumbled this time, and I shook my head violently, cussing fervently as I got my feet under me. Ironville. I oughta knowed—Bill Cairn, which they called the Ironville Blacksmith, the hardest hitter in the game! This was his home town, and this was him!

Fighting mad, I bounded up, but Cairn was so close to me that he reached me with one of his pile-driving left hooks before I was balanced, and down I went again. Now the yelling was kinda dim and the lights was quaking and rocking. I crouched, taking a count which Honest Jim was reeling off a lot faster than necessary. Bill Cairn! The kayo king of the heavyweights, with thirty or forty knockouts in a row, and never been socked off his feet, himself. He was in line for a crack at the champ—and I was supposed to flatten this grizzly in four rounds!

I was up at nine, and, ducking a savage drive for the face, I clinched. By golly, it was like tying up a grizzly. But I ain't no chicken myself. I gripped him in a desperate bear-hug whilst him and the referee cussed and strained, and the crowd begged him to shake me loose and kill me.

"You side-show rat!" he gritted between his teeth. "Leggo whilst I rip yore head off! How can I show my best stuff with you hangin' on like a leech?"

"This is cheap stuff for a headliner like you!" I snarled, red-eyed.

"Givin' my home town folks a free show," he grinned, nastily. "It was just my luck to have a mug like you blow in whilst I was visitin' back home."

Oh, I see the idee all right. It was a big joke with him to knock me off and give his friends a treat—show off before the home-folks! He was laughing at me and so was all them Ironville lubbers. Well, I thought, grinding my teeth with red rage, they's many a good man punched hisself into fistic oblivion on my iron jaw.

I let go of Cairn and throwed my right at his jaw like it was a hammer. He pulled away from it and—*bang!* It mighta been a left hook to the head. It felt like a handspike. And the next instant, whilst my eyes was still full of stars, I felt another jolt like a concentrated earthquake.

Purty soon I heered somebody say, "Seven!" and I instinctively clumb up and looked about for my foe. I didn't locate him, as he was evidently standing behind me, but I did locate a large gloved mauler which crashed under my ear and nearly unjinted my neck. I done a beautiful dive, ploughing my nose vigorously into the resin, whilst the crowd wept with delight, and then I heered a noise like a sleigh-bell and was aware of being dragged to my corner.

A SNIFTER OF ammonia brung me to myself, and I discovered I was propped on my stool and being worked over by my handlers and Joe, who was bleeding from a cut over the temple.

"How'd you get that?" I asked groggily.

"One of these eggs hit me with a bottle," he said. "They claim I jerked the gong too soon. Listen at 'em! Toughest crowd I ever seen."

They sure was. They was rumbling and growling, just seething for a scrap, but stopping now and then to cheer Cairn, which was bowing and smirking in his corner.

"I knew I'd seen him," said Joe, "and Ace Brelen, his manager. The lousy chiselers! You ain't got a chance, Steve—"

At this moment a rough-whiskered mug stuck his head through the ropes and waved a coil of rope at Joe.

"We're on to you, you rat!" he bellered. "None of your side-show tricks, understand? If you try anything dirty, we'll stretch your neck. And that goes for you, too, you tin-eared gorilla!"

"So's your old man!" I roared, kicking out with all my might. My heel crunched solid on his jaw, and he shot back into the first row amongst a tangle of busted seats and cussing customers, from which he emerged bleeding at the mouth and screaming with rage. He was fumbling for a gun in his shirt, but just then the gong sounded and me and Cairn went for each other.

I come in fast, and figgered on beating him to the punch, but he was too quick for me. He wasn't so clever, but he moved like a big cat, and the very power of his punches was a swell defense. No man couldst keep his balance under them thundering smashes, even if they didn't land on no vital spot. Just trying to block 'em numbed my arms.

Zip! His left whizzed past my jaw like a red-hot brick. *Zinggg!* His right burned my ear as it went by. I seen a opening and shot my right with everything I had. But I was too eager; my arm looped over his shoulder and he banged his left into my ribs, which I distinctly felt bend almost to the breaking point as my breath went outa me in a explosive grunt.

I throwed my arms about him in a vain effort to clinch, but he pushed me away and slammed a full-armed right to my jaw. *Crash!* I felt myself turning a complete somersault in the air, and I landed on my belly with my head sticking out under the ropes and ogling glassily down at the ecstatic customers. One of these riz up and slashed his thigh with his hat and, sticking his face almost into mine, yelled, "Well, you carnival punk, how do you like *those?*"

"Like this!" I roared, catching him on the whiskers with a unexpected bash that sunk his nose in the sawdust. I then rolled over on my back and, observing that the referee had rapidly counted up to nine, I ariz and, abandoning my scanty boxing skill, started slugging wild and ferocious in the hope of landing a haymaker.

But that was Cairn's game; he blocked my punches for a second or so, then *bang!* he caught me square on the chin with one of them thunderbolt rights which shot me back into the ropes, and I rebounded from 'em square into a whistling left hook that dropped me face-down in the resin.

I couldst dimly hear the crowd yelling like wolves. When the average man falls face-first he's through, but nobody never accused me of being a average man. At nine I was up as usual, reeling, and Cairn approached me with a look of disgust on his brutal face.

"Will you stay down?" he gritted, and, measuring me with a left, he crashed his right square into my mouth, and I went down like a pole-axed ox.

"That finishes him!" I heered somebody yelp, and evidently Cairn thought so too, because he give a scornful laugh and started toward his corner where his manager was getting his bathrobe ready. But I got my legs under me and at nine I staggered up, as is my habit.

"Come back here, you big sissy!" I roared groggily, spitting out fragments of a tooth. "This fight ain't over by a devil of a ways!"

The mob screamed with amazement, and Cairn, swearing ferociously, turned and rushed at me like a tiger. But though I reeled on buckling knees, I didn't go down under his smashing left hooks.

"Why don't you get a ax, you big false-alarm?" I sneered, trying to shake the blood outa my eyes. "What you got in them gloves—powder puffs?"

At that he give a roar which made the ring lights shimmy, and brought one up from the canvas which hung me over the top rope just as the gong sounded. Joe and his merry men untangled my limp carcass and held me on the stool while they worked despairingly over me.

"Drop it, Steve," urged Joe. "Cairn will kill you."

"How many times was I on the canvas that round?" I asked.

"How should I know?" he returned, peevishly, wringing the gore out of my towel. "I ain't no adding machine."

"Well, try to keep count, willya?" I requested. "It's important; I can tell how much he's weakenin' if you check up on the knockdowns from round to round."

Joe dropped the sponge he was fixing to throw into the ring.

"Ye gods! Are you figgerin' on continuin' the massakree?"

"He can't keep this pace all night," I growled. "Lookit Brelen talkin' to his baby lamb!"

Ace was gesticulating purty emphatic, and Cairn was growling back at him and glaring at me and kneading his gloves like he wisht it was my goozle. I knowed that Brelen was telling him this scrap was getting beyond the point of a joke, and that it wasn't helping his reputation none for me to keep getting up on him, and for him to make it another quick kayo. Ha, ha, thought I grimly, shaking the blood outa my mangled ear, let's see how quick a kayo Bill Cairn can make where so many other iron-fisted sluggers has failed.

At the gong I was still dizzy and bleeding copiously, but that's a old story to me.

CAIRN, INFURIATED AT not having finished me, rushed outa his corner and throwed over a terrible right, which I seen coming like a cannonball, and ducked. His arm looped over my shoulder and his shoulder rammed into my neck with such force that we both crashed to the canvas.

Cairn untangled hisself with a snarl of irritation, and, assisted by the fair-minded referee, arose, casually kicking me in the face as he done so. I ariz likewise, and, enraged by my constant position on the canvas, looped a whistling left at his head that would of undoubtedly decapitated him hadst it landed—but luck was against me as usual. My foot slipped in a smear of my own blood, my swing was wild, and I run smack into his ripping right.

I fell into Cairn, ignoring an uppercut which loosened all my lower teeth, and tied him up.

"Leggo, you tin-eared baboon!" he snarled, heaving and straining. "Try to show me up, wouldja? Try to make a monkey outa me, wouldja?"

"Nature's already attended to that, you lily-fingered tap-dancer," I croaked. "A flapper with a powder-puff couldst do more damage than you can with them chalk-knuckled bread-hooks."

"So!" he yelled, jerking away and crashing his right to my jaw with every ounce of his huge frame behind it. I revolved in the air like a spin-wheel, felt the ropes scrape my back, and realized that I was falling through space. *Crash!* My fall was cushioned by a mass of squirming, cussing fans, else I would of undoubtedly broke my back.

I looked up, and high above me, it seemed, I seen the referee leaning over the ropes and counting down at me. I began to kick and struggle, trying to get up, and a number of willing hands—and a few hobnailed boots—hoisted me offa the squawking fans, and I grabbed the ropes and swung up.

Somebody had a grip on my belt, and I heard a guy growl. "You're licked, you fool! Take the count. Do you want to get slaughtered?"

"Leggo!" I roared, kicking out furiously. "I ain't never licked!"

I tore loose and crawled through the ropes—it looked like I'd never make it—and hauled myself up just as the referee was lifting his arm to bring it down on "Ten!" Cairn didn't rush this time; he was scowling, and I noticed that sweat was streaming down his face, and his huge chest was heaving.

Some of the crowd yelled, "Stop it!" but most of 'em whooped, "Now you got him, Bill. Polish him off!"

Cairn measured me, and smashed his right into my face. The top-rope snapped as I crashed back against it, but I didn't fall. Cairn swore in amazement, and drawed back his right again, when the gong sounded. He hesitated, then lemme have it anyway—a pile-driving smash that nearly lifted me offa my feet. And the crowd cheered the big egg. My handlers jostled him aside and, as they pulled me offa the ropes, Cairn sneered and walked slowly to his corner.

SUPPORTED ON MY stool, I seen Joe pick up a sponge stealthily.

"Drop that sponge!" I roared, and Joe, seeing the baleful light in my one good eye, done so like it was red-hot.

"Lemme catch you throwin' a sponge in for me!" I growled. "Gimme ammonia! Dump that bucket of water over me! Slap the back of my neck with a wet towel! One more round to go, and I gotta save that fifty bucks!"

Swearing dumfoundedly, my handlers did as they was bid, and I felt better and stronger every second. Even they couldn't understand how I couldst take such a beating and come back for more. But any slugger which depends on his ruggedness to win his fights understands it. We got to be solid iron—and we are.

Besides, my recent rough-and-ready life hadst got me into condition such as few men ever gets in, even athaletes. This, coupled with my amazing recuperative powers, made me just about unbeatable. Cairn could, and had, battered me from pillar to post, knocked me down repeatedly, and had me groggy and glassy-eyed, but he hadn't sapped the real reservoir of my vitality. Being groggy and being weak is two different things. Cairn hadn't weakened me. The minute my head cleared under the cold water and ammonia, I was as good as ever. Well, just about, anyhow.

So I come out for the fourth round raring to go. Cairn didn't rush as usual. In fact, he looked a little bit sick of his job. He walked out and lashed at my head with his left. He connected solid, but I didn't go down. And for the first time I landed squarely. *Bang.* My right smashed under his ear, and his head rocked on his bull's neck.

With a roar of fury, he come back with a thundering right to the head, but it only knocked me to my knees, and I was up in a instant. I was out-lasting him! His blows was losing their dynamite! This realization electrified me, and I bored in, slashing with both hands.

A left to the face staggered but didn't stop me, and I ripped a terrific left hook under his heart. He grunted and backed away. He wasn't near as good at taking punishment as he was at handing it out. I slashed both hands to his head, and the blood flew. With a deafening roar, he sunk his right mauler clean outa sight in my belly.

I thought for a second that my spine was broke, as I curled up on the canvas, gasping. The referee sprang forward and began counting, and I looked for Cairn, expecting to see him standing almost astraddle of me, as usual, waiting to slug me down as I got up. He wasn't; but was over against the ropes, holding onto 'em with one mitt whilst he wiped the blood and sweat outa his eyes with the other'n. And I seen his great chest heaving, his belly billowing out and in, and his leg muscles quivering.

Grinning wolfishly, I drawed in great gulps of air and beat the count by a second. Cairn lurched offa the ropes at me, swinging a wide left, but I went under it and crashed my right to his heart. He rolled like a ship in a heavy gale, and I knowed I had him. That last punch which had floored me had been his dying effort. He'd fought hisself clean out on me, as so many a man had didst. Strategy, boy, strategy!

I went after him like a tiger after a bull, amid a storm of yells and curses and threats. The crowd, at first dumfounded, was now leaping up and down and shaking their fists and busting chairs and threatening me with torture and sudden death if I licked their hero. But I was seeing red. Wait'll you've took the beating I'd took and then get a chance to even it up! I ripped both hands to Cairn's quivering belly and swaying head, driving him to the ropes, off of which he rolled drunkenly.

I HEERED A gong sounding frantically; Brelen hadst knocked the time-keeper stiff with a blackjack and was trying to save his man.

Also the referee was grabbing at me, trying to push me away. But I give no heed. A left and right under the heart buckled Cairn's knees, and a blazing right to the temple glazed his eyes. He reeled, and a trip-hammer left hook to the jaw that packed all my beef sent him crashing to the canvas, just as the crowd come surging into the ring, tearing down the ropes. I seen Joe take it on the run, ducking out under the wall of the tent, and yelling, "Hey, Rube!"

Then me and the handlers was engulfed. Half a hundred hands grabbed at me, and fists, boots and chairs swung for me. But I ducked, ripping off my gloves, and come up fighting like a wild man.

I swung my fists like they was topping-mauls, and ribs snapped and noses and jaw-bones cracked, whilst through the melee I caught glimpses of Brelen and his men carrying out their battered gladiator. He was still limp.

Just as the sheer number of maddened citizens was dragging me down, a gang of frothing razor-backs come through the tent like a whirlwind, swinging pick handles and tent-stakes.

Well, I ain't seen many free-for-alls to equal that 'un! The circus war-whoop of "Hey, Rube!" mingled with the blood-thirsty yells of the customers. The Iron-villians outnumbered us, but we give 'em a bellyful. In about three seconds the ring was tore to pieces and the storm of battle surged into the tent-wall, which collapsed under the impact.

Knives was flashing and a few guns barking, and all I wonder is that somebody wasn't kilt. The athaletic tent was literally ripped plumb to ribbons, and the battle surged out onto the grounds and raged around the other tents and booths.

Then a wild scream went up: "Fire!" And over everything was cast a lurid glow. Somehow or other the main top hadst caught in the melee—or maybe some fool set it on fire. A strong wind was fanning the flames, which mounted higher each second. In a instant the fight was abandoned. Everything was in a tumult, men running and yelling, children squalling, women screaming. The circus-people was running and hauling the cages and wagons outa the animal tent, which was just catching. The critters was bellering and howling in a most hair-raising way, and I remembered Mike in Oswald's cage. I started for there on the run, when there riz a most fearful scream above all the noise: "The animals are loose!"

EVERYBODY HOLLERED AND tore their hair and ran, and here come the elephants like a avalanche! They crashed over wagons and cages and booths, trumpeting like Judgment Day, and thundered on into the night. How they got loose nobody never exactly knowed. Anything can happen in a fire. But, in stampeding, they'd bumped into and busted open some more cages, letting loose the critters inside.

And here *they* come roaring—Sultan, the tiger, and Amir, the leopard, killers both of 'em. A crowd of screaming children rushed by me, and right after them come that striped devil, Sultan, his eyes blazing. I grabbed up a heavy tent-stake and leaped betweenst him and the kids. He roared and leaped with his talons spread wide, and I braced my feet and met him in mid-air with a desperate smash that had every ounce of my beef behind it. The impact nearly knocked me offa my feet, and the stake splintered in my hand, but Sultan rolled to the ground with a shattered skull.

And almost simultaneously a terrible cry from the people made me wheel just in time to see Amir racing toward me like a black shadder with balls of fire for eyes. And, just as I turned, he soared from the ground straight at my throat. I didn't have time to do nothing. He crashed full on my broad breast, and his claws ripped my hide as the impact dashed me to the earth. And at the same instant I felt another shock which knocked him clear of me.

I scrambled up to see a squat white form tearing and worrying at the limp body of the big cat. Again Mike had saved my worthless life. When Amir hit me, he hit Amir and broke his neck with one crunch of his iron jaws. He'd squoze out between the bars of Oswald's cage and come looking for me.

He lolled out his tongue, grinning, and vibrated his stump tail, and all to once I heered my name called in a familiar voice. Looking around, I seen a battered figger crawl out from under the ruins of a band-wagon, and, in the lurid light of the burning tents, I reckernized him.

"Jerusha!" I said. "The Old Man! What you doin' under that wagon?"

"I crawled under there to keep from bein' trampled by the mob," he said, working his legs to see if they was broke. "And it was a good idee, too, till a elephant run over the wagon. By gad, if I ever get safe to sea once more I'll never brave the perils of the land again, I wanta tell ya!"

"Did you see me lick Bill Cairn?" I asked.

"I ain't see nothin' but a passel of luneyticks," he snapped. "I arrived just as the free-for-all was ragin'. I don't mind a rough-house, but when they drags in a fire and a stampede of jungle-critters, I'm ready to weigh anchor! And you!" he added, accusingly. "A merry chase you've led me, you big sea-lion! I've come clean from Frisco, and it looked for a while like I wouldn't never find this blame circus."

"What you wanta find it for?" I growled, the thought of my wrongs renewing itself.

"Steve," said the Old Man, "I done you a injustice! It was the cabin-boy which put that pole-cat in my bunk—I found it out after he jumped ship. Steve, as champeen of the old *Sea Girl,* I asks you—let bygones be gone-byes! Steve, me and the crew has need of your mallet-like fists. At Seattle, a few weeks ago, I shipped on a fiend in human form by the name of Monagan, which immediately set hisself up as the bully of the fo'c'le. I had to put in Frisco because of shortage of hands. Even now, Mate O'Donnell, Mushy Hanson and Jack Lynch lies groanin' in their bunks from his man-handlin', and he has likewise licked Bill O'Brien, Maxie Heimer and Sven Larsen. He has threatened to hang me on my own bow-sprit by my whiskers. I dast not fire him, for fear of my life. Steve!" the Old Man's voice trembled with emotion, "I asks you—forgive and forget! Come back to the *Sea Girl* and demonstrate the eternal brotherhood of man by knockin' the devil outa this demon Monagan before he destroys us all! Show the monster who's the real champeen of the craft!"

"Well," I said, "I got some money comin' to me from Larney—but let it go. He'll need it repairin' his show. Monagan, of Seattle—bah! I hammered him into a pulp in Tony Vitello's poolroom three years ago, and I can do it again. Calls hisself champeen of the *Sea Girl,* huh? Well, when I kick his battered carcass onto the wharf, he'll know who's champeen of the craft. They never was, and they ain't now, and they never will be but one champeen of her, and that's Steve Costigan, A.B. Let's go! I wasn't never cut out for no peaceful landlubber's existence, nohow."

Vikings of the Gloves

By R. E. HOWARD

Hakon's eyes blazed. He was berserk, like the Vikings of old who were his ancestors. And all the Irish fighting madness took hold of Steve Costigan, and they ripped and tore like tigers. For a fighting man is a fighting man in any language.

VIKINGS OF THE GLOVES

NO SOONER HAD the *Sea Girl* docked in Yokohama than Mushy Hansen beat it down the waterfront to see if he couldst match me at some good fight club. Purty soon he come back and said: "No chance, Steve. You'd have to be a Scandinavian to get a scrap right now."

"What you mean by them remarks?" I asked, suspiciously.

"Well," said Mushy, "the sealin' fleet's in, and so likewise is the whalers, and the port's swarmin' with squareheads."

"Well, what's that got to do—?"

"They ain't but one fight club on the waterfront," said Mushy, "and it's run by a Dutchman named Neimann. He's been puttin' on a series of elimination contests, and, from what I hear, he's been cleanin' up. He matches Swedes against Danes, see? Well, they's hundreds of squareheads in port, and naturally each race turns out to support its countryman. So far, the Danes is ahead. You ever hear of Hakon Torkilsen?"

"You bet," I said. "I ain't never seen him perform, but they say he's the real goods. Sails on the *Viking*, outa Copenhagen, don't he?"

"Yeah. And the *Viking's* in port. Night before last, Hakon flattened Sven Tortvigssen, the Terrible Swede, in three rounds, and tonight he takes on Dirck Jacobsen, the Gotland Giant. The Swedes and the Danes is fightin' all over the waterfront," said Mushy, "and they're bettin' their socks. I sunk a few bucks on Hakon myself. But that's the way she stands, Steve. Nobody but Scandinavians need apply."

"Well, heck," I complained, "how come I got to be the victim of race prejerdice? I need dough. I'm flat broke. Wouldn't this mug Neimann gimme a preliminary scrap? For ten dollars I'll fight any three squareheads in port—all in the same ring."

"Naw," said Mushy, "they ain't goin' to be no preliminaries. Neimann says the crowd'll be too impatient to set through 'em. Boy, oh boy, will they be excitement! Whichever way it goes, they's bound to be a rough-house."

"A purty lookout," I said bitterly, "when the *Sea Girl,* the fightenest ship on the seven seas, ain't represented in the melee. I gotta good mind to blow in and bust up the whole show—"

At this moment Bill O'Brien hove in sight, looking excited.

"Hot dawg!" he yelled. "Here's a chance for us to clean up some dough!"

"Stand by to come about," I advised, "and give us the lay."

"Well," Bill said, "I just been down along the waterfront listening to them squareheads argy—and, boy, is the money changin' hands! I seen six fights already. Well, just now they come word that Dirck Jacobsen had broke his wrist, swinging for a sparrin' partner and hittin' the wall instead. So I run down to Neimann's arena to find out if it was so, and the Dutchman was walkin' the floor and tearin' his hair. He said he'd pay a hundred bucks extra, win or lose, to a man good enough to go in with Torkilsen. He says if he calls the show off, these squareheads will hang him. So I see where we can run a *Sea Girl* man in and cop the jack!"

"And who you think we can use?" I asked skeptically.

"Well, there's Mushy," began Bill. "He was raised in America, of course, but—"

"Yeah, there's Mushy!" snapped Mushy, bitterly. "You know as well as I do that I ain't no Swede. I'm a Dane myself. Far from wantin' to fight Hakon, I hope he knocks the block offa whatever fool Swede they finds to go against him."

"That's gratitude," said Bill, scathingly. "How can a brainy man like me work up anything big when I gets opposition from all quarters? I lays awake nights studyin' up plans for the betterment of my mates, and what do I get? Argyments! Wisecracks! Opposition! I tellya—"

"Aw, pipe down," I said. "There's Sven Larson—he's a Swede."

"That big ox would last about fifteen seconds against Hakon," said Mushy, with gloomy satisfaction. "Besides, Sven's in jail. He hadn't been in port more'n a half hour when he got jugged for beatin' up a cop."

Bill fixed a gloomy gaze on me, and his eyes lighted.

"Hot dawg!" he whooped. "I got it! Steve, you're a Swede!"

"Listen here, you flat-headed dogfish," I began, in ire, "me and you ain't had a fight in years, but by golly—"

"Aw, try to have some sense," said Bill. "This is the idee: You ain't never fought in Yokohama before. Neimann don't know you, nor anybody else. We'll pass you off for Swede—"

"Pass *him* off for a Swede?" gawped Mushy.

"Well," said Bill, "I'll admit he don't look much like a Swede—"

"*Much* like a Swede!" I gnashed, my indignation mounting. "Why, you son of a—"

"Well, you don't look *nothin'* like a Swede then!" snapped Bill, disgustedly, "but we can pass you off for one. I reckon if we tell 'em you're a Swede, they can't prove you ain't. If they dispute it, we'll knock the daylights outa 'em."

I thought it over.

"Not so bad," I finally decided. "We'll get that hundred extra—and, for a chance to fight somebody, I'd purtend I was a Eskimo. We'll do it."

"Good!" said Bill. "Can you talk Swedish?"

"Sure," I said. "Listen: Yimmy Yackson yumped off the Yacobladder with his monkey-yacket on. Yimminy, what a yump!"

"Purty good," said Bill. "Come on, we'll go down to Neimann's and sign up. Hey, ain't you goin', Mushy?"

"No, I ain't," said Mushy sourly. "I see right now I ain't goin' to enjoy this scrap none. Steve's my shipmate but Hakon's my countryman. Whichever loses, I won't rejoice none. I hope it's a draw. I ain't even goin' to see it."

Well, he went off by hisself, and I said to Bill, "I gotta good mind not to go on with this, since Mushy feels that way about it."

"Aw, he'll get over it," said Bill. "My gosh, Steve, this here's a matter of business. Ain't we all busted? Mushy'll feel all right after we split your purse three ways and he has a few shots of hard licker."

"Well, all right," I said. "Let's get down to Neimann's."

SO ME AND Bill and my white bulldog, Mike, went down to Neimann's, and, as we walked in, Bill hissed, "Don't forget to talk Swedish."

A short, fat man, which I reckoned was Neimann, was setting and looking over a list of names, and now and then he'd take a long pull out of a bottle, and then he'd cuss fit to curl your toes, and pull his hair.

"Well, Neimann," said Bill, cheerfully, "what you doin'?"

"I got a list of all the Swedes in port which think they can fight," said Neimann, bitterly. "They ain't one of 'em would last five seconds against Torkilsen. I'll have to call it off."

"No you won't," said Bill. "Right here I got the fightin'est Swede in the Asiatics!"

Neimann faced around quick to look at me, and his eyes flared, and he jumped up like he'd been stung.

"Get outa here!" he yelped. "You should come around here and mock me in my misery! A sweet time for practical jokes "

"Aw, cool off," said Bill. "I tell you this Swede can lick Hakon Torkilsen with his right thumb in his mouth."

"Swede!" snorted Neimann. "You must think I'm a prize sucker, bringin' this black-headed mick around here and tellin' me—"

"Mick, baloney!" said Bill. "Lookit them blue eyes—"

"I'm lookin' at 'em," snarled Neimann, "and thinkin' of the lakes of Killarney all the time. Swede? Ha! Then so was Jawn L. Sullivan. So you're a Swede, are you?"

"Sure," I said. "Aye bane Swedish, Mister."

"What part of Sweden?" he barked.

"Gotland," I said, and simultaneous Bill said, "Stockholm," and we glared at each other in mutual irritation.

"Cork, you'd better say," sneered Neimann.

"Aye am a Swede," I said, annoyed. "Aye want dass fight."

"Get outa here and quit wastin' my valuable time," snarled Neimann. "If you're a Swede, then I'm a Hindoo Princess!"

At this insulting insinuation I lost my temper. I despises a man that's so suspicious he don't trust his feller men. Grabbing Neimann by the neck with a viselike grip, and waggling a huge fist under his nose, I roared, "You insultin' monkey! Am I a Swede or ain't I?"

He turned pale and shook like an aspirin-leaf.

"You're a Swede," he agreed, weakly.

"And I get the fight?" I rumbled.

"You get it," he agreed, wiping his brow with a bandanner. "The squareheads may stretch my neck for this, but maybe, if you keep your mouth shut, we'll get by. What's your name?"

"Steve—" I began, thoughtlessly, when Bill kicked me on the shin and said, "Lars Ivarson."

"All right," said Neimann, pessimistically, "I'll announce it that I got a man to fight Torkilsen."

"How much do I—how much Aye bane get?" I asked.

"I guaranteed a thousand bucks to the fighters," he said, "to be split seven hundred to the winner and three hundred to the loser."

"Give me das loser's end now," I demanded. "Aye bane go out and bet him, you betcha life."

So he did, and said, "You better keep offa the street; some of your countrymen might ask you about the folks back home in dear old Stockholm." And, with that, he give a bitter screech of raucous and irritating laughter, and slammed the door; and as we left, we heered him moaning like he had the bellyache.

"I don't believe he thinks I'm a Swede," I said, resentfully.

"Who cares?" said Bill. "We got the match. But he's right. I'll go place the bets. You keep outa sight. Long's you don't say much, we're safe. But, if you go wanderin' around, some squarehead'll start talkin' Swedish to you and we'll be sunk."

"All right," I said. "I'll get me a room at the sailor's boardin' house we seen down Manchu Road. I'll stay there till it's time for the scrap."

SO BILL WENT off to lay the bets, and me and Mike went down the back alleys toward the place I mentioned. As we turned out of a side street into Manchu Road, somebody come around the corner moving fast, and fell over Mike, who didn't have time to get outa the way.

The feller scrambled up with a wrathful roar. A big blond bezark he was, and he didn't look like a sailor. He drawed back his foot to kick Mike, as if it was the dog's fault. But I circumvented him by the simple process of kicking him severely on the shin.

"Drop it, cull," I growled, as he begun hopping around, howling wordlessly and holding his shin. "It wasn't Mike's fault, and you hadn't no cause to kick him. Anyhow, he'd of ripped yore laig off if you'd landed—"

Instead of being pacified, he gave a bloodthirsty yell and socked me on the jaw. Seeing he was one of them bull-headed mugs you can't reason with, I banged him once with my right, and left him setting dizzily in the gutter picking imaginary violets.

Proceeding on my way to the seamen's boardin's house, I forgot all about the incident. Such trifles is too common for me to spend much time thinking about. But, as it come out, I had cause to remember it.

I got me a room and stayed there with the door shut till Bill come in, jubilant, and said the crew of the *Sea Girl* hadst sunk all the money it could borrow at heavy odds.

"If you lose," said he, "most of us will go back to the ship wearin' barrels."

"Me lose?" I snorted disgustedly. "Don't be absurd. Where's the Old Man?"

"Aw, I seen him down at that dive of antiquity, the Purple Cat Bar, a while ago," said Bill. "He was purty well lit and havin' some kind of a argyment with old Cap'n Gid Jessup. He'll be at the fight all right. I didn't say nothin' to him; but he'll be there."

"He'll more likely land in jail for fightin' old Gid," I ruminated. "They hate each other like snakes. Well, that's his own lookout. But I'd like him to see me lick Torkilsen. I heered him braggin' about the squarehead the other day. Seems like he seen him fight once some place."

"Well," said Bill, "it's nearly time for the fight. Let's get goin'. We'll go down back alleys and sneak into the arena from the rear, so none of them admirin' Swedes can get ahold of you and find out you're really a American mick. Come on!"

So we done so, accompanied by three Swedes of the *Sea Girl*'s crew who was loyal to their ship and their shipmates. We snuck along alleys and slunk into the back rooms of the arena, where Neimann come in to us, perspiring freely, and told us he was having a heck of a time keeping Swedes outa the dressing-room. He said numbers of 'em wanted to come in and shake hands with Lars Ivarson before he went out to uphold the fair name of Sweden. He said Hakon was getting in the ring, and for us to hustle.

So we went up the aisle hurriedly, and the crowd was so busy cheering for Hakon that they didn't notice us till we was in the ring. I looked out over the house, which was packed, setting and standing, and squareheads fighting to get in when they wasn't room for no more. I never knowed they was that many Scandinavians in Eastern waters. It looked like every man in the house was a Dane, a Norwegian, or a Swede—big, blond fellers, all roaring like bulls in their excitement. It looked like a stormy night.

NEIMANN WAS WALKING around the ring, bowing and grinning, and every now and then his gaze wouldst fall on me as I set in my corner and he wouldst shudder viserbly and wipe his forehead with his bandanner.

Meanwhile, a big Swedish sea captain was acting the part of the announcer, and was making quite a ceremony out of it. He wouldst boom out jovially, and the crowd wouldst roar in various alien tongues, and I told one of the Swedes from the *Sea Girl* to translate for me, which he done so in a whisper, while pertending to tie on my gloves.

This is what the announcer was saying: "Tonight all Scandinavia is represented here in this glorious forthcoming struggle for supremacy. In my mind it brings back days of the Vikings. This is a Scandinavian spectacle for Scandinavian sailors. Every man involved in this contest is Scandinavian. You all know Hakon Torkilsen, the pride of Denmark!" Whereupon, all the Danes in the crowd bellered. "I haven't met Lars Ivarson, but the very fact that he is a son of Sweden assures us that he will prove no mean opponent for Denmark's favored son." It was the Swedes' turn to roar. "I now present the referee, Jon Yarssen, of Norway! This is a family affair. Remember, whichever way the fight goes, it will lend glory to Scandinavia!"

Then he turned and pointed toward the opposite corner and roared, "Hakon Torkilsen, of Denmark!"

Again the Danes thundered to the skies, and Bill O'Brien hissed in my ear. "Don't forget when you're interjuiced say 'Dis bane happiest moment of my life!' The accent will convince 'em you're a Swede."

The announcer turned toward me and, as his eyes fell on me for the first time, he started violently and blinked. Then he kind of mechanically pulled hisself together and stammered, "Lars Ivarson—of—of—Sweden!"

I riz, shedding my bathrobe, and a gasp went up from the crowd like they was thunderstruck or something. For a moment a sickening silence reigned, and then my Swedish shipmates started applauding, and some of the Swedes and Norwegians took it up, and, like people always do, got louder and louder till they was lifting the roof.

Three times I started to make my speech, and three times they drowned me out, till I run outa my short stock of patience.

"Shut up, you lubbers!" I roared, and they lapsed into sudden silence, gaping at me in amazement. With a menacing scowl, I said, "Dis bane happiest moment of my life, by thunder!"

They clapped kind of feebly and dazedly, and the referee motioned us to the center of the ring. And, as we faced each other, I gaped, and he barked, "Aha!" like a hyena which sees some critter caught in a trap. The referee was the big cheese I'd socked in the alley!

I didn't pay much attention to Hakon, but stared morbidly at the referee, which reeled off the instructions in some Scandinavian tongue. Hakon nodded and responded in kind, and the referee glared at me and snapped something and I nodded and grunted, "Ja!" just as if I understood him, and turned back toward my corner.

He stepped after me, and caught hold of my gloves. Under cover of examining 'em he hissed, so low my handlers didn't even hear him, "You are no Swede! I know you. You called your dog 'Mike.' There is only one white bulldog in the Asiatics by that name! You are Steve Costigan, of the *Sea Girl*."

"Keep it quiet," I muttered nervously.

"Ha!" he snarled. "I will have my revenge. Go ahead—fight your fight. After the bout is over, I will expose you as the imposter you are. These men will hang you to the rafters."

"Gee whiz," I mumbled, "what you wanta do that for? Keep my secret and I'll slip you fifty bucks after the scrap."

He merely snorted, "Ha!" in disdain, pointing meaningly at the black eye which I had give him, and stalked back to the center of the ring.

"What did that Norwegian say to you?" Bill O'Brien asked.

I didn't reply. I was kinda wool-gathering. Looking out over the mob, I admit I didn't like the prospects. I hadst no doubt that them infuriated squareheads would be maddened at the knowledge that a alien had passed hisself off as one of 'em—and they's a limit to the numbers that even Steve Costigan can vanquish in mortal combat! But about that time the gong sounded, and I forgot everything except the battle before me.

FOR THE FIRST time I noticed Hakon Torkilsen, and I realized why he had such a reputation. He was a regular panther of a man—a tall, rangy, beautifully built young slugger with a mane of yellow hair and cold, steely eyes. He was six feet one to my six feet, and weighed 185 to my 190. He was trained to the ounce, and his long, smooth muscles rippled under his white skin as he moved. My black mane musta contrasted strongly with his golden hair.

He come in fast and ripped a left hook to my head, whilst I come back with a right to the body which brung him up standing. But his body muscles was like iron ridges, and I knowed it wouldst take plenty of pounding to soften him there, even though it was me doing the pounding.

Hakon was a sharpshooter, and he begunst to shoot his left straight and fast. All my opponents does, at first, thinking I'm a sucker for a left jab. But they soon abandons that form of attack. I ignores left jabs. I now walked through a perfect hail of 'em and crashed a thundering right under Hakon's heart which brung a astonished grunt outa him. Discarding his jabbing offensive, he started flailing away with both hands, and I wanta tell you he wasn't throwing no powder-puffs!

It was the kind of scrapping I like. He was standing up to me, giving and taking, and I wasn't called on to run him around the ring like I gotta do with so many of my foes. He was belting me plenty, but that's my style, and, with a wide grin, I slugged merrily at his body and head, and the gong found us in the center of the ring, banging away.

The crowd give us a roaring cheer as we went back to our corners, but suddenly my grin was wiped off by the sight of Yarssen, the referee, cryptically indicating his black eye as he glared morbidly at me.

I determined to finish Torkilsen as quick as possible, make a bold break through the crowd, and try to get away before Yarssen had time to tell 'em my fatal secret. Just as I started to tell Bill, I felt a hand jerking at my ankle. I looked down into the bewhiskered, bewildered and bleary-eyed face of the Old Man.

"Steve!" he squawked. "I'm in a terrible jam!"

Bill O'Brien jumped like he was stabbed. "Don't yell 'Steve' thataway!" he hissed. "You wanta get us all mobbed?"

"I'm in a terrible jam!" wailed the Old Man, wringing his hands. "If you don't help me, I'm a rooined man!"

"What's the lay?" I asked in amazement, leaning through the ropes.

"It's Gid Jessup's fault," he moaned. "The serpent got me into a argyment and got me drunk. He knows I ain't got no sense when I'm soused. He hornswoggled me into laying a bet on Torkilsen. I didn't know you was goin' to fight—"

"Well," I said, "that's tough, but you'll just have to lose the bet."

"I can't!" he howled.

Bong! went the gong, and I shot outa my corner as Hakon ripped outa his.

"I can't lose!" the Old Man howled above the crowd. *"I bet the Sea Girl!"*

"What!" I roared, momentarily forgetting where I was, and half-turning toward the ropes. *Bang!* Hakon nearly tore my head off with a free-swinging right. Bellering angrily, I come back with a smash to the mush that started the claret, and we went into a slug-fest, flailing free and generous with both hands.

That Dane was tough! Smacks that would of staggered most men didn't make him wince. He come ploughing in for more. But, just before the gong, I caught him off balance with a blazing left hook that knocked him into the ropes, and the Swedes arose, whooping like lions.

BACK ON MY stool I peered through the ropes. The Old Man was dancing a hornpipe.

"What's this about bettin' the *Sea Girl*?" I demanded.

"When I come to myself a while ago, I found I'd wagered the ship," he wept, "against Jessup's lousy tub, the *Nigger King,* which I find is been condemned by the shippin' board and wouldn't clear the bay without goin' to the bottom. He took a unfair advantage of me! I wasn't responsible when I made that bet!"

"Don't pay it," I growled, "Jessup's a rat!"

"He showed me a paper I signed while stewed," he groaned. "It's a contrack upholdin' the bet. If it weren't for that, I wouldn't pay. But if I don't, he'll rooin my reputation in every port of the seven seas. He'll show that contrack and gimme the name of a welsher. You got to lose!"

"Gee whiz!" I said, badgered beyond endurance. "This is a purty mess—"

Bong! went the gong, and I paced out into the ring, all upset and with my mind elsewhere. Hakon swarmed all over me, and drove me into the ropes, where I woke up and beat him off, but, with the Old Man's howls echoing in my ears, I failed to follow up my advantage, and Hakon come back strong.

The Danes raised the roof as he battered me about the ring, but he wasn't hurting me none, because I covered up, and again, just before the gong, I snapped outa my crouch and sent him back on his heels with a wicked left hook to the head.

The referee gimme a gloating look, and pointed at his black eye, and I had to grit my teeth to keep from socking him stiff. I set down on my stool and listened gloomily to the shrieks of the Old Man, which was getting more unbearable every minute.

"You got to lose!" he howled. "If Torkilsen don't win this fight, I'm rooined! If the bet'd been on the level, I'd pay—you know that. But, I been swindled, and now I'm goin' to get robbed! Lookit the rat over there, wavin' that devilish paper at me! It's more'n human flesh and blood can stand! It's enough to drive a man to drink! You *got* to lose!"

"But the boys has bet their shirts on me," I snarled, fit to be tied with worry and bewilderment. "I can't lay down! I never throwed a fight. I don't know how—"

"That's gratitood!" he screamed, busting into tears. "After all I've did for you! Little did I know I was warmin' a serpent in my bosom! The poorhouse is starin' me in the face, and you—"

"Aw, shut up, you old sea horse!" said Bill. "Steve—I mean Lars—has got enough to contend with without you howlin' and yellin' like a maneyack. Them squareheads is gonna get suspicious if you and him keep talkin' in English. Don't pay no attention to him, Steve—I mean Lars. Get that Dane!"

Well, the gong sounded, and I went out all tore up in my mind and having just about lost heart in the fight. That's a most dangerous thing to have happen, especially against a man-killing slugger like Hakon Torkilsen. Before I knowed what was goin' on, the Swedes rose with a scream of warning and about a million stars bust in my head. I realized faintly that I was on the canvas, and I listened for the count to know how long I had to rest.

I heered a voice droning above the roar of the fans, but it was plumb meaningless to me. I shook my head, and my sight cleared. Jon Yarssen was standing over me, his arm going up and down, but I didn't understand a word he said! He was counting in Swedish!

Not daring to risk a moment, I heaved up before my head had really quit singing an' Hakon come storming in like a typhoon to finish me.

But I was mad clean through and had plumb forgot about the Old Man and his fool bet. I met Hakon with a left hook which nearly tore his head off, and the Swedes yelped with joy. I bored in, ripping both hands to the wind and heart, and, in a fast mix-up at close quarters, Hakon went down—more from a slip than a punch. But he was wise and took a count, resting on one knee.

I watched the referee's arm so as to familiarize myself with the sound of the numerals—but he wasn't counting in the same langwidge as he had over me! I got it, then; he counted over me in Swedish and over Hakon in Danish. The langwidges is alike in many ways, but different enough to get me all mixed up, which didn't know a word in either tongue, anyhow. I seen then that I was going to have a enjoyable evening.

Hakon was up at nine—I counted the waves of the referee's arm—and he come up at me like a house afire. I fought him off half-heartedly, whilst the Swedes shouted with amazement at the change which had come over me since that blazing first round.

Well, I've said repeatedly that a man can't fight his best when he's got his mind on something else. Here was a nice mess for me to worry about. If I quit, I'd be a yeller dog and despize myself for the rest of my life, and my shipmates would lose their money, and so would all the Swedes which had bet on me and was now yelling and cheering for me just like I was their brother. I couldn't throw 'em down. Yet if I won, the Old Man would lose his ship, which was all he had and like a daughter to him. It wouldst beggar him and break his heart. And, as a minor thought, whether I won or lost, that scut Yarssen was going to tell the crowd I wasn't no Swede, and get me mobbed. Every time I looked at him over Hakon's shoulder in a clinch, Yarssen wouldst touch his black eye meaningly. I was bogged down in gloom, and I wished I could evaporate or something.

Back on my stool, between rounds, the Old Man wept and begged me to lay down, and Bill and my handlers implored me to wake up and kill Torkilsen, and I thought I'd go nuts.

I WENT OUT for the fourth round slowly, and Hakon, evidently thinking I'd lost my fighting heart, if any, come with his usual tigerish rush and biffed me three times in the face without a return.

I dragged him into a grizzly-like clinch which he couldn't break, and as we rassled and strained, he spat something at me which I couldn't understand, but I understood the tone of it. He was calling me yellow! Me, Steve Costigan, the terror of the high seas!

With a maddened roar, I jerked away from him and crashed a murderous right to his jaw that nearly floored him. Before he couldst recover his balance, I tore into him like a wild man, forgetting everything except that I was Steve Costigan, the bully of the toughest ship afloat.

Slugging right and left, I rushed him into the ropes, where I pinned him, while the crowd went crazy. He crouched and covered up, taking most of my punches on the gloves and elbows, but I reckoned it looked to the mob like I was beating him to death. All at once, above the roar, I heered the Old Man screaming, "Steve, for cats' sake, let up! I'll go on the beach, and it'll be your fault!"

That unnerved me. I involuntarily dropped my hands and recoiled, and Hakon, with fire in his eyes, lunged outa his crouch like a tiger and crashed his right to my jaw.

Bang! I was on the canvas again, and the referee was droning Swedish numerals over me. Not daring to take a count, and maybe get counted out unknowingly, I staggered up, and Hakon come lashing in. I throwed my arms around him in a grizzly hug, and it took him and the referee both to break my hold.

Hakon drove me staggering into the ropes with a wild-man attack, but I'm always dangerous on the ropes, as many a good man has found out on coming to in his dressing room. As I felt the rough strands against my back, I caught him with a slung-shot right uppercut which snapped his head right back betwixt his shoulders, and this time it was him which fell into a clinch and hung on.

Looking over his shoulder at that sea of bristling blond heads and yelling faces, I seen various familiar figgers. On one side of the ring—near my corner—the Old Man was dancing around like he was on a red-hot hatch, shedding maudlin tears and pulling his whiskers; and, on the other side, a skinny, shifty-eyed old seaman was whooping with glee and waving a folded paper. Cap'n Gid Jessup, the old cuss! He knowed the Old Man would bet anything when he was drunk—even bet the *Sea Girl,* as sweet a ship as ever rounded the Horn, against that rotten old hulk of a *Nigger King,* which wasn't worth a cent a ton. And, near at hand, the referee, Yarssen, was whispering tenderly in my ear, as he broke our clinch, "Better let Hakon knock you stiff—then you won't feel so much what the crowd does to you when I tell them who you are!"

Back on my stool again, I put my face on Mike's neck and refused to listen either to the pleas of the Old Man or to the profane shrieks of Bill O'Brien. By golly, that fight was like a nightmare! I almost hoped Hakon would knock my brains out and end all my troubles.

I went out for the fifth like a man going to his own hanging. Hakon was evidently puzzled. Who wouldn't of been? Here was a fighter—me—who was performing in spurts, exploding in bursts of ferocious battling just when he appeared nearly out, and sagging half heartedly when he looked like a winner.

He come in, lashed a vicious left to my mid-section, and dashed me to the canvas with a thundering overhand right. Maddened, I arose and dropped him with a wild round-house swing he wasn't expecting. Again the crowd surged to its feet, and the referee got flustered and started counting over Hakon in what sounded like Swedish.

Hakon bounded up and slugged me into the ropes, offa which I floundered, only to slip in a smear of my own blood on the canvas, and again, to the disgust of the Swedes, I found myself among the resin.

I looked about, heard the Old Man yelling for me to stay down, and saw Old Cap'n Jessup waving his blame-fool contrack. I arose, only half aware of what I was doing, and *bang!* Hakon caught me on the ear with a hurricane swing, and I sprawled on the floor, half under the ropes.

Goggling dizzily at the crowd from this position, I found myself staring into the distended eyes of Cap'n Gid Jessup, which was standing up, almost touching the ring. Evidently froze at the thought of losing his bet—with me on the canvas—he was standing there gaping, his arm still lifted with the contrack which he'd been waving at the Old Man.

With me, thinking is acting. One swoop of my gloved paw swept that contrack outa his hand. He yawped with suprise and come lunging half through the ropes. I rolled away from him, sticking the contrack in my mouth and chawing as fast as I could. Cap'n Jessup grabbed me by the hair with one hand and tried to jerk the contrack outa my jaws with the other'n, but all he got was a severely bit finger.

At this, he let go of me and begun to scream and yell. "Gimme back that paper, you cannibal! He's eatin' my contrack! I'll sue you—!"

MEANWHILE, THE DUMBFOUNDED referee, overcome with amazement, had stopped counting, and the crowd, not understanding this by-play, was roaring with astonishment. Jessup begun to crawl through the ropes, and Yarssen yelled something and shoved him back with his foot. He started through again, yelling blue murder, and a big Swede, evidently thinking he was trying to attack me, swung once with a fist the size of a caulking mallet, and Cap'n Jessup bit the dust.

I arose with my mouth full of paper, and Hakon promptly banged me on the chin with a right he started from his heels. Ow, Jerusha! Wait'll somebody hits you on the jaw when you're chawing something! I thought for a second every tooth in my head was shattered, along with my jaw-bone. But I reeled groggily back into the ropes and begun to swaller hurriedly.

Bang! Hakon whanged me on the ear. "Gulp!" I said. *Wham!* He socked me in the eye. "Gullup!" I said. *Blop!* He pasted me in the stummick. "Oof—glup!" I said. *Whang!* He took me on the side of the head. "*Gulp!*" I swallered the last of the contrack, and went for that Dane with fire in my eyes.

I banged Hakon with a left that sunk outa sight in his belly, and nearly tore his head off with a paralyzing right before he realized that, instead of being ready for the cleaners, I was stronger'n ever and ra'ring for action.

Nothing loath, he rallied, and we went into a whirlwind of hooks and swings till the world spun like a merry-go-round. Neither of us heered the gong, and our seconds had to drag us apart and lead us to our corners.

"Steve," the Old Man was jerking at my leg and weeping with gratitude, "I seen it all! That old pole-cat's got no hold on me now. He can't prove I ever made that fool bet. You're a scholar and a gent—one of nature's own noblemen! You've saved the *Sea Girl*!"

"Let that be a lesson to you," I said, spitting out a fragment of the contrack along with a mouthful of blood. "Gamblin' is sinful. Bill, I got a watch in my pants pocket. Get it and bet it that I lay this squarehead within three more rounds."

And I come out for the sixth like a typhoon. "I'm going to get mobbed by the fans as soon as the fight's over and Yarssen spills the beans," I thought, "but I'll have my fun now."

For once I'd met a man which was willing and able to stand up and slug it out with me. Hakon was as lithe as a panther and as tough as spring-steel. He was quicker'n me, and hit nearly as hard. We crashed together in the center of the ring, throwing all we had into the storm of battle.

Through a red mist I seen Hakon's eyes blazing with a unearthly light. He was plumb berserk, like them old Vikings which was his ancestors. And all the Irish fighting madness took hold of me, and we ripped and tore like tigers.

We was the center of a frenzied whirlwind of gloves, ripping smashes to each other's bodies which you could hear all over the house, and socks to each other's heads that spattered blood all over the ring. Every blow packed dynamite and had the killer's lust behind it. It was a test of endurance.

At the gong, we had to be tore apart and dragged to our corners by force, and, at the beginning of the next round, we started in where we'd left off. We reeled in a blinding hurricane of gloves. We slipped in smears of blood, or was knocked to the canvas by each other's thundering blows.

The crowd was limp and idiotic, drooling wordless screeches. And the referee was bewildered and muddled. He counted over us in Swedish, Danish and Norwegian alike. Then I was on the canvas, and Hakon was staggering on the ropes, gasping, and the befuddled Yarssen was counting over me. And, in the dizzy maze, I recognized the langwidge. He was counting in Spanish!

"You ain't no Norwegian!" I said, glaring groggily up at him.

"Four!" he said, shifting into English. "—As much as you're a Swede! Five! A man's got to eat. Six! They wouldn't have given me this job—seven!—if I hadn't pretended to be a Norwegian. Eight! I'm John Jones, a vaudeville linguist from Frisco. Nine! Keep my secret and I'll keep yours."

THE GONG! OUR handlers dragged us off to our corners and worked over us. I looked over at Hakon. I was marked plenty—a split ear, smashed lips, both eyes half closed, nose broken—but them's my usual adornments. Hakon wasn't marked up so much in the face—outside of a closed eye and a few gashes—but his body was raw beef from my continuous body hammering. I drawed a deep breath and grinned gargoylishly. With the Old Man and that fake referee offa my mind, I couldst give all my thoughts to the battle.

The gong banged again, and I charged like a enraged bull. Hakon met me as usual, and rocked me with thundering lefts and rights. But I bored in, driving him steadily before me with ripping, bone-shattering hooks to the body and head. I felt him slowing up. The man don't live which can slug with me!

Like a tiger scenting the kill, I redoubled the fury of my onslaught, and the crowd arose, roaring, as they foresaw the end. Nearly on the ropes, Hakon rallied with a dying burst of ferocity, and momentarily had me reeling under a fusillade of desperate swings. But I shook my head doggedly and plowed in under his barrage, ripping my terrible right under his heart again and again, and tearing at his head with mallet-like left hooks.

Flesh and blood couldn't stand it. Hakon crumpled in a neutral corner under a blasting fire of left and right hooks. He tried to get his legs under him, but a child couldst see he was done.

The referee hesitated, then raised my right glove, and the Swedes and Norwegians came roaring into the ring and swept me offa my feet. A glance showed Hakon's Danes carrying him to his corner, and I tried to get to him to shake his hand, and tell him he was as brave and fine a fighter as I ever met—which was the truth and nothing else—but my delirious followers hadst boosted both me and Mike on their shoulders and were carrying us toward the dressing-room like a king or something.

A tall form come surging through the crowd, and Mushy Hansen grabbed my gloved hand and yelled, "Boy, you done us proud! I'm sorry the Danes had to lose, but, after a battle like that, I can't hold no grudge. I couldn't stay away from the scrap. Hooray for the old *Sea Girl,* the fightin'est ship on the seven seas!"

And the Swedish captain, which had acted as announcer, barged in front of me and yelled in English, "You may be a Swede, but if you are, you're the most unusual looking Swede I ever saw. But I don't give a whoop! I've just seen the greatest battle since Gustavus Adolphus licked the Dutch! Skoal, Lars Ivarson!"

And all the Swedes and Norwegians thundered, *"Skoal, Lars Iverson!"*

"They want you to make a speech," said Mushy.

"All right," I said. "Dis bane happiest moment of my life!"

"Louder," said Mushy. "They're makin' so much noise they can't understand you, anyhow. Say somethin' in a foreign langwidge."

"All right," I said, and yelled the only foreign words I couldst think of, *"Parleyvoo Francais! Vive le Stockholm! Erin go bragh!"*

And they bellered louder'n ever. A fighting man is a fighting man in any langwidge!

NIGHT OF BATTLE

By R. E. HOWARD

Singapore . . . slinking shapes . . . villainous plans afoot . . . and through the menacing waterfront shadows the roaring, roistering figures of Steve Costigan and Black Jack O'Brien, bent on a leather-pusher's holiday . . .

NIGHT OF BATTLE

I'M BEGINNING TO believe that Singapore is a jinx for me. Not that I don't always get a fight there; I do. But it looks, by golly, like a lot of dirty luck is always throwed in with the fight.

Rumination of them sort was in my mind as I clumb the rickety stairs of the Seaman's Deluxe Boarding House and entered my room, tightly gripping the fifty bucks which constituted my whole wad.

I'd just been down to see Ace Larnigan, manager of the Arena, and had got matched with Black Jack O'Brien for ten rounds or less, that night. And I was wondering where I could hide my roll. I had the choice of taking it with me and getting it stole outa my britches whilst I was in the ring, or leaving it in my room and getting it hooked by the Chino servants from which you couldn't hide nothing.

I set on my ramshackle bed and meditated, and I had about decided to let my white bulldog, Mike, hold the roll in his mouth while I polished off Black Jack, with a good chance of him swallering it in his excitement, when all of sudden I heered sounds of somebody ascending the stairs about six steps at a jump, and then running wildly down the hall.

I paid no heed; guests of the Deluxe is always being chased into the dump or out of it by the cops. But instead of running into his own room and hiding under the bed, as was the usual custom, this particular fugitive blundered headlong against my door, blowing and gasping like a grampus. Much to my annoyance, the door was knocked violently open, and a disheveled shape fell all over the floor.

I riz with dignity. "What kind of a game is this?" I asked, with my instinctive courtesy. "Will you get outa my room or will I throw you out on your ear?"

"Hide me, Steve!" the shape gasped. "Shut the door! Hide me! Give me a gun! Call the cops! Lemme under the bed! Look out the window and see if you see anybody chasing me!"

"Make up your mind what you want me to do; I ain't no magician," I said disgustedly, recognizing the shape as Johnny Kyelan, a good-hearted but soft-headed sap of a kid which should of been jerking soda back home instead of trying to tend bar in a tough waterfront joint in Singapore. Just one of them fool kids which is trying to see the world.

He grabbed me with hands that shook, and I seen the sweat standing out on his face.

"You got to help me, Steve!" he babbled. "I came here because I didn't know anybody else to go to. If you don't help me, I'll never live to see another sunrise. I've stumbled onto something I wasn't looking for. Something that it's certain death to know about. Steve, I've found out who The Black Mandarin is!"

I grunted. This is serious.

"You mean you know who it is that's been committin' all these robberies and murders, dressed up in a mask and Chinee clothes?"

"The same!" he exclaimed, trembling and sweating. "The worst criminal in the Orient!"

"Then why in heck don't you go to the police?" I demanded.

He shook like he had aggers. "I don't dare! I'd never live to get to the police station. They're watching for me—it isn't one man who's been doing all these crimes; it's a criminal organization. One man is the head, but he has a big gang. They all dress the same way when they're robbing and looting."

"How'd you get onto this?" I asked.

"I was tending bar," he shuddered. "I went into the cellar to get some wine—it's very seldom I go there. By pure chance, I came onto a group of them plotting over a table by a candle-light. I recognized them and heard them talking—the fellow who owns the saloon where I work is one of them—and I never had an inkling he was a crook. I was behind a stack of wine-kegs, and listened till I got panicky and made a break. Then they saw me. They chased me in and out among those winding alleys till I thought I'd die. I shook them off just a few minutes ago, and reached here. But I don't dare stir out. I don't think they saw me coming in, but they're combing the streets, and they'd see me going out."

"Who is the leader?" I asked.

"They call him the Chief," he said.

"Yeah, but who is he?" I persisted, but he just shook that much more.

"I don't dare tell." His teeth was chattering with terror. "Somebody might be listening."

"Well, gee whiz," I said, "you're in bad with 'em already—"

But he was in one of them onreasoning fears, and wouldn't tell me nothing.

"You'd never in the world guess," he said. "And I just don't dare. I get goose-pimples all over when I think about it. Let me stay with you till tomorrow morning, Steve," he begged, "then we'll get in touch with Sir Peter Brent, the Scotland Yard guy. He's the only man of authority I trust. The police have proven themselves helpless—nobody ever recognized one of that Mandarin gang and lived to tell about it. But Sir Peter will protect me and trap these fiends."

"Well," I said, "why can't we get him now?"

"I don't know where to reach him," said Johnny. "He's somewhere in Singapore—I don't know where. But in the morning we can get him at his club; he's always there early in the morning. For heavens' sake, Steve, let me stay!"

"Sure, kid," I said. "Don't be scairt. If any them Black Mandarins comes buttin' in here, I'll bust 'em on the snoot. I was goin' to fight Black Jack O'Brien down at the Arena tonight, but I'll call it off and stick around with you."

"No, don't do that," he said, beginning to get back a little of his nerve. "I'll lock the door and stay here. I don't think they know where I am; and, anyway, with the door locked they can't get in to me without making a noise that would arouse the whole house. You go ahead and fight Black Jack. If you didn't show up, some of that gang might guess you were with me; they're men who know us both. Then that would get you into trouble. They know you're the only friend I've got."

"Well," I said, "I'll leave Mike here to purteck you."

"No! No!" he said. "That'd look just as suspicious, if you showed up without Mike. Besides, they'd only shoot him if they came. You go on, and, when you come back, knock on the door and tell me who it is. I'll know your voice and let you in."

"Well, all right," I said, "if you think you'll be safe. I don't think them Mandarins would have sense enough to figger out you was with me, just because I didn't happen to show up at the Arena—but maybe you know. And say, you keep this fifty bucks for me. I was wonderin' what to do with it. If I take it to the Arena, some dip will lift it offa me."

So Johnny took it, and me and Mike started for the Arena, and, as we went down the stairs, I heered him lock the door behind us. As I left the Deluxe, I looked sharp for any slinking figgers hanging around watching the house, but didn't see none, and went on down the street.

THE ARENA WAS just off the waterfront, and it was crowded like it always is when either me or Black Jack fights. Ace had been wanting to get us together for a long time, but this was the first time we happened to be in port at the same time. I was in my dressing-room putting on my togs when in stormed a figger I knowed must be my opponent. I've heered it said me and Black Jack looked enough alike to be brothers; he was my height, six feet, weighed same as me, and had black hair amd smoldering blue eyes. But I always figgered I was better looking than him.

I seen he was in a wicked mood, and I knowed his recent fight with Bad Bill Kearney was still rankling him. Bad Bill was a hard-boiled egg which run a gambling hall in the toughest waterfront district of Singapore and fought on the side. A few weeks before, him and O'Brien had staged a most vicious battle in the Arena, and Black Jack had been knocked cold in the fifth round, just when it looked like he was winning. It was the only time he'd ever been stopped, and, ever since, he'd been frothing at the mouth and trying to get Bad Bill back in the ring with him.

He give a snarling, blood-thirsty laugh as he seen me.

"Well, Costigan," he said, "I guess maybe you think you're man enough to stow me away tonight, eh? You slant-headed goriller!"

"I may not lick you, you black-jowled baboon," I roared, suspecting a hint of insult in his manner, "but I'll give you a tussle your great-grandchildren will shudder to hear about!"

"How strong do you believe that?" he frothed.

"Strong enough to kick your brains out here and now," I thundered.

Ace got in between us.

"Hold it!" he requested. "I ain't goin' to have you boneheads rooin'in' my show by massacreein' each other before the fight starts."

"What you got there?" asked O'Brien,suspiciously, as Ace dug into his pockets.

"Your dough," said Ace sourly, bringing out a roll of bills. "I guaranteed you each fifty bucks, win, lose or draw."

"Well," I said, "we don't want it now. Give it to us after the mill."

"Ha!" sneered Ace. "Keep it and get my pockets picked? Not me! I'm givin' it to you now. You two can take the responsibility. Here—take it! Now I've paid you, and you got no kick comin' at me if you lose it. If the dips get it offa you, that ain't my lookout."

"All right, you white-livered land-shark," sneered Black Jack, and turned to me. "Costigan, this fifty says I lays you like a carpet."

"I takes you!" I barked. "My fifty says you leaves that ring on a shutter. Who holds stakes?"

"Not me," said Ace, hurriedly.

"Don't worry," snapped Black Jack, "I wouldn't trust a nickel of my dough in your greasy fingers. Not a nickel. Hey Bunger!"

At the yell, in come a bewhiskered old wharf-rat which exuded a strong smell of trader's rum.

"What you want?" he said. "Buy me a drink, Black Jack."

"I'll buy you a raft of drinks later," growled O'Brien. "Here, hold these stakes, and if you let a dip get 'em, I'll pull out all your whiskers by the roots."

"They won't get it offa me," promised old Bunger. "I know the game, you bet."

Which he did, having been a dip hisself in his youth; but he had one virtue—when he was sober, he was as honest as the day is long with them he considered his friends. So he took the two fifties, and me and O'Brien, after a few more mutual insults, slung on our bathrobes and strode up the aisle, to the applause of the multitude, which cheered a long-looked-for melee.

The *Sea Girl* wasn't in port—in fact, I'd come to Singapore to meet her, as she was due in a few days. So, as they was none of my crew to second me, Ace had provided a couple of dumb clucks.

He'd also give Black Jack a pair of saps, as O'Brien's ship, the *Watersnake,* wasn't in port either.

THE GONG WHANGED, the crowd roared, and the dance commenced. We was even matched. We was both as tough as nails, and aggressive. What we lacked in boxing skill, we made up for by sheer ferocity. The Arena never seen a more furious display of hurricane battling and pile-driving punching; it left the crowd as limp as a rag and yammering gibberish.

At the tap of each gong we just rushed at each other and started slugging. We traded punches 'til everything was red and hazy. We stood head to head and battered away, then we leaned on each other's chest and kept hammering, and then we kept our feet by each resting his chin on the other's shoulder, and driving away with short-arm jolts to the body. We slugged 'til we was both blind and deaf and dizzy, and kept on battering away, gasping and drooling curses and weeping with sheer fighting madness.

At the end of each round our handlers would pull us apart and guide us to our corners, where they wouldst sponge off the blood and sweat and tears, and douse us with ice-water, and give us sniffs of ammonia, whilst the crowd watched, breathless, afeared neither of us would be able to come up for the next round. But with the marvelous recuperating ability of the natural-born slugger, we would both revive under the treatments, and stiffen on our stool, glaring red-eyed at each other, and, with the tap of the gong, it would begin all over again. Boy, that was a scrap, I'm here to tell you!

Time and again either him or me would be staggering on the ragged edge of a knockout, but would suddenly rally in a ferocious burst of battling which had the crowd delirious. In the eighth he put me on the canvas with a left hook that nearly tore my head off, and the crowd riz, screaming. But at "eight" I come up, reeling, and dropped him with a right hook under the heart that nearly cracked his ribs. He lurched up just before the fatal "ten," and the gong sounded.

The end of the ninth found us both on the canvas, but ten rounds was just too short a time for either of us to weaken sufficient for a knockout. But I believe, if it had gone five more rounds, half the crowd would of dropped dead. The finish found most of 'em feebly flapping their hands and croaking like frogs. At the final gong we was standing head to head in the middle of the ring, trading smashes you couldst hear all over the house, and the referee pulled us apart by main strength and lifted both our hands as an indication that the fight was a draw.

* * *

DRAWING ON HIS bathrobe, Black Jack come over to my corner, spitting out blood and the fragments of a tooth, and he said, grinning like a hyena, "Well, you owe me fifty bucks which you bet on lickin' me."

"And, by the same token, you owe me fifty," I retorted. "your bet was you'd flatten me. By golly, I don't know when I ever enjoyed a scrap more! I don't see how Bad Bill licked you."

O'Brien's face darkened like a thunder-cloud.

"Don't mention that egg to me," he snapped. "I can't figger it out myself. You hit me tonight a lot harder'n he ever did. I'd just battered him clean across the ring, and he was reelin' and rockin'—then it happened. All I know is that he fell into me, and we in a sort of half-clinch—then *bing!* The next thing I knowed, they was pourin' water on me in my dressin'-room. They said he socked me on the jaw as we broke, but I never seen the punch—or felt it."

"Well," I said, "forget it. Let's get our dough from old Bunger and go get a drink. Then I gotta go back to my room."

"What you turnin' in so soon for?" he scowled. "The night's young. Let's see if we can't shake up some fun. They's a couple of tough bouncers down at Yota Lao's I been layin' off to lick a long time—"

"Naw," I said, "I got business at the Deluxe. But we'll have a drink, first."

So we looked around for Bunger, and he wasn't nowhere to be seen. We went back to our dressing-rooms, and he wasn't there either.

"Now, where is the old mutt?" inquired Black Jack, fretfully. "Here's us famishin' with thirst, and that old wharf-rat—"

"If you mean old Bunger," said a lounger, "I seen him scoot along about the fifth round."

"Say," I said, as a sudden suspicion struck me, "was he drunk?"

"If he was, I couldn't tell it," said Black Jack.

"Well," I said, "I thought he smelt of licker."

"He always smells of licker," answered O'Brien, impatiently. "I defies any man to always know whether the old soak's drunk or sober. He don't ack no different when he's full, except you can't trust him with dough."

"Well," I growled, "he's gone, and likely he's blowed in all our money already. Come on; let's go hunt for him."

So we donned our street clothes, and went forth. Our mutual battering hadn't affected our remarkable vitalities none, though we both had black eyes and plenteous cuts and bruises. We went down the street and glanced in the dives, but we didn't see Bunger, and purty soon we was in the vicinity of the Deluxe.

"Come on up to my room," I said. "I got fifty bucks there. We'll get it and buy us a drink. And listen, Johnny Kyelan's up there, but you keep your trap shut about it, see?"

"Okay," he said. "If Johnny's in a jam, I ain't the man to blab on him. He ain't got no sense, but he's a good kid."

SO WE WENT up to my room; everybody in the house was either asleep or had gone out some place. I knocked cautious, and said, "Open up, kid; it's me, Costigan."

They wasn't no reply. I rattled the knob impatiently and discovered the door wasn't locked. I flang it open, expecting to find anything. The room was dark, and, I switched on the light. Johnny wasn't nowhere to be seen. The room wasn't mussed up nor nothing, and though Mike kept growling deep down in his throat, I couldn't find a sign of anything suspicious. All I found was a note on the table. I picked it up and read, "Thanks for the fifty, sucker! Johnny."

"Well, of all the dirty deals!" I snarled. "I took him in and perteckted him, and he does me outa my wad!"

"Lemme see that note," said Black Jack, and read it and shook his head. "I don't believe this here's Johnny's writin'," he said.

"Sure it is," I snorted, because I was hurt deep. It's bad to lose your dough; but it's a sight worse to find out that somebody you thought was your friend is nothing but a cheap crook. I ain't never seen any of his writin' before, but who else would of writ it? Nobody but him knowed about my wad. Black Mandarins my eye!"

"Huh?" Black Jack looked up quick, his eyes glittering; that phrase brung interest to anybody in Singapore. So I told him all about what Johnny had told me, adding disgustedly, "I reckon I been took for a sucker again. I bet the little rat had got into a jam with the cops, and he just seen a chance to do me out of my wad. He's skipped; if anybody'd got him, the door would be busted, and somebody in the house would of heered it. Anyway, the note wouldn't of been here. Dawggonit, I never thought Johnny was that kind."

"Me neither," said Black Jack, shaking his head, "and you don't figger he ever saw them Black Mandarins."

I don't figger they is any Black Mandarins," I snorted, fretfully.

"That's where you're wrong," said O'Brien. "Plenty of people has seen 'em—and others saw 'em and didn't live to tell who they was. I said all the time it was more'n any one man which was doin' all these crimes. I thought it was a gang—"

"Aw, ferget it," I said. "Come on. Johnny's stole my wad, and old Bunger has gypped the both of us. I'm a man of action. I'm goin' to find the old buzzard if I have to take Singapore apart."

"I'm with you," said Black Jack, so we went out into the street and started hunting old Bunger, and, after about a hour of snooping into low-class dives, we got wind of him.

"Bunger?" said a bartender, twisting his flowing black mustaches. "Yeah, he was here earlier in the evenin'. He had a drink and said he was goin' to Kerney's Temple of Chance. He said he felt lucky."

"Lucky?" gnashed Black Jack. "He'll feel sore when I get through kickin' his britches up around his neck. Come on, Steve. I oughta thought about that before. When he's lit, he always thinks he can beat that roulette wheel at Kerney's."

SO WE WENT into the mazes of the waterfront till we come to Kerney's Temple, which was as little like a temple as a critter couldst imagine. It was kinda underground, and, to get to it, you went down a flight of steps from the street.

We went in, and seen a number of tough-looking eggs playing the various games or drinking at the bar. I seen Smoky Rourke, Wolf McGernan, Red Elkins, Shifty Brelen, John Lynch, and I don't know how many more—all shady characters. But the hardest looking one of 'em was Bad Bill hisself—one of these square-set, cold-eyed thugs which sports flashy clothes, like a gorilla in glad rags. He had a thin, sneering gash of a mouth, and his big, square, hairy hands glittered with diamonds. At the sight of his enemy, Black Jack growled deep in his throat and quivered with rage.

Then we seen old Bunger, leaning disconsolately against the bar, watching the clicking roulette wheel. Toward him we strode with a beller of rage, and he started to run, but seen he couldn't get away.

"You old mud-turtle!" yelled Black Jack. "Where's our dough?"

"Boys," quavered old Bunger, lifting a trembling hand, "don't jedge me too harsh! I ain't spent a cent of that jack."

"All right," said Black Jack, with a sigh of relief. "Give it to us."

"I can't," he sniffled, beginning to cry. "I lost it all on this here roulette wheel!"

"What!" our maddened beller made the lights flicker.

"It was this way, boys," he whimpered. "Whilst I was watchin' you boys fight, I seen a dime somebody'd dropped on the floor, and I grabbed it. And I thought I'd just slip out and get me a drink and be back before the scrap was over. Well, I got me the drink, and that was a mistake. I'd already had a few, and this'n kinda tipped me over the line. When I got some licker in me, I always get the gamblin' craze. To-night I felt onusual lucky, and I got the idea in my head that I'd beat it down to Kerney's, double or triple this roll, and be that much ahead. You boys would get back your dough, and I'd be in the money, too. It looked like a great idea, then. And I was lucky for a while, if I'd just knowed when to quit. Once I was a hundred and forty-five dollars ahead, but the tide turned, and, before I knowed it, I was cleaned."

"Dash-blank-the-blank-dash!" said Black Jack, appropriately.

"This here's a sweet lay! I oughta kick you in the pants, you white-whiskered old mutt!"

"Aw," I said, "I wouldn't care, only that was all the dough I had, except my lucky half-dollar."

"That's me," snarled O'Brien. "Only I ain't got no half-dollar."

About this time up barged Bad Bill.

"What's up, boys?" he said, with a wink at the loafers.

"You know what's up, you louse!" snarled Black Jack. "This old fool has just lost a hundred bucks on your crooked roulette game."

"Well," sneered Bad Bill, "that ain't no skin offa your nose, is it?"

"That was our money," howled Black Jack. "And you gotta give it back!"

Kerney laughed in his face. He took out a roll of bills and fluttered the edges with his thumb.

"Here's the dough he lost," said Kerney. "Mebbe it was yours, but it's mine now. What I wins, I keeps—onless somebody's man enough to take it away from me, and I ain't never met anybody which was. And what you goin' to do about it?"

BLACK JACK WAS so mad he just strangled, and his eyes stood out. I said, losing my temper, "I'll tell you what we're goin' to do, Kerney, since you wanta be tough. I'm goin' to knock you stiff and take that wad offa your senseless carcass."

"You are, hey?" he roared, blood-thirstily. "Lemme see you try it, you black-headed sea-rat! Wanta fight, eh? All right. Lemme see how much man you are. Here's the wad. If you can lick me, you can have it back. I won it fair and square, but I'm a sport. You come around here cryin' for your money back—all right, we'll see if you're men enough to fight for it!"

I growled deep and low, and lunged, but Black Jack grabbed me.

"Wait a minute," he yelped. "Half that dough's mine. I got just as much right to sock this polecat as you has, and you know it."

"Heh! Heh!" sneered Kerney, jerking off his coat and shirt. "Settle it between yourselves. If either one of you can lick me, the dough's yours. Ain't that fair, boys?"

All the assembled thugs applauded profanely. I seen at a glance they was all his men—except old Bunger, which didn't count either way.

"It's my right to fight this guy," argued Black Jack.

"We'll flip a coin," I decided, bringing out my lucky half-dollar. "I'll take—"

"I'll take heads," busted in Black Jack, impatiently.

"I said it first," I replied annoyedly.

"I didn't hear you," he said.

"Well, I did," I answered pettishly. "You'll take tails."

"All right, I'll take tails," he snorted in disgust. "Gwan and flip."

So I flopped, and it fell heads.

"Didn't I say it was my lucky piece?" I crowed jubilantly, putting the coin back in my pocket and tearing off my shirt, whilst Black Jack ground his teeth and cussed his luck something terrible.

"Before I knock your brains out," said Kerney, "you got to dispose of that bench-legged cannibal."

"If you mean Mike, you foul-mouthed skunk," I said, "Black Jack can hold him."

"And let go of him so he can tear my throat out just as I got you licked," sneered Kerney. "No, you don't. Take this piece of rope and tie him up, or the scrap's off."

So, with a few scathing remarks which apparently got under even Bad Bill's thick hide, to judge from his profanity, I tied one end of the rope to Mike's collar and the other'n to the leg of a heavy gambling table. Meanwhile, the onlookers had cleared away a space between the table and the back wall, which was covered by a matting of woven grass. To all appearances, the back wall was solid, but I thought they must be a lot of rats burrowing in there, because every now and then I heered a kind of noise like something moving and thumping around.

WELL, ME AND Kerney approached each other in the gleam of the gas-lights. He was a big, black-browed brute, with black hair matted on his barrel chest and on his wrists, and his hands was like sledge-hammers. He was about my height, but heavier.

I started the scrap like I always do, with a rush, slugging away with both hands. He met me, nothing loath. The crowd formed a half-circle in front of the stacked-up tables and chairs, and the back wall was behind us. Above the thud and crunch of blows I couldst hear Mike growling as he strained at his rope, and Black Jack yelling for me to kill Kerney.

Well, he was tough and he could hit like a mule kicking. But he was fighting Steve Costigan. There, under the gas-lights, with the mob yelling, and my bare fists crunching on flesh and bone, I was plumb in my element. I laughed at Bad Bill as I took the best he could hand out, and come plunging in for more.

I worked for his belly, repeatedly sinking both hands to the wrists, and he began to puff and gasp and go away from me. My head was singing from his thundering socks, and the taste of blood was in my mouth, but that's a old, old story to me. I caught him on the ear and blood spattered. Like a flash, up come his heavy boot for my groin, but I twisted aside and caught him with a terrible right-hander under the heart. He groaned and staggered, and a ripping left hook to the body sent him down, but he grabbed my belt as he fell and dragged me with him.

On the floor he locked his gorilla arms around me, and spat in my eye, trying to pull my head down where he could sink his fangs in my ear. But my neck was like iron, and I pulled back, fighting mad, and, getting a hand free, smashed it savagely three times into his face. With a groan, he went slack. And just then a heavy boot crashed into my back, purty near paralyzing me, and knocking me clear of Kerney.

It was John Lynch which had kicked me, and even as I snarled up at him, trying to get up, I heered Black Jack roar, and I heered the crash of his iron fist under Lynch's jaw, and the dirty yegg dropped amongst the stacked-up tables and lay like a empty sack.

The thugs surged forward with a menacing rumble, but Black Jack turned on 'em like a maddened tiger, his teeth gleaming in a snarl, his eyes blazing, and they hesitated. And then I climbed on my feet, the effecks of that foul lick passing. Kerney was slavering and cursing and trying to get up, and I grabbed him by his hair and dragged him up.

"Stand on your two feet and fight like as if you was a man," I snarled disgustedly, and he lunged at me sudden and unexpected, trying to knee me in the groin. He fell into me, and, as I pulled out of a half-clinch, I heered Black Jack yell suddenly, *"Look out, Steve!* That's the way he got me!"

And simultaneous I felt Kerney's hand at the side of my neck. Instinctively, I jerked back, and as I did, Kerney's thumb pressed cunning and savage into my neck just below the ear. Jiu-jitsu! Mighty few white men know that trick—the Japanese death-touch, they call it. If I hadn't been going away from it, so he didn't hit the exact nerve he was looking for, I'd of been temporarily paralyzed. As it was, my heavy neck muscles saved me, though for a flashing instant I staggered, as a wave of blindness and agony went all over me.

Kerney yelled like a wild beast, and come for me, but I straightened and met him with a left hook that ripped his lip open from the corner of his mouth to his chin, and sent him reeling backward. And, clean maddened by the dirty trick he had tried on me, I throwed every ounce of my beef into a thundering right swing that tagged him square on the jaw.

It was just a longshoreman's haymaker with my whole frame behind it, and it lifted him clean offa his feet and catapulted him bodily against the back wall. *Crash!* The matting tore, the wood behind it splintered, and Kerney's senseless form smashed right on through!

THE FORCE OF my swing throwed me headlong after Kerney, and I landed with my head and forearms through the hole he'd made. The back wall wasn't solid! They was a secret room beyond it. I seen Kerney lying in that room with his feet projecting through the busted partition, and beyond I seen another figger—bound and gagged and lying on the floor.

"Johnny!" I yelled, scrambling up, and behind me rose a deep, ominous roar. Black Jack yelled, "Look out, Steve!" and a bottle whizzed past my ear and crashed against the wall. Simultaneous come the thud of a sock and the fall of a body, as Black Jack went into action, and I wheeled as Kerney's thugs come surging in on me.

Black Jack was slugging right and left, and men were toppling like ten-pins, but they was a whole room full of 'em. I saw old Bunger scooting for the exit, and I heered Mike roaring, lunging against his rope. I caught the first thug with a smash that near broke his neck, and then they swarmed all over me, and I cracked Red Elkins' ribs with my knee as we went to the floor.

I heered Black Jack roaring and battling, and I shook off my attackers and riz, fracturing Shifty Brelen's skull, and me and Black Jack stiffened them deluded mutts till we was treading on a carpet of senseless yeggs, but still they come, with bottles and knives and chair-legs, till we was both streaming blood.

Black Jack hadst just been felled with a table-leg, and half a dozen of 'em was stomping on my prostrate form, whilst I was engaged in gouging and strangling three or four I had under me, when Mike's rope broke under repeated gnawings and lunges. I heered him beller, and I heered a yegg yip as Mike's iron fangs met in his meat. The clump on me bust apart, and I lurched up, roaring like a bull and shaking the blood in a shower from my head.

Black Jack come up with the table-leg he'd been floored with, and he hit Smoky Rourke so hard they had to use a pulmotor to bring Smoky to. The battered mob staggered dizzily back, and scattered as Mike plunged and raged amongst them.

Spang! Wolf McGernan had broke away from the melee and was risking killing some of his mates to bring us down. They run for cover, screeching. Black Jack throwed the table-leg, but missed, and the three of us—him and Mike and me—rushed McGernan simultaneous.

His muzzle wavered from one to the other as he tried to decide quick which to shoot, and then *crack!* Wolf yelped and dropped his gun; he staggered back against the wall, grabbing his wrist, from which blood was spurting.

The yeggs stopped short in their head-long fight for the exit, and me and Black Jack wheeled. A dozen policemen was on the stairs with drawed guns and one of them guns was smoking.

* * *

THE THUGS BACKED against the wall, their hands up, and I run into the secret room and untied Johnny Kyelan.

All he could say was, "Glug ug glug!" for a minute, being nearly choked with fear and excitement and the gag. But I hammered him on the back, and he said, "They got me, Steve. They sneaked into the hall and knocked on the door. When I stooped to look through the key-hole, as they figgered I'd do—its a natural move—they blew some stuff in my face that knocked me clean out for a few minutes. While I was lying helpless, they unlocked the door with a skeleton key and came in. I was coming to myself, then, but they had guns on me and I didn't dare yell for help.

"They searched me, and I begged them to leave your fifty dollars on the table because I knew it was all the money you had, but they took it, and wrote a note to make it look like I'd skipped out with the money. Then they blew some more powder in my face, and the next thing I knew I was in a car, being carried here.

"They were going to finish me before daylight. I heard the Chief Mandarin say so."

"And who's he?" we demanded.

"I don't mind telling you now," said Johnny, looking at the yeggs which was being watched by the cops, and at Bad Bill, who was just beginning to come to on the floor. "The Chief of the Mandarins is *Bad Bill Kerney!* He was a racketeer in the States, and he's been working the same here."

An officer broke in: "You mean this man is the infamous Black Mandarin?"

"You're darn tootin'," said Johnny, "and I can prove it in the courts."

WELL, THEM COPS pounced on the dizzy Kerney like gulls on a fish, and in no time him and his gang, such as was conscious, was decorated with steel bracelets. Kerney didn't say nothing, but he looked black murder at all of us.

"Hey, wait!" said Black Jack, as the cops started leading them out. "Kerney's got some dough which belongs to us."

So the cop took a wad offa him big enough to choke a shark, and Black Jack counted off a hundred and fifty bucks and give the rest back. The cops led the yeggs out, and I felt somebody tugging at my arm. It was old Bunger.

"Well, boys," he quavered," don't you think I've squared things? As soon as the roughhouse started, I run up into the street screamin' and yellin' till all the cops within hearin' come on the run!"

"You've done yourself proud, Bunger," I said. "Here's a ten spot for you."

"And here's another'n," said Black Jack, and old Bunger grinned all over.

"Thank you, boys," he said, ruffling the bills in his eagerness. "I gotta go now—they's a roulette wheel down at Spike's I got a hunch I can beat."

"Let's all get outa here," I grunted, and we emerged into the street and gazed at the street-lamps, yellow and smoky in the growing daylight.

"Boy, oh, boy!" said Johnny. "I've had enough of this life. It's me for the old U.S.A. just as soon as I can get there."

"And a good thing," I said gruffly, because I was so glad to know the boy wasn't a thief and a cheat that I felt kinda foolish. "Snappy kids like you got no business away from home."

"Well," said Black Jack, "let's go get that drink."

"Aw, heck," I said, disgustedly, as I shoved my money back in my pants, "I lost my good-luck half-dollar in the melee."

"Maybe this is it," said Johnny, holding it out. "I picked it up off the floor as we were coming out."

"Gimme it," I said, hurriedly, but Black Jack grabbed it with a startled oath.

"Good luck piece?" he yelled. "Now I see why you was so insistent on takin' heads. This here blame half-dollar is a trick coin, and it's got heads on both sides! Why, I hadn't a chance. Steve Costigan, you did me out of a fight, and I resents it! You got to fight me."

"All right," I said. "We'll fight again tonight at Ace's Arena. And now let's go get that drink."

"Good heavens," said Johnny, "It's nearly sun-up. If you fellows are going to fight again tonight, hadn't you better get some rest? And some of those cuts you both got need bandaging."

"He's right, Steve," said Black Jack. "We'll have a drink and then we'll get sewed up, and then we'll eat breakfast, and after that we'll shoot some pool."

"Sure," I said, "that's a easy, restful game, and we oughta take things easy so we can be in shape for the fight tonight. After we shoot some pool, we'll go to Yota Lao's and lick some bouncers you was talkin' about."

THE SLUGGER'S GAME

Mauling fists on the Hong Kong waterfront—
and the comedy of the vanished bulldog.

By ROBERT E. HOWARD

THE SLUGGER'S GAME

I WAS BROODING over my rotten luck in the Sweet Dreams bar on the Hong Kong waterfront, when in come that banana peel on the steps of progress, Smoky Jones. I ain't got no use for Smoky, and he likes me just about as much. But he is broad-minded, as he quickly showed.

"Quick!" quoth he. "Lemme have fifty bucks, Steve."

"Why shouldst I loan you fifty smackers?" I demanded.

"I got a sure-fire tip," he yipped, jumping up and down with impatience. "A hundred-to-one shot which can't lose! You'll get back your dough tomorrer. C'mon, kick in."

"If I had fifty bucks," I returned bitterly, "do you think I'd be wasting my time in a port which don't appreciate no fistic talent?"

"What?" hollered Smoky. "No fifty bucks? After all I've did for you?"

"Well, I can't help it if these dopey promoters won't gimme a fight, can I?" I said fiercely. "Fifty bucks! Fifty bucks would get me to Singapore, where I can always talk myself into a scrap. I'm stuck here with my white bulldog, Mike, and can't even get a ship to sign on. If I don't scram away from here soon, I'll be on the beach, and you demands fifty bucks!"

A number of men at the bar was listening to our altercation with great interest, and one of 'em, a big, tough-looking guy, bust into a loud guffaw, and said: "Blimey! If the regular promoters turn you down, mate, why don't you try Li Yun?"

"What d'you mean?" I demanded suspiciously.

All the others was grinning like jassacks eating prickly pears.

"Well," he said, with a broad smirk, "Li Yun runs a small menagerie to cover his real business which is staging animal fights, like mongooses and cobras, and pit-terriers, and game-cocks. He's got a big gorilla he ought to sign you up with. I'd like to see the bloody brawl myself; with that pan of yours, it'd be like twin brothers fighting."

"Lissen here, you," I said, rising in righteous wrath—I never did like a limey much anyhow—"I may have a mug like a gorilla, but I figger your'n could be improved some—like this!"

And so saying, I rammed my right fist as far as it would go into his mouth. He reeled and come back bellowing like a typhoon. We traded some lusty swats and then clinched and went head-long into the bar, which splintered at our impact, and the swinging lamp fell down from the ceiling. It busted on the floor, and you should of heard them fellers holler when the burning ile splashed down their necks. Everything was dark in there, and some was scrambling out of winders and doors, and some was stomping out the fire, and somehow me and my opponent got tore loose from each other in the rush.

My eyes was full of smoke, but as I groped around I felt a table-leg glance off my head, so I made a grab and got hold of a human torso. So I throwed him and fell on him and begun to maul him. I musta softened him considerable already, I thought, because he felt a lot flabbier than he done before, and he was hollering a lot louder. Then somebody struck a light, and I found I was hammering the fat Dutch bartender. The limey was gone, and somebody hollered the cops was coming. So I riz and fled out the back way in disgust. That limey had had the last lick, and it's a p'int of honor with me to have the last lick myself. I hunted him for half a hour, aiming to learn him to hit a man with a table-leg and then run, but I didn't find him.

Well, my clothes was singed and tore, so I headed for my boarding-house, the Seamen's Delight, which was down on the waterfront and run by a fat half-caste. He was lying in the hall dead-drunk as usual, and I was glad because when he was sober he was all the time bellyaching about my board bill. Didn't seem to be nobody else in the house.

I went upstairs to my room and opened the door, calling Mike. But Mike didn't come, and I smelt a peculiar smell in the air. I smelt that same smell once when some crimps tried to shanghai me. And the room was empty. My bed was still warm where Mike had been curled up on it, sleeping, but he was gone. I started to go outside and call him, when I seen a note stuck to the wall. I read it and turned cold all over.

It said:

If you want to ever see yure dog agane leeve fiftey dolers in the tin can outside the alley dore of the Bristol Bar at the stroak of leven-thirty tonight. Put the money in the can and go back in the sloon and cloase the dore. Count a hunderd and then you will find yure dog in the ally.

—A Man What Meens Bizziness.

I run downstairs and shook the landlord and hollered: "Who's been here since I been gone?"

But all he done was grunt and mutter: "Fill 'er up again, Joe!"

I give him a hearty kick in the pants and run out on the street, plumb distracted. Me and Mike has kicked around together for years; he's saved my worthless life a dozen times. Mike is about the only difference between me and a bum. I don't give a cuss what people think about me, but I always try to conduct myself so my dog won't be ashamed of me. And now some dirty mug had stole him and I hadn't no dough to buy him back.

I sot down on the curb and held my throbbing head and tried to think, but the more I thought, the more mixed up things got. When I'm up against something I can't maul with my fists, I'm plumb off my course and no chart to steer by. Finally I riz up and sot out at a run for the Quiet Hour Arena. They was a fight card on that night, and though I'd already tried to get signed up and been turned down by the promoter, in my desperation I thought I'd try again. I intended appealing to his better nature, if he had one.

From the noise which issued from the building as I approached, I knowed the fights had already started, and my heart sunk, but I didn't know nothing else to try. The back door was locked, but I give it a kind of tug and it come off the hinges and I went in.

They was nobody in sight in the narrer hallway running between the dressing-rooms, but as I run up the hall, a door opened and a big man come out in a bathrobe, follered by a feller with towels and buckets. The big man ripped out a oath and throwed out his arm to stop me. It was the limey I'd fit in the Sweet Dreams bar.

"So that table-leg didn't do the business, eh?" he inquired nastily. "Looking for another dose of the same, are you?"

"I got no time to fight you now," I muttered, trying to crowd past him. "I'm lookin' for Bisly, the promoter."

"What you shaking about?" he sneered, and I seen he had his hands taped. "Why are you so pale and sweating? Scared of me, eh? Well, I'm due up in that ring right now, but first I'm going to polish you off, you Yankee swine!" And with that he give me a open-handed swipe across the face.

I dunno when anybody ever dared *slap* me. For a second everything floated in a crimson haze. I dunno what kind of a lick I handed that Limey ape. I don't even remember hitting him. But I must of, because when I could see again, there he was on the floor, with his jaw split open from the corner of his mouth to the rim of his chin, and his head gashed where it hit the door jamb.

The handler was trying to hide under a bench, and somebody else was hollering like he had a knife stuck in him. It was the promoter of the joint, and he was jumping up and down like a cat on a red-hot hatch.

"What 'ave you done?" he squalled. "Oh, blimey, what *'ave* you done? A packed 'ouse 'owlin' for h'action, and one of the principals wyting in the bleedin' ring—and 'ere you've lyed out the other! Oh, my 'at! What a bloody go!"

"You mean this here scut was goin' to fight in the main event?" I asked stupidly, because my head was still going around.

"What else?" he howled. "Ow, murder! What am I to do?"

"Well, you limeys certainly stick together," I said. And then a vast light dazzled me. I gasped with the force of the idea which had just hit me, so to speak. I laid hold on Bisly so forcibly he squealed, thinking I was attacking him.

"How much you payin' this rat?" I demanded, shaking him in my urgency.

"Fifty dollars, winner tyke all!" he moaned.

"Then I'm your man!" I roared, releasing him so vi'lently he sprawled his full length on the floor. "You been refusin' to let me fight in your lousy club account of your prejudice against Americans, but this time you ain't got no choice! That mob out there craves gore, and if they don't see some, they'll tear down your joint! Lissen at 'em!"

He done so, and shuddered at the ferocious yells with which the house was vibrating. The crowd was tired of waiting and was demanding action in the same tone them old Roman crowds used when they yelped for another batch of gladiators to be tossed to the lions.

"You want to go out there and tell 'em the main event's called off?" I demanded.

"No! No!" he said hastily, mopping his brow with a shaky hand. "Have you got togs and a handler?"

"I'll get 'em," I answered. "Hop out there and tell them mugs that the main event will go on in a minute!"

So he went out like a man going to keep a date with the hangman, and I turned to the feller which was still trying to wedge hisself under the bench—a dumb cluck hired by the club to scrub floors and second fighters which didn't have none theirselves. I handed him a hearty kick in the rear, and sternly requested, "Come out here and help me with this stiff!"

He done so in fear and trembling, and we packed the limey battler into his dressing-room, and laid him on a table. He was beginning to show some faint signs of life. I took off his bathrobe and togs and clamb into 'em myself, whilst the handler watched me in a kind of pallid silence.

"Pick up them buckets and towels," I commanded. "I don't like your looks, but you'll have to do. Any handler is better'n none—and the best is none too good. Come on!"

Follered close by him, I hurried into the arener to be greeted by a ferocious uproar as I come swinging down the aisle. Bisly was addressing 'em, and I caught the tag-end of his remarks which went as follows: "—and so, if you gents will be pytient, Battler Pembroke will be ready for the go in a moment—in fact, 'ere 'e comes now!"

And so saying, Bisly skipped down out of the ring and disappeared. He hadn't had nerve enough to tell 'em that a substitution had been made. They glanced at me, and then they glared, with their mouths open, and then, just as I reached the ring, a big stoker jumped and roared: "*You* ain't Battler Pembroke! At him, mates—!"

I clouted him on the button and he done a nose-dive over the first row ringside. I then faced the snarling crowd, expanding my huge chest and glaring at 'em from under my battered brows, and I roared: "Anybody else thinks I ain't Battler Pembroke?"

They started surging towards me, growling low in their throats, but they glanced at my victim and halted suddenly, and crowded back from me. With a snort of contempt, I turned and clamb into the ring. My handler clumb after me and commenced to massage my legs kind of dumb-like. He was one of these here sap-heads, and things was happening too fast for him to keep up with 'em.

"What time is it?" I demanded, and he pulled out his watch, looked at it carefully, and said, "Five minutes after ten."

"I got well over a hour," I muttered, and glanced at my opponent in the oppersite corner. I knowed he must be popular, from the size of the purse; most performers at the Quiet Hour got only ten bucks apiece, win, lose or draw, and generally had to lick the promoter to get that. He was well built, but pallid all over, with about as much expression as a fish. They was something familiar about him, but I couldn't place him.

The crowd was muttering and growling, but the announcer was a stolid mutt which didn't have sense enough to be afraid of anybody, even the customers which frequents the Quiet Hour. To save time, he announced whilst the referee was giving the usual instructions, and said he: "In that corner, Sailor Costigan, weight—"

"Where's Pembroke?" bellered the crowd. "That ain't Pembroke! That's a bloody Yankee, the low-lifed son of a canine!"

"Nevertheless," said the announcer, without blinking, "he weighs one-ninety; and the other blighter is Slash Jackson, of Cardiff; weight, one-eighty-nine."

The maddened mob frothed and commenced throwing things, but then the gong clanged and they calmed down reluctantly to watch the show, like a fight crowd will. After all, what they want is a fight.

At the whang of the gong I tore out of my corner with the earnest ambition of finishing that fight with the first punch, if possible. It was my intention to lay my right on his jaw, and I made no secret of it. I scorns deception. If he'd ducked a split second slower, the scrap would of ended right there.

But I didn't pause to meditate. I sent my left after my right, and he grunted poignantly as it sunk under his heart. Then his right flicked up at my jaw, and from the way it cut the air as it whistled past, I knowed it was loaded with dynamite. Giving him no time to get set, I slugged him back across the ring and into the ropes on the other side. The crowd screamed blue murder, but I wasn't hurting him as much as they thought, or as much as I wanted to. He was clever at rolling with a punch, and he was all elbows. Nor he wasn't too careful where he put 'em, neither. He put one in my stummick and t'other'n in my eye, which occasioned some bitter profanity on my part. He also stomped heartily on my insteps.

Little things like them is ignored in the Quiet Hour; the audience merely considers 'em the spice of the sport, and the referee is above noticing 'em.

But I was irritated, and in my eagerness to break Jackson's neck with a swinging overhand punch, I exposed myself to his right, which licked out again like the flipper of a seal. I just barely managed to duck it, and it ripped the skin off my chin as it grazed me. And as I stabbed him off balance with a straight left to the mouth, that peculiar lick of his set me to wondering again, because it reminded me of something, I couldn't remember what.

He now brung his left into play with flashy jabs and snappy hooks, but it didn't pack the power his right did, and all he done was to cut my lips a little. He kept his right cocked, but I was watching it, and when he shot it again I went inside it and battered away at his midriff with both hands. He was steel springs and whale-bone under his white skin, but he didn't like 'em down below. He was backing and breaking ground when the gong ended the round.

I sunk onto my stool in time to receive a swipe across the eyes with the towel my handler was trying to fan me with, and whilst I was shaking the stars out of my vision, he emptied a whole bucket of ice water over my head. This was wholly unnecessary, as I p'inted out to him with free and fervent language, but he had a one-track mind. He'd probably seen a fighter doused thusly, and thought it *had* to be did, whether the fighter needed it or not.

I was still remonstrating with him concerning his dumbness when the bell rung, and as a result, Jackson, who shot out of his corner like a catapult, caught me before I could get into the center of the ring, shooting his left and throwing his right after it. *Zip!* It come through the air like a hammer on a steel spring!

I side-stepped and ripped my left to his midriff. He gasped and staggered, and I set myself like a flash and throwed my right at his head with all my beef behind it. But I'd forgot I was standing where the canvas was soaked with the water my dumb handler had poured over me. My foot slipped on a sliver of ice just as I let go my swing, and before I could recover myself, that T.N.T. right licked out, and this time it didn't miss.

Jerusha! It wasn't like being hit by a human being. I felt like a fire-works factory hadst exploded in my skull. I seen comets and meteors and sky-rockets, and somebody was trying to count the stars as they flew past. Then things cleared a little bit, and I realized it was the referee which was counting, and he was counting over me.

I was on my belly in the resin, and bells seemed to be ringing all over the house. I could'st hardly hear the referee for 'em, but he said "Nine!" so I riz. That's a habit of mine. I make a specialty of getting up. I have got up off the floor of rings from Galveston to Shanghai.

My legs wasn't exactly right—one had a tendency to steer south by west, while the other'n wanted to go due east—and I had a dizzy idee that a typhoon was raging outside. I coulds't hear the waters rising and the winds roaring, but realized that it was my own ears ringing after that awful clout.

Jackson was on me like a hunting panther, just about as light and easy. He was too anxious to use his right again. He thought I was out on my feet and all he had to do was to hit me. Any old-timer could of told him that leading to me with his right, whether I was groggy or not, was violating a rule of safety which is already becoming a ring tradition.

He simply cocked his right and let it go, and I beat it with a left hook to the body. He turned kinda green in the face, like anybody is liable to which has just had a iron fist sunk several inches into their belly. And before he could strike again, I fell into him and hugged him like a grizzly.

I knowed him now! They wasn't but one man in the world with a right-hand clout like that—Torpedo Willoughby, the Cardiff Murderer. Whiskey and women kept him from being a champ, and kept him broke so much he often performed in dumps like the Quiet Hour under a assumed name, but he was a mankiller, the worst England ever produced.

I shook the blood and sweat outa my eyes, and took my time about coming out of that clinch, and when the referee finally broke us, I was ready. Willoughby come slugging in, and I crouched and covered up, weaving always to his left, and hooking my left to his ribs and belly. My left carried more dynamite than his left did, and I didn't leave no openings for that blasting right. I didn't tin-can; I dunno how and wouldn't if I could. But I retired into my shell whilst pounding his mid-section, and he got madder and madder, and flailed away with that right fiercer than ever. But it was glancing off my arms and the top of my head, and my left was digging into his guts deeper and deeper. It ain't a spectacular way of battling, but it gets results in the long run.

I was purty well satisfied at the end of that round. Fighting like I was didn't give Willoughby no chance to blast me, and eventually he was going to weaken under my body-battering. It might take five or six rounds, but the bout was scheduled for fifteen frames, and I had plenty of time.

But that don't mean I was happy as I sot in my corner whilst my handler squirted lemon juice in my eye, trying to moisten my lips, and give me a long, refreshing drink of iodine in his brainless efforts to daub a cut on my chin. I was thinking of Mike, and a chill trickled down my spine as I wondered what them devils which stole him wouldst do to him if the money wasn't in the tin can at exactly eleven-thirty.

"What time is it?" I demanded, and my handler hauled out his watch and said, "Five minutes after ten."

"That's what you said before!" I howled in exasperation. "Gimme that can!"

I grabbed it and glared, and then I shook it. It wasn't running. It didn't even sound like they was any works inside of it. Stricken by a premonishun, I yelled to the referee, "What time is it?"

He glanced at his watch. "Seconds out!" he said, and then: "Fifteen minutes after eleven!"

Fifteen minutes to go! Cold sweat bust out all over me, and I jumped up offa my stool so suddenly my handler fell backwards through the ropes. *Fifteen minutes!* I couldn't take no five or six rounds to lick Willoughby! I had to do it in this round if winning was going to do me any good.

I throwed all my plans to the winds. I was trembling in every limb and glaring across at Willoughby, and when he met the glare in my eyes he stiffened and his muscles tensed. He sensed the change in me, though he couldn't know why; he knowed the battle was to be to the death.

The gong whanged and I tore out of my corner like a typhoon, to kill or be killed. I'm always a fighter of the iron-man type. When I'm nerved up like I was then, the man ain't born which can stop me. There wasn't no plan or plot or science about that round—it was just raw, naked, primitive manhood, sweat and blood and fists flailing like mallets without a second's let-up.

I tore in, swinging like a madman, and in a second Willoughby was fighting for his life. The blood spattered and the crowd roared and things got dim and red, and all I seen was the white figger in front of me, and all I knowed was to hit and hit and keep hitting till the world ended.

I dunno how many times I was on the canvas.

Every time he landed solid with that awful right I went down like a butchered ox. But every time I come up again and tore into him more furious than ever. I was crazy with fear, like a man in a nightmare, thinking of Mike and the minutes that was slipping past.

His right was the concentrated essence of hell. Every time it found my jaw I felt like my skull was caved in and every vertebrae of my spine was dislocated. But I'm used to them sensations. They're part of the slugger's game. Let these here classy dancing-masters quit when their bones begins to melt like wax, and their brains feels like they was being jolted loose from their skull. A slugger lowers his head and wades in again. That's his game. His ribs may be splintered in on his vitals, and his guts may be mashed outa place, and his ears may be streaming blood from veins busted inside his skull, but them things don't matter; the important thing is winning.

No white man ever hit me harder'n Torpedo Willoughby hit me, but I was landing too, and every time I sunk a mauler under his heart or smashed one against his temple, I seen him wilt. If he could of took it like he handed it out, he'd been champeen. But at last I seen his pale face before me with his lips open wide as he gulped for air, and I knowed I had him, though I was hanging to the ropes and the crowd was yelling for the kill. They couldn't see the muscles in his calves quivering, nor his belly heaving, nor the glaze in his eyes. They couldn't understand that he'd hammered me till his shoulder muscles was dead and his gloves was like they was weighted with lead, and the heart was gone out of him. All they couldst see was me, battered and bloody, clinging to the ropes, and him cocking his right for the finisher.

It come over, slow and ponderous, and glanced from my shoulder as I lurched off the ropes. And my own right smashed like a caulking mallet against his jaw, and down he went, face-first in the resin.

When they fall like that, they don't get up. I didn't even wait to hear the referee count him out. I run across the ring, getting stronger at every step, tore off my gloves and held out my hand for my bathrobe. My gaping handler put the sponge in it.

I throwed it in his face with a roar of irritation, and he fell outa the ring headfirst into a water bucket, which put the crowd in such a rare good humor that they even cheered as I run down the aisle, and not over a dozen empty beer bottles was throwed at me.

Bisly was waiting in the corridor, and I grabbed the fifty bucks outa his hand as I went by on the run. He follered me into the dressing-room and offered to help me put on my clothes, but knowing he hoped to steal my wad whilst helping me, I throwed him out bodily, jerked on my street clothes, and sallied forth at top speed.

The Bristol Bar was a low-class dive down on the edge of the native quarters. It took me maybe five minutes to get there, and a clock behind the bar showed me that it lacked about a minute and a fraction of eleven-thirty.

"Tony," I panted to the bartender, who gaped at my bruised and bloody face, "I want the back room to myself. See that nobody disturbs me."

I run to the back door and throwed it open. It was dark in the alley, but I seen a empty tobacco tin setting close to the door. I quickly wadded the money into it, stepped into the room and shut the door. I reckon somebody was hiding in the alley watching, because as soon as I shut the door, I heard a stirring around out there. I didn't look. I wasn't taking no chances on them doing anything to Mike.

I heard the tin scrape against the stones, and they was silence whilst I hurriedly counted up to a hundred. Then I jerked open the door, and joyfully yelled: "*Mike!*" They was no reply. The tin can was gone, but Mike wasn't there.

Cold, clammy sweat bust out all over me, and my tongue stuck to the roof of my mouth. I rushed down the alley like a wild man, and just before I reached the street, where a dim street-lamp shone, I fell over something warm and yielding which groaned and said: "Oh, my head!"

I grabbed it and dragged it into the light, and it was Smoky Jones. He had a lump on his head and the tin can in his hand, but it was empty.

I must of went kinda crazy then. Next thing I knowed I had Smoky by the throat, shaking him till his eyes crossed, and I was mouthing, "What you done with Mike, you dirty gutter rat? *Where is he?*"

His hands were waving around, and I seen he couldn't talk. His face was purple and his eyes and tongue stuck out remarkable. So I eased up a bit, and he gurgled, "I dunno!"

"You do know!" I roared, digging my thumbs into his unwashed neck. "You was the one which stole him. You wanted that fifty bucks to bet on a horse. I see it all, now. It's so plain even a dumb mutt like me can figure it out. You got the money—where's Mike?"

"I'll tell you everything," he gasped. "Lemme up, Steve. You're chockin' me to death. Lissen—it was me which stole Mike. I snuck in and doped him and packed him off in a sack. But I didn't aim to hurt him. All I wanted was the fifty. I figgered you could raise it if you had to . . . I'd taken Mike to Li Yun's house, to hide him. We put him in a cage before he come to—that there dog is worse'n a tiger. . . I was to hide in the alley till you put out the dough, and meanwhile one of Li Yun's Chinees was to bring Mike in a auto, and wait at the mouth of the alley till I got the money. Then, if everything was OK, we was going to let the dog out into the alley and beat it in the car. . . . Well, whilst I hid in the alley I seen the Chinee drive up and park in the shadows like we'd agreed, so I signalled him and went on after the dough. But as I come up the alley with the money, *wham!* that double-crossin' heathen riz up out of the dark and whacked me with a black-jack. And now he's gone and the auto's gone and the fifty bucks is gone!"

"And where's Mike?" I demanded.

"I dunno," he said. "I doubt if that Chinee ever brung him here at all. Oh, my head!" he said, holding onto his skull.

"That ain't a scratch to what I'm goin' to do to you when you get recovered," I promised him. "Where at does Li Yun live at?"

"In that old warehouse down near the wharf the natives call the Dragon Pier," said Smoky. "He's fixed up some rooms for livin' quarters, and—"

That was all I wanted to know. The next second I was headed for the Dragon Pier. I run down alleys, crossed dark courts, turned off the narrer side street that runs to the wharf, ducked through a winding alley, and come to the back of the warehouse I was looking for. As I approached, I seen a back door hanging open; and a light shining through.

I didn't hesitate, but bust through with both fists cocked. Then I stopped short. They was nobody there. It was a great big room, electrically lighted, with a switch on the wall, and purty well fixed up generally. Leastways it had been. But now it was littered with busted tables and splintered chairs, and there was blood and pieces of silk on the floor. They had been some kind of a awful fight in there, and my heart was in my mouth when I seen a couple of empty cages. There was white dog hair scattered on the floor, and some thick darkish hair in big tufts that couldn't of come from nothing but a gorilla.

I looked at the cages. One was a bamboo cage, and some of the bars had been gnawed in two. The lock on the steel cage was busted from the inside. It didn't take no detective to figger out what had happened. Mike had gnawed his way out of the bamboo cage and the gorilla had busted out of his cage to get at him. But where was they now? Was the Chinees and their gorilla chasing poor old Mike down them dark alleys, or had they took his body off to dispose of it after the gorilla had finished him?

I felt weak and sick and helpless; Mike is about the only friend I got. Then things begun to swim red around me again. They was one table in that room yet unbusted. I attended to that. They was no human for me to lay hands on, and I had to wreck something.

Then a inner door opened and a fat white man with a cigar in his mouth stuck his head in and stared at me.

"What was that racket?" he said. "Hey, who are you? Where's Li Yun?"

"That's what I want to know," I snarled. "Who are you?"

"Name's Wells, if it's any of your business," he said, coming on into the room. His belly bulged out his checked vest, and his swagger put my teeth on edge.

"What a mess!" he said, flicking the ashes offa his cigar in a way which made me want to kill him. It's the little things in life which causes murder. "Where the devil is Li Yun? The crowd's gettin' impatient."

"Crowd?" I interrogated. As I spoke, it seemed like I did hear a hum up towards the front of the building.

"Why," he said, "the crowd which has come to watch the battle between Li Yun's gorilla and the fightin' bull-dog."

"Huh?" I gawped.

"Sure," he said. "Don't you know about it? It's time to start now. I'm Li Yun's partner. I finances these shows. I've been up at the front of the buildin', sellin' tickets. Thought I heard a awful racket back here awhile ago, but was too busy haulin' in the dough to come back and see. What's happened, anyhow? Where's the Chinees and the animals? Huh?"

I give a harsh, rasping laugh that made him jump. "I see now," I said betwixt my teeth. "Li Yun wanted Mike for his dirty fights. He seen a chance to make fifty bucks and stage a show too. So he double-crossed Smoky, and—"

"Go find Li Yun!" snapped Wells, biting off the end of another cigar. "That crowd out there is gettin' mad, and they're the scrapin's off the docks. Hurry up, and I'll give you half a buck—"

I then went berserk. All the grief and fury which had been seething in me exploded and surged over like hot lava out of a volcano. I give one yell, and went into action.

"Halp!" hollered Wells. "He's gone crazy!" He grabbed for a gun, but before he could draw I caught him on the whiskers with a looping haymaker and he done a classy cart-wheel head-on into the wall. The back of his skull hit the light-switch so hard it jolted it clean outa the brackets, and the whole building was instantly plunged in darkness. I felt around till my groping hands located a door, and I ripped it open and plunged recklessly down a narrer corridor till I hit another door with my head so hard I split the panels. I jerked it open and lunged through.

I couldn't see nothing, but I felt the presence of a lot of people. They was a confused noise going up, a babble of Chinese and Malay and Hindu, and some loud cussing in English and German. Somebody bawled, "Who turned out them lights? Turn on the lights! How can we see the scrap without no lights?"

Somebody else hollered, "They've turned the animals into the cage! I hear 'em!"

Everybody begun to cuss and yell for lights, and I groped forward until I was stopped by iron bars. Then I knowed where I was. That corridor I'd come through served as a kind of chute or runway into the big cage where the fights was fit. I reached through the bars, groped around and found a key sticking in the lock of the cage door. I give a yell of exultation which riz above the clamor, turned the key, throwed open the door and come plunging out. Them rats enjoyed a fight, hey? Well, I aimed they shouldn't be disappointed. Two men fighting for money, of their own free will, is one thing. Making a couple of inoffensive animals butcher each other just for the amusement of a gang of wharf rats is another'n.

I came out of that cage crazy-mad and flailing with both fists. Somebody grunted and dropped, and somebody else yelled, "Hey, who hit me?" and then the whole crowd began to mill and holler and strike out wild at random, not knowing what it was all about. It was a regular bedlam, with me swinging in the dark and dropping a man at each slam, and then a window got busted, and as I moved across a dim beam of light which come through, one guy give a frantic yell, "Run! Run! *The griller's loose!*"

At that, hell bust loose. Everybody stampeded, screaming and hollering and cussing and running over each other, and me in the middle of 'em, slugging right and left.

"You all wants a fight, does you?" I howled. "Well, here's some to tote home with you!"

They hit the door like a herd of steers and splintered it and went storming through, them which was able to storm. Some had been stomped in the rush, and plenty had stopped my iron fists in the dark. I come ravin' after 'em. Just because them rats wanted to see gore spilt—by somebody else—Mike, my only friend in the Orient, had to be sacrificed. I could of kilt 'em all.

Well, they streamed off down the street in full cry, and as I emerged, I fell over a innocent passerby which had been knocked down by the stampede. By the time I riz, they was out of my reach, though the sounds of their flight come back to me.

The fire of my rage died down to ashes. I felt old and sick and worn out. I wasn't young no more, and Mike was gone. I stooped to pick up the man I had fell over, idly noticing that he was a English captain whose ship was tied up at a nearby wharf, discharging cargo.

"Say," he said, gasping to get his breath back, "aren't you Steve Costigan?"

"Yeah," I admitted, without enthusiasm.

"Good!" he said. "I was looking for you. They told me it was your dog."

I sighed. "Yeah," I said. "A white bulldog that answered to the name of Mike. Where'd you find his body?"

"Body?" he said. "My word! The bally brute has been pursuing four Chinamen and a bloody gorilla up and down the docks for half an hour, and now he has them treed in the rigging of my ship, and I want you to come and call him off. Can't have that, you know!"

"Good old Mike!" I whooped, jumping straight into the air with joy and exultation. "Still the fightin'est dog in the Asiatics! Lead on, matey! I craves words with his victims. I got nothin' against the griller, but them Chinees has got fifty bucks belongin' to me and Mike!"

General Ironfist

"Lose the fight, and you lose your head" was the suave dictum of General Yun. Costigan, in the clutch of the revolutionists, was on the spot!

By Robert E. Howard

GENERAL IRONFIST

AS I CLUMB into the ring that night in the Pleasure Palace Fight Club, on the Hong Kong waterfront, I was low in my mind. I'd come to Hong Kong looking for a former shipmate of mine. I'd come on from Tainan as fast as I could, even leaving my bulldog Mike aboard the *Sea Girl,* which wasn't due to touch at Hong Kong for a couple of weeks yet.

But Soapy Jackson, the feller I was looking for, had just dropped plumb out of sight. Nobody'd saw him for weeks, or knowed what had become of him. Meanwhile my dough was all gone, so I accepted a bout with a big Chinese fighter they called the Yeller Typhoon.

He was a favorite with the sporting crowd and the Palace was jammed with both white men and Chineses that night, some very high class. I noticed one Chinee in particular, whilst setting in my comer waiting for the bell, because his European clothes was so swell, and because he seemed to take such a burning interest in the goings on. But I didn't pay much attention to the crowd; I was impatient to get the battle over with.

The Yeller Typhoon weighed three hundred pounds and he was a head taller'n me; but most of his weight was around his waist-line, and he didn't have the kind of arms and shoulders that makes a hitter. And it don't make no difference how big a Chinaman is, he can't take it.

I wasn't in no mood for classy boxing that night. I just walked into him, let him flail away with both hands till I seen a opening, and then let go my right. He shook the ring when he hit the boards, and the brawl was over.

Paying no heed to the howls of the dumbfounded multitude, I hastened to my dressing-room, donned my duds, and then hauled a letter from my britches pocket and studied it like I'd done a hundred times before.

It was addressed to Mr. Soapy Jackson, American Bar, Tainan, Taiwan, and was from a San Francisco law firm. After Soapy left the *Sea Girl,* he tended bar at the American, but he'd been gone a month when the *Sea Girl* docked at Tainan again, and the proprietor showed me that letter which had just come for him. He said Soapy had went to Hong Kong, but he didn't know his address, so I took the letter and come on alone to find him, because I had a idea it was important. Maybe he'd been left a fortune.

But I'd found Hong Kong in turmoil, just like all the rest of China. Up in the hills a lot of bandits, which called themselves revolutionary armies, was raising hell, and all I couldst hear was talk about General Yun Chei, and General Whang Shan, and General Feng, which they said was really a white man. Folks said Yun and Feng had joined up against Whang, and some tall battling was expected, and the foreigners was all piling down out of the interior. It was easy for a white sailorman with no connections to drop out of sight and never be heard of again. I thought what if Soapy has got hisself scuppered by them bloody devils, just when maybe he was on the p'int of coming into big money.

Well, I stuck the letter in my pocket, and sallied forth into the lamp-lit street to look for Soapy some more, when somebody hove up alongside of me, and who should it be but that dapper Chinee in European clothes I'd noticed in the first row, ringside, at the fight.

"You are Sailor Costigan, are you not?" he said in perfect English.

"Yeah," I said, after due consideration.

"I saw you fight the Yellow Typhoon tonight," he said. "The blow you dealt him would have felled an ox. Can you always hit like that?"

"Why not?" I inquired. He looked me over closely, and nodded his head like he was agreeing with hisself about something.

"Come in and have a drink," he said, so I follered him into a native joint where they wasn't nothing but Chineses. They looked at me with about as much expression as fishes, and went on guzzling tea and rice wine out of them little fool egg-shell cups. The mandarin, or whatever he was, led the way into a room which the door was covered with velvet curtains and the walls had silk hangings with dragons all over 'em, and we sot down at a ebony table and a Chinaboy brung in a porcelain jug and the glasses.

The mandarin poured out the licker, and, whilst he was pouring mine, such a infernal racket arose outside the door that I turned around and looked, but couldn't see nothing for the curtains, and the noise quieted down all of a sudden. Them Chineses is always squabbling amongst theirselves.

So the mandarin said, "Let us drink to your vivid victory!"

"Aw," I said, "that wasn't nothin'. All I had to do was hit him."

But I drank, and I said, "This is funny tastin' stuff. What is it?"

"Kaoliang," he said. "Have another glass." So he poured 'em, and nigh upsot my glass with his sleeve as he handed it to me.

So I drank it, and he said, "What's the matter with your ears?"

"You oughta know, bein' a fight fan," I said.

"This fight tonight was the first I have ever witnessed," he confessed.

"I'd never thought it from the interest you've taken in the brawl," I said. "Well, these ears is what is known in the vernacular of the game as cauliflowers. I got 'em, also this undulatin' nose, from stoppin' gloves with human knuckles inside of 'em. All old-timers is similarly decorated, unless they happen to be of the dancin'-school variety."

"You have fought in the ring many times?" he inquired.

"Oftener'n I can remember," I answered, and his black eyes gleamed with some secret pleasure. I took another snort of that there Chinese licker out of the jug, and I begun to feel oratorical and histrionic.

"From Savannah to Singapore," I said, "from the alleys of Bristol to the wharfs of Melbourne, I've soaked the resin dust with my blood and the gore of my enermies. I'm the bully of the *Sea Girl,* the toughest ship afloat, and when I set foot on the docks, strong men hunt cover! I—"

I suddenly noticed my tongue was getting thick and my head was swimming. The mandarin wasn't making no attempt to talk. He was setting staring at me kinda intense-like, and his eyes glittered through a mist which was beginning to float about me.

"What the heck!" I said stupidly. Then I heaved up with a roar, and the room reeled around me. "You yeller-bellied bilge-rat!" I roared drunkenly. "You done doped my grog! You—"

I grabbed him by the shirt with my left, and dragged him across the table top, drawing back my right, but before I could bash him with it, something exploded at the base of my skull, and the lights went out.

I MUST OF been out a long time. Once or twice I had a sensation of being tossed and jounced around, and thought I was in my bunk and a rough sea running, and then again I kinda vaguely realized that I was bumping over a rutty road in a automobile, and I had a feeling that I ought to get up and knock somebody's block off. But mostly I just laid there and didn't know nothing at all.

When I did finally come to myself, the first thing I discovered was that my hands and feet was tied with ropes. Then I seen I was laying on a camp cot in a tent, and a big Chinaman with a rifle was standing over me. I craned my neck, and seen another man setting on a pile of silk cushions, and he looked kinda familiar.

At first I didn't recognize him, because now he was dressed in embroidered silk robes, Chinese style, but then I seen it was the mandarin. I struggled up to a sitting position, in spite of my bonds, and addressed him with poignancy and fervor.

"Why," I concluded passionately, "did you dope my licker? Where am I at? What've you done with me, you scum of a Macao gutter?"

"You are in the camp of General Yun Chei," he said. "I transported you hither in my automobile while you lay senseless."

"And who the devil are you?" I demanded.

He gave me a sardonic bow. "I am General Yun Chei, your humble servant," he said.

"The hell you are!" I commented with a touch of old-world culture. "You had a nerve, comin' right into Hong Kong."

"The Federalist fools are blind," he said. "Often I play my own spy."

"But what'd you kidnap *me* for?" I yelled with passion, jerking at my cords till the veins stood out on my temples. "I can't pay no cussed ransom."

"Have you ever heard of General Feng?" he asked.

"And what if I has?" I snarled, being in no mood for riddles.

"He is camped nearby," said he. "He is a white foreign-devil like yourself. You have heard his nickname—General Ironfist?"

"Well?" I demanded.

"He is a man of great strength and violent passions," said General Yun. "He has acquired a following more because of his personal fighting ability than because of his intellect. Whomever he strikes with his fists falls senseless to the ground. So the soldiers call him General Ironfist.

"Now, he and I have temporarily allied our forces, because our mutual enemy, General Whang Shan, is somewhere in the vicinity. General Whang has a force greater than ours, and he likewise possesses an airplane, which he flies himself. We do not know exactly where he is, but, on the other hand, he does not know our position, either, and we are careful to guard against spies. No one leaves or enters our camp without special permission.

"Though General Ironfist and myself are temporary allies, there is no love lost between us, and he constantly seeks to undermine my prestige with my men. To protect myself I must retaliate—not so as to precipitate trouble between our armies, but in such a way as to make him lose face.

"General Feng boasts that he can conquer any man in China with his naked fists, and he has frequently dared me to pit my hardiest captains against him for the sheer sport of it. He well knows that no man in my army could stand up against him, and his arrogance lowers my prestige. So I went secretly to Hong Kong to find a man who might have a fighting chance against him. I contemplated the Yellow Typhoon, but when you laid him low with a single stroke, I knew you were the man for whom I was looking. I have many friends in Hong Kong. Drugging you was easy. The first time a pre-arranged noise at the door distracted your attention. But that was not enough, so I contrived to dope your second drink under cover of my sleeve. By the holy dragon, you had enough drug in you to have overcome an elephant before you succumbed!

"But here you are. I shall present you to General Feng, before all the captains, and challenge him to make good his boast. He cannot with honor refuse; and if you beat him, he will lose face, and my prestige will rise accordingly, because you represent me."

"And what do I get out of it?" I demanded.

"If you win," he said, "I will send you back to Hong Kong with a thousand American dollars."

"And what if I lose?" I said.

"Ah," he smiled bleakly, "a man whose head has been removed by the executioner's sword has no need of money."

I burst into a cold sweat and sot in silent meditation.

"Do you agree?" he asked at last.

"I'd like to know what choice I got," I snarled. "Take these here cords offa me and gimme some grub. I won't fight for nobody on a empty belly."

He clapped his hands, and the soldier cut my cords with his bayonet, and another menial come in with a big dish of mutton stew and some bread and rice wine, so I fell to and lapped it all up in a hurry.

"As a token of appreciation," said General Yun, "I now make you a present of this unworthy trinket."

And he hauled out the finest watch I ever seen and give it to me.

"If the gift pleases you," he said, noting my gratification, "let it nerve your thews against General Ironfist."

"Don't worry about that," I said, admiring the watch, which was gold with dragons carved on it. "I'll bust him so hard he'll be loopin' the loop for a week."

"Excellent!" beamed General Yun. "If you could contrive to deal him a fatal injury during the combat, it could simplify matters greatly. But come! I shall tangle General Feng in his own web!"

I FOLLERED HIM out of the tent, and seen a lot of other tents and ragged soldiers drilling amongst 'em, and off to one side another camp with more yeller-bellied gunmen in it. It was still kinda early in the morning, and I gathered it had tooken us all night to get there in Yun's auto. We was away up in the hills, and they was no sign of civilization anywheres.

General Yun headed straight for a big tent in the middle of the camp, and I follered him in. A lot of officers in all kinds of uniforms riz and bowed, except one big man who sot on a camp stool. He was a white man in faded khaki and boots and a sun helmet; his fists was as big as mauls, and his hairy arms was thick with muscles. His face and corded neck was burned brick-colored by the sun, and he wore a expression like he habitually hankered for somebody to give him a excuse to slug 'em.

"General Yun—" he begun in a harsh voice, then stopped and glared at me. "What the hell are you doing here?" he demanded.

"Joel Ballerin!" I said, staring at him. I might of knowed. Wherever they was war, you'd usually find Joel Ballerin right in the middle of it. He was from South Australia, and had a natural instinct for carnage. He was famed as a fighting man all over South Africa, Australia and the South Seas. Gunrunner, blackbirder, smuggler, pirate, pearler, or what have you, but always a scrapper from the word go, with a constant hankering to bounce his enormous fists offa somebody's conk. I'd never fit him, but I'd saw some of his handiwork. The ruin he could make of a human carcass was plumb appalling.

He glared at me with no love, because I got considerable reputation as a man-mauler myself, and fighting men is jealous of each other's fame. I couldst feel my own short hairs bristle as I glared at him.

"You have boasted much of your prowess with the clenched fist," said Yun Chei, softly. "You have repeatedly assured me that there was not a man in my army, including my unworthy self, whom you could not subdue with ease. I have here one of my followers whom I venture to back against you."

"That's Steve Costigan, an American sailor," snarled Ballerin. "He's no man of yours."

"On the contrary!" said General Yun. "Do you not see that he wears my dragon watch, entrusted only to my loyal henchmen?"

"Well," growled Ballerin, "there's something fishy about this. When you bring that cabbage-eared gorilla up here—"

"Hey!" I said indignantly. "You cease heavin' them insults around! If you ain't got the guts to fight, why, say so!"

"Why, you blasted fool!" he roared, jumping up off his stool like it was red hot. "I'll break your infernal head right here and now—"

General Yun got between us and smiled blandly and said, "Let us be dignified in all things. Let it be a public exhibition. I fear this tent would not prove a proper arena for two such gladiators. I shall have a ring constructed at once."

Ballerin turned away, grunting, "All right; fix it any way you want to." Then he wheeled back, his eyes flaming, and snarled at me, "As for you, you Yankee ape, you're going out of this camp feet-first!"

"Big talk don't bust no chins," I retorted. "I never did like you anyway, you nigger-stealin' pearl-thief!"

He looked like he was going to bust some blood-vessels, but he just give a ferocious snarl and plunged out of the tent. General Yun motioned me to foller him, and his officers tagged after us. The others follered General Feng. They didn't seem to be no love lost betwixt them two armies.

"General Ironfist is caught in his own snare!" gurgled General Yun, hugging hisself with glee. "He lusts for battle, but is furious and suspicious because I trapped him into it. All the men of both armies shall see his downfall. Call in the patrols from the hills! General Ironfist! Ha!"

GENERAL YUN DIDN'T take me back to his tent, but he put me in another'n and told me to holler if I wanted anything. He said I'd be guarded so's Ballerin couldn't have me bumped off, but I seen I was as good as a prisoner.

Well, I sot in there, and heard some men come marching up and surround the tent, and somebody give orders in broken Chinese, and cussed heartily in English, and I stuck my head out of the door and hollered, *"Soapy!"*

There he was, all right, commanding the guard, with a old British army coat three sizes too small for him, and a sword three sizes too big. He nigh dropped his sword when he seen me, and bellered, "Steve! What you doin' here?"

"I come up to lick Joel Ballerin for Yun Chei," I said. And he said, "So that's why they're buildin' that ring! Nobody but the highest officers knows what's goin' on."

"What you doin' here?" I demanded.

"Aw," he said, "I got tired tendin' bar and decided to become a soldier of fortune. So I skipped to Hong Kong and beat it up into the hills and joined Yun Chei. But Steve, the life ain't what it's cracked up to be. I don't mind the fightin' much, cause it's mostly yellin' and shootin' and little damage done, but marchin' through these hills is hell, and the food is lousy. We don't get paid regular, and no place to spend the dough when we do get it. For ten cents I'd desert."

"Well, lissen," I said, "I got a letter for you." I reached into my britches pocket, and then I give a yelp. "I been rolled!" I hollered. "It's gone!"

"What?" he said.

"Your letter," I said. "I was lookin' for you to give it to you. It come to the American Bar at Tainan. A letter from the Ormond and Ashley law firm, 'Frisco."

"What was in it?" he demanded.

"How should I know?" I returned irritably. "I didn't open it. I thought maybe somebody had left you a lot of dough, or somethin'."

"I've heard pa say he had wealthy relatives," said Soapy, doubtfully. "Look again, Steve."

"I've looked," I said. "It ain't here. I bet Yun Chei took it offa me whilst I was out. I'll go over and bust him on the jaw—"

"Wait!" hollered Soapy. "You'll get us both shot! You ain't supposed to leave this tent, and I got to guard you."

"Well," I said, "t'aint likely they was any money in the letter.

Likely they was just tellin' you where to go to get the dough. I remember the address, and when I get back to Hong Kong, I'll write and tell 'em I got you located."

"That's a long time to wait," said Soapy, pessimistically.

"Not so long," I said. "As soon as I lick Ballerin, I'll start for Hong Kong—"

"No, you won't" said Soapy. "No ways soon, anyhow."

"What d'you mean?" I asked. "Yun said he'd send me back if I licked Ballerin."

"He didn't say when, did he?" inquired Soapy. "He ain't goin' to take no chance of you going back and talkin' and revealin' our position to Whang's spies. No, sir; he'll keep you prisoner till he's ready to change camp, and that may be six months."

"Me stay in this dump six months?" I exclaimed fiercely. "I won't do it!"

"Maybe you won't at that," he said cheeringly. "A lot of things can happen unexpected around a rebel Chinee camp. I see you're wearin' Yun Chei's dragon watch."

"Yeah," I said. "Ain't it a beaut? Yun Chei give it to me."

"Well" he said, "that watch has been give away before, but it has a way of comin' back to Yun Chei after the owner's demise, which is generally sudden and frequent. Four men that I know of has already been made a present of that watch, and none of 'em is now alive."

"The hell you say!" I said, beginning to perspire copiously. "This is a nice, friendly place I got into. Do *you* want to stay here?"

"No, I don't!" he replied bitterly. "I didn't want to before, and when I thinks they's maybe a million dollars waitin' somewhere for me to spend, I feels like throwin' down this fool sword and headin' for the coast."

"Well," I said, "I ain't goin' to spend no six months here. Yet I wants that thousand bucks. Let's us make a break tonight, after I collects."

"They'd run us down before we'd went far," he said despondently. "I got one of the few good horses in camp, but it couldn't carry us both at any kind of a clip. All the other nags are fastened up and guarded so nobody can desert and carry news of our whereabouts to General Whang, which would give a leg to know, so he could raid us. Yun Chei knows he can trust me not to, because Whang wants to cut off my head. I stole a batch of his eatin' chickens onst when we was fightin' him over near Kauchau."

"Well," I begun hotly, "I'll be derned if *I'm* goin' to—"

"Shhh!" he said. "We got to change guard now; here comes the other squad. I'm goin' off somewheres and think."

Another gang of Chinamen come up with a native officer in

charge, and Soapy and his men marched off, and I sot and wound my dragon watch, and tried to think of something, but didn't have no success, as usual.

TIME DRAGGED SLOW, but finally about the middle of the afternoon, a mob of captains or something come and led me out of the tent and escorted me to the ring which had been built about halfway between the camps. They was already a solid bank of soldiers around it, Yun Chei's on one side and General Feng's on the other, with their rifles. The ring was just four posts stuck in the ground, with ropes stretched between 'em, and a bare floor of boards elevated maybe a yard or more. General Yun was setting in a camp chair on one side, with his officers around him, and a big Chinee, which was naked to the waist, was standing right behind him. The other officers and the common soldiers of both armies sot on the ground or stood up.

I didn't see Soapy nowheres, and they wasn't no seconds nor handlers. The Chineses didn't know nothing about such things. I clumb into the ring and examined the ropes, which was too loose, for one thing, and the floor, which was solid enough but none too even, and no padding of any kind on it. They had had sense enough to put camp stools in the corners, so I shed my cap, coat and shirt, and sot down. General Yun then riz and come over to me and smiled gently and said, "Smite the dog as you smote the Yellow Typhoon. If you lose the fight, you will lose your head in this very ring."

"I ain't goin' to lose," I snarled, being fed up on that kind of talk, and he smiled benevolently and retired to his chair. Just then somebody yanked my pants leg, and I looked down and seen Soapy. He was shaking with excitement.

"Don't talk, Steve!" he whispered. "Just lissen! Yun Chei thinks I'm encouragin' you for the battle. But lissen: I've fixed it! I got wind of a Federal army camped in a valley to the south. They don't know nothin' about us, but I found a man who swore I could trust him, and I smuggled him off on my horse. He'll guide 'em back here, and they'll break up this den of thieves. When the shootin' starts, we'll duck and run for the Federal lines. I sent my man right after I talked to you this mornin', so they oughta get here in maybe an hour or so."

"Well," I said, "I hope they don't get here too soon; I want to collect my thousand bucks from Yun Chei before I run."

"I'm goin' to snoop amongst Feng's men," he hissed, and just then the crowd on the opposite side of the ring divided, and here come Feng hisself, alias Joel Ballerin.

He was stripped to the waist, and he wore his fighting scowl. His short blond hair bristled, and his men sent up a cheer. He *was* big, and well built for speed and power. He had broad, square shoulders, a big arching chest, and a heavy neck, and his muscles fairly bulged under his sun-reddened skin with every move he made. He stood square on his wide-braced legs, and they showed plenty of power and drive. He was a fraction of a inch taller'n me, and weighed about 200 to my 190, all bone and muscle and hellfire.

Looking back on that fight, it was one of the strangest I ever mixed in. They wasn't no referee. They was a Chinaman who whanged a gong every now and then when he remembered to, but he wasn't no-ways consistent in his time-keeping. Some of the rounds lasted thirty seconds and some lasted nine or ten minutes. When one of us went down, they wasn't no counting. The idea was that we should just keep on battling till one of us wasn't able to get up at all. We hadn't no gloves. Bare knuckles don't jolt like the mitts, but they cut and bruise. It's hard to knock out a tough man in good condition with one lick or half a dozen licks of your bare maulers. You got to plumb butcher him.

They was few preliminaries. Ballerin vaulted into the ring, kicked his stool through the ropes, and yelled, "Hit that gong, Wu Shang!" Wu Shang hit it, and Ballerin come for me like a cross between a bucking bronco and a China typhoon.

We met in the center of the ring like a thunder-clap, and his first lick split my left cauliflower, and my first clout laid his jaw open to the bone. After that it was slaughter and massacre.

There wasn't nothing fancy about our battling. It was toe to toe, and breast to breast, bare knuckles crunching against muscle and bone. Before the first round was over we was slipping in smears of our own blood. In the second Ballerin nearly fractured my jaw with a blazing left hook that stretched me on the floor. But I was up and slugging like mad at the bell. We begun the third by rushing from our corners with such fury that we had a head-on collision which dumped us both to the boards nigh senseless. Ballerin's scalp was laid open, and my head had a bump on it as big as a egg. The Chineses screamed with amazement, seeing us both writhing on the floor, but we staggered up about the same time and begun swinging at each other when Wu Shang got rattled and hit the gong.

AT THE BEGINNING of the fourth I started bombarding Ballerin's mid-section whilst he pounded my head till my ears was ringing like all the ship bells in Frisco harbor, and the blood got in my eyes till I couldn't see and was hitting by instinct. I could hear him gasping and panting as my iron maulers sunk deeper and deeper into his suffering belly, and finally, with a maddened roar, he grappled me and throwed me, and, setting astraddle of me, begun pounding my head against the boards, to the great glee of his warriors.

As Wu Shang seemed inclined to let that round go on forever, I resorted to some longshoreman tactics myself, kicked General Ironfist lustily in the back of the head, arched my body and throwed him off of me, and pasted him beautifully in the eye as he riz.

This reduced his available sight by half, and didn't improve his temper none, as he proved by giving vent to a screech like a steam whistle, and letting go a hurricane swing that caught me under the ear and wafted me across the ring into the ropes. Them being too loose, I continued my flight unchecked and lit headfirst in the laps of the soldiers outside.

I riz and started to climb back through the ropes, necessarily tromping on my victims as I done so, and one would've stabbed me with his bayonnet by way of reprisal if I hadn't thoughtfully kicked him in the jaw first. Then I seen Ballerin crouching at the ropes, grinning fiercely at me as he dripped blood and weighed his huge fists, and I seen his intention of socking me as I clumb through. I said, "Get back from them ropes and let me in, you scum of the bilge!"

"That's up to you, you wind-jamming baboon!" he laughed brutally. So I unexpectedly reached through the ropes and grabbed his ankle and dumped him on his neck, and before he could rise, I was back in the ring. He riz ravening, and just then Wu Shang decided to hit the gong.

At the beginning of the fifth we came together and slugged till we was blind and deaf and dizzy, and when we finally heard the gong, we dropped in our tracks and lay there side by side, gasping for breath, till the gong announced the opening of the sixth, and we riz up and started in where we'd left off.

We was exchanging lefts and rights like a hail storm when he brung one up from the floor so fast I never seen it coming. The first part of me that hit the boards was the back of my head, and it nigh caved in the floor. I riz and tore into him, slugging with frenzied abandon, and battered him back across the ring, but I was so blind I missed him as he side-stepped, and fell into the ropes, and he smashed me three times behind the ear, and then, as I wheeled groggily, he caught me square on the button with a most awful right swing. *Wham!* I don't remember falling, but I must of, because the next thing I knowed I was down on the boards and Ballerin was stomping in my ribs with his boots. Away off I could hear Wu Shang banging his gong, but Ballerin give no heed, and I felt myself slipping into dreamland.

Then my blood-misted gaze, wandering at random, rested on General Yun in his camp chair. He smiled at me grimly, and that half-naked Chinaman behind him drawed a great curved sword and run his thumb along the edge.

With a howl of desperation I steadied my tottering brain, and I fought my way to my feet in spite of all Ballerin could do, and I pasted him with a left that tore his ear nearly off his head, and he went reeling into the ropes. He come back with a roar and a tremendous clout that missed me and splintered one of the ring posts, and I heaved my right under his heart with all my beef behind it. I heard a couple of his ribs crack under it, and I follered it with a hurricane of lefts and rights that drove him staggering before me like a ship in a typhoon. A thundering right to the head bent him back over the ropes, and then, just as I was setting myself for the finisher, I felt somebody jerking my pants leg and heard Soapy hollering to me amidst the roar of the mob, "Steve! Ballerin's got fifty rifles trained on you right now. If you drop him, you'll never leave that ring alive."

I SHOOK THE blood outa my eyes and cast a desperate glare over my shoulder. The front ranks of General Feng's warriors still leaned on their rifles, but behind 'em I caught a glimmer of black muzzles.

Ballerin pitched off the ropes, swinging a wild overhand right that missed by a yard, and he would of tumbled to the boards if I hadn't grabbed him and held him up.

"What'm I goin' to do?" I howled. "If I don't drop him, Yun Chei'll cut off my head, and if I do, his men'll shoot me!"

"Stall, Steve!" begged Soapy. "Keep it up as long as you can; somethin' might happen any minute now."

I cast a glance at the sun, and sweated with despair. But I held Ballerin up as long as I dared, and then I pushed him away from me and swung wide at him. He reeled and I tried to catch him, but he pitched face-first, and I ducked as I heard a click of rifle bolts. But he was trying to climb up again, and I never hoped to see a opponent rise like I hoped to see him rise. He grabbed the ropes and hauled hisself up, and stared around, one eye closed and t'other glassy.

He was out on his feet, but his fighting instinct kept him going. He come blundering out into the ring, swinging blind, and I swung wide, but he fell into it somehow, and I hit him in spite of myself. Soapy give a lamentable howl, and Ballerin pitched back into the ropes, and I was on him and locked him in a despairing grasp before he could fall. He was dead weight in my arms, out cold, his legs dragging, and I was so near out myself I wondered how long I couldst hold him up. Over his shoulder I see General Yun looking at me impatient; even a Chinese revolutionist could see that General Ironfist was ready for the cleaners. But I held on; if I let go, I knowed Ballerin wouldn't get up again, and his men would start target practice on me.

Then above the noise of the crowd I heard a low roar. I looked out over their heads, and beyond the ridge of a distant hill something come soaring. It was a airplane, and nobody but me had seen it. I wrestled my limp victim to the ropes, and gasped the news to Soapy. He was too smart to look, but he hissed, "Keep stallin'! Hold him up! The Federals have sent a plane to our rescue! Everything's jake!"

General Yun had got suspicious. He jumped up and shook his fist at me, and hollered, and his derned executioner grinned and drawed his sword again—and then, with a rush and zoom, the airplane swooped down on us like a hawk. Everybody looked up and yelled, and as it passed right over the ring, I seen something tumble from it and flash in the sun. And Soapy yelled, "Look out! There's a dragon painted on it! That ain't a Federal plane—that's *Whang Shan!*"

I throwed Ballerin bodily over the ropes as far as I could heave him, and div after him, and the next instant—*blam!*—the ring went up in smoke, and pieces flew every which way.

BOMBS WAS FALLING and crashing and tents going sky-high, and men yelling and shooting and running and falling over each other, and the roar of that cussed plane was in my ears as I headed for the tall timber. I was vaguely aware that Soapy was legging it alongside me, hollering, "That Chinaman of mine never went to the Federals, the dirty rat! I see it all now! He was one of Whang Shan's spies. No wonder he was so anxious to help! He wanted my horse—hey, Steve! This way!"

I seen Soapy do a running dive into General Yun's auto, which was setting in front of his tent, and I follered him. We went roaring away just as a bomb hit where the car had been a second before, and spattered us with dirt. I dunno where General Yun was, though I caught a glimpse of a silk-robed figure, which might of been him, scudding for the hills.

We went through that camp like a tornado, with all hell popping behind us. Whang was sure giving his enermies the works in that one plane of his'n. They was such punk shots they couldn't hit him with their rifles, and all he had to do was heave bombs into the thick of 'em.

I don't remember much about that ride. Soapy was hanging to the wheel and pushing the accelerator through the floor, and I was holding onto the seat and trying to stay with the derned craft which was bucking over that awful road like a skiff in a squall. Presently we hit a bump that throwed me clean over the seat into the back, and when I come up for air I had something clutched in my hand, at the sight of which I give a yell of joy—and bit my tongue savagely as we hit another bump.

I clumb back into the front seat like I was crawling along the cross-trees of the main-mast in a typhoon, and tried to tell Soapy what I'd found, but we was going so fast the wind blowed the words clean outa my mouth.

It wasn't till we had dropped down out of the higher hills along about sundown and was coasting along a comparatively better road amongst fields and mud huts that I got a chance to catch my breath.

"I found your letter," I said. "It was in the bottom of the car. It must of slipped outa my pocket whilst I was tied up."

"Read it to me," he requested, and I said, "Wait till I see is my watch intact. I didn't get my thousand bucks for lickin' Ballerin, and I want to be sure I got *somethin*, for goin' through what I been through."

So I looked at the watch, which must of been worth five hundred dollars anyway, and it was unscratched, so I opened the letter and read: "Ormond and Ashley, attorneys at law, San Francisco, California, U. S. A. Dear Mister Jackson: This is to inform you that you are being sued by Mrs. J. A. Lynch for a nine months board bill, amounting to exactly—"

Soapy give a ear-splitting yell and wrenched the wheel over.

"What you doin', you idjit?" I howled, as the car r'ared and skidded and lurched around like a skiff in a tide-rip.

"I'm goin' back to Yun Chei!" he screeched. "My expectations is bust! I thought I was a heiress, but I'm still a bum! I ain't got the—"

Crash! We left the road, rammed a tree, and went into a perfect tailspin.

The evening shadders was falling as I crawled out from under the debris and untangled one of the wheels from around my neck. I looked about for Soapy's remains, and seen 'em setting on a busted headlight, brooding somberly.

"You might at least ask if I'm hurt," I said resentfully.

"What of it?" he asked bitterly. "We're ruined. I ain't got not fortune."

"I was ruined when I first met a hoodoo like you," I said fiercely. "Anyway, I still got Yun Chei's watch." And I reached into my pocket. And then I gave a poignant shriek. That watch must of absorbed the whole jolt of the smash. I had a handful of metal scraps and wheels and springs which nobody could tell was they meant for a watch or what. Thereafter, a figure might have been seen flitting through the twilight, hotly pursued by another, bulkier figure, breathing threats of vengeance, in the general direction of the coast.

SLUGGERS OF THE BEACH

A Sailor Costigan Story

It started in the ring and ended in the ring, with a strange interlude in the searing sunlight of the blue Pacific, between them the pact: "Winner takes the treasure!"

By Robert E. Howard

SLUGGERS ON THE BEACH

THE MINUTE I seen the man which was going to referee my fight with Slip Harper in the Amusement Palace Fight Club, Shanghai, I takes a vi'lent dislike to him. His name was Hoolihan, a fighting sailor, same as me, and he was a big red-headed gorilla with hands like hairy hams, and he carried hisself with a swagger which put my teeth on edge. He looked like he thought he was king of the waterfront, and that there is a title I aspires to myself.

I detests these conceited jackasses. I'm glad that egotism ain't amongst my faults. Nobody'd ever know, from my conversation, that I was the bully of the toughest ship afloat, and the terror of bucko mates from Valparaiso to Singapore. I'm that modest I don't think I'm half as good as I really am.

But Red Hoolihan got under my hide with his struttings and giving instructions in that fog-horn beller of his'n. And when he discovered that Slip Harper was a old shipmate of his'n, his actions growed unbearable.

He made this discovery in the third round, whilst counting over Harper, who hadst stopped one of my man-killing left hooks with his chin.

"Seven! Eight! Nine!" said Hoolihan, and then he stopped counting and said: "By golly, ain't you the Johnny Harper that used to be bos'n aboard the old *Saigon*?"

"Yuh—yeah!" goggled Harper, groggily, getting his legs under him, whilst the crowd went hysterical.

"What's eatin' you, Hoolihan?" I roared indignantly. "G'wan countin'!"

He gives me a baleful glare.

"I'm refereein' this mill," he said. "You tend to your part of it. By golly, Johnny, I ain't seen you since I broke jail in Calcutta—"

But Johnny was up at last, and trying to keep me from taking him apart, which all that prevented me was the gong.

Hoolihan helped Harper to his corner, and they kept up an animated conversation till the next round started—or rather Hoolihan did. Harper wasn't in much condition to enjoy conversation, having left three molars embedded in my right glove.

Whilst we was whanging away at each other during the fourth, I was aware of Hoolihan's voice.

"Stand up to him, Johnny," he said. "I'll see that you get a square deal. G'wan, sink in your left. That right to the guts didn't hurt us none. Pay no attention to them body blows. He's bound to weaken soon."

Enraged beyond control, I turned on him and said, "Look here, you red-headed baboon, are you a referee or a second?"

I dunno what retort he was fixing to make, because just then Harper takes advantage of my abstraction to slam me behind the ear with all he had. Maddened by this perfidy, I turned and sunk my left to the hilt in his midriff, whereupon he turned a beautiful pea-green.

"Tie into him, Johnny," urged Hoolihan.

"Shut up, Red," gurgled Harper, trying to clinch. "You're makin' him mad, and he's takin' it out on *me*!"

"Well, we can take it," begun Hoolihan, but at that moment I tagged Harper on the ear with a meat-cleaver right, and he done a nose-dive, to Hoolihan's extreme disgust.

"One!" he hollered, waving his arm like a jib-boom. "Two! Three! Get up, Johnny. This baboon can't fight."

"Maybe he can't," said Johnny, dizzily, squinting up from the canvas, with his hair full of resin, "but if he hits me again like he just done, I'll be a candidate for a harp. And I hate music. You can count all night if you want to, Red, but as far as I'm concerned, the party's over!"

Hoolihan give a snort of disgust, and grabbed my right arm and raised it and hollered: "Ladies and gents, it is with the deepest regret that I announce this bone-headed gorilla as the winner!"

With a beller of wrath, I jerked my arm away from him and hung a clout on his proboscis that knocked him headfirst through the ropes. Before I couldst dive out on top of him, as was my firm intention, I was seized from behind by ten special policemen—rough-houses is so common in the Amusement Palace that the promoter is always prepared. Whilst I was being interfered with by these misguided idjits, Hoolihan riz from amongst the ruins of the benches and customers, and tried to crawl back into the ring, bellering like a bull and spurting blood all over everything. But a large number of people fell on him with piercing yells and dragged him back and set on him.

Meanwhile forty or fifty friends of the promoter hadst come to the rescue of the ten cops, and eventually I found myself back in my dressing-room without having been able to glut my righteous wrath on Red Hoolihan's huge carcass. He'd been carried out through one door whilst several dozen men was hauling me through another. It's a good thing for them that I'd left my white bulldog Mike aboard the *Sea Girl*.

I WAS SO blind mad I couldn't hardly get my clothes on, and by the time I hadst finished I was alone in the building. Gnashing my teeth slightly, I prepared to sally forth and find Red Hoolihan. Shanghai was too small for both of us.

But as I started for the door that opened into the corridor, I heard a quick rush of feet in the alley outside, and the back door of the dressing-room bust open. I wheeled, with my fists cocked, thinking maybe it was Red—and then I stopped short and gawped in surprise. It wasn't Red. It was a girl.

She was purty as all get-out, but now she was panting and pale and scared-looking. She shut the door and leaned against it.

"Don't let them get me!" she gurgled.

"Who?" I asked.

"Those Chinese devils!" she gasped. "The terrible Whang Yi!"

"Who's them?" I inquired, considerably bewildered.

"A secret society of fiends and murderers!" she said. "They chased me into that alley! They'll torture me to death!"

"They won't, neither," I said. "I'll mop up the floor with 'em. Lemme look!"

I pushed her aside and opened the door and stuck my head out in the alley. "I don't see nobody," I said.

She leaned back against the wall, with one hand to her heart. I looked at her with pity. Beauty in distress always touches a warm spot in my great, big, manly bosom.

"They're hiding out there, somewhere," she whimpered.

"What they chasin' you for?" I asked, forgetting all about my hurry to smear the docks with Red Hoolihan.

"I have something they want," she said. "My name is Laura Hopkins. I do a dance act at the European Grand Theater—did you ever hear of Li Yang?"

"The bandit chief which was raising Cain around here a couple of years ago?" I said. "Sure. He raided all up and down the coast. Why?"

"Last night I came upon a Chinaman dying in the alley behind the theater," she said. "He'd been stabbed. But he had a piece of paper in his mouth, which had been overlooked by the men who killed him. He had been one of Li Yang's soldiers. He gave me that paper, when he knew he was dying. It was a map showing where Li Yang had hidden his treasure."

"The heck you say!" I remarked, much interested.

"Yes. And the spot is less than a day's journey from here," she said. "But somehow the killers learned that I had this map. They call themselves the Whang Yi. They are the men who were the enemies of Li Yang in his lifetime. They want the treasure themselves. So they're after me. Oh, what shall I do?" she said, wringing her hands.

"Don't be afraid," I said. "I'll pertect you from them yeller-bellied rats."

"I want to get away," she whimpered. "I'm afraid to stay in Shanghai. They'll kill me. I dare not try to find the treasure. I'd give them the map if they'd only spare my life. But they'll kill me just for knowing about it. Oh, if I only had money enough to get away! I' d sell the map for fifty dollars."

"You would?" I ejaculated. "Why, that there treasure is likely to be a lot of gold and silver and jewerls and stuff. He was a awful thief."

"It won't do me any good dead," she answered. "Oh, what shall I do?"

"I'll tell you," I said, digging into my britches. "Sell it to me. I'll give you fifty bucks."

"Would you?" she cried, jumping up, her eyes shining. "No—oh, no; it wouldn't be fair to you. It's too dangerous. I'll tear the map up, and—"

"Wait a minute!" I hollered. "Don't do that, dern it! I'll take the risks. I ain't scared of no yeller bellies. Here, here's the fifty. Gimme the map."

"I'm afraid you'll regret it," she said. "But here it is."

Whilst she was counting the fifty, I looked at the map, feeling like I was holding a fortune in my hand. It seemed to represent a small island laying a short distance offa the mainland, with trees and things growing on it. One of these trees was taller'n the others and stood off to itself. A arrer run from it to a spot on the beach, which was marked with a "x." There was a lot of Chinese writing on the edge of the map, and a line of English.

"Fifty paces south of that tall tree," said Miss Hopkins. "Five feet down in the loose sand. The island is only a few hours run from the port, if you take a motor launch. Full directions are written out there in English."

"I'll find it," I promised, handling the map with awe and reverence. "But before I start, I'll see you home so them Whang Yis won't try to grab you."

But she said, "No, I'll go out the front way and hail a cab. Tomorrow night I'll be safe on the high seas. I'll never forget what you've done for me."

"If you'll give me the address of where you're goin'," I said, "I'll see that you get a share of the treasure if I finds it."

"Don't worry about that," she said. "You've already done more for me than you realize. Goodbye! I hope you find all you deserve."

And she left in such a hurry I hardly realized she had went till she was gone.

WELL, I WASTED no time. I forgot all about Red Hoolihan—a man with millions on his mind ain't got no time for such hoodlums—and I headed for a certain native quarter of the waterfront as fast as I could leg it. I knowed a Chinese fisherman named Chin Yat who had a motor launch which he rented out, and being as I had given all my money to Miss Hopkins, I didn't have no dough, and he was the only one which I knowed would let me have his boat on credit.

It was late, because the fight card had been a unusually long one. It was away past midnight when I got to Chin Yat's, and I seen him and a big white man puttering around the boat, under the light of torches burning near the wharves. I bust into a run, because I was afraid he'd rent the boat before I could get there, though I couldn't figger what any white man would want with a boat that time of night.

As I hove up, I hollered, "Hey Chin, I wanta rent your boat—"

The big white man turned around, and the torchlight fell on his face. It was Red Hoolihan.

"What you doin' here?" he demanded, clenching his fists.

"I got no time to waste on you," I snarled. "I'll fix you later. Chin, I gotta have your motor-boat."

He shook his head and sing-songed, "Velly solly. No can do."

"What you mean?" I hollered. "How come you can't?"

"'Cause it's already rented to me," said Hoolihan, "and I've done paid him his dough in advance."

"But this here's important," I bellered. "I *got* to have that boat! It means a lot of dough."

"What d'you know about a lot of dough?" snorted Hoolihan. "I need that boat because I'm goin' after more dough than you ever dreamed of, you bone-headed ape! You know why I ain't takin' the time to caulk the wharf-timbers with your gore? Well, I'll tell you, so you won't get no false ideas. I ain't got the time to waste on a baboon like you. I'm goin' after hidden treasure! When I come back, that boat'll be loaded to the gunnels with gold!"

And so saying, he waved a piece of paper in my face.

"Where'd you get that?" I yelped.

"None of your business," he said. "That's—hey, leggo that!"

I had made a grab for it, in my excitement, and he took a poke at me. I busted him in the snout in return, and he nearly went over the lip of the wharf. He managed to catch hisself—and then he let out a agonized beller. The paper had slipped outa his hand and vanished in the black water.

"Now look what you done!" he howled frantically. "You've lost me a fortune. Put up your mitts, you spawn of the devil's gutter! I'm goin' to knock—"

"Did your map look like this?" I asked, pulling out mine and showing it to him in the torchlight. The sight sobered him quick.

"By Judas!" he bawled. "The same identical map! Where'd you get it?"

"Never mind about that," I said. "The p'int is, we both knows what the other'n's after. We both wants the treasure Li Yang hid before the Federalists bumped him off. I got a map but no boat, you got a boat but no map. Let's go!"

"Before I'd share anything with you," he said bitterly, "I'd lose the whole shebang."

"Who said anything about sharin' anything?" I roared. "The best man takes the loot. I still got a score to settle with you. We finds the plunder, and then we settles our argument. Winner takes the treasure!"

"Okay with me," he agreed, blood-thirstily. "Come on!"

But as we sputtered outa the harbor in the starlight, a sudden thought hit me.

"Hold on!" I said. "Does this here island lie south or north of the port?"

"Cut off the engine and we'll look at the map," he said, holding up a lantern. I done so, and we peered at the line of English which was writ in a very small, femernine hand.

"That's a 'n'," said Red, pointing at it with his big, hairy finger. "It means the island lies north of the harbor."

"It looks like a 's' to me," I said. "I believe it means the island's south of the harbor."

"I say north!" exclaimed Hoolihan, angrily.

"South!" I snarled.

"We goes north!" bellered Hoolihan, brandishing his fists. He hadn't no control over his temper at all. "We goes north or nowheres!"

As I started to rise, my foot hit something in the bottom of the launch. It was a belaying pin. I ain't a man to be gypped out of a fortune account of the stubbornness of some misguided jackass. I laid that belaying pin over Red Hoolihan's ear with a full-arm swing.

"We goes south," I repeated truculently, and they was no opposing voice.

FEELING YOUR WAY along that coast at night in a motor-launch ain't no picnic. Hoolihan come to just about daylight, and he got up and rubbed the lump over his ear, and cussed free and fervent.

"I won't forget this," he said. "This here is another score to settle with you. Where at are we?"

"There's the island, dead ahead," I answered.

He scowled over the map, and said, "It don' t look like the one on the map."

"You expect a ignerant Chinese to draw a perfect map?" I retorted. "It's bound to be the one. Look for a tall tree standing kinda out alone. It oughta be on this end of the island."

But it wasn't; they wasn't nothing there but low, thick bushes rising outa marshy land. We tried the other end of the island, and I said: "This is it. The Chinee made another mistake. He put the tree on the wrong end of the island. There's a sandy beach and a tall palm standin' out from the rest of the growth."

Hoolihan had forgot all about his doubts. He was as impatient as me to get ashore. We run in and tied up in a narrow cove, and tramped through the deep sand to the trees, packing the picks and shovels we had brung along, and my heart beat faster as I realized that in a short time I wouldst be a millionaire.

That tall palm was a lot closer to the water than it looked like on the map. When we'd stepped off fifty paces to the south, we was waist-deep in water!

"I see where we meets with engineerin' problems in our excavations," I said, but Hoolihan scowled and flexed his enormous arms, and said, "That ain't worryin' me. I'm thinkin' about somethin' else. Here we are, there's the treasure, lyin' under five foot of sand and water. All we got to do is dig it up. But we ain't settled yet whose treasure it is."

"All right," I said, shedding my shirt, "we settles it now."

With a roar, Hoolihan ripped off his shirt and squared off, the morning sun gleaming on the red hair of his gigantic chest, and the muscles standing out in knots all over his arms and shoulders. He come plunging in like the wild bull of Bashen, and I met him breast to breast with both maulers flailing.

He'd never been licked in a ring or out, they said. He was two hundred pounds of bone and bulging muscle, and he was quick as a cat on his feet. Or he would of been, if'n he'd had a chance to be.

We was standing ankle-deep in sand. They wasn't no chance for foot-work. It was like dragging our feet through hot mush. The sun riz higher and beat down on us like the pure essence of hell-fire, and it soaked vitality out of us like water out of a sponge. And that awful sand! It was worse'n having iron weights fastened to our ankles. There wasn't no foot-work, side-stepping—nothing but slug, slug, slug! Toe to toe, leaning head to head, with our four maulers working like sledge-hammers fastened on pistons.

I dunno how long we fought. It musta been hours, because the sun crawled up and up, and beat down on us like red hot lances. Everything was floating red before me; I couldn't hear nothing except Red's gusty panting, the scruff of our feet through that hellish sand, and the thud and crunch of our fists.

Talk about the heat Jeffries and Sharkey fought in at Coney Island, and the heat of the ring at Toledo! Them places was Eskimo igloos compared to that island, under that awful sun! I got so numb I could scarcely feel the jolt of Hoolihan's iron fists. I'd done quit any attempt at defense, and so had he. We was just driving in our punches wide open and with all we had behind 'em.

One of my eyes was closed, the brow split and the lid sagging down like a curtain. Half the hide was missing from my face, and one cauliflowered ear was pounded into a purple pulp. Blood was oozing from my lips, nose and ears. Sweat poured off my chest and run down my legs till I was standing in mud. We was both slimy with sweat and blood. I could hear the agonized pound of my own heart, and it felt like it was going to bust right through my ribs. My calf muscles and thigh muscles was quivering cords of fire, where they wasn't numb and dead. Every time I dragged a foot through that clinging, burning sand it felt like the joints of my limbs was giving apart.

But Hoolihan was reeling like a stabbed ox, staggering and blowing. His breath was sobbing through his busted teeth, and blood streamed down his chin. His belly was heaving like a sail in the wind, and his ribs was raw beef from my body punching.

I was driving him before me, step by step. And the next thing I knowed, we was under the shade of that big palm tree, and the sun wasn't flaying my back no more. It was almost like a dash of cold water. It revived Hoolihan a little, too. I seen him stiffen and lift his head, but he was done. My body beating hadst took all the starch outa his spine. My legs were dead, and I couldn't rush him no more, but I fell into him and, as I fell, I crashed my right overhand to his jaw with my last ounce of strength.

It connected, and we went down together, him under me. I laid there for a second, and then I groped around and caught hold of the tree and hauled myself to my feet. Hanging on with one hand, I shook the blood and sweat outa my eyes, and begun counting. I was so dopey and groggy I got mixed up three or four times and had to start over, and finally I passed out on my feet, cause when I come to I was still counting up around thirty or forty. Hoolihan hadn't moved.

I tried to say, "By golly, the dough's mine!" But all I could do was gulp like a dying fish. I took one staggering step towards the picks and shovels, and then my legs give way and I went headfirst into the sand. And there I laid, like a dead man.

IT WAS THE sound of a motor putt-putting above the wash of the surf which first roused me. Then, a few minutes later, I heard feet scruff through the sand, and men talking and laughing. Then somebody swore loud and freely.

I shook the red glare outa my eyes and blinked up. Four men was standing there, with picks and shovels in their hands, staring down at me, and I rekernized 'em: Smoky Harrigan, Bat Schimmerling, Joe Donovan and Tom Storley, as dirty a set of rats as ever infested a wharf.

"Well, by Jupiter!" said Smoky, with the sneer he always wore. "What do you know about this? Costigan and Hoolihan! How come these gorillas to land on *this* island?"

I tried to get up, but my legs wouldn't work, and I sunk back into the sand. Hoolihan groaned and cussed groggily somewhere near me. Harrigan stooped and picked up something which I seen was my map which had fell into the sand.

He showed it to the others and they laughed loud and jeeringly, which dully surprised me. My brain was still too numb from Hoolihan's punching and that awful sun to hardly know what it was all about.

"Put that map down before I rises and busts you in half," I mumbled through pulped lips.

"Oh, is it yours?" asked Smoky, sardonically.

"I bought it offa Miss Laura Hopkins," I said groggily. "It's mine, and so is the dough. Gimme it before I lays you like a carpet."

"Laura Hopkins!" he sneered. "That was Suez Kit, the slickest girl-crook that ever rolled a drunk for his wad. She worked the same gyp on that big ox Hoolihan. I saw her take him as he left the fight club."

"What d'you mean?" I demanded, struggling up to a sitting posture. I still couldn't get on my feet, and Hoolihan was in even worse shape. "She sold the same map to Hoolihan? Is that where he got his'n?"

"Why, you poor sucker!" sneered Harrigan. "Can't you understand nothing? Them maps was fakes. I dunno what you're doin' here, but if you'd followed 'em, you'd been miles away to the north of the harbor, instead of the south."

"And there ain't no treasure of Li Yang?" I moaned.

"Sure there is," he said. "What's more, it's hid right here on this island. And this is the right map." He waved a strip of parchment all covered with lines and Chinese writing. "There's treasure here. Li Yang didn't hide it here hisself, but it was left here for him by a smuggler. Li Yang got bumped off before he could come for it. An old Chinee fence named Yao Shan had the map. Suez Kit bought it off him with the hundred bucks she gypped out of you and Hoolihan. He must have been crazy to sell it, but you can't never tell about them Chineses."

"But thc Whang Yis?" I gasped wildly.

"Horseradish!" sneered Smoky. "A artistic touch to put the story over. But if it'll make you feel any better, I'll tell you that Suez Kit lost the map after all. I'd been follerin' her for days, knowin' she was up to something, though I didn't know just what. When she got the map from old Yao Shan, I tapped her on the head and took it. And here we are!"

"The treasure's as much our'n as it is your'n," I protested.

"Heh! heh! heh!" he replied. "Try and get it. Gwan, boys, get to work. These big chumps has fought each other to a frazzle, and we got nothin' to fear from 'em."

So I laid there and et my soul out whilst they set about stealing our loot right under our noses. Smoky paid no attention to the palm tree. Studying the map closely, he located a big rock jutting up amongst some bushes, and he stepped off ten paces to the west. "Dig here," he said.

They pitched in digging a lot harder'n I had any idee them rats could work, and the sand flew. Purty soon Bat Schimmerling's pick crunched on something solid, and they all yelled.

"Look here!" yelled Tom Storley. "A lacquered chest, bound with iron bands!"

They all yelled with joy, and Hoolihan groaned dismally. He'd come to in time to get what it was all about.

"Gypped!" he moaned. "Cheated! Swindled! Framed! And now them thieves is robbin' us right before us!"

I HAULED MYSELF painfully across the sands, and stared down into the hole, and my heart leaped as I seen the top of a iron-bound chest at the bottom. A wave of red swept all the weakness and soreness outa my frame.

Smoky turned and yelled at me, "See what you've missed, you dumb chump? See that chest? I dunno what's in it, but whatever it is, it's worth millions! 'More precious than gold,' old Yao Shan said. And it's our'n! While you and that other gorilla are workin' out your lives haulin' ropes and eatin' resin dust, we'll be rollin' in luxury!"

"You'll roll in somethin' else first!" I yelled, heaving up amongst 'em like a typhoon. Harrigan swung up a pick, but before he couldst bring it down on my head, I spread his nose all over his face with a left hook which likewise deprived him of all his front teeth and rendered him *horse-de-combat.* At this moment Bat Schimmerling broke a shovel over my head, and Tom Storley run in and grappled with me. This was about the least sensible thing he could of done, as he instantly realized, and just before he lapsed into unconsciousness he hollered for Donovan to get a gun.

Donovan took the hint and run for the launch, where he procured a shotgun and come back on the jump. He hesitated to fire at long range, because I was so mixed up with Storley and Schimmerling that he couldn't hit me without riddling them. But about that time I untangled myself from Storley's senseless carcass and caressed Schimmerling's chin with a right uppercut which stood him on his head in the hole on top of the chest.

Donovan then give a yelp of triumph and throwed the gun to his shoulder—but Hoolihan had crawled up behind him on all-fours, and as Joe pulled the trigger, Red swept his legs out from under him. The charge combed my hair, it missed me that close, and Donovan crashed down on top of Hoolihan, who stroked his whiskers with a right that nearly tore his useless head off.

Hoolihan then crawled to the edge of the hole and looked down.

"It's your'n," he gulped. "You licked me. But it busts my heart to think of the dough I've lost."

"Aw, shut up," I growled, grabbing Schimmerling by the hind laig and dragging him out of the hole. "Help me get this chest outa here. Whatever's in it, you get half."

Hoolihan gaped at me.

"You mean that?" he gasped.

"He may, but I don't!" broke in a hard, femernine voice, and we whirled to behold Miss Laura Hopkins standing before us. But they was considerable change in her appearance. She wore a man's shirt, for one thing, and khaki pants and boots, and her face was a lot harder'n I remembered it. Moreover, they was a bandage on her head under her sun-helmet, and she had a pistol in her hand, p'inting at us. She looked like Suez Kit now, all right.

She give a sneer at Smoky and his minions, which was beginning to show signs of life.

"That fool thought he'd finished me, eh? Pah! I don't kill that easy," she said. "Stole my map, the rat! How did you two gorillas get here? Those maps I sold you were for an island half a day from here."

"It was my mistake," I said, and I added, limping disconsolately towards her, "I believed you. I thought you was in distress."

"The more fool you," she sneered. "I *had* to have a hundred dollars to buy Yao Shan's map. That gyp I worked on you and Hoolihan was the best one I could think of, at the spur of the moment. Now get to work and hoist that chest out, and load it in my boat. You're a sap to trust anybody—*ow!*"

I'd slapped the gun out of her hand so quick she didn't have time to pull the trigger. It went spinning into the water and sunk.

"Just because *you're* smart, you think everybody else is a sap," I snorted. "C'mon, Red, le's get our chest out."

SUEZ KIT STOOD staring wildly at us. "But it's mine!" she hollered. "I gave Yao Shan a hundred dollars—"

"You give him our hundred," I snorted. "You make me sick."

Me and Red bent down and got hold of the chest and rassled it out of the hole. Suez Kit was doing a war-dance all over the beach.

"You dirty, double-crossing rats!" she wept. "I might have known I couldn't trust any man! Robbers! Bandits! Oh, this is too much!"

"Oh, shut up," I said wearily. "We'll give you some of the

loot—gimme that rock, Red. The lock is plumb rotten."

I took the stone and hit the lock a few licks, and it come all to pieces. Smoky and his gang had come to, and they watched us wanly. Suez Kit fidgeted around behind us, and I heard her breath coming in pants. Red throwed open the lid. They was a second of painful silence, and then Suez Kit let out an awful scream and staggered back, her hands to her head. Hanigan and his mob lifted up their voices in lamentation.

That chest wasn't full of silver, nor platinum, nor jewels. It was full of machine-gun cartridges!

"Bullets!" said Hoolihan, kinda numbly. "No wonder Yao Shan was willing to sell the map. 'More precious than gold,' he said. Of course, this ammunition *was* more precious than gold to a bandit chief. Steve, I'm sick!"

So was Smoky and his gang. And Suez Kit wept like she'd sot on a hornet.

"Steve," said Red, as him and me limped towards our boat whilst the sounds of weeping and wailing riz behind us, "was it because I kept Donovan from blowin' your head off that you decided to split the treasure with me?"

"Do I look like a cheapskate?" I snapped. "I knowed from the first that I was going to split with you."

"Then why in the name of thunderation," he bellered, turning purple in the face, "did you have to beat me up like you done, when you was intendin' to split anyway? What was we fightin' about, anyway?"

"You might of been fightin' for the loot," I roared, brandishing my fists in his face, "but I was merely convincin' you who was the best man."

"Well, I ain't convinced," he bellered, waving *his* fists. "It was the sand and the sun which licked me, not you. We'll settle this in the ring tonight, at the Amusement Palace."

"Let's go!" I yelled, leaping into the launch. "I'm itchin' to prove to the customers that you're as big a flop as a fighter as you were as a referee."

Alleys of Darkness

By PATRICK ERVIN

A story of Singapore and Dennis Dorgan, hardest-fisted slugger in the merchant marine, and the maze of intrigue that enmeshed him

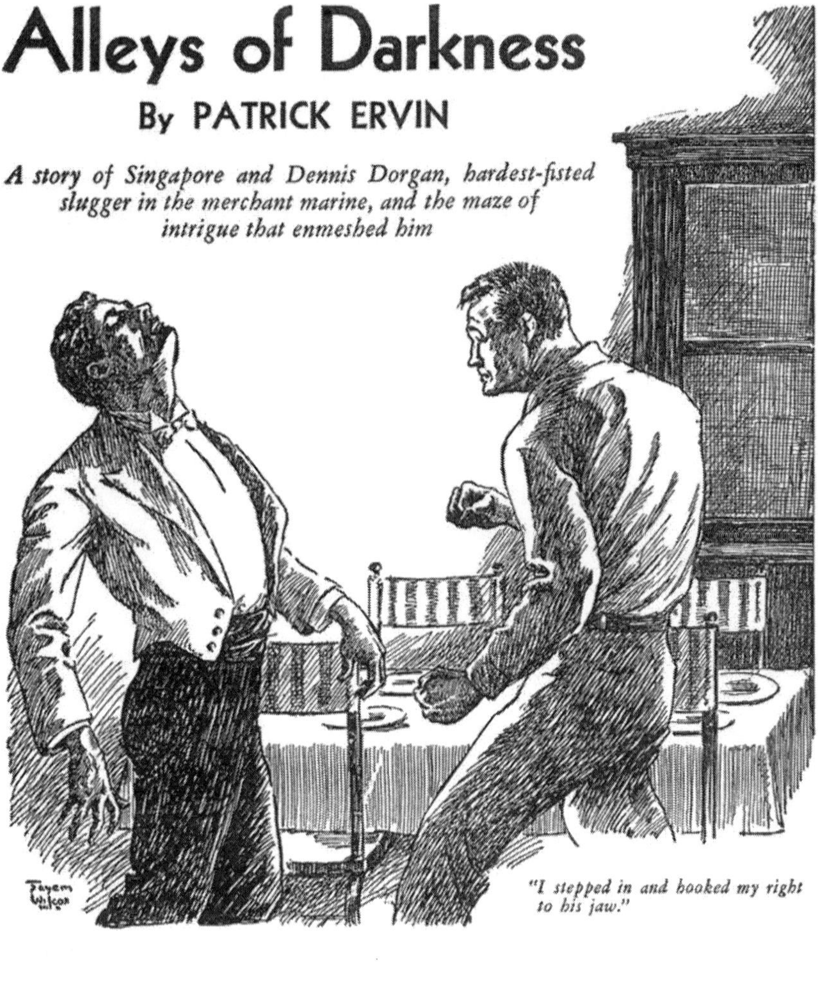

"I stepped in and hooked my right to his jaw."

ALLEYS OF DARKNESS

WHEN THE GONG ended my fight with Kid Leary in the Sweet Dreams Fight Club, Singapore, I was tired but contented. The first seven rounds had been close, but the last three I'd plastered the Kid all over the ring, though I hadn't knocked him out like I'd did in Shanghai some months before, when I flattened him in the twelfth round. The scrap in Singapore was just for ten; another round and I'd had him.

But anyway, I'd shaded him so thoroughly I knowed I'd justified the experts which had made me a three to one favorite. The crowd was applauding wildly, the referee was approaching, and I stepped forward and held out my glove hand—when to my utter dumfoundment, he brushed past me and lifted the glove of the groggy and bloody Kid Leary!

A instant's silence reigned, shattered by a nerve-racking scream from the ringside. The referee, Jed Whithers, released Leary, who collapsed into the rosin, and Whithers ducked through the ropes like a rabbit. The crowd riz bellowing, and recovering my frozen wits, I gave vent to lurid langwidge and plunged outa the ring in pursuit of Whithers. The fans was screaming mad, smashing benches, tearing the ropes offa the ring and demanding the whereabouts of Whithers, so's they could hang him to the rafters. But he had disappeared, and the maddened crowd raged in vain.

I found my way dazedly to my dressing-room, where I set down on a table and tried to recover from the shock. Bill O'Brien and the rest of the crew was there, frothing at the mouth, each having sunk his entire wad on me. I considered going into Leary's dressing-room and beating him up again, but decided he'd had nothing to do with the crooked decision. He was just as surprised as me when Whithers declared him winner.

Whilst I was trying to pull on my clothes, hindered more'n helped by my raging shipmates, whose langwidge was getting more appalling every instant, a stocky bewhiskered figger come busting through the mob, and done a fantastic dance in front of me. It was the Old Man, with licker on his breath and tears in his eyes.

"I'm rooint!" he howled. "I'm a doomed man! Oh, to think as I've warmed a sarpint in my boozum! Dennis Dorgan, this here's the last straw!"

"Aw, pipe down!" snarled Bill O'Brien. "It wasn't Denny's fault. It was that dashety triple-blank thief of a referee—"

"To think of goin' on the beach at my age!" screamed the Old Man, wringing the salt water outa his whiskers. He fell down on a bench and wept at the top of his voice. "A thousand bucks I lost—every cent I could rake, scrape and borrer!" he bawled.

"Aw, well, you still got your ship," somebody said impatiently.

"That's just it!" the Old Man wailed. "That thousand bucks was dough owed them old pirates, McGregor, McClune & McKile. Part of what I owe, I mean. They agreed to accept a thousand as part payment, and gimme more time to raise the rest. Now it's gone, and they'll take the ship! They'll take the *Python!* All I got in the world! Them old sharks ain't got no more heart than a Malay pirate. I'm rooint!"

The crew fell silent at that, and I said: "Why'd you bet all that dough?"

"I was lickered up," he wept. "I got no sense when I'm full. Old Cap'n Donnelly, and McVey and them got to raggin' me, and the first thing I knowed, I'd bet 'em the thousand, givin' heavy odds. Now I'm rooint!"

He throwed back his head and bellered like a walrus with the belly-ache.

I just give a dismal groan and sunk my head in my hands, too despondent to say nothing. The crew bust forth in curses against Whithers, and sallied forth to search further for him, hauling the Old Man along with them, still voicing his woes in a voice like a steamboat whistle.

PRESENTLY I RIZ with a sigh and hauled on my duds. They was no sound outside. Apparently I was alone in the building except for Spike, my white bulldog. All at once I noticed him smelling of a closed locker. He whined, scratched at it, and growled. With a sudden suspicion I strode over and jerked open the door. Inside I seen a huddled figger. I jerked it rudely forth and set it upright. It was Jed Whithers. He was pale and shaking, and he had cobwebs in his hair. He kind a cringed, evidently expecting me to bust into loud cusses. For once I was too mad for that. I was probably as pale as he was, and his eyes dilated like he seen murder in mine.

"Jed Whithers," I said, shoving him up against the wall with one hand whilst I knotted the other'n into a mallet, "this is one time in my life when I'm in the mood for killin'."

"For God's sake, Dorgan," he gurgled, "you can't murder me!"

"Can you think of any reason why I shouldn't put you in a wheelchair for the rest of your life?" I demanded. "You've rooint my friends and all the fans which bet on me, lost my skipper his ship—"

"Don't hit me, Dorgan!" he begged, grabbing my wrist with shaking fingers. "I had to do it; honest to God, Sailor, I *had* to do it! I know you won—won by a mile. But it was the only thing I *could* do!"

"What you mean?" I demanded suspiciously.

"Lemme sit down!" he gasped.

I reluctantly let go of him, and he slumped down onto a near-by bench. He sat there and shook, and mopped the sweat offa his face. He was trembling all over.

"Are the customers all gone?" he asked.

"Ain't nobody here but me and my man-eatin' bulldog," I answered grimly, standing over him. "Go on—spill what you got to say before I start varnishin' the floor with you."

"I was forced to it, Sailor," he said. "There's a man who has a hold on me."

"What you mean, a hold?" I asked suspiciously.

"I mean, he's got me in a spot," he said. "I have to do like he says. It ain't myself I have to think of—Dorgan, I'm goin' to trust you. You got the name of bein' a square shooter. I'm goin' to tell you the whole thing.

"Sailor, I got a sister named Constance, a beautiful girl, innocent as a newborn lamb. She trusted a man, Sailor, a dirty, slimy snake in human form. He tricked her into signin' a document—Dorgan, that paper was a confession of a crime he'd committed himself!"

Whithers here broke down and sobbed with his face in his hands. I shuffled my feet uncertainly, beginning to realize they was always more'n one side to any question.

He raised up suddenly and said: "Since then, that man's been holdin' that faked confession over me and her like a club. He's forced me to do his filthy biddin' time and again. I'm a honest man by nature, Sailor, but to protect my little sister"—he kinda choked for a instant—"I've stooped to low deeds. Like this tonight. This man was bettin' heavy on Leary, gettin' big odds—"

"Somebody sure was," I muttered. "Lots of Leary money in sight."

"Sure!" exclaimed Whithers eagerly. "That was it; he made me throw the fight to Leary, the dirty rat, to protect his bets."

I begun to feel new wrath rise in my gigantic breast.

"You mean this low-down polecat has been blackmailin' you on account of the hold he's got over your sister?" I demanded.

"Exactly," he said, dropping his face in his hands. "With that paper he can send Constance to prison, if he takes the notion."

"I never heered of such infermy," I growled. "Whyn't you bust him on the jaw and take that confession away from him?"

"I ain't no fightin' man," said Whithers. "He's too big for me. I wouldn't have a chance."

"Well, *I* would," I said. "Listen, Whithers, buck up and quit cryin'. I'm goin' to help you."

His head jerked up and he stared at me kinda wild-eyed.

"You mean you'll help me get that paper?"

"You bet!" I retorted. "I ain't the man to stand by and let no innercent girl be persecuted. Besides, this mess tonight is his fault."

Whithers just set there for a second, and I thought I seen a slow smile start to spread over his lips, but I mighta been mistook, because he wasn't grinning when he held out his hand and said tremulously: "Dorgan, you're all they say you are!"

A remark like that ain't necessarily a compliment; some of the things said about me ain't flattering; but I took it in the spirit in which it seemed to be give, and I said: "Now tell me, who is this rat?"

He glanced nervously around, then whispered: "Ace Bissett!"

I grunted in surprize. "The devil you say! I'd never of thought it."

"He's a fiend in human form," said Whithers bitterly. "What's your plan?"

"Why," I said, "I'll go to his Diamond Palace and demand the confession. If he don't give it to me, I'll maul him and take it away from him."

"You'll get shot up," said Whithers. "Bissett is a bad man to fool with. Listen, I got a plan. If we can get him to a certain house I know about, we can search him for the paper. He carries it around with him, though I don't know just where. Here's my plan—"

I listened attentively, and as a result, perhaps a hour later I was heading through the narrer streets with Spike, driving a closed car which Whithers had produced kinda mysteriously. Whithers wasn't with me; he was gone to prepare the place where I was to bring Bissett to.

I driv up the alley behind Ace's big new saloon and gambling-hall, the Diamond Palace, and stopped the car near a back door. It was a very high-class joint. Bissett was friends with wealthy sportsmen, officials, and other swells. He was what they call a soldier of fortune, and he'd been everything, everywhere—aviator, explorer, big game hunter, officer in the armies of South America and China—and what have you.

A native employee stopped me at the door, and asked me what was my business, and I told him I wanted to see Ace. He showed me into the room which opened on the alley, and went after Bissett—which could not of suited my plan better.

Purty soon a door opened, and Bissett strode in—a tall, broad-shouldered young fellow, with steely eyes and wavy blond hair. He was in a dress suit, and altogether looked like he'd stepped right outa the social register. And as I looked at him, so calm and self-assured, and thought of poor Whithers being driv to crime by him, and the Old Man losing his ship on account of his crookedness, I seen red.

"Well, Dorgan, what can I do for you?" he asked.

I said nothing. I stepped in and hooked my right to his jaw. It caught him flat-footed, with his hands down. He hit the floor full length, and he didn't twitch.

I bent over him, run my hands through his clothes, found his six-shooter and throwed it aside. Music and the sounds of revelry reached me through the walls, but evidently nobody had seen or heard me slug Bissett. I lifted him and histed him onto my shoulders—no easy job, because he was as big as me, and limp as a rag.

But I done it, and started for the alley. I got through the door all right, which I was forced to leave open, account of having both hands full, and just as I was dumping Ace into the back part of the car, I heered a scream. Wheeling, I seen a girl had just come into the room I'd left, and was standing frozen, staring wildly at me. The light from the open door shone full on me and my captive. The girl was Glory O'Dale, Ace Bissett's sweetheart. I hurriedly slammed the car door shut and jumped to the wheel, and as I roared off down the alley, I was vaguely aware that Glory had rushed out of the building after me, screaming blue murder.

IT WAS PURTY late, and the route I took they wasn't many people abroad. Behind me I begun to hear Bissett stir and groan, and I pushed Spike over in the back seat to watch him. But he hadn't fully come to when I drawed up in the shadows beside the place Whithers had told me about—a ramshackle old building down by a old rotting, deserted wharf. Nobody seemed to live anywheres close around, or if they did, they was outa sight. As I clum outa the car, a door opened a crack, and I seen Whithers' white face staring at me.

"Did you get him, Sailor?" he whispered.

For answer I jerked open the back door, and Bissett tumbled out on his ear and laid there groaning dimly. Whithers started back with a cry.

"Is he dead?" he asked fearfully.

"Would he holler like that if he was?" I asked impatiently. "Help me carry him in, and we'll search him."

"Wait'll I tie him up," said Whithers, producing some cords, and to my disgust, he bound the unconscious critter hand and foot.

"It's safer this way," Whithers said. "He's a devil, and we can't afford to take chances."

We then picked him up and carried him through the door, into a very dimly lighted room, across that 'un, and into another'n which was better lit—the winders being covered so the light couldn't be seen from the outside. And I got the surprise of my life. They was five men in that room. I wheeled on Whithers. "What's the idee?" I demanded.

"Now, now, Sailor," said Whithers, arranging Bissett on the

bench where we'd laid him. "These are just friends of mine. They know about Bissett and my sister."

I heered what sounded like a snicker, and I turned to glare at the assembled "friends". My gaze centered on a fat, flashy-dressed bird smoking a big black cigar; diamonds shone all over his fingers, and in his stick-pin. The others was just muggs.

"A fine lot of friends you pick out!" I said irritably to Whithers. "Diamond Joe Galt is been mixed up in every shady deal that's been pulled in the past three years. And if you'd raked the Seven Seas you couldn't found four dirtier thugs than Limey Teak, Bill Reynolds, Dutch Steinmann, and Red Partland."

"Hey, you—" Red Partland riz, clenching his fists, but Galt grabbed his arm.

"Stop it, Red," he advised. "Easy does it. Sailor," he addressed me with a broad smile which I liked less'n I'd liked a scowl, "they's no use in abuse. We're here to help our pal Whithers get justice. That's all. You've done your part. You can go now, with our thanks."

"Not so fast," I growled, and just then Whithers hollered: "Bissett's come to!"

We all turned around and seen that Bissett's eyes was open, and blazing.

"Well, you dirty rats," he greeted us all and sundry, "you've got me at last, have you?" He fixed his gaze on me, and said: "Dorgan, I thought you were a man. If I'd had any idea you were mixed up in this racket, you'd have never got a chance to slug me as you did."

"Aw, shut up," I snarled. "A fine nerve you've got, talkin' about men, after what you've did!"

Galt pushed past me and stood looking down at Bissett, and I seen his fat hands clenched, and the veins swell in his temples.

"Bissett," he said, "we've got you cold and you know it. Kick in—where's that paper?"

"You cursed fools!" Bissett raved, struggling at his cords till the veins stood out on his temples too. "I tell you, the paper's worthless."

"Then why do you object to givin' it to us?" demanded Whithers.

"Because I haven't got it!" raged Bissett. "I destroyed it, just as I've told you before."

"He's lyin'," snarled Red Partland. "He wouldn't never destroy such a thing as that. It means millions. Here, I'll make him talk—"

He shouldered forward and grabbed Bissett by the throat. I grabbed Red in turn, and tore him away.

"Belay!" I gritted. "He's a rat, but just the same I ain't goin' to stand by and watch no helpless man be tortured."

"Why, you—" Red bellered, and swung for my jaw.

I ducked and sunk my left to the wrist in his belly and he dropped like his legs had been cut out from under him. The others started forward, rumbling, and I wheeled towards 'em, seething with fight. But Galt got between us and shoved his gorillas back.

"Here," he snapped. "No fightin' amongst ourselves! Get up, Red. Now, Sailor," he begun to pat my sleeves in his soothing way, which I always despises beyond words, "there ain't no need for hard feelin's. I know just how you feel. But we got to have that paper. You know that, Sailor—"

Suddenly a faint sound made itself evident. "What's that?" gasped Limey, going pale.

"It's Spike," I said. "I left him in the car, and he's got tired of settin' out there, and is scratchin' at the front door. I'm goin' to go get him, but I'll be right back, and if anybody lays a hand on Bissett whilst I'm gone, I'll bust him into pieces. We'll get that paper, but they ain't goin' to be no torturin'."

I strode out, scornful of the black looks cast my way. As I shut the door behind me, a clamor of conversation bust out, so many talking at wunst I couldn't understand much, but every now and then Ace Bissett's voice riz above the din in accents of anger and not pain, so I knowed they wasn't doing nothing to him. I crossed the dim outer room, opened the door and let Spike in, and then, forgetting to bolt it—I ain't used to secrecy and such—I started back for the inner room.

BEFORE I REACHED the other door, I heered a quick patter of feet outside. I wheeled—the outer door bust violently open, and into the room rushed Glory O'Dale. She was panting hard, her dress was tore, her black locks damp, and her dark eyes was wet and bright as black jewels after a rain. And she had Ace's six-shooter in her hand.

"You filthy dog!" she cried, throwing down on me.

I looked right into the muzzle of that .45 as she jerked the trigger. The hammer snapped on a faulty cartridge, and before she could try again, Spike launched hisself from the floor at her. I'd taught him never to bite a woman. He didn't bite Glory. He throwed hisself bodily against her so hard he knocked her down and the gun flew outa her hand.

I picked it up and stuck it into my hip pocket. Then I started to help her up, but she hit my hand aside and jumped up, tears of fury running down her cheeks. Golly, she was a beauty!

"You beast!" she raged. "What have you done with Ace? I'll kill you if you've harmed him! Is he in that room?"

"Yeah, and he ain't harmed," I said, "but he oughta be hung—"

She screamed like a siren. "Don't you dare! Don't you touch a hair of his head! Oh, Ace!"

She then slapped my face, jerked out a handful of hair, and

kicked both my shins.

"What I can't understand is," I said, escaping her clutches, "is why a fine girl like you ties up with a low-down rat like Bissett. With your looks, Glory—"

"To the devil with my looks!" she wept, stamping on the door. "Let me past; I know Ace is in that room—I heard his voice as I came in."

They wasn't no noise in the inner room now. Evidently all of them was listening to what was going on out here, Ace included.

"You can't go in there," I said. "We got to search Ace for the incriminatin' evidence he's holdin' against Jed Whithers' sister—"

"You're mad as a March hare," she said. "Let me by!"

And without no warning she back-heeled me and pushed me with both hands. It was so unexpected I ignominiously crashed to the floor, and she darted past me and throwed open the inner door. Spike drove for her, and this time he was red-eyed, but I grabbed him as he went by.

Glory halted an instant on the threshold with a cry of mingled triumph, fear and rage. I riz, cussing beneath my breath and dusting off my britches. Glory ran across the room, eluding the grasping paws of Joe Galt, and throwed herself with passionate abandon on the prostrate form of Ace Bissett. I noticed that Ace, which hadn't till then showed the slightest sign of fear, was suddenly pale and his jaw was grim set.

"It was madness for you to come, Glory," he muttered.

"I saw Dorgan throw you into the car," she whimpered, throwing her arms around him, and tugging vainly at his cords. "I jumped in another and followed—blew out a tire a short distance from here—lost sight of the car I was following and wandered around in the dark alleys on foot for awhile, till I saw the car standing outside. I came on in—"

"Alone? My God!" groaned Ace.

"Alone?" echoed Galt, with a sigh of relief. He flicked some dust from his lapel, stuck his cigar back in his mouth at a cocky angle, and said: "Well, now, we'll have a little talk. Come here, Glory."

She clung closer to Ace, and Ace said in a low voice, almost a whisper: "Let her alone, Galt." His eyes was like fires burning under the ice.

Galt's muggs was grinning evilly and muttering to theirselves. Whithers was nervous and kept mopping perspiration. The air was tense. I was nervous and impatient; something was wrong, and I didn't know what. So when Galt started to say something, I took matters into my own hands.

"Bissett," I said, striding across the room and glaring down at him, "if they's a ounce of manhood in you, this here girl's devotion oughta touch even your snakish soul. Why don't you try to redeem yourself a little, anyway? Kick in with that paper! A man which is loved by a woman like Glory O'Dale loves you, oughta be above holdin' a forged confession over a innocent girl's head."

Bissett's mouth fell open. "What's he talking about?" he demanded from the world at large.

"I don't know," said Glory uneasily, snuggling closer to him. "He talked that way out in the other room. I think he's punch-drunk."

"Dorgan," said Bissett, "you don't belong in this crowd. Are you suffering from some sort of an hallucination?"

"Don't hand me no such guff, you snake!" I roared. "You know why I brung you here—to get the confession you gypped outa Whithers' sister, and blackmailed him with—just like you made him throw my fight tonight."

Bissett just looked dizzy, but Glory leaped up and faced me.

"You mean you think Ace made Whithers turn in that rotten decision?" she jerked out.

"I don't think," I answered sullenly. "I know. Whithers said so."

She jumped like she was galvanized.

"Why, you idiot!" she hollered, "they've made a fool of you! Jed Whithers hasn't any sister! He lied! Ace had nothing to do with it! Whithers was hired to throw the fight to Leary! Look at him!" Her voice rose to a shriek of triumph, as she pointed a accusing finger at Jed Whithers. "Look at him! Look how pale he is! He's scared witless!"

"It's a lie!" gulped Whithers, sweating and tearing at his crumpled collar like it was choking him.

"It's not a lie!" Glory was nearly hysterical by this time. "He was paid to throw the fight! And there's the man who paid him!" And she dramatically pointed her finger at Diamond Joe Galt!

GALT WAS ON HIS feet, his small eyes glinting savagely, his jaws grinding his cigar to a pulp.

"What about it, Galt?" I demanded, all at sea and bewildered.

He dashed down his cigar with a oath. His face was dark and convulsed.

"What of it?" he snarled. "What you goin' to do about it? I've stood all the guff out of you I'm goin' to!"

His hand snaked inside his coat and out, and I was looking into the black muzzle of a wicked stumpy automatic.

"You can't slug this like you did Red, you dumb gorilla," he smirked viciously. "Sure, the dame's tellin' the truth. Whithers took you in like a sucklin' lamb.

"When you caught him in your dressin'-room, he told you the first lie that come to him, knowin' you for a soft sap where women's concerned. Then when you fell for it, and offered to help him, he thought fast and roped you into this deal. We been tryin' to get hold of Bissett for a long time. He's got somethin' we want. But he was too smart and too tough for us. Now, thanks to you, we got him, *and* the girl. Now we're goin' to sweat what we want out of him, and you're goin' to keep your trap shut, see?"

"You mean they ain't no Constance Whithers, and no confession?" I said slowly, trying to get things straight. A raucous roar of mirth greeted the remark.

"No, sucker," taunted Galt; "you just been took in, you sap."

A wave of red swept across my line of vision. With a maddened roar, I plunged recklessly at Galt, gun and all. Everything happened at once. Galt closed his finger on the trigger just as Spike, standing beside him all this time, closed his jaws on Galt's leg. Galt screamed and leaped convulsively; the gun exploded in the air, missing me so close the powder singed my hair, and my right mauler crunched into Galt's face, flattening his nose, knocking out all his front teeth, and fracturing his jaw-bone. As he hit the floor Spike was right on top of him.

The next instant Galt's thugs was on top of me. We rolled across the room in a wild tangle of arms and legs, casually shattering tables and chairs on the way. Spike, finding Galt was out cold, abandoned him and charged to my aid. I heered Red Partland howl as Spike's iron fangs locked in his britches. But I had my hands full. Fists and hobnails was glancing off my carcass, and a thumb was feeling for my eye. I set my teeth in this thumb and was rewarded by a squeal of anguish, but the action didn't slow up any.

It was while strangling Limey Teak beneath me, whilst the other three was trying to stomp my ribs in and kick my head off, that I realized that another element had entered into the fray. There was the impact of a chair-leg on a human skull, and Jed Whithers give up the ghost with a whistling sigh. Glory O'Dale was taking a hand.

Dutch Steinmann next gave a ear-piercing howl, and Bill Reynolds abandoned me to settle her. Feeling Limey go limp beneath me, I riz, shaking Steinmann offa my shoulders, just in time to see Reynolds duck Glory's chair-leg and smack her down. Bissett give a most awful yell of rage, but he wasn't no madder than me. I left the floor in a flying tackle that carried Reynolds off his feet with a violence which nearly busted his skull against the floor. Too crazy-mad for reason, I set to work to hammer him to death, and though he was already senseless, I would probably of continued indefinite, had not Dutch Steinmann distracted my attention by smashing a chair over my head.

I riz through the splinters and caught him with a left hook that tore his ear nearly off and stood him on his neck in a corner. I then looked for Red Partland and seen him crawling out a winder which he'd tore the shutters off of. He was a rooin; his clothes was nearly all tore offa him, and he was bleeding like a stuck hawg and bawling like one, and Spike didn't show no intentions of abandoning the fray. His jaws was locked in what was left of Red's britches, and he had his feet braced against the wall below the sill. As I looked, Red gave a desperate wrench and tumbled through the winder, and I heered his lamentations fading into the night.

SHAKING THE BLOOD and sweat outa my eyes, I glared about at the battlefield, strewn with the dead and dying—at least with the unconscious, some of which was groaning loudly, whilst others slumbered in silence.

Glory was just getting up, dizzy and wobbly. Spike was smelling each of the victims in turn, and Ace was begging somebody to let him loose. Glory wobbled over to where he'd rolled offa the bench, and I followed her, kinda stiffly. At least one of my ribs had been broke by a boot-heel. My scalp was cut open, and blood was trickling down my side, where Limey Teak had made a ill-advised effort to knife me. I also thought one of them rats had hit me from behind with a club, till I discovered that sometime in the fray I'd fell on something hard in my hip pocket. This, I found, was Ace Bissett's pistol, which I'd clean forgot all about. I throwed it aside with disgust; them things is a trap and a snare.

I blinked at Ace with my one good eye, whilst Glory worked his cords offa him.

"I see I misjudged you," I said, lending her a hand. "I apolergize, and if you want satisfaction, right here and now is good enough for me."

"Good Lord, man," he said, with his arms full of Glory. "I don't want to fight you. I still don't know just what it was all about, but I'm beginning to understand."

I set down somewhat groggily on a bench which wasn't clean busted.

"What I want to know is," I said, "what that paper was they was talkin' about."

"Well," he said, "about a year ago I befriended a half-cracked Russian scientist, and he tried in his crazy way to repay me. He told me, in Galt's presence, that he was going to give me a formula that would make me the richest man on earth. He got blown up in an explosion in his laboratory shortly afterward, and an envelope was found in his room addressed to me, and containing a formula. Galt found out about it, and he's been hounding me ever since, trying to get it. He thought it was all the Russian claimed. In reality it was merely the disconnected scribblings of a disordered mind—good Lord, it claimed to be a process for the manufacture of diamonds! Utter insanity—but Galt never would believe it."

"And he thought I was dumb," I cogitated. "But hey, Glory, how'd you know it was Galt hired Whithers to throw my fight to Leary?"

"I didn't," she admitted. "I just accused Galt of it to start you fellows fighting among yourselves."

"Well, I'll be derned," I said, and just then one of the victims which had evidently come to while we was talking, riz stealthily to his all fours and started crawling towards the winder. It was Jed Whithers. I strode after him and hauled him to his feet.

"How much did Galt pay you for throwin' the bout to Leary?" I demanded.

"A thousand dollars," he stuttered.

"Gimme it," I ordered, and with shaking hands he hauled out a fold of bills. I fluttered 'em and saw they was intact.

"Turn around and look out the winder at the stars," I commanded.

"I don't see no stars," he muttered.

"You will," I promised, as I swung my foot and histed him clean over the sill.

As his wails faded up the alley, I turned to Ace and Glory, and said: "Galt must of cleaned up plenty on this deal, payin' so high for his dirty work. This here dough, though, is goin' to be put to a good cause. The Old Man lost all his money account of Whithers' crooked decision. This thousand bucks will save his ship. Now let's go. I wanta get hold of the promoter of the Sweet Dreams, and get another match tomorrer night with Kid Leary—this time with a honest referee."

19343799R00186

Made in the USA
San Bernardino, CA
23 February 2015